LIES IN WHITE DRESSES

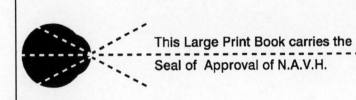

This Large Print Book carries the Seal of Approval of N.A.V.H.

LIES IN WHITE DRESSES

SOFIA GRANT

THORNDIKE PRESS
A part of Gale, a Cengage Company

LIBRARY OF CONGRESS CIP DATA ON FILE.
CATALOGUING IN PUBLICATION FOR THIS BOOK
IS AVAILABLE FROM THE LIBRARY OF CONGRESS

ISBN-13: 978-1-4328-7672-2 (hardcover alk. paper)

Published in 2020 by arrangement with William Morrow, an imprint of HarperCollins Publishers

Printed in Mexico
Print Number: 01   Print Year: 2020

For Caitlin,
my Reno girl

CHAPTER 1
FRANCIE

May 1952

It couldn't be Margie, because she would cry, and besides, she might bring the children, which would turn the whole thing into a circus. Jimmy hadn't come out and said it, because he was trying to spare her feelings, but he was playing golf with his father today — the club had called to confirm their tee time.

That left Alice. As usual.

"Mother, do you want the blue with the feather or the tan?" Alice called from upstairs. She had skipped her painting class this morning to help Francie finish packing and to say goodbye to Vi. Vi's two boys worked for their father's publicity firm, and all three of them were currently in the middle of the Mojave Desert getting ready to launch a client's nuclear tourism business. It was just like Harry to leave his wife to make her shameful departure from an empty house, even when he was the one who'd smashed their sacred vows into smithereens.

"Oh, the blue, I suppose," Francie called. "Though it hardly matters, does it?"

"Don't be glum." Alice came down the stairs carrying the hat under one arm, leaving the other free to hold on to the handrail. "It's going to be lovely, Mother. You just need to think of it as a vacation. You and Vi have talked about going to Reno together for ages."

"Yes, but not like this. There won't be any snow and we'll be coming back divorced."

Francie put on the blue hat, checking her reflection in the hall mirror. How had she let this happen? It had been a decade at least since Vi first broached the idea of visiting her hometown — she wanted to show Francie the house she grew up in, to visit her parents' graves, to see the mountains covered in all that lovely snow. There'd be ice skating, Vi had promised, and walks along the river, and drinks at the Sky Room on top of the Mapes Hotel.

But it had never seemed like the right time. There'd been graduations and weddings and engagements and grandchildren, and it had seemed as though they had all the time in the world.

Before Alice could respond, the front door opened and Vi walked in. She hadn't bothered to knock since she and Harry had moved across the street from the Meekers three decades earlier, when she was pregnant with Frank, and Francie's firstborn, Margie, was only a baby.

"Good morning, Francie. Hello, Alice, darling."

"Well, you don't have to sound like you dropped your ice-cream cone," Francie scolded. "Alice was just telling me to keep my chin up, and you'll simply have to do the same."

The driver followed behind Vi timidly. Harry always hired men who were afraid of him. "Should I get the bags, ma'am?"

"Yes, please." Francie grabbed Alice's hand and gave it a squeeze. "I suppose this is goodbye, then. Are you sure you'll be all right?"

"Of course I will."

Dear Alice — she was as brave as she was thoughtful. "Just call Dad for anything you need. Don't try to do everything yourself." For the ten-thousandth time, Francie sent up her prayer — *Dear Lord, take care of Alice* — a habit like breathing.

"I'll miss you too, Auntie Vi," Alice said, kissing her on the cheek.

Francie was gathering her purse and gloves when she saw Vi do something she'd never done before — she placed her hands on either side of Alice's face and pressed her forehead to hers. Didn't say anything, just stood like that for a moment.

Vi had never been the demonstrative sort. Was this what she was in for, Francie wondered, six weeks of maudlin fussing? All because of Harry — who, in Francie's opinion, wasn't worth wasting a single tear on.

"Let's go," she said, too sharply. "I want to get on the train before they start letting the coach passengers on."

The train would be departing at nine, but at eight-thirty the sleeping-car passengers had been allowed to board. Francie had been determined to settle into their compartment before the hall became congested with other passengers.

The porter looked at their tickets, then at his clipboard. "Madam? You wanted pillow service?"

"Yes, please," Francie said tiredly. "I know we're only going as far as Reno, but if you would be so kind . . ."

"Of course." He was back in minutes to turn down the beds. "Have a nice trip."

"Do you remember," Vi said dreamily, once he was gone. "The year Frank broke his arm, and we had to drive all the way back from Yosemite in the dark?"

"Oh, I do. Jimmy was so upset that he missed feeding the bears."

"What I remember most is that you didn't think twice, you just started packing up the station wagon. You could have stayed and enjoyed the rest of the trip, but you and Arthur and the kids all came back so my boys wouldn't feel like they missed out."

"Of course we did!" Francie said. "You would have done the same for me."

"*I* would have. But Harry wouldn't. It's funny — when I think back over the years, you were there for me all the times that he wasn't. Sometimes I wish I could have married you instead of him."

For a moment both of them were quiet. "I believe I'll lie down," Francie finally said. "I didn't sleep well last night. What about you, dear?"

"I think I'll read the paper."

"If you're sure."

Francie kicked off her shoes and climbed into the lower berth. She knew Vi wouldn't mind; Francie wasn't built for going up and down ladders, but Vi was still as thin as a whip and agile as a cat after all these years.

11

It felt strange to pull the bed linens up when she was fully clothed. The cotton sheets glided over her stockings; her woolen skirt twisted around her hips. She closed her eyes, but moments later opened them again. She reminded herself to check her makeup and wondered how much rouge she was leaving on the pillowcase.

Vi had barely moved. She was staring out the window, the newspaper untouched in her lap. *Of course, it's different for her,* Francie thought. Harry didn't care a bit about Vi's humiliation. Arthur, for all his faults, had always been kind.

She watched her friend as the train sped through the bright morning, enjoying its hypnotic rocking. Outside the door to their compartment, she could hear the voices of the porters. Vi sighed and pressed a hand to her cheek, but her expression didn't change. Should Francie say something? Offer some sort of comfort? Vi had never welcomed that kind of attention.

Francie let her eyelids slowly drift down. She felt both deliciously indolent and uncomfortably warm. How lovely it would be to strip down to her camisole and slip.

This is how it began, then, the transformation she had never asked for. In six weeks she would return, a divorcée. Arthur had rented his North Beach apartment several years ago, though very few people knew; he stayed there only a few days a month. While she was away, he would arrange for the rest of his things to be moved. He'd asked for so little from the house — but then again, nearly all of it had been bought with the money she'd brought into the marriage.

It was as though time were moving backward, a loose thread being wound around the spool. The apartment was on Powell, a ten-minute taxi ride from the Arcadia Dance Pavilion, where they had first been introduced. Breathtakingly handsome in his uniform, Arthur was serving as a coast artillery soldier at Fort Winfield Scott on the Presidio; all day long he fired enormous guns at targets out in the sea, while Army Air Corps pilots flew overhead, dipping their wings when a target was hit.

How could she not have fallen in love with him?

She woke several hours later, groggy from a dream in which she was riding on the lower wing of a biplane while shouting for Arthur to take her home, but he couldn't hear her.

For a moment Francie stared up at the wooden struts supporting the upper bunk, slowly remembering the purpose of the trip, the reason she was here. She glanced over at Vi and was not surprised to see her sitting exactly as she had been before, though now her eyes were closed.

Francie faked a little cough, as a courtesy. Funny, in all the time they'd known each other, they'd never slept in the same room. Vi started awake, and for the briefest second, a look of panic crossed her face. But then she was herself again, smoothing her skirt and giving Francie a sphinxlike smile.

"Did you sleep well?"

"If you can call that sleep," Francie said, easing herself out of the bunk and putting her stockinged feet on the floor. How anyone could spend an entire night in these things was a mystery. "I feel bounced about like a cart going to market."

"We've stopped half a dozen times. We're in Roseville now, but they just announced that we'll be moving again in a moment."

Francie hadn't heard a thing — the last announcement she remembered was when they were pulling out of the station on Market. She had been sleeping more soundly than she realized. She looked down at the mother-of-pearl face of the dainty platinum watch Arthur had given her for their twenty-fifth wedding anniversary.

"We should get to the dome car for lunch,"

she said. "I'm ravenous — I haven't eaten a thing all day."

"I think I'll stay back here." Vi's smile slipped a little. "I'm not hungry."

"Oh no you won't," Francie said firmly. "I won't have you moping around all day."

Vi shrugged and took a compact from her purse. From the corner of her eye as she touched up her own makeup and patted her hair in place, Francie watched Vi gaze at her reflection as though she were looking at a stranger. Finally, Vi put the compact away, sighed, and stood up.

"Lead on," she said.

The dome car of the *City of San Francisco* had been a thing of fascination for Francie's son, Jimmy. Arthur had brought him to the station for the unveiling of the new train when it debuted; he reported that Jimmy — ten or eleven at the time — had stared, enraptured, through the curved glass panels that allowed uninterrupted views, even though it was the same platform and tracks he'd visited many times before. Of course, Jimmy had long ago lost his love of trains; these days it was all work, work, work at the bank.

All these years later, the car's banquettes had been reupholstered in turquoise leatherette, the fussy dining area replaced with

15

club chairs in a coral jacquard. The waiters wore snappy bow ties. As the maître d' was showing them to their seats, moving the table so that Francie could more easily shoehorn her derriere into the booth, he suddenly frowned. "Excuse me, ladies. I'll be right back."

He strode to the entrance of the car, where a tentative young woman stood, holding the hand of a little girl with blond curls.

"Miss, this dining room is only for the use of sleeping-car passengers," he said, more loudly than necessary. "I'm sure you'll find the other dining car more than adequate for your needs."

The woman blushed furiously but held her ground. "We won't be but a minute," she pleaded. "It's just that I promised her. It's the only thing she wanted to see."

"That's out of the question, I'm afraid."

Francie felt her hackles rise. Perhaps it was the years of forging a path for Alice, plunging into social encounters with the ferocity of a mother bear, insisting that she be treated like any other child — but Francie could not stand to see the young mother be humiliated in front of the well-heeled passengers.

"Sir, those are our guests," she said loudly. "Please show them to our table."

16

Conversation stopped. Vi flinched. Francie didn't care. Her pride had already taken a beating; how much worse could it get? She looked around at the other passengers' curious gazes and gave them the regal demi-smile she'd cultivated all those years ago as the richest girl at Lowell High School, then turned her attention back to the maître d', who sagged under the weight of her chilly gaze. In his profession, it was to his advantage to recognize money when he saw it. "Of course," he said, obsequious in defeat.

"Oh, I don't —" the young woman blurted.

"We're so *glad* to see you," Francie called. Hesitantly, the woman and her daughter approached the table. Other diners looked on approvingly; the court of public opinion was clearly on the side of the pretty stranger and her adorable child. The maître d' didn't bother to help them into their seats, so Francie rolled her eyes and patted the bench next to her. "Here, darling, you sit with me — there's more room for your mother with Mrs. Carothers."

"I'll bring two more menus," the maître d' said, but Francie ignored him.

"Thank you," the young woman said, looking as though she was about to burst into tears. "I don't know what I would have

17

done — I didn't realize, you see, I've never — I thought anyone could visit the dining car. I didn't know there were two of them."

"It's silly, isn't it?" Vi said. Kindness came naturally to her. "What's your name, young lady?"

"Patty," the little girl said softly, looking to her mother for confirmation.

"And how old are you?"

Instead of answering, Patty gravely held up four fingers.

"Four!" Francie exclaimed. "What a delightful age to be. Good for you. I'm Francine Meeker, but I'm called Francie by my friends. And this is Violet Carothers."

"Please, call me Vi."

"I'm June. June Samples."

She wore a dress that would have fit a woman fifteen pounds heavier, the wool shiny with wear, the style several years out of date. Her shoes were the sort one buys if one can afford only a single pair for church and town — too plain for one, too dressy for the other.

She wore no wedding ring.

"We're heading for Reno," Francie said.

"Reno!" June looked taken aback. "That's — but that's where we're going too!"

"Well, then, you must dine with us, so we can get acquainted."

18

"Oh, we couldn't impose. And besides, we already ate."

"Mama, I'm hungry," Patty said in a voice barely louder than a whisper.

"I have sandwiches," June said rather desperately. "We'll go back to our seats and —"

"I really wish you'd allow us to treat you to lunch," Vi said. "You see, my husband made me promise to enjoy this trip. I mustn't let him down. And it will be so much nicer if you stay. I've known Francie for thirty years, and I've run out of things to say to her."

There was a brief, shocked silence, and then Francie burst into laughter. "What's gotten into you, Vi? Oh, never mind — since Harry is treating, let's order every lovely thing on the menu!"

CHAPTER 2
VIRGIE

"Hey, Virgie," a voice called from one of the open doors down the carpeted second-floor hall. "Come here a minute, will you?"

Virgie Swanson slowed her step, tucking the mail she was carrying into the big patch pocket of her pinafore. Her mother, the owner and manager of the Holiday Ranch hotel, had sewn the pinafore herself. It was made of white cotton duck with cheerful red rickrack trim, and in addition to the large pocket there was a smaller one that contained a notepad and several pencils, for writing down the guests' requests and messages, and a metal ring to hook the supply-closet key to. There was also a tiny pocket sewn onto the inside of the pinafore where Virgie stashed the tips that the guests gave her until she was back in her room and could hide them in the baking-powder tin behind the wall.

The voice summoning Virgie was hoarse

and a bit pitiful, the way the ladies sometimes got after they stayed out too late. Virgie hoped it was the girl from Las Vegas.
She had seemed nice enough when she
checked in two weeks ago, but more important, she probably had money. Her mother
drew this conclusion from the girl's suitcases
and her coat; she said you could learn a lot
about a person from observing them carefully, a skill that Virgie was trying hard to
learn on her own, as she planned to be a
detective when she grew up. Indeed, she
recorded in the back of her diary all kinds
of useful observations, mostly gleaned from
eavesdropping.

She was also collecting information for
another of her projects, which was to become poised and beautiful, like Ava Gardner
in *Pandora and the Flying Dutchman*. (She
wasn't allowed to see the film, but she'd
snuck into the Majestic with her friend
Pearl, whose father was their dairyman.)
The guests were very useful on this front:

Use safety pin to seperate eye lashes after
putting on mascarra
OVAL is best face shape!!!
Don't chew gum it is COMMON
Cream on neck EVERY night NOT JUST
  FACE

Virgie followed the source of the voice down the hall. No light spilled from the door, suggesting that the occupant hadn't opened the drapes yet, despite the fact that it was nearly lunchtime. On hot afternoons, guests often left their doors open in hopes of getting a bit of a cross breeze. On rainy or snowy days, it wasn't uncommon to see them wandering between their rooms in their wrappers and slippers, as if they were attending a giant pajama party.

A face peeped out. The girl from Las Vegas had a pretty smile and lively eyes, but Mother had observed that it was her bombshell figure that had gotten her to the altar the first time and, if she played her cards right, might get her there again. (Virgie had written *bombshell figure* in her notebook, along with a question mark, as she wasn't entirely sure what one was.)

"Remember me, honey?" the girl said. "I'm called Willy. Listen, can you run down to the store for me?" She held out a quarter between her fingertips, as if she were holding a cigarette. Virgie often practiced holding cigarettes — the candy ones, anyway — and blowing pretend rings of smoke.

"What do you need from the store, Miss Willy?" Virgie asked politely.

"Get me the new issue of *Life*. Make sure

it's the new one, with Diana Lynn on the cover. And a packet of matches." She coughed delicately. An odor issued from the room, a not very pleasant odor with notes of perfume and hairspray masking something sour and stale. The robe Willy was wearing could stand a washing too. The hotel did a brisk business with the ladies' laundry. Pearl's father sent a boy to pick up their dirty things each morning and then a different one brought back the clean, folded bundles right before suppertime — and Mother charged the guests a bit extra for her trouble.

"Yes, Miss."

"And you can keep the change for yourself, how's that?"

"Thank you!" Virgie beamed. "I'll go right now."

Life cost twenty cents and matches were free, and that left a nickel that she could put in the baking-powder tin. Other than Nancy Drew mysteries — Virgie already had twenty-two of them, lined up neatly on her bookshelf — she had few expenses, and there was already sixteen dollars and forty-two cents in the bank. She needed forty-nine dollars by next summer to attend the Hector Y. Brown Private Detective Academy, which, after two weeks of intensive study, would confer on her an official certificate allowing her to work as a private eye anywhere in the state of Nevada.

"Your mother won't mind?" Willy asked. Up close, Virgie could see that her cheeks were smeared with last night's rouge, and her eyeliner had smudged, making her look a bit like a raccoon. "I don't want you to get into trouble."

"My mother doesn't care." That wasn't true, but her mother was too busy to know where Virgie was all day long, especially now that school was out for the summer.

"You sure are a sassy little thing, aren't you?" Willy said, yawning. She covered her mouth with her fingers, and Virgie stared at her shiny red fingernails, filed to points.

"I don't know, Miss." Virgie smiled — Mother said to *always* smile when talking to the guests, even if they were complaining about something — and dropped the quarter into the pocket with the notepad. "Are you going to throw your wedding ring into the river?"

"I don't know about that. It cost a lot of money."

"It doesn't have to be your real one," Virgie offered. "Woolworths sells cheap ones. Lots of ladies keep the real ones and throw the fake ones in the river. I can get one for

24

you, if you like."

"Aren't you enterprising?" Willy laughed. "How old are you, anyway?"

"Twelve." Virgie stood up straight, counting on every one of her fifty-nine inches to make up for what she lacked in age.

"Well, Virgie, how much would such a ring cost me?"

"Eighty cents."

"But that's not what it costs at Woolworths, is it?"

For a moment, Virgie considered lying, but her woman's intuition — Nancy Drew said that every girl had one — told her not to.

"No, Miss," she admitted. "They're sixty-five cents. But the extra fifteen cents is —"

"Relax, honey," Willy interrupted. "Of course you've got to have a markup. Frankly, I think it should be more. Tell you what, come and see me — not this afternoon, I'm feeling a bit unwell — but come up later this week and we'll work on your pitch. Okay?"

Virgie wasn't sure what a pitch was, but she was intrigued by the thought of gaining entrance into a den of indolence, which was what her mother called the rooms occupied by the richest, laziest girls. "Okay. I'll be back soon with your magazine."

"Just slide it under the door, honey. I'm going to lie down." Willy yawned again. "I had no idea how exhausting it is to get a divorce."

CHAPTER 3
FRANCIE

Francie studied their new friend while pretending to read the menu. She already knew what she was going to order, having remembered the menu from her last trip on the *City of San Francisco,* when she'd gone to see her elderly aunt in Sacramento shortly before her death last year. That time, she'd ordered the cottage cheese and pineapple plate, in a vain attempt to watch her waistline — but ever since Francie had decided to divorce, she'd given up dieting and still the weight seemed to be coming off of its own accord. Most likely, it was because with Arthur out of the house she'd been skipping meals, but she couldn't help wondering if there were other forces at work.

It had taken her much too long to come to the conclusion that heading into her golden years as a divorcée was preferable to a life that felt like a vigil before her own death. Now, having freed both herself and

Arthur from the shackles of their marriage, life presented a shocking number of decisions. Arthur was lucky, in a way — he knew exactly what he wanted and was well on his way to having it. Francie, on the other hand, had no idea.

Except: "I'm going to order the veal chop in paprika cream sauce," she announced, and then, catching June's eye, added, "and I think you should do the same, dear. You look like you could use the iron."

"Oh," June said, startled. "I thought perhaps the ham and cheese sandwich."

The sandwich was the least expensive item on the menu; the chop was the most, at $2.25. Francie summoned the waiter with a nod, and before he could speak, she said, "I think we're ready to order, young man. I shall have the veal chop and so will my friend. A nice piece of fried chicken for the child, I think, and some peaches. Do you like peaches, darling?"

Patty looked to her mother, who had recovered herself enough to say, "She likes them very much, don't you?"

"And you, madam?" the waiter asked Vi.

She set down her menu. "I'm not all that hungry, actually. I suppose the broiled sole. And iced tea."

"Yes, tea for all of us, except the young

28

lady. If it's all right with her mother, please bring her a Shirley Temple. With extra cherries, please. And do bring a dish for the stems."

As the waiter hurried away, Vi remarked, "Wasn't it Alice who loved the cherries?"

"It was! Alice is my youngest," Francie explained to June. "Patty, I'm sure you can hardly believe it, as I am a grandmother now, but I was once a young mother just like your own. Though never as pretty."

June blushed furiously, gazing down at the tablecloth.

"Oh, but you are," Vi said, perking up a bit. "The two of you! Those beautiful curls. Do you have to put in papers every night?"

"No, they're — they just do this on their own. Patty's are very hard to comb sometimes. They tangle so." She touched Patty's head lightly. "How many children do you have, Francie?"

"Three, dear. Margie's my eldest — she and her husband have three little girls, age four, two, and Dorrie's ten months. Then there's Jimmy, who was married last year to a lovely girl named Evelyn. And my Alice is twenty-five." Then, to save Vi the trouble, she did her list too. "Vi's got Charlie and Frank. All our boys were in the service — Jimmy went in the air force and Vi's boys

29

joined the marines. Frank's twenty-eight and Charlie's twenty-seven, and they're both still single, just to give their mother fits. They're both bright as pennies and they work with their father."

"Oh?" June said politely. "What does your husband do, Vi?"

The waiter had brought rolls and a dish of butter, which Patty was eyeing hungrily. Francie took a roll and broke it into pieces and buttered them, just as she used to do for her own children.

"He's a . . ." Vi cleared her throat, her face a little pink. "He owns an event management and promotion company, but mostly he's a J-A-C-K-A-S-S."

Francie burst into laughter. "He certainly is! Good for you, dear." She set the buttered roll on Patty's bread plate. "Do start, sweetheart, you're famished. June, you are having a wonderful effect on Vi here — I've been trying to get her to admit that for ages."

"I'm sorry," Vi said, with a hint of a smile. "I really am. It's just — Well. You see, Francie and I are both taking the Reno cure. And my husband has insisted on this divorce despite the fact that his own comportment has hardly been that of a gentleman."

"One cannot say more in polite company,"

30

Francie said, eyeing the little girl, who was already nearly finished with the roll. "But let's just say that Mr. Carothers's attention often strayed."

"I'm terribly sorry," June said. After a moment she added, "Though I do understand."

"You've experienced something similar," Francie said. It wasn't a question; a girl like June didn't end up on a journey like this unless she'd been forced to. Though Francie had never known want, she could imagine that the security of a marriage was a powerful glue when a girl had no means to support her child.

June blinked several times and gave a faltering smile but said no more. Poor thing, traveling alone, with no friend or sister or mother to console her — who did she have to confide in?

"Where will you be staying in Reno, June?" Vi asked gently.

"We have a room at the Twilight Inn," June said. "We're expected for a week, and after that I'm not sure. I'll be looking for work, you see."

"Pardon me, ladies."

The three turned to see a white-haired man in a perfectly tailored suit, dining alone with a newspaper folded next to his plate. "I'm terribly sorry, but I'm guilty of eaves-

31

dropping. Please forgive me, but it isn't every day that I can enjoy the conversation of such lovely ladies as yourselves."

Francie allowed herself a very small snort; she'd never been fond of men who indulged in hyperbole.

"This is very forward of me," he continued, "but I feel it is my duty to most strenuously encourage you to consider other lodging, Miss. The Twilight is a rough place, and the men who lodge there are rougher still. It's no place for a child or her mother."

"I see," Francie said, revising her opinion of the man. "You are familiar with the area?"

"You might say that," he said. He took a card from his pocket and handed it to her. "Lawrence Wheeler, at your service. I grew up in Reno, lived there seventy years next December. Practiced law most of 'em, right downtown. I'm happy to recommend more suitable lodging, if you wish."

"Thank you, but that won't be necessary," Vi said. "Mrs. Samples can stay with me. I have a suite, you see — I've no idea what I would have done with the extra room."

"Oh — but I couldn't —"

"Thank you," Francie interrupted. "As you can see, Mr. Wheeler, we have matters well in hand. Good day."

He nodded and returned to his newspaper.

"Truly, Vi, we can't impose on you," June said. "You've been so kind already, and you must be — that is, it isn't easy — not that I know —"

"You'll be doing me a favor," Vi said calmly. "Harry — my husband — booked a suite because he's trying to assuage his own guilt. I told him it was an unnecessary expense, but now I see that it was meant to be. You'll have your own room, and we can have a cot sent in for Patty, and you can take meals with us. Really, it will be much more pleasant for everyone."

"Seeing as she has nothing to say to me anymore, I agree," Francie teased. Secretly, she was delighted. Maybe the young woman's company would be just the thing to cheer Vi up. And Patty! It was no secret that Vi longed for grandchildren of her own, but since Charlie had broken up with his girl months ago, and Frank showed every sign of remaining a bachelor forever, Vi had been forced to settle for being an honorary auntie to Francie's grandchildren. "And I shall take us all out for dinner at the Mapes Sky Room tonight as a celebration of our first night in Reno. Please, say you will, so we can eat our lunch."

A battle of emotions played across June's face. The waiter approached with a cart laden with dishes covered with gleaming silver lids. The cloth in front of Patty was littered with crumbs, her chin shiny with butter.

"Well, all right," June finally said. "But only to be polite."

Francie grinned and gave Vi a wink. Their new friend, it seemed, had an impish side.

It would come in handy, if the rumors were to be believed. According to Harry, who was currently promoting nuclear tourism in the desert near Las Vegas, there were all sorts of entertainments on offer for the soon-to-be-single ladies of Reno.

Harry was a fool if he thought that the prospect of gambling or horseback riding or nightclubs would appeal to his wife. Francie, on the other hand, thought she might have to see what was on offer. After all, why bother shaking up her entire life if she was just going to stay in and mope?

CHAPTER 4

As the *City of San Francisco* rolled into Reno, her whistle announcing their arrival, Vi pressed her nose to the window at the breathtaking view. Mountains rose up in the distance to the east and south, the highest peaks topped with snow despite the warmth of late spring.

They were back in their sleeping compartment, having arranged to meet June and Patty on the platform after June retrieved their bags.

"It's beautiful," Francie said. "You must be so happy to see the mountains again."

"Oh yes." Vi sighed. "I haven't made a snowball in — well, as long as I can remember. Mother used to let me play outside for hours after big snowstorms, until I couldn't feel my fingers and toes."

Francie shuddered. "That sounds horrid."

"It was wonderful! Mother made hot cocoa and toasted cheese sandwiches when

35

I finally came in." She turned away from the window, her eyes animated and shining. "And Papa would pull me on the sled all the way up the hill, over and over so I could come zipping down. I don't know how many times I fell off and ended up facedown in a drift!"

"Vi, are you sure you don't want to try to visit family while you're here?" Francie asked. "I'm sure they'd be thrilled to see you again."

The light left Vi's eyes and Francie could have kicked herself. "I'd be too ashamed," she said. "I haven't spoken to any of my cousins in years — I don't even know if any of them are still in the area. And none of my aunts and uncles are even alive anymore."

That damn Harry. It was his fault that Vi'd lost touch with her family, in Francie's opinion — there were only so many times Vi could stand to hear him dismiss her relatives as uneducated country folk before she gave up and quit suggesting they visit.

A sharp rap at the door was accompanied by the porter's announcement that the train would be pulling into the station and that their bags would be brought to them on the platform.

"Well — are we ready?" Francie said.

"I suppose so. Though I have half a mind to stay on and ride this train right back to San Francisco."

"Whatever for? You've been wanting to come back as long as I've known you."

"Yes, but not for this. I wish it could be the way it used to be, back when I was just a girl. But everything is different now. Nothing stays the same."

"No," Francie said sadly. "No, I don't suppose it does."

"I wish —" Vi caught herself and shook her head.

"What, dear? Tell me."

"I just wish that I'd made time to come back when . . . during happier times. When the boys were younger, and I could have shown them around. Maybe made a vacation of it — we could have brought the kids and taken them horseback riding."

Francie made a face. "Arthur would never have gotten on a horse — he thinks they're filthy beasts."

"Just the two of us, then, and the kids. They're all grown up now — you've got grandchildren."

"Well, then, we'll simply have to bring all of them. Soon you'll have grandchildren of your own, you'll see." Francie was doing her best to cheer Vi up. "Oh, look — there's June."

They filed onto the platform with the other passengers to wait for their bags, enjoying the sun on their faces and the smell of creosote that always reminded Francie of childhood visits to her relatives, most of whom had been gone for years. A few blocks away, the gaudy neon signs she'd seen on television rose up over the casinos: the Apache Casino had an Indian head on top, complete with blinking feather headdress, and across the street the Pioneer Club cowboy tipped his neon hat. Towering over the rest was the bucking mule atop the Prospector, the brand-new casino that was rumored to have cost more than eight million dollars to build.

For all the traveling Francie had done in her life, she'd never seen a city quite like this, with the frenetic bustle and brilliant lights of Times Square, nestled in the bosom of nature's stately majesty.

"Have you *ever,*" June said and sighed, as Patty craned her neck to look in every direction, her eyes as big as saucers.

"I believe I see our ride," Vi said. Leaning against the bumper of a battered Ford pickup truck that had been patched in several shades of paint was a grizzled-looking gent in a black cowboy hat and boots, smoking a cigarette and holding up a sign with their names written in neat block letters. They waved at him, and he flicked the butt to the ground and crushed it with the toe of his boot. After tossing the sign into the back of the truck and wiping his hands on his pants, he ambled over.

"Hello," Francie said. "I'm Mrs. Meeker and this is Mrs. Carothers, and we've been joined by Mrs. Samples and her daughter, Patty."

"They'll be staying in my suite with me," Vi added.

"It's a pleasure to meet you," the man said, removing his hat. Underneath, his hair was thick as a teenager's but shot through with gray. "My name's Clyde Hardy. Mrs. Swanson sent me to bring you back to the hotel. See here, though, I wasn't expecting but the two of you. I couldn't bring the car because Mrs. Swanson had to go to court this morning."

"But there's no way we'll all fit," Vi fretted, peering into the truck's cab. "Mr. Hardy, I am afraid you will have to make two trips. I will wait here while you take the others and then you can return for me."

"Nonsense," Francie said. "You three go first, Vi, so you can get June and Patty

39

settled in your suite. I'm sure I'll be just fine."

She was sure of no such thing — the train station seemed a bit dodgy, with shady-looking men loitering outside — but Vi tended to be easily upset by changes in plans. Besides, an adventurous spirit had come over her when they invited June and Patty to join them.

"We'll just ride in the back!" June said brightly, already dragging her suitcase toward the rear of the truck. Patty followed like a little duckling after its mother. "I rode in the back of my daddy's truck all the time when I was growing up."

"It's only two miles up the river," Clyde said, obviously relieved not to have to make the second trip. "And I'll drive nice and slow. I've even got a couple of old buckets back there to sit on."

Francie stilled Vi's protest with a squeeze of her hand. She'd ridden in the back of a truck once herself — before meeting Arthur, she'd dated a boy whose father was a cotton farmer in the Imperial Valley, and on a visit home, he drove them through what seemed like endless white fields. She remembered being pleasantly terrified as she clung to the side of the truck bed for dear life, watching the dirt road rushing by, the

40

smell of cut hay in the air — so strange to remember that she had been a bit of a thrill-seeker in her day.

Clyde pulled down the tailgate to start loading their bags. June had only a single suitcase, a sorry-looking thing held together with twine, and after Clyde had lifted it into the truck bed June scrambled nimbly up, holding the hem of her skirt. When Clyde lifted Patty up into the truck bed, he pretended to stagger under her weight.

"What are you made of, girl — iron ore?"

Patty squealed with laughter. Clyde went back for more suitcases, making several trips to carry everything Francie and Vi had brought for their six-week stay. He closed the tailgate and came around to the passenger side to assist the ladies, who squeezed together on the bench seat. The cab smelled of motor oil and tobacco and the dashboard held two packs of Pall Malls, one crumpled and the other half empty, but it was fairly clean. Clyde adjusted the mirror and lit a fresh cigarette before pulling out of the parking lot into the street.

"I hear you ladies are from San Francisco, so I know you're used to city ways," he said. "But Reno's a heck of a town. We like to say it's the biggest little city on the map."

Francie twisted in her seat to check on

June, who was perched on a bucket with Patty in her arms. Her curls had escaped their pins and were being whipped by the wind, but she was smiling.

"Now, right there, that's the Virginia Street Bridge," Clyde was saying. "Nowadays some folks call it the Wedding Ring Bridge, on account of ladies coming out of the courthouse with their divorce papers and celebrating by throwing their rings into the Truckee River. She's a beauty, ain't she? But don't be fooled just because she's behaving today — she gets wild now and then. Two years ago on Thanksgiving Day, she busted clear through the Boca Reservoir and made a real mess. And with all the rains we had last month, she's itching to do it again."

Francie peered down at the water. Clyde was right — it was running high and brackish, carrying downed branches and submerging much of the vegetation along the banks. People leaned over the bridge rails to watch.

"Now, over there's the Mapes Hotel — tallest building in Nevada. You can see the entire Sierra Nevada range on a clear day from those windows up on the top floor."

"I've seen pictures," Vi said, "but it's even more remarkable in person."

42

"You don't know the half of it," Clyde said, obviously enjoying his role as guide. "Prettiest chorus girls anywhere — those New York City Rockettes don't have anything on the Skylettes."

"I can't believe how many casinos there are!" Francie said, as they passed the Silver Spur, the Senator, the Prospector — and those were just the biggest; tucked between them were smaller joints, card clubs and bingo rooms. "Can there really be enough gamblers for all of them?"

Clyde chuckled. "Yes, ma'am, there sure are, and ever since the state got smart and started taxing gambling income Reno's been doing real well. And now, of course, we've got you ladies spending money here too. Divorcées pouring in from all over the country create a lot of jobs. If Mrs. Swanson hadn't hired me, I probably would have spent my golden years sitting on my porch and talking to my dog."

The downtown casinos and businesses gave way to homes as they drove west. On the other side of the river, the bank rose up into tall cliffs with mansions perched on the top, but on this side were more modest bungalows with well-tended flowerbeds and porches looking out onto the river, which in turn gave way to rich bottomland. Clyde turned into a circular drive bordered by a split-log fence.

"Here we are," he said cheerfully. "The Holiday Ranch, in all its glory."

The sprawling three-story hotel was hardly a ranch, but it did remind Francie of a summer camp her mother had sent her to when she was a girl. Francie had been an awkward child, constantly bumping into things and knocking things over and failing the most basic lessons of comportment. The camp was in the Sierra foothills an hour or two to the south and was comprised of a dozen cabins nestled in an evergreen forest. There was a large stone fire ring for roasting marshmallows, three other girls in her cabin who all thought she was clever, name tags sewn into all her clothes, and wholesome exercise from sunup to sundown.

There, Francie had felt at ease; her stout legs were fine for shinnying up trees and her sunburnt arms propelled her silently through the water during twilight swims. Francie had been happy there.

Like the camp's dining hall, the Holiday Ranch hotel was sided with whitewashed shingles and trimmed with green shutters with cutouts in the shape of Christmas trees. Rustic beams hewn from the trunks of enormous trees supported the slate roof,

44

and stripped lodgepole pine logs served as porch posts. There were wooden rocking chairs and hanging baskets of flowers and a hitching post out front, along with a decorative wishing well. The Western theme continued into the parking lot on the side of the building, which was enclosed by a split-rail fence to which several sets of steer horns and a bleached-white cow skull were attached. On the other side of the hotel was a garden divided by stone walkways and arches blooming with climbing roses, all arranged around a fountain, the water arcing up from an old cattle trough before splashing down into a mossy, rock-lined pool.

Clyde came around and opened the door of the truck for Francie and Vi, then helped June and Patty down from the truck bed.

"Any worse for wear, Miss?"

"Only my hair!" June laughed, attempting to pat it into place.

"How about you, young lady? Catch any flies with your tongue?"

"No," Patty replied seriously. "But I saw some ducks. Do you live here?"

"No, I just work here. But maybe you can help me with my chores. I'll pay you a penny, how does that sound?"

"He's teasing, sweetie," June said. "But

isn't this the loveliest place you've ever seen?"

Francie suppressed a smile. Though the setting and the view were spectacular, *lovely* wasn't the word that came to mind. The brochure had made much of the fact that the hotel had once been the summer mansion of a turn-of-the-century railroad baron before it was renovated and expanded to meet the needs of divorcées flocking to town in recent years. The rooms were richly appointed, the food was supposed to be excellent, and the prices were certainly extravagant — but the ersatz Western features were . . . well, Francie had promised herself that she'd do her best to get into the spirit of things, so she decided they were *fun.*

"It's quite nice, isn't it?" Vi agreed.

"I've only stayed in a motel once before," June confessed. "On my wedding night. It was supposed to have a view of Folsom Lake, but we got stuck in a room over the restaurant and it smelled like bacon and burnt coffee and all we could see was the parking lot."

Clyde had obviously been listening as he lifted down their bags. He picked up June's suitcase first, treating it with exaggerated care as though it were made of fine Italian leather instead of battered pasteboard. Francie decided she liked him fine.

"That's your suite right up there," he said, pointing to where white lace curtains fluttered in an open window on the third floor. "Best view in the whole place. And a bathtub with feet like a giant crow."

He pretended to claw at the air with his work-scarred hands, his thick yellowed nails. Patty shrieked with laughter and hid behind her mother.

"Is my room close to theirs?" Francie asked. "I did request it."

"No, ma'am, it's on the second floor, but it has the same view. Trust me, you'll be glad you're in the old part of the building. If you ask me, they cut corners on the newer rooms. Now, follow me, and you can check in while I take your things up to your rooms. By the time you've got your keys, you can go on up and relax."

"Where are the horses?" Patty asked.

"I'm sorry, Miss Patty, but this isn't that kind of a ranch. But we've got a library, and a card room, and a very nice lounge, and a fancy dining room. And of course, there's Miss Virgie, I believe she's only a year or two older than you. Didn't you tell me you were ten?"

Patty stared at him. "I'm *four,*" she said sternly.

"Oh, well, so she's a bit older. But she's a real firecracker, you'll see. And out back by the shed, we've got the meanest cat in the West. Goes by Petunia. We keep her around for safety — she brought down two mountain lions last week. Got their bones stuck in her teeth. Gotta watch out for her — if she's hungry she might try to take a bite of your leg."

Patty's eyes widened with alarm.

"He's just teasing, dear," Vi said reassuringly. "I'm quite sure there are no mountain lions to worry about, and Petunia will be too busy to bother you. Isn't that right, Mr. Hardy?"

Taking her tone, Clyde chuckled. "I'm sure you're right. With Petunia on the prowl, this is the safest place to be in all of Nevada."

The door flew open and a girl of eleven or twelve came flying out, all knobby knees and skinny freckled limbs in a yellow romper and socks bagging around her ankles. Her long yellow hair was escaping its pigtails and she had a book in her hand. She paid no attention to them as she raced past, down the street toward town.

"That," Clyde said with something akin to admiration, "was Miss Virginia Swanson."

CHAPTER 5

Clyde escorted them up the wide porch steps and through a pair of heavy Dutch doors made to look as if they came from a barn, the top half open to let the breeze in. Directly in front of them was a desk with a bored-looking young man sitting behind it, wearing a white shirt and a string tie and a fake sheriff's star stamped with the word *Security.*

"Howdy, ladies, welcome to the Holiday!" he said.

"This is Paul," Clyde said. "He's here to keep you safe and to make sure you meet the residency requirement. Mrs. Swanson will serve as your resident witness when you go to court, and the sign-in records provide evidence of your uninterrupted residence."

"I'll sign you in and out every time you come through the door, even if you're just going out for a stroll," Paul said. "The only exception is the garden off the dining room.

49

It's completely fenced, and to get from the garden to any other part of the grounds, you'll have to come back in and out the front door."

"There are fire doors at the end of each wing and in the back," Clyde said, "but only the staff can bypass them. Anyone else goes out, the alarm will sound, and nobody wants that, because then I have to go room to room checking on you girls."

"You certainly take the rules seriously," Vi observed. "Is all this caution really necessary?"

"Well, ma'am, if Mrs. Swanson speaks for you in court but can't prove you were on site at least an hour each day, she could go to jail for perjury. She wouldn't be the first — and the minimum sentence is ten years. Not to mention the fact that your case would be thrown out."

"Well, we can't have that," Francie said. "I didn't go to all this trouble just to lose my court case over a silly clerical error."

"Don't worry," Clyde reassured her. "There's one of these fellows on duty around the clock. You'll need to show your key every time you enter until they recognize you by sight. Guests are allowed in the first-floor public areas, but only after the security guard signs them in."

He led them past the desk, through a reception hall anchored by a huge fireplace flanked by leather couches and a coffee table made from a wagon wheel, with a glass top. Above the mantel hung an oil painting of a cattle drive, and the day's papers were stacked in an old copper coal shuttle. The reception desk was built from knotty pine, and the woman who came out to greet them wore cowboy boots and a checked kerchief knotted over her blouse.

"We've got our work cut out with this one, Mrs. Swanson," Clyde said, nudging Patty. "I expect she'll be wanting her dinner before long. She mentioned that she has a hankering for a side of roasted river rhinoceros."

"That will be all, Mr. Hardy," Mrs. Swanson responded unsmilingly. "Do tell Mr. Yang that Archie's been late with the linens again. He was nearly twenty minutes late yesterday, which makes it very difficult for Flossie to finish, as you might imagine."

"Sure, sure. I'll make sure he's here pronto. Good day, ladies." He tipped his hat, then hefted June's suitcase and headed up the stairs, whistling.

Francie considered Mary Swanson with interest. She'd rarely seen a woman order a grown man around like that, unless he was a servant or a merchant, and even then, most women she knew enlisted their husbands to get them in line. Mary Swanson was plain and short and doughy, but her confidence signaled a force to be reckoned with — exactly the kind of woman she'd want to vouch for her in court.

"I'm Francis Meeker, and this is Vi Carothers, June Samples, and Miss Patty Samples. I trust you were expecting us?"

Mrs. Swanson drew two heavy keys from her pocket but didn't hand them over. "I was only expecting you and Mrs. Carothers. As you'll remember from my letter, no overnight guests are allowed. I'm afraid there are no exceptions to that policy."

"I'm quite sure you're mistaken," Vi said firmly. "I made it clear when I spoke to your assistant on the phone that I was traveling with my cousin and her child."

"I'm not sure who you spoke to, but no one informed me."

"Her husband has abandoned her, and she is of limited means," Vi continued, "and her mother prevailed upon me to bring her with me when she heard about my circumstances. It certainly seemed like a sensible solution. Tell me, why would I request your largest suite if I was traveling alone?"

"I'm sure I don't know — I do not make

a practice of speculating on my guests' concerns."

"Admirable. All the same, it would be a shame for you to have to find another guest to take the suite at this late date, since I'll obviously be forced to cancel if you can't accommodate us."

Francie said nothing while the two stared at each other like cats facing off in an alley. She was mystified by Vi's behavior; ordinarily she didn't speak up for herself, even when she was in the right. Whatever was responsible for Vi's new attitude, Francie thought it was an improvement.

Finally, Mrs. Swanson dropped her gaze. "Very well," she said. "But the child must not disturb the other guests. Children's meals are one-half the adult fee, and no special requests will be considered. She must eat the same as everyone else."

"She's a good eater," June piped up. "And she's well behaved. You'll have no trouble from her, I promise."

"Now that that's taken care of, we would like reservations for dinner at the Mapes Hotel tonight," Francie said. "Seven-thirty would be ideal. I trust you can take care of that for us?"

"Of course, Mrs. Meeker. Shall I arrange for a taxi?"

"Yes, please. And can arrangements be made for Patty? She's had quite a long day, and I'm sure she'll go to bed early, but perhaps someone could see to her dinner and stay with her until our return."

"My daughter, Virginia, will be happy to help," Mrs. Swanson said. "I'll send her up at seven-fifteen."

"I'm sure your daughter is a lovely girl," June said hesitantly. "I believe we saw her leave, actually, but is she . . . that is to say, she seems very young —"

"Virginia has been babysitting since she was ten. She's a very responsible girl. And she charges just twenty-five cents an hour."

"There's no need to decide now," Francie said. "Let's see how Patty is doing when we're ready to leave. Perhaps a nap would do her good?"

"I'm not sleepy," Patty protested, though she looked ready to collapse, her dress wilted and her hair in tangles from the drive.

"Vi, let's see June to the suite, and then you can come to my room with me," Francie suggested. "We'll let June and Patty get their rest, and you can help me settle in. Mrs. Swanson, could you send some lemonade up? And perhaps a cookie or two?"

"Tea and sherry are served in the lounge at five," Mrs. Swanson said. "There's no service to the rooms, I'm afraid. Breakfast and lunch are to be taken in the dining room only, and dinner requires reservations by noon. There will be a sign-up sheet here every morning but Saturday, when no dinner is served."

"How wonderfully civilized," Francie said. "Not having to cook or do dishes for six weeks might just make this ordeal worth it."

CHAPTER 6

"Did you see her looking around the suite? It's as if she'd never seen anything like it before."

Francie and Vi were reclining in a pair of green club chairs that flanked the fireplace in Francie's room, their feet up on the matching ottomans.

"She probably hadn't," Vi said. "I don't believe *I've* ever seen a lampshade made from cowhide before. And I can't imagine how she'll sleep with a painting of some poor fool about to be gored to death hanging over the bed."

"How do you know the bull wins the fight? My money's on the cowboy."

"And that suitcase," Vi continued. "Practically falling apart, and all she had were those four sad dresses. Thank goodness we're the same size — though I had to beg her to borrow one of mine."

"But she had twice as many clothes for

Patty." Francie, who'd been forced to learn embroidery as a girl, had examined the fine handwork and lavished June with compliments after she admitted that she sewed Patty's clothes from her mother-in-law's hand-me-downs.

"What kind of man lets his wife walk around in rags while he does whatever he pleases?"

"We don't know that," Francie scolded. "And besides, she won't be his wife for much longer."

Despite the house rules prohibiting food in the rooms, they'd found an electric teakettle already filled with water and a selection of teas in an alabaster box. Francie had brewed a pot of lichee black tea and they were sipping lazily as the sun sank over the river, the view as magnificent as Clyde had promised.

"I don't mean to sound like June, but this is one of the nicest hotels I've ever stayed in," Vi said. "Do you know, even on our honeymoon Harry refused to book a suite. He said it would be a waste since he didn't plan to get out of bed the entire time. And he kept his promise — had me calling for room service three times a day and got crumbs everywhere."

"He feels guilty," Francie said. "That's

why he got you a suite."

"Actually, *I* arranged for the suite," Vi admitted. "I didn't tell you before, but he booked me a single in the new wing, the cheapest rooms in the hotel. I called back and said he'd made a mistake. Mrs. Swanson doesn't remember, but she was more than happy to switch it. I doubt Harry even looked at the bill."

"Oh, Vi, I wish you'd started standing up for yourself ages ago."

"At least I am now." Vi's expression grew serious. "Did you notice that June unpacked two short-sleeved dresses — and yet on the hottest day so far this year, she was wearing sleeves down to her wrists?"

Francie didn't comment on Vi's change of subject. "She was, now that you mention it."

"And there were faded marks on the side of her neck. I wouldn't be surprised if there were more of them under her clothes."

"Do you think that's why she was so reluctant to stay with you?"

"Maybe. Though I think it was mostly just shame. I doubt that girl's got enough money to see her through the week."

"I'd like a word with her husband. At least Harry never beat you." Something occurred to Francie. "He hasn't, has he? You'd tell

58

me, dear, wouldn't you?"

Vi laughed. "Oh, Fran, you don't need to worry about that. I suppose I should be grateful, really. The worst thing Harry is guilty of is a wandering eye."

"And a wandering *pecker.*"

"Francie!"

It was Francie's turn to laugh. "If we can't say what we please here in Reno, then where can we? They say girls dance on tables in the nightclubs, that they gamble at the poker tables alongside the men. Just think of it — we can carry on like a couple of drunk sailors, and no one back home will ever know."

"Well, still — it's a bit shocking to hear that sort of language come out of your mouth. If I had a nickel for every time you threatened to wash Jimmy's mouth out with soap!"

"But I sort of enjoyed saying it. It felt quite freeing." Francie grinned. "Pecker. Prod. Ding-dong!"

"Please!" Vi shrieked, covering her ears with her hands. "I don't think I can bear it."

"Oh, fine, I'll save it for when I'm smoking cigars and drinking whiskey and whatever other trouble I can find. But seriously, dear, it does feel good to be able to talk about things we never talked about at home, doesn't it?"

Tentatively, Vi took her hands away from her ears. "I'm not sure I like where this is going . . ."

Francie took pity on her best friend. After all, even if this wasn't the first or even the fifth girl Harry had taken up with, it was definitely the first one he'd left her for. Arthur, on the other hand, had been apologizing for his trespasses for nearly two decades now. She'd had plenty of time to get used to the idea, even if she'd never accept it. Dear old Arthur — he'd given her the best he could, and if that love was never quite enough, at least it kept her from having to feel the loneliness that seemed to follow Vi around like a kicked dog.

"Vi," she said hesitantly. "If you ever did want to talk about it — if you ever needed someone to listen — I wouldn't tell a soul. You know that, don't you? Because I couldn't bear it if —"

Vi snatched the napkin from her lap and dabbed at her eyes. "Don't," she pleaded. "If I start, I'll never stop. And since you've promised me dinner at the Sky Room, I really must hold myself together."

"All right," Francie said quietly. Every time she'd tried to talk to Vi about her sadness, she'd been rebuffed. She wished she could breach the wall Vi kept around her, convince her that only good could come from unburdening herself. The truth was that she had a secret too, and she longed to finally share it with another living soul. Vi was the only person Francie trusted, not just because she'd take her secrets to her grave, but because Vi would see past the shocking facts and understand that Arthur was no monster, that he was decent in nearly every way.

Life wasn't fair. Good people suffered. But that wasn't news; Francie had seen the proof too many times. When Francie's mother died two days shy of meeting her first grandchild. When the boys returned from the war and so many of their friends didn't. When Alice had been born and the nurses whisked her away, refusing to look at Francie until the doctor came to examine the baby and told her, with as much concern as if he were weighing a calf, that her daughter had a condition called fibular hemimelia. "She's lucky," he'd said, after explaining that Alice's left leg would always be several inches shorter than her right. "At least her foot is only mildly deformed."

People could be as unkind as Fate herself, which was why a friendship like theirs was so precious. Sometimes Francie thought there was nothing she couldn't endure, as long as she had Vi.

She reached out and took Vi's hand. "Not one more tear tonight. But just wait until I get you as drunk as a skunk one of these days."

This was an easy threat to make because Vi almost never touched a drop of liquor — but Vi surprised her today. "If I ever *do* take a drink, it's not me you need to worry about."

Francie wondered if Harry knew just how close to disaster he'd come.

CHAPTER 7
VIRGIE

After dropping off Willy's magazine, Virgie took the back stairs to her room to avoid passing by the lobby. Whenever possible, she liked to conceal her comings and goings from her mother.

Virgie's room was in the basement. When her mother had first bought the Holiday with the money from her divorce, when Virgie was only a baby, they'd moved into the maid's quarters behind the kitchen, where Virgie slept in her mother's bed and then, when she got bigger, on a cot. As the hotel began turning a profit, her mother had expanded into what had been the morning room, remodeling the space into a roomy apartment. But Virgie still slept on the cot until her tenth birthday, when her mother finally allowed her to move to the basement.

Clyde walled off a corner of the basement that had decent light coming in a window well, tiled the floor and lined the walls with beadboard. He'd installed a wall of shelves he'd picked up secondhand from a law office that was being demolished, and her mother bought her a bed with a painted headboard and matching desk. Virgie finally had a place to display the treasures she collected and her Nancy Drew books, and a good hiding place for her journals and savings. On rainy days her room smelled faintly of onion skins and mildew, but it was a small price to pay for a place of her own.

Once inside, she turned the deadbolt and began preparing for her babysitting job. She would be watching a four-year-old in Room 302, the largest suite in the hotel. Mother said that two cousins were staying there, in a voice that implied she didn't approve, but she refused to explain why. The ladies were going to the Sky Room for dinner and so Virgie knew they would probably be gone for hours. Ladies who could afford the Sky Room sometimes paid Virgie extra. One time a lady gave her a crisp five-dollar bill after her four-year-old vomited on Virgie's sweater.

She checked her babysitting kit, a collection of toys and games she stored in an old tackle box that Clyde had given her. In the compartments meant for lures were jacks and marbles and pipe cleaners, while the large compartment held coloring books and crayons and scratch paper and the dolls that Virgie had outgrown ages ago. Four-year-olds were more interesting than babies, but they were also fast-moving and curious and didn't have a lick of sense. Virgie would have to be vigilant.

Up on the third floor, things were quiet. The ladies who booked suites tended to keep to themselves, though they could be demanding. Mother said that the richer people were, the more they expected to be waited on, but the flip side was that they rarely damaged anything or tried to sneak guests upstairs.

Room 302 was next to the third-floor supply closet, which Virgie sometimes used for eavesdropping, pressing her ear against the wall it shared with the suite. There was another closet directly below on the second floor, and once, when Virgie was eavesdropping there, she had overheard a guest in the adjoining room arguing on the phone with her husband and learned a number of fascinating things. Virgie already knew the basics about sex from a book she'd found in the library, but the guest was telling her husband all the ways that he wasn't very good at it, including some shocking claims about what he did before and during the act, as well as another thing they did that apparently involved him licking her between her legs. Virgie couldn't imagine why he would do such a thing and was certain she'd misunderstood, but she'd written it all down in her diary anyway.

Virgie stood outside the door for a moment, listening for voices, but all was silent. She knocked and a skinny older lady in a fancy blue dress answered the door.

"Well, hello there. You must be Virginia. I'm Mrs. Carothers." The lady had a friendly smile and short dark hair like Jean Simmons. She wore pearl earrings and a matching necklace, a gold wedding ring, and on her other hand, a ring with a giant red stone surrounded by two rounds of diamonds. Virgie couldn't help staring at it — she'd recently cut out an article from one of her mother's magazines and pasted it in her notebook, about the most romantic engagement ever: Norma Shearer's movie executive boyfriend called her into his office at MGM and presented her with a tray full of rings and told her to choose whichever she liked. She ended up choosing one that cost the unimaginable sum of nineteen thousand dollars — and it wasn't even as big and fancy as Mrs. Carothers's ring!

Virgie realized that Mrs. Carothers was

waiting for her to reply. "Yes, ma'am. And that must be Patty I hear in the other room?"

"Oh, yes. Her mother's just finishing getting ready — won't you come in?"

Virgie entered the room, casing it the way she had learned from the Post's Junior Detective Corps manual that Wally Heard, the hotel chef, had given her. Virgie knew all the rooms at the Holiday Ranch like the back of her hand, since they had been her nursery, her playroom, her kindergarten back when her mother had done much of the cleaning herself. In fact, she had probably played on this very same floor.

Using the tips in the manual, Virgie had trained herself to notice only what was different. The telephone had been moved as far as the cord would reach, to one of the built-in shelves, as had the bowl of wax fruit, probably to keep them out of Patty's reach. A lightweight sweater was draped over the arm of one of the chairs, and an empty teacup rested on the table next to it. On top of the little table under the mirror was a large black alligator-skin purse with a gold buckle.

"Make yourself comfortable, Virginia. I just need to use the bathroom quickly, and Mrs. Samples should be out shortly."

Virgie nodded in response.

She didn't have to wait long before a much younger woman came out of the small room, leading a little girl by the hand. The woman was wearing a beautiful shimmering green dress with tiny sleeves that barely covered her shoulders and a full skirt that danced around her legs as she walked — but her stockings had runs in them and her shoes were old and scuffed, the heels worn down, with the leather coming off. Her only jewelry was a tiny gold cross on a thin chain. She wore no makeup, but she had a pretty face.

The stockings and shoes were a mystery that bore further scrutiny. Virgie wondered if this was what had caught her mother's attention — that or the fact that there was such a large age difference between the two women. Although Flossie had cousins that were young enough to be her children, so maybe it didn't mean anything.

"Oh, hello," the woman said. "I'm Mrs. Wen— *Samples,* and this is my daughter, Patty."

"Hello," Virgie said, not missing the woman's slip of the tongue. Interesting. She seemed nervous, too.

She and Patty gazed at each other. Virgie liked the looks of the kid — serious, with

68

hair as unmanageable as her own, the kind that probably drove her mother crazy.

"She's had her dinner," Mrs. Samples said, "and she's tired from our trip, so she'll be ready for bed. I usually sing to her when I put her to bed. Maybe you could, if you know some songs . . . ?"

What kind of question was that? "I know lots of songs, Mrs. Samples."

"Shall we be going?" Mrs. Carothers asked, emerging from the bathroom with a freshly powdered nose.

"Just a second," Mrs. Samples said, leading Patty into the bathroom. When they walked out a moment later, Patty's curls had been dampened to coax them into behaving.

Mrs. Samples knelt and kissed Patty's cheek. "Be good for Virginia."

"Why?" Patty asked.

"I'm going to have dinner with Mrs. Carothers."

"Why?"

Mrs. Samples stood. "We'd better leave now," she said worriedly, "before I change my mind."

"All right, then," Mrs. Carothers said. "Goodbye, Patty. Goodbye, Virginia."

After she closed the door, Patty gazed up at Virgie with eyes as round as silver dollars.

"They sure were in a hurry, weren't they?" Virgie said — just as Patty started to wail.

CHAPTER 8
FRANCIE

"All better, dear?" Francie asked when the driver dropped them in front of the Mapes Hotel. She had a feeling that the cab driver Mrs. Swanson had summoned had overcharged them and figured he was paying her a little something for the referral. No harm in that — Francie admired any woman who ran a business, something she'd sometimes wondered if she might like to try.

"Yes, much, thank you." June had confided when they got in the cab that she'd never left her baby with a stranger before — had barely left her at all, Francie surmised. June's husband apparently refused to be left alone with her, and she had no family back in Roseville.

A doorman in a red velvet jacket held the door open. "Madam," he said with a slight bow. Francie caught Vi's eye and winked as she slipped her arm through June's and they walked in together.

The lobby was breathtaking, with red carpets on the polished marble floors and heavy silk drapes. Beautifully dressed men and women came and went from the entrance to the casino, as the sounds of laughter and slot machines drifted out.

They took the elevator to the twelfth floor, where the doors opened directly onto the large dining room lined with windows on all sides. Tuxedoed waiters moved smoothly among the tables carrying trays, while busboys discreetly swept crumbs from the tablecloths and whisked away dishes. The distinguished-looking maître d' looked up from his post at a polished wood stand with a welcoming smile. But most impressive of all was the view from the large windows on two sides of the room, the neon lights coming on in the purpling twilight as the moon rose in the sky, and the dark band of the river winding as far as the eye could see.

"I — I don't think I should be here," June said, hanging back in the elevator.

"Madam?" the operator said, his hand on the button.

"I'm sorry, I'm so sorry, I need to go back. I don't belong, I can't —" Her face was contorted with fear.

Francie took her arm and led her out, nodding at the operator. "Come here, dear, let's talk over here where we can have some privacy, all right?"

"But —"

"Just for a minute," Vi chimed in.

Francie held up a finger at the maître d'. "One moment, please."

They guided June to a little nook around the corner from the coat check. "What's wrong, darling?"

June clutched her purse handle for dear life. "I've never been anywhere like this before. I don't know what to do. How to act."

Vi took her hand. "It's really not so different from a diner. They just dirty a lot more dishes and give you less food. Just follow my lead and do what I do, all right?"

"But, Patty —"

"Patty's playing as nice as you please right now," Francie said firmly. "I'm sure she only cried for a few minutes. My kids were the same way, crying for show and then forgetting all about me once I was out the door. Virginia seems smart as a whip, and did you see the kit she brought with her? You'll see, Patty will have the time of her life."

"But what if she's scared?"

"This is good for her. I promise." Francie had barely let Alice out of her sight until she started school, too worried about the cruel things people might say, the way they stared. As a result, poor Alice had been painfully shy, and it had taken years for her to come out of her shell. If Francie had it to do over, she would have done as she had with her other children and let Alice learn to take her knocks and pick herself back up again.

She led the way back to the maître d' and announced, "We are ready to be seated now, please. The name is Meeker."

"Yes, madam. This way."

He led them to a table near the window, where Francie stood aside so June could have the seat next to the window. A glowing rim of orange was all that remained of the sun as it sank behind the mountains.

June watched Francie and Vi and followed their lead, laying her napkin in her lap and picking up her menu and sipping from her water only after they did so first. She listened attentively as the waiter described the specials, but when he left, she visibly relaxed.

"I've never heard anyone go on so about dinner," she said. "I'm not even sure what most of those dishes were."

"Well, I think the rabbit sounds delicious," Vi said. "And the asparagus should be very fresh this time of year."

"Just pick something that sounds good," Francie said. "And we'll ask the sommelier to help choose the wine."

"Remember, all the people who work here — their job is to make sure you have a nice time," Vi added.

Once they had ordered, and Francie selected a bottle of Bordeaux, June seemed to start enjoying herself. She delighted over the basket of rolls, the little silver tongs the waiter used to set one on her plate. She exclaimed over the little pats of butter molded into fleur-de-lis, the pool of creamy sauce under the asparagus. When the waiter wielded a giant pepper grinder over her chicken divan, her eyes went wide.

"Oh," she said, after taking a bite of the chicken. She closed her eyes and chewed rapturously. "I've never tasted anything so delicious!"

"Life is full of surprises," Vi said. "Who knows what you'll try next? I wish I'd been more adventurous when I was young."

"What on earth do you mean?" Francie asked, picking at her New York strip. It was quite good, but she didn't have much of an appetite tonight. There was simply too much to think about. "You married Harry three months after meeting him and moved to the big city — that seems pretty adventurous considering you'd barely been out of Reno."

"I was only doing what was expected." Vi shrugged. "My parents worked their fingers to the bone so that I could go to college. They wanted to see me move up in the world. Harry had a good job and a nice car and you know how he talks — my parents thought he was the second coming."

"The things we do just because we're *expected*," Francie said. "It's a shame — by the time you figure out what you really want out of life, you're someone's wife and mother and you don't even have time to read a book or see a movie."

"It's true," Vi said. "Once I was married we always did what Harry wanted — he didn't like it when I made a fuss. He insisted that we go to the Thunderbird Lodge every summer, even after the boys had gotten bored with it. He wouldn't let me ride the horses or take photography classes. And you know how he was about restaurants — when it was just the two of us, we hardly went anywhere but the Tadich Grill, and he always ordered the same thing."

Vi had never talked like this — she'd almost never complained about Harry until now. "Are you saying you wish you hadn't married him?"

"Not at all — if I hadn't, I wouldn't have my boys!"

"And I wouldn't have Patty," June agreed. "I can't imagine life without her."

"If only there was a way to have our children without men being involved. Divine birth worked for the Virgin Mary, didn't it?"

"Francie!" Vi chided. June looked as if she were about to choke.

"Oh, I'm just teasing. Pay no attention to me."

"I still believe in marriage," Vi said thoughtfully. "It's weddings I'm not so sure about."

"What do you mean?" June asked.

"Well, just think about it. Little girls are told they'll marry handsome princes. They start dreaming of weddings before they can even read the announcements in the papers. I had paper dolls with an entire trousseau, right down to the monogrammed tea towels."

"My mom let me play with her veil," June said. "She kept it in a hatbox, but her dress was packed up in the attic for when I got married."

"Did you wear it?"

"I did," June said sadly. "I was keeping it for Patty, but . . ."

Francie patted her hand, wondering what else the poor thing had been forced to leave behind.

"But that's just it," Vi said. "We're taught to dream about the dress, the flowers, the ring — and none of it matters in the end. It's — it's just a bunch of lies. A fancy wedding gown can't make your husband treat you well. It doesn't matter how beautiful and happy you look on your wedding day, you won't even remember it when life gets hard. And it does, doesn't it? Everyone's life gets hard eventually."

Francie looked at her friend in alarm. They'd only just arrived in Reno; they'd have plenty of time to be morose later. Tonight was supposed to be for celebrating — especially since poor June had been through so much already.

"Well, now's your chance!" she said, forcing herself to sound cheerful. "You can do whatever you like now, Vi. Make your life whatever you want it to be. Move into a new house — as long as it's still close to me, of course — or take up new hobbies, join clubs, take up a cause, anything at all!"

"But, Francie, I don't want to do any of that. I'm perfectly content with my life just as it is. All I meant was that I should have been braver when I was *young.*" After a moment, Vi gave a funny little smile and added, "Nowadays, I think I'm just brave enough."

It was an odd thing to say, but Francie let it pass; Vi probably just meant her decision to go ahead with the divorce. "Well, *I* want to try some new things."

"Like what?" June asked.

"Chinese food," Francie said immediately. "It sounds so interesting. Even the names sound so exotic — chop suey and the like."

"We'll ask Mrs. Swanson for a recommendation, then," Vi said. "I'm sure she knows a good Chinese restaurant. What else?"

"Don't laugh — but I want to learn to ride a bicycle. I never did, as a child. My mother thought it wasn't ladylike." She had a sudden inspiration. "And I want to learn to ski! We could come back here next winter — you could teach me!"

"I can't even imagine skiing," June said. "I've only seen snow once — one winter it got so cold in Roseville we got some flurries, but it melted when it hit the ground. I mean, until yesterday, when I saw the snow on the mountains. But it's different when it's so far away."

"Then you can go with Francie," Vi said. "What else?"

"Let's see." Francie and Arthur had had

some wonderful adventures together. They'd been to Europe and Mexico and made many trips to New York. They'd taken a tour of Yellowstone National Park and gone to Chicago to see an exhibit of fifteenth-century German book illustrations after he had inherited the family printing business. They'd ridden in a hot-air balloon and taken a raft down the American River and gone to the movies in every theater in the city.

But as content as they'd been as companions, there was still a loneliness inside Francie that ached more every year. She didn't want another husband. Even a courtship seemed unlikely and not all that appealing. In truth she thought it might actually be a relief to live alone, to have her single status finally acknowledged so she could stop pretending her marriage was fine.

But she was afraid it wouldn't be enough. As the years with Arthur went by, she had tried to bury the part of her that wasn't needed or wanted. When it wouldn't be ignored, she'd tried to drown it by keeping busy. She'd been cheerful — oh, how cheerful she had tried to be — and supportive; she'd managed the household with efficiency and good humor. She'd joined charitable organizations and helped in the children's schools and given dinner parties for Arthur's clients; and she'd managed their finances too, meeting with the trustees of her fortune and keeping track of her investments. At the end of each day she took off her tasteful dresses and suits and put on an equally tasteful nightgown, applied a good night cream and flossed and brushed her teeth, and went to bed knowing that she'd done all she could.

But, oh, how that emptiness ached.

She suddenly became aware of the others waiting expectantly.

"I'd like to dye my hair red," she announced.

Vi looked surprised. "You always said it wasn't worth the bother to cover the gray."

"But I don't want to just *cover* it," Francie said. "I don't want my dull old brown anymore."

"Do you mean true red, or just strawberry blond?"

"Bright, flaming red! What's wrong with that? If I don't like it, it will grow out. And also, I want to redecorate the living room. Now that Arthur is gone, and the children are grown, I think it might be time for a change."

"What sort of change?"

Francie turned to June. "Vi doesn't like

change," she confided. "She came with me when I chose the furniture for that room twenty years ago. Remember?"

"You wanted the green drapes," Vi said. "And Arthur said they'd make the room feel like a jungle."

"He did. I think I'll make an appointment when we get home. You'll come, won't you?"

"Mmm."

But that was still six weeks away. "What about you, June? What sorts of things will you do differently now?"

June set down her fork. She'd practically cleaned her plate, though her wine remained untouched.

"A job," she said. "I have to get a job. I've never had money of my own, not since our neighbor used to pay me to sit with her father-in-law and make sure he didn't go wandering the neighborhood."

"Vi and I will help you find one, then. I'm sure you're clever at all sorts of things. What sort of work are you interested in?"

"I was in secretarial school when I met my husband. I got good marks. And I was one of the fastest typists in the class." She blushed. "I loved filing. I like to organize things, to take a mess and put it in order. It could be anything — an overgrown garden, a toolshed, a box of photographs."

"Maybe you could finish school while you're here," Vi said. "We could loan you the tuition and you could pay us back when you start working."

"And we could help with Patty," Francie added, thinking it would give her something to do. "You could do your studying at night."

"Oh dear, we've made you anxious," Vi said.

Indeed, June looked slightly nauseated. She was saved from responding by the waiter, who asked if they were finished and refilled Vi's and Francie's wineglasses.

"I see you enjoyed your dinner," he said, winking at June. When she blushed, Francie could have stabbed him.

When he was gone, she said, "I once had an appetite like yours — I was thin as a rail too. Maybe the mountain air will encourage me to get more exercise. I could even look into a reducing program."

"There are the most wonderful trails here for hiking," Vi said.

"Now you can see them again."

But Vi merely shrugged. "It was so long ago. I doubt I could make it halfway up those trails anymore."

"*I'd* love to see them," June said, "if you ever wanted company."

"Thank you, that's very kind."

"And *I* can't wait to see the house you grew up in," Francie said. "You said it's next to the cemetery, right? We can go with you to visit your parents' graves, if you like."

"Sure," Vi said. "That would be nice. There's a plot there for me, you know. My dad bought all three on a payment plan years ago. I want to be buried there when I die."

It hadn't occurred to Francie to wonder where she would be buried now — she'd always assumed that someday she'd be laid to rest next to Arthur, and there was no room near her parents' graves. What would become of her — would they bury her with all her distant relatives in the far corner of the family section of the cemetery, so that future generations would wonder how a Meeker ended up among all those Knopfs? "Let's not think about that now."

"If not now, when?" Vi drained her wine. She'd drunk more tonight than Francie had ever seen her drink before. "It's the sort of thing people should know, isn't it? And I don't want to burden the boys with it."

"Well — you can tell your lawyer, then," Francie said. "Send him a letter. But tonight we're celebrating and I won't hear another word on the subject."

84

There was a sudden commotion across the room, raised voices and the sound of breaking glass. Everyone turned to stare at the maître d', who was attempting to lead a disheveled man away from the dining room. At their feet, a floral arrangement lay in ruins, the vase shattered, the blooms trampled by the stranger's heavy boots.

"You're a goddamn liar!" he shouted, slurring his words, his face bright red. "I know she's here!"

The maître d' spoke quietly while trying to steer the man away, but the stranger shook him off. He lunged for the reservation book just as a huge man in a stained white apron emerged from the kitchen. He yanked the book out of the stranger's hands and handed it to the maître d', then grabbed the stranger's arm and dragged him, cursing, to the elevator. As he pushed the button the stranger landed a kick on his shin, so the large man wrapped his meaty arm around his neck and held him while he writhed and choked until the elevator arrived. Then he dragged the man inside.

"My goodness!" Francie said, as conversation resumed all around them. "I wonder what that was about."

Only then did she notice that June was white as a sheet.

CHAPTER 9
VIRGIE

Virgie had dealt with crying children before, but Patty was keeping it up longer than most. When Virgie tried to pick her up, Patty stiffened her spine and Virgie nearly dropped her, so she tried begging.

"Please, Patty, please stop crying, just for a minute? We can play house or choo-choo or explorers. We can play anything you like. I have a coloring book, do you want to make a picture?"

If Virgie couldn't get her to stop soon, the neighboring guests would call the desk to complain and her mother would come up to investigate, and she might even decide that Virgie couldn't handle Patty and insist on taking over. Which would be terrible, because then Virgie wouldn't be paid.

She looked around for a doll, a stuffed bear, anything that might distract the little girl. "Stay right here. I'm going to see if I can find your toys."

The door to the smaller bedroom was open and Virgie slipped inside, turning on the light. She was an expert in covering her tracks; she'd snuck into the guest rooms ever since her mother gave her a copy of the master key.

A battered suitcase sat open on the luggage rack, but it was empty. Four dresses hung in the closet — strangely, they were mere rags, patched and faded from washing. The desk was empty save for a small, worn Bible.

Virgie checked the dresser and found a stack of pretty child's dresses, neatly folded, and half a dozen pairs of little socks. A small frame on the dresser held a blurry photo of what might have been a younger version of Mrs. Samples with an older couple.

Virgie was so intent on her search that she almost missed the fact that the crying had stopped. Silence — blessed silence — filled the air. Patty stood in the doorway, watching her curiously.

"I'm only looking for a toy," Virgie said. "I know you don't trust me yet, but I'm your friend."

At the sound of her voice, Patty's expression shifted; she looked as if she was going to start crying again. Virgie had had quite enough, and she picked Patty up. "Before you start up again, let's think about this. You're stuck here for six weeks. There aren't any other little kids staying here right now, and your mother is probably going to act a little funny for a while. Trust me, kid, you're going to need a friend. So give me a chance, and we can have some fun. How about it?"

Patty regarded her owlishly. "Draw picture," she finally said.

"Draw picture, now that's a good idea," Virgie said. "How about I make you a picture and you can color it in? What are you in the mood for? Kitties? Birthday cakes?"

These were the subjects her last charges had demanded. But Patty looked at her with a serious expression and said, "Pony. And a spoon. Put me down."

Virgie did. Maybe this kid wasn't so bad after all — here was something she could work with. Within an hour they'd turned out a dozen pictures, all drawn by Virgie and colored enthusiastically by Patty in big scribbles — a turtle and a hairbrush and a portrait of Virgie herself, her face rendered in green with a wild halo of pink hair — and the artist had fallen asleep on the floor. Virgie carried her to the bedroom and laid her on the bed. She was just draping a blanket over the little girl when there was a knock at the door.

She raced for the door, fearful the sound would wake the sleeping child. Willy waited, dressed in a red silk robe over matching pajamas and wearing slippers decorated with tufts of dyed rabbit fur.

"Hello, Virgie," Willy said. "How's tricks?"

"Fine, thank you."

"Mind if I come in? I heard you were babysitting, but it looks like you got the little brat to sleep."

Virgie wasn't at all sure if she should let her in, but Willy sashayed past her without waiting for permission and took a look around, whistling when she saw the velvet chairs, the marble hearth, the cashmere sweater.

"Nice digs," she said. "Bet they cost a pretty penny. Is she famous?"

"I don't think so," Virgie said, eyeing the clock on the mantel, hoping the residents of the suite were still at dinner. "What can I help you with?"

Willy laughed and dropped onto one of the chaises, her voluptuous body draped like a length of satin, effortless and elegant. She took a pack of cigarettes from the pocket of her robe and lit one. "Got an ashtray, sweetheart?"

Virgie dutifully retrieved one from the

breakfront and set it on the little table between the chaises, then sat cross-legged on the other one.

"So," Willy said, after a few puffs. "I know you're a clever girl, and I need some discreet advice. Do you know what *discreet* means?"

"Ummm . . ."

"It means you can't tell anyone. Cross your heart and hope to die. Can I count on you?"

"Yes, I won't tell a soul."

Virgie had learned at an early age that an important service her mother provided was to keep her guests' secrets. The day Mother had given Virgie the master key, she'd reminded her that no information was to be given out about any guest — not even to confirm whether she was staying at the hotel — and that if Virgie was asked, she was to direct all inquiries to her mother.

Willy took another puff and let the smoke trail slowly from her lips. Then she nodded.

"I believe you, Virgie Swanson. Okay, so it's like this. I need to see a doctor who specializes in ladies' concerns, one who's just as good at keeping his mouth shut as you are. See what I mean?"

Virgie thought she might. She'd overheard her mother referring guests to a certain Dr. Peabody who worked not in a clinic or

90

hospital but at a location that required complicated directions that her mother wrote out on hotel stationery but handed over only after instructing the ladies not to share the address with anyone else. However, Virgie had no idea what the doctor actually *did,* only that it was something other doctors didn't, which caused the ladies considerable agitation.

"Maybe," she hedged, thinking it through. "But I'd have to know what you need him for. And then I could find out for sure."

"I see," Willy said. "Well, listen, Virgie, I don't mean to insult your intelligence, because you're obviously wise beyond your years, but do you know what a venereal disease is?"

Virgie shook her head; there was no way to fake this one.

"All right. Fetch me a pen and paper and I'm going to write something down, then you show it to this doctor, and he'll let you know if he can help me or not. I'll pay you either way. How does three dollars sound?"

"Fine," Virgie said, a little too quickly. For that kind of money she was sure she could figure it out. She got a pen and a piece of stationery from the drawer in the side table, and Willy wrote something down and folded the paper twice before handing it back.

"When do you think you might have an answer for me?"

Virgie was saved from having to respond by the sound of a key in the door. Willy stabbed her cigarette out in the ashtray, while Virgie thought, *Oh no, oh no.* She leapt up and went to the door, blocking the view of the room.

"Hello!" she said brightly. "Patty was very good, and we played and made drawings, and then she got tired, and she fell asleep on the floor, but after a while I put her to bed and she didn't even wake up and I've been checking her a lot and she's just fine and then Miss" — oh no, what was her last name, had she ever told Virgie? — "Miss Willy from down the hall stopped by to borrow a needle and thread and she was just leaving." She dug out the sewing kit she kept in the pocket of her smock and removed a needle she'd threaded with white cotton, which suited most fixes she was called upon to perform, and handed it to Willy.

"I see," Mrs. Carothers said, nodding as if it made perfect sense, even though Willy made no move to leave and didn't even adjust her robe to conceal the lacy bodice of her pajamas.

"I'm Wilhelmina Carroll," she said. "Willy

for short. How do you do?"

June said hello and disappeared into the bedroom, but Mrs. Carothers and Mrs. Meeker introduced themselves and chatted with Willy about the pleasant weather, the need to find a good hairdresser, the quality of the food at the Sky Room, while Virgie's heart slowed to a normal rate.

June returned, looking much more relaxed. "Thank you for taking such good care of Patty, Virginia."

"We were wondering if you might stay just a little longer," Mrs. Meeker said. "We thought we might get a nightcap at Gwin's. We saw it when we drove in."

"Sure." Virgie was surprised — usually it was the younger ladies who ventured out in the evenings to the roadhouse up the street.

"Oh, there's no need," June said quickly. "I'll just stay here with Patty."

"Have you been before?" Willy asked. "To Gwin's, I mean."

"No, we've only just arrived today," Mrs. Meeker said.

"Then I'll be happy to take you. I'm known there — in fact, I sing there sometimes."

"You're a performer?" Mrs. Meeker asked politely, though there was something about the way she said it that made Virgie think she didn't believe it.

"Sure, I've had gigs at Dusty's and the Live Oak Club in Sacramento — have you heard of them?"

"I'm afraid I haven't."

Willy looked disappointed. "They're very nice. Anyway, we'll get top service at Gwin's. I just need a minute to change."

Mrs. Meeker and Mrs. Carothers exchanged a look. "Why not?" Mrs. Carothers said. "You only live once!"

CHAPTER 10
FRANCIE

It took Willy more than a minute to return — more like fifteen — which gave Francie and Vi time to try to cajole June into joining them. "She's sleeping like a log, dear," Francie pointed out.

"I really couldn't," June said. "I ate so much it made me sleepy. And Patty's likely to be up with the birds."

Willy came back in a blouse tied at the waist over cigarette pants and ankle-strap sandals that seemed like a poor idea for a walk along the uneven river path, but soon she and Francie and Vi were outside strolling under the bright moon. As they approached the tavern, the sound of laugher and piano music spilled from the open windows.

Willy led them through a gravel parking lot crowded with cars, up the steps to a long porch where half a dozen women and a couple of men lounged on wicker chairs, smoking. Inside, a pair of brass chandeliers provided barely enough light to see, but as her eyes adjusted, Francie took in the patrons lined up at the bar and crowded around the tables, the little wooden stage with an upright piano being played by a woman in a checked Western shirt, the rows of bottles behind the bar, and the bloodred wallpaper. A few people were dancing in front of the stage in the small roped-off area that passed for a dance floor.

There were men in cowboy hats and men in shirts and ties, but they were outnumbered at least two to one, and only one had been brave enough to venture onto the dance floor, where he was leading his partner in a very badly executed East Coast Swing, out of time with the music. As the pianist played the last few bars of "Hoop-Dee-Doo," the bartender rang a bell and a woman at the end of the bar let out a whoop and everyone in the bar cheered, including Willy.

"They do that whenever someone gets her papers. It's a tradition — you get to drink on the house all night. You can bet I'll be here when it's my turn!"

"When will that be?" Francie inquired.

"I've got another four and a half weeks," Willy said, her ebullience fading.

"How did you get the job here so quickly?" Vi asked.

"Oh, it's not really a job, nothing regular anyway — it's mostly to pass the time. I know the pianist — she and I did a gig together in Nevada City a while back. She's really good. Speaking of drinks —"

"A grand idea," Vi said. "What shall we have?"

Francie was relieved to see her friend in better spirits. At dinner, after the incident with the vagrant, she'd become silent and withdrawn. It had been happening frequently in the last week or two — ever since she'd relented and agreed to go through with the divorce. Francie intended to do her best to banish Vi's second thoughts, if that's what they were.

"What do you think, Willy?" Vi asked. "Something we can't get in San Francisco."

"I've got just the thing," Willy said. "Don't worry, I'll have them run a tab. Be right back."

As they watched her flounce her way to the bar, Francie said, "A tab in *your* name, I'll bet."

Vi shrugged. "Who cares? It's Harry's money."

"Darling, you're sure that Mr. Yeske understands the situation?"

Francie had asked around, and the attorney Vi had engaged did have a sterling reputation, but Vi had refused to allow Francie to accompany her to see him, and Francie was concerned that Harry might be hiding money in accounts Vi didn't know about.

"It's all taken care of," Vi said. There was a strange energy to her mood, probably owing to the amount she'd had to drink. "You know what I'd like to do?"

"I can't imagine."

"Dance. Just for fun — you and me."

Before Francie could protest, Vi had grabbed her hand and tugged her toward the little dance floor. Vi's hand was warm and so familiar — the hand that had held hers the day the telegram arrived announcing that Francie's mother had died; the hand that had seized hers with joy the day the doctor had confirmed that Vi and Harry were expecting their second child. Oh, how she'd come to rely on this hand, with its neat buffed nails and the garnet ring that had been Vi's mother's that looked so out of place on Vi's slender hand — it had checked her children's foreheads for fevers almost as often as her own, had rolled wartime bandages at her side, had divided bulbs to share so the same flowers bloomed every spring in their window boxes.

But for all the parties and charity balls that the two couples had attended together, the only time Francie had ever seen Vi dance was at Margie's and Jimmy's weddings, when Harry led her onto the dance floor as though it were the first day of cotillion, stiff as a board and heavy on his feet.

This Vi was nothing like the one who'd rested her hand on Harry's shoulder and tried to avoid getting stepped on. She tried the Lindy Hop, laughing as she kept moving in the wrong direction, then giving up and putting her arm around Francie's waist and steering her in circles, spinning until Francie was dizzy. The music changed, and Vi giggled and linked arms with Francie and pranced in a high-stepping Cakewalk, and soon others on the dance floor joined in. Francie's breasts and belly jiggled, and she was out of breath in minutes, but she felt more alive than she had in ages.

They danced until the pianist announced she was taking a break, and Francie, still laughing, turned to see Willy watching them. She was seated at the bar, wearing an intent expression that dissolved into a grin when their eyes met.

"I can't move another step," Francie said. "I've got to catch my breath."

99

"All right, but wasn't that wonderful? I'd given up on ever dancing again, since Frank and Charlie don't seem inclined to marry."

"One of those girls Frank brings around is bound to settle him down," Francie predicted. "And there's a girl out there for Charlie who's just as sweet and kind as he is, you'll see."

"You two were cutting quite the rug!" Willy said, handing them each a glass filled with ice and long strips of lemon peel and amber liquid. "These are called Saddle Sores. Shirley says they were invented right here at Gwin's."

Francie's first sip made her eyes water. "What *is* that?"

"Rum, chartreuse, and ginger ale. Go easy," Willy cautioned belatedly. "They pour heavy here, especially for the new girls — they want you to keep coming back. There's a table there in the corner — shall we?"

They took their drinks to a round table that had just been vacated by a couple leaning on each other drunkenly as they made their way to the door, the man in a fine sport coat and the woman, whose skirt swirled around her thighs, in a patterned dress. She couldn't have been more than twenty-two, and he was fifty if he was a day.

"Now, those two? I'd bet a dollar they'll

be hitched just the minute her divorce goes through," Willy said mischievously. "Wonder if her soon-to-be ex-husband knows his replacement is in town?"

The light in Vi's eyes dimmed and she stared into her drink, no doubt thinking about Harry's new flame. Francie couldn't bear to see Vi's fun come to an abrupt end, so she changed the subject.

"So tell us about you. What's your story?"

"Oh, it's nothing special," Willy said. "I married a boy when we were both too young to know better — we were seventeen. We grew up together in a little town outside Bakersfield. His daddy grew grapes and my daddy sold him pallets and crates. I wore my Sunday dress, and Peter borrowed a tie from his brother, and we moved into a cottage on his father's land."

"That sounds romantic," Vi said.

"Maybe, but the reality was about as romantic as a run-over skunk. There wasn't any plumbing, and Peter was up before dawn every day to go to work for a farmer up the road. By our first anniversary we could barely stand the sight of each other, but neither of us was the type to give up easy, and it took us a while to get used to the idea that we'd made a terrible mistake." Her smile slipped a little. "Well, a few mistakes, to tell you the truth."

"Is that when you decided to come to Reno?"

Willy laughed. "Oh no, not right away. We didn't have the money for a single night in a motel, let alone six weeks. And it didn't seem important at the time. Peter stayed and I moved to San Francisco and got a job and a place with some other girls. It was a gas, to tell you the truth, and it wasn't until I fell in love with a fellow who could afford to pay for it that I decided to get my divorce so I'd be free to marry again."

A bad feeling took root in Francie's gut. "How interesting. What does your fellow do that he can afford such a nice place for you to stay?"

Never mind that the question was terribly gauche — Willy didn't seem to notice as she took a long sip of her drink. "He's in promotions," she said proudly. "He works with all kinds of wonderful acts. He's going to get me an audition with a band that plays all the best clubs in San Francisco."

Vi had gone pale. Francie reached for her hand under the table, already gathering her purse.

"That's nice," she said, her face aching from smiling. "What's his name?"

"Harold," Willy said, "but everyone calls

him Harry."

"We have to go," Francie said, pushing back her chair with such force that it slammed into the neighboring table, causing drinks to slosh out of the glasses. She pulled Vi up from her seat as Willy's face registered confusion.

"What do you —"

"Allergies, I'm allergic," Francie said, the first thing that popped into her head. "We'll see you around."

"But —"

Whatever Willy had to say was lost in the din. Francie put her arm around Vi's waist and pulled her along, but the moment they were outside, Vi shook her off and stalked alone down the street.

"Vi, wait!" Francie called, trying to catch up. "It might not be the same Harry —"

"It doesn't matter," Vi said. "I've known what he was up to — does it really matter which girl it is? One's the same as another. Oh, I'm such a fool."

"You're *not* a fool, you're better than any girl in that place, better than all of them put together. And Harry is a — a stupid gollumpus."

Vi stopped in her tracks. She turned to look at Francie and burst into laughter. "Say it again."

"What?" Francie said. It hardly seemed like a laughing matter.

"*Gollumpus* — oh, it's just too funny. I wish Harry was here, so I could say that to his face." She gazed out over the river; the moon's reflection floated like a yellow rubber ball on the inky water. "He really is a ridiculous man, isn't he? I wish — I just wish I'd chosen better, for the boys' sakes. Think of it, Francie — what are they going to do when their father announces he's going to marry that girl? She can't even be as old as Alice! I can't believe he'd date someone so . . ."

"Gaudy?" Francie said, not knowing whether to be heartened or worried by this outpouring of uncharacteristic venom. "Tawdry?"

Vi laughed again. "I was going to say naïve. But it isn't really her fault, is it? Harry probably told her I'm a miserable shrew."

"Oh, Vi . . . you're too good. I'd like to go back there and teach her a lesson she'll never forget. No — I take it back. I'd like to teach *Harry* a lesson. Hire one of his skywriters to take him up and drop him on a spiked iron fence."

"Let's not waste another minute thinking about him," Vi said decisively. "It's too lovely a night. Do you see that moon? Let's go down to the water and watch it float. Better yet — let's throw pennies and make wishes. Maybe if they land in the moon's reflection they'll be more likely to come true."

She led Francie down the footpath to a stone outcropping that jutted from the bank, smoothed by centuries of people sitting there to enjoy the view. The smell of the river, briny and sweet and grassy, rose up to meet them to the tune of a hermit thrush's song.

"I've only got two," Vi said, pressing a coin into Francie's hand. "So you've got to use it for your very best wish."

She cupped her hands together and closed her eyes, a little smile playing at the edge of her lips. Then she opened her eyes and tossed the penny high in the air, moonlight winking off its surface as it spun before landing with a quiet splash.

"What did you wish for?" Francie asked. A strange feeling had overtaken her — her heart was heavy and light at the same time, the things she didn't dare say fluttering in her mouth like the wings of a moth.

"You know I can't tell, or it won't come true! Now you do yours."

So Francie did. She squeezed the coin, then wound up and threw it as if she were fifteen and pitching against the team from Anna Head, and the penny arced through the air trailing her wish behind it like a comet's tail:

Let Vi be happy now.

Chapter 11
June

Patty stirred, making sweet snuffling sounds and pressing closer against June's side, her little forehead damp with sweat. June waited until her big blue eyes finally popped open to push the hair off her face.

"I'm hungry, Mama. Can I have ham again?"

"We'll see."

June dressed herself and Patty as quietly as she could. The wall between the bedrooms was thin; June remembered how her own mother had struggled to sleep once the change began, and she didn't want to disturb Vi. She dabbed on a bit of powder and swiped on the lipstick that was worn down to next to nothing; then she took the key from the top of the dresser, and they left.

Only one other woman was sitting at a table in the dining room. The clock on the wall said it was almost six.

"Good morning," June said shyly, but the woman barely looked up from her coffee. Her eyes were rimmed with red and her hand trembled on the handle of her cup. *Heartbroken,* June thought.

"I'm hungry," Patty repeated, her eyes on the sideboard, which was covered in a white cloth and laden with silver chafing dishes, a toaster, and a basket of bread. There were dishes of butter and a jug of cream, pitchers of orange juice and milk, a jar of raspberry preserves and another of honey.

"All right, darling."

Suddenly she heard men's rough voices, the tread of boots in the hall. June cringed, trying to make out their words.

". . . a fisherman setting his lines down near Lockwood."

An answering woman's voice, the words muffled.

"We're not asking you to wake the whole damn place, ma'am."

A moment later Mrs. Swanson hurried down the hall but stopped short when she spotted June. In the second that it took to press her thin lips into a strained smile, June grew very afraid. She'd seen that look before, on nurses who'd seen the injuries from her latest "fall down the stairs," on the neighbor whose bedroom window was only a few yards from theirs.

"Mrs. Samples," Mrs. Swanson said. "I wonder — that is, the police have come . . . This is Officer Crandall and Officer Franklin. Mrs. Samples shares a suite with Mrs. Carothers."

Officer Crandall, a portly gentleman with a hopeful little moustache, took off his cap, but Officer Franklin — who had a bit of blood-dotted toilet paper stuck to his neck where he'd cut himself — merely stared at her, causing June to pull her cardigan tighter across her chest.

"Would you mind fetching Mrs. Carothers, ma'am?" Officer Crandall asked.

Another woman might have demanded to know why. June nodded dumbly.

"Leave the little one with me," Mrs. Swanson said. "I'll fix her something to eat. Is that all right?"

"It's fine," June said, finding her voice. "I'll be right back."

Then she was rushing back up the stairs, away from the policemen, who, in her experience, never understood what was right in front of them and left things worse in their wake.

CHAPTER 12
VIRGIE

Virgie stood on her bed, looking up into the window well, even though all she could see was the dark rubber tires of the police car. She had been carrying a pail filled with coffee grounds and eggshells, sent by her mother to work them into the soil around the rosebushes, when they pulled into the drive. When Virgie saw the car coming she dropped the bucket at the edge of the garden and sprinted around the side of the main house to the back door, down the stairs to her room, where she closed and locked the door behind her. Then she went to the cigar box where she kept her smallest treasures and took out the thing she had taken and searched the room for a better hiding place.

Owing to its past as the cold storage for the hotel, Virgie's room was fitted with shelves and hooks that had once held cured hams and salted fish, onions and potatoes, and cheeses. Most of the shelves were filled now with books and interesting rocks and scavenged parts of radios and things left behind by guests, but one narrow cubby held a coffee can filled with hair ribbons. This was a trick, because anyone who checked the contents of the can would consider the twelve-year-old girl who lived there and move on. (With the exception, perhaps, of a girl who actually wore ribbons in her hair, but the would-be thieves Virgie worried about weren't girls but thugs and crooks like the ones Nancy Drew dealt with all the time.)

She took out the can and reached into the back of the cubby, slipping her fingertips into a gap between the shelf and the rough painted boards, which allowed her to nudge a loose board up. Behind was a narrow space with a horizontal framing board forming a shelf, on which sat a leatherette case that had once held a necklace a hotel guest had received from her lover. When the guest checked out, she left the case in the trash can, and Virgie had taken it to store the most precious things she'd found — a single gold hoop earring, a stick pin missing a jet bead, a Canadian dime.

She dropped her new treasure inside the case and gazed at it, the tiny diamonds surrounding the huge red stone sparkling brilliantly against the black velvet. She snapped the lid shut and returned the case, the board, and the coffee can, then climbed up on her bed to keep an eye out, praying that the police would get back in the car and leave. Instead, they seemed to have begun a search, because there were more voices now, some of them distraught.

She never should have taken it! Only, she'd been so shocked to come across it among the belongings of someone who was not the rightful owner. Who had, she was certain, stolen it. Virgie was only keeping it safe until she could find a way to return it, but what a mess she had made — the owner obviously discovered it missing and called the police, and now if they searched the thief's room it wouldn't be there, and justice would be delayed. And how could Virgie even give it back now without attracting attention to herself?

Adults never believed her — not the ones she knew, at any rate. Though to be fair she had given them reasons to doubt her. Virgie rarely got caught anymore, but when she'd been younger and dumber she'd been caught in lies often enough to get a reputation. Her mother and even the staff suspected her whenever things were broken or missing.

Upstairs, people rushed around, their footsteps muffled. She heard her mother's voice, arguing with someone. Were the police demanding to come down and search the cellar? Would her mother be able to stop them?

Trepidation was instantly replaced by guilt, because Virgie knew that her mother lacked guile. The coppers would see right through her lies; they might consider her an accomplice. And while Virgie had accepted that her life in the shadows might lead to danger and even imprisonment, her mother wouldn't be able to bear life in prison, with no emery boards or hot tea or visits to the salon.

Virgie had to do something to save her. She squared her shoulders and headed up the stairs, with her fingers crossed for luck.

CHAPTER 13
JUNE

June burst through the door and was met by silence. The suite was as empty as Jesus's tomb, and even though Vi's pocketbook was resting on the coffee table, her sweater still draped over the chair, June knew even before she turned the knob on the door of Vi's room that she was gone.

That was why, when her eyes fell upon the neatly made bed, the clothes undisturbed in the closet, the suitcases lined up in the corner, it wasn't shock she felt in her heart but grim fear. Vi was missing and the police were downstairs, and why hadn't June known something was wrong? There had been a kinship between the two women, an unspoken recognition of the melancholy and perpetual watchfulness of those who'd endured their husband's abuse for many years, whether it took the form of physical scars or the ones on the inside.

June had been so worried that Stan would

somehow track her down despite the pre-cautions she had taken, and she'd been right — somehow, he'd shown up last night in the very restaurant where she was eating dinner. Luckily, he hadn't seen her before he was thrown out, and now all she could do was pray he didn't know where she was staying, though it was probably only a matter of time.

Maybe Vi hadn't been careful enough either.

June turned on her heel and dashed back downstairs.

"She's gone," she reported breathlessly to the police and Mrs. Swanson and the handful of curious guests who'd joined them in the hall — and Francie, whose fingers worried a linen napkin she didn't seem to know she was holding.

"But I saw her go in!" Francie looked wildly from one policeman to the other. "I was *with* her. We said good night in the hall and then she . . . Why are you here? *Why?*"

Officer Crandall shared a look with Mrs. Swanson, who made the sign of the cross.

"Mrs. Samples," she said gravely. "Mrs. Meeker. You'll need to go with the officers now. I'll follow in my car and I can bring you back after."

"We can drive them, ma'am," Officer

Crandall said.

"I'd rather you didn't. I'm sure you can understand that I don't need police cars in my drive any more than necessary."

Officer Franklin gestured impatiently toward the door. "Ladies?"

"But where are you taking us?"

The policemen looked at each other, while all around them the assembled guests — in robes and housedresses, curlers and head rags and papers — watched with silent pity.

"I'll explain on the way," Officer Crandall said, while Franklin signaled for the other guests to stand back.

"Let them pass," he said. "Let the ladies pass."

CHAPTER 14
FRANCIE

They rode in silence, Francie in front with Officer Crandall and June in back with Franklin. Francie cradled her pocketbook in her lap and worried her teeth with her tongue, a nervous habit that hadn't plagued her in years. She had never ridden in a police car before, had never had any dealings with the police at all aside from the San Francisco sergeant who had brought his squad car to the school playground every year. She stared straight ahead, wondering what strangers must think of her, if they would assume she'd been arrested.

She noticed the smell of tobacco, a torn scrap of paper that had fallen to the floor, the way the young police officer in the back kept clearing his throat. It wasn't until they'd driven through town and turned onto the bridge at Sutro Street that Officer Crandall finally spoke. "A body fitting Mrs. Carothers's description was discovered early this morning about three miles downriver," he said. "She had a Holiday Ranch key in her pocket."

The breath left Francie. "Body?"

"She was, er, drowned. She was wearing a blue dress and she had dark hair and gray eyes, five foot seven, pearl earrings and necklace, and a gold wedding ring. Mrs. Swanson remembered what Mrs. Carothers was wearing on account of she saw you leaving for dinner."

"But *you've* never seen her before," Francie protested. "Mrs. Swanson doesn't even *know* her."

Officer Franklin spoke up from the backseat. "That doesn't stop us from making her ID from —"

"All right, that's enough, Franklin." The older officer didn't take his eyes from the road, but his partner shut up.

"But why would Vi — why would *anyone* be in the river?" Francie pressed, her heart chasing its tail in her chest. *Vi — oh, Vi. Please, please don't let it be you.*

"River's running high this year," Crandall said as he pulled into the parking lot of a new brick-and-steel building. "Lot of rain. People don't realize how quick it can pull you under."

"But Vi didn't swim. She never would

118

have risked standing too close to the edge, she wouldn't take the chance." But that wasn't true — it was Vi who suggested going down to the bank last night, who sat down on the flat rock to watch the moon's reflection shimmering on the water.

"Be that as it may, ma'am," Officer Crandall said. "The body wasn't in the water long, which is . . . well, it will make it easier to identify."

He pulled into a space at the back of the building, turned off the engine, and shifted in his seat to face her. His eyes held sympathy.

"There will be a sheet," he went on. "They won't pull it down until you're ready."

A car pulled into the next space over. Mrs. Swanson got out and stood with her arms crossed, waiting with the air of someone who'd seen all this before.

Francie took June's arm when they got out of the car; she needed something to hold on to. Officer Crandall held the door while Mrs. Swanson and Officer Franklin took up the rear. They filed silently through the halls and down the stairs to the basement, to a door marked "Washoe County Regional Medical Examiner." Inside was a cramped waiting room with a few chairs against the wall, an empty desk, and another door with a square of opaque glass.

Officer Crandall rapped on the glass, and a man in a white gown and gloves opened it, a paper mask pulled down around his neck.

"Hello, Joe. This is Mrs. Meeker and Mrs. Samples, and Mrs. Swanson from the hotel."

"I'll wait outside," Mrs. Swanson said.

They followed the pathologist in, Francie holding June's arm more tightly, and June covering Francie's hand with her own. Only one of the steel tables held a body, draped with a sheet.

"Are you ready?" the pathologist asked, and though Francie wasn't — she would never be — she gave a tiny, stiff nod and he picked up the corner of the sheet almost reverently and slowly pulled it down.

It was Vi, her hair coiled thinly at her nape, her lips and eyelids pale as paper, purple smudges under her eyes. She could have been sleeping.

"No," Francie whispered. "No, no, don't . . ."

"Is it Mrs. Carothers, ma'am?" Officer Crandall prompted gently. "Just say yes or no."

But Francie couldn't, because then it would be true. Instead she collapsed against

June, who held her and murmured, "There, there, there," like a woman who's only ever given comfort, never expecting any for herself.

CHAPTER 15
VIRGIE

Flossie was cleaning down the hall, but Virgie took a chance and slipped into the room next to Mrs. Meeker's after knocking first to make sure the guest was out. If she'd answered, Virgie planned to say that she'd come to collect the soiled linens, but it was a fine spring day and most of the guests had joined a group going to Pyramid Lake for a picnic. By now all of them had probably heard that a guest had drowned last night, and human nature being what it was, they probably hoped Mrs. Swanson would share the details. If so, they were in for a disappointment — her mother had gathered the staff to remind them that no one was to discuss the tragedy and any inquiries should be directed only to her.

Virgie glanced quickly around the room — this guest was one of the neat ones, who seemed to take comfort in keeping things spotless and orderly. The rooms were cleaned once a week, but Flossie and Ruth would have an easy job with this one.

She pressed her ear to the wall and heard Mrs. Meeker crying — great, gusty sobs. Mrs. Meeker had returned only an hour earlier, supported by both Mrs. Samples and Virgie's mother, who practically carried her up the stairs to the suite Mrs. Carothers had been sharing with Mrs. Samples, the police officers trailing behind. Virgie's mother came downstairs moments later and sent Virgie up with hot tea and a plate of ginger cookies, despite the rule about no food in the rooms.

Virgie knocked softly and the door swung open. She could hear the police officers talking in low voices in Mrs. Carothers's bedroom, but Mrs. Meeker was slumped in one of the upholstered chairs with her eyes closed while Mrs. Samples sat silently watching her.

"There's milk, and sugar if you want it," Virgie had said as she set the tray down on the coffee table, but Mrs. Meeker didn't move.

When Mrs. Samples thanked her in a voice barely above a whisper, Virgie glared at her and said, "I'm sure Mrs. Meeker would like some time to herself," just as firmly as her mother would have. June swallowed and looked over her shoulder, but didn't budge, so it was left to Virgie to march into the bedroom, where the older policeman was on all fours peering under the bed while the younger one pawed through a dresser drawer, a white silk slip in his hand.

Positively indecent — that's what her mother would have said if she were here. Virgie cleared her throat. "Mrs. Meeker needs to lie down," she said with as much authority as she could muster. "Can she go to her own room now?"

"Sure, kid," the young cop said, earning a glare from the older one.

"In a few minutes," Crandall said. "We're almost done here, but I may have a question or two for her. There's no need for you to stay, young lady. It's nice of you to be concerned, but we'll make sure she gets to her room."

Virgie held her chin up as she left, but the knowledge that she'd been dismissed burned. Everyone thought she was just a dumb kid, even though she could tell them things that would shock them. She was probably twice as observant as the younger cop, who didn't even know that his fly was unzipped.

On the way out of the suite Virgie nodded

124

stiffly to Mrs. Samples and cast a sympathetic look at Mrs. Meeker, who had slumped further into the chair, clutching a tear-dampened handkerchief to her cheek.

She had reported to her mother that she'd delivered the tea and that Mrs. Meeker looked well enough, considering, and that the cops were almost done searching the suite. Then Virgie announced she was going to return a library book, but instead she doubled back and slipped into the pantry and waited half an hour to make sure the cops were gone before sneaking up the back staircase.

Now she listened to Mrs. Meeker cry and grew madder and madder. Mrs. Meeker obviously loved her friend very much, and her heart was broken, and all the while Mrs. Samples had just sat there pretending to care! Where were *her* tears, if they were really cousins? Virgie hadn't yet figured out why they were traveling together, but something fishy was definitely going on: when they returned from the morgue, Mrs. Samples was *wearing one of Mrs. Carothers's dresses,* a scarlet serge Virgie recognized from exploring Mrs. Carothers's closet the night before while babysitting. It took a lot of nerve to steal from a dead woman, in Virgie's opinion, but underneath Mrs. Samples's shy, timid act there appeared to be a cool, calculating mind at work.

And there was another thing. Mrs. Samples had asked another guest, an older lady from Utah, to watch Patty while she went to the morgue with the cops and Mrs. Meeker. Why not ask Virgie, since she was right there and had done such a good job last night? Mrs. Meeker had even given her an extra dollar as a tip and called her babysitting kit "clever"!

The obvious reason Mrs. Samples asked someone else was that she was onto Virgie. Virgie had been careful, but maybe she'd disturbed something in Mrs. Samples's room while she was investigating last night. Mrs. Samples might have even set a trap, like the one described in her treasured copy of George Barton's *Great Cases of Famous Detectives,* where a crook had rigged a thread to his desk drawer that would break when it was opened, so he would know if someone had searched it.

Though why would anyone take such care to trap an intruder but not hide the loot better? Maybe it was because Mrs. Samples was waiting for Mrs. Carothers to go out to dinner, so she had to just stash it the first place she could think of — her ratty old vanity case on the shelf in the bathroom,

126

hidden under her toothbrush and cold cream.

Which brought up one more angle of the mystery: What was with Mrs. Samples's old, worn luggage and the ragged dresses hanging in her closet? If Mrs. Carothers had bought a new wardrobe for her stay in Reno, it might explain why Mrs. Meeker hadn't noticed that Mrs. Samples was wearing her friend's clothes, since they were very close in size. But if Mrs. Samples was so down on her luck, where had she gotten the outfit she'd worn last night? Was she just *pretending* to be poor?

Virgie knew better than to leap to conclusions, but everything she was learning was starting to point to a very sinister explanation for Mrs. Samples's behavior. Virgie dug out her notebook and started making a list.

1. Mrs. S is pretending to be Mrs. C's Long Lost cousin.
2. Also she is pretending to be POOR. Because she wants to steal from Mrs. C but she needed to Gain Her Trust. So she Lied and said she was getting a Divorce when she found out Mrs. C was getting Her Own Divorce so Mrs. C would let her stay with her.

3. She saw her chance to Steal the ring when Mrs. C took it off in the Bathroom and put it in her train case. Because it didn't go with her dinner outfit??? Since Mrs. S found it in the Bathroom she put it in her own case but she was probably planning to move it later but when she got back it was GONE.
4. Now she can't leave until she gets it back. And also if Mrs. C saw it was missing she would tell the police and they would know Mrs. S took it because No One else was in the room.

"Except for me," Virgie said out loud, chewing on her pencil. "And Mrs. Meeker."

5. DID MRS. S KILL MRS. C?????
6. Is Patty even her real baby? Why does Patty cry so much and Also she doesn't look like Mrs. S.
7. Why did she steal a baby?

Virgie stared at the list. These were shocking conclusions, but Virgie had heard Mrs. Meeker telling the police that Mrs. Carothers couldn't swim. All Mrs. Samples would have had to do would be to invite her on a late-night stroll, and when they got to the

128

bend where the water was deeper, push her in.

Virgie was getting a very bad feeling.

If Mrs. Samples had killed Mrs. Carothers to keep her from calling the police about the ring, what would she do to *her*? Virgie was going to have to be very careful from here on. Now that she thought about it, it was for the best that Mrs. Samples had found another babysitter — Virgie needed to avoid being alone with her.

She had a sudden, terrible thought. Mrs. Carothers certainly looked ill when she arrived, and she was too thin. What if Mrs. Samples had been slowly poisoning her, like the woman in England who'd put tiny amounts of arsenic in her husband's tea for weeks until he died? But then why steal the ring now when she could have just waited until Mrs. Carothers was dead?

Mrs. Meeker's sobs were subsiding into a muffled moan. Virgie knew how these things went, how you could tire yourself out crying. Soon she'd fall asleep.

Virgie opened the door a crack and checked up and down the hall before leaving the room. She patted her pocket, where she'd stashed her book. She still had time to get to the library to return it before her mother expected her back.

CHAPTER 16
FRANCIE

The police allowed Mrs. Swanson to drive them back, but insisted on coming upstairs to search Vi's room, saying it was standard in a case like this. *Like what?* Francie had asked, distraught at the thought of them going through her things, but the police officers had glanced at each other and declined to answer.

She and June sat silently in the living room as the officers moved around the suite. Virgie came by with cookies sent by her mother, but Francie couldn't even muster a polite thanks, and the girl soon left. Mercifully, the search was mostly focused on Vi's bedroom and didn't take long.

"Are you finished?" she asked when they came out.

"For now," Officer Crandall said. "We'll be in touch if we need anything more from you. And you should call if . . . anything

130

else occurs to you."

"And that's it? You've decided it was an accident?"

"That'll be the official report, yes." Crandall looked at her meaningfully. "It's for the best."

"We, uh, saw her rosary," Franklin said quietly.

Defeated, Francie gave up and ushered them out of the suite. They were right — ruling Vi's death a suicide would cause a scandal among her family, her church, everyone she knew. And it wasn't like the police could have told her anything she didn't already know.

"I'm going to take some of her things to my room," she said to June once they were gone. "It's not that I don't trust you — you must know that. I just . . ."

She just wanted them close. She'd make sure it all got back to Harry — or rather, to the boys — but she needed something, anything of Vi's now.

"I understand," June said. "I'm so sorry. I don't know what to say. Is there anything I can do?"

"No, but thank you," Francie said, starting to go through Vi's purse. She'd watched the cops go through it already, and there was nothing she hadn't seen a hundred times before. She took the wallet and Vi's address book and dropped them in her own pocketbook.

She checked the bathroom, but there was only Vi's train case sitting on a shelf next to June's old, worn vanity case. Francie opened it and took her bottle of Ma Griffe — the only scent Vi ever wore — and sprayed a bit on her wrist before putting the perfume in her purse. Francie was about to leave the room when she spotted Vi's hairbrush with a few strands of her hair caught in the bristles. She picked it up and smelled it — and a sob escaped her; when she closed her eyes, Vi might as well have been standing right there, asking her to zip her dress.

She slipped the brush in her purse with a feeling of shame. No one would understand why she had to have it — she wasn't sure she understood herself.

In the bedroom, she was disappointed to find nothing personal, just Vi's clothes, a book that looked as if she hadn't even opened it, a water glass with an inch of water and a smudge of lipstick on the rim. Francie looked over her shoulder to make sure June hadn't followed her into the room, and then she drank the water.

She was looking for clues, but Vi had left no trace of herself here. Whatever secrets

132

she'd kept had died with her.

"I think I'll go lie down," she said when she came out, not meeting June's eyes. "I'm sorry you got caught up in all of this."

"Oh, please, don't say that," June said, wringing her hands. "Please don't worry about me at all."

"Goodbye," Francie said, then stopped herself at the door. "What about Patty? Don't you need to go get her?"

"Yes, but I thought . . . I didn't want you to be alone."

The poor girl, she'd probably been worried sick about her daughter. "That was very thoughtful, but I'm fine."

Francie wasn't the least bit fine, but it wouldn't do to burden June, who, despite her kindness, was a stranger. She couldn't think of anything else to say and so she went downstairs without even waiting for June to lock the door. Francie was aware that she was being rude, but she couldn't help it — the social grace that had become second nature after all these years had deserted her.

The minute she was alone in her room, she called Arthur. When she heard his familiar, kindly voice, she burst into tears.

"What's wrong?" he asked in alarm.

Francie managed to compose herself enough to get the story out — the official version, that it had been an accident. Arthur was shocked, of course — and terribly sad; he and Vi had always been close. But he immediately started trying to console her; he'd always been good at making people feel better.

"I'll come as soon as I can," he said.

"Oh, Arthur, you needn't rush. You'll come for the service, of course — it would mean a great deal to the boys. But there's so much to do, so many people to notify, and all that travel and lodging to arrange . . . you do think it's the right thing to do, don't you? Lay her to rest with her parents?"

"Yes, if that's what she wanted. Although Harry may disagree." Arthur had always tried to conceal his dislike of Harry, but for decades the two men had almost nothing to talk about. "But her wishes are all that matter, I suppose."

"I know people will talk — but I just can't bear the thought of her lying next to him for eternity, when he's been carrying on right under her nose all this time."

"Let them talk." Brave words, coming from Arthur. "Shall I tell the children?"

Francie hadn't thought that far ahead. Vi had been part of the family — of course the children should know right away. "If you would . . . Tell them I'll call with the details of the funeral just as soon as I can. Oh, and please ask Alice to find my black crape. And she'll need — never mind, I'll call her myself tonight."

"I'll talk to them. And I'll make arrangements for John to take over, so I can take some time off." John was Arthur's most trusted employee, someone he was grooming to run the printing business when he eventually retired.

"Really, you should take your time. I'll be fine."

"You know I don't mind, Francie. Just because we're . . ." His voice trailed off. Both had avoided saying the word *divorce* whenever possible; it had hung between them like an impending surgery, something necessary but dreaded. "You know I would never let you go through this alone."

Francie sat in silence for a while after they hung up. She was new at shouldering burdens without Arthur — for decades they had shared every sorrow and joy. Getting through the coming days without him was unthinkable; returning to San Francisco as a single woman and living alone in that big empty house, unimaginable. For a moment she wondered if she'd made a mistake in giving him the divorce.

But in the next moment she thought of

135

how his eyes had filled with cautious hope when she proposed the idea, how even as he assured her that he would always love her, that they would always be close, she could hear in his voice that already he was moving away from her toward his new life. She could not take that away from him.

She went into the bathroom to splash water on her face. There was much to be done.

CHAPTER 17

It took three calls, fifty dollars, and more than two hours to reach Harry Carothers — and when Francie finally did, she was immediately reminded of what an important person he considered himself to be.

She'd called his San Francisco office first, and Eugenia — a grandmotherly woman with an unfortunate birthmark on her cheek, whom Harry had hired as penance after Vi found out about his affair with her predecessor — had given her the phone number of the hotel where he and the boys were staying in Las Vegas. Eugenia also confided that the police had called not an hour before with the terrible news and that she'd been trying to reach Harry before they did, to no avail.

The girl at the front desk at the El Rancho Vegas told Francie that all three Mr. Carothers had left that morning for the test site in the desert, where they were overseeing the grand opening. There was no way to reach them by phone, but Francie was unwilling to have Charlie and Frank find out the news from a stranger. Knowing better than to make her case to someone with no power to help, she politely asked the girl if she could be connected to the hotel manager, adding that she'd be sure to tell him how efficient his front desk staff was.

The hotel manager came on the line and asked how he could be of service and Francie summoned her most imperious voice and explained that a tragedy had taken place. Mr. Carothers must be notified as soon as possible, she explained, even if that meant the hotel manager had to drive into the desert himself. When she explained that she was willing to pay handsomely, the manager called the valet supervisor, who promised that he'd leave immediately.

Then Francie waited, pacing the room and smoking. As the minutes turned into an hour, and then another, despair caught up with her. She lay down on the bed and hugged the pillow to her chest and whispered Vi's name and started crying again. She tried to muffle the sound with a pillow, but the grief poured from her and there was no way to contain it; it seemed to expand to fill the room — and then, gently, the tide

138

turned, and the tears dried up and she was left spent and exhausted.

She'd been lying like that, the pillowcase damp beneath her cheek, when the phone rang.

"Hello?"

"Francie, it's Harry. How on earth did you convince that kid to drive out here? I had to hitch a ride to a lumberyard forty-five minutes away just to find a phone."

"Harry," Francie said, remembering that Harry had an irregular heartbeat and also had loved Vi in his own selfish, thoughtless, cruel way. She pictured him out on that sweltering stretch of sand, about to have his world turned upside down. "Are the boys with you?"

"Frank's back at the site — I sent Charlie out to fetch lunch."

"I'm afraid I have some terrible, terrible news."

"What? Yeah, I know. Cops showed up an hour before the fellow from the hotel. Reno cops called up, had the Vegas chief send a couple of guys out here." Somewhat belatedly, he added, "I can't believe she took a chance like that. Poor Vi."

He *knew*? "A chance like what?"

"Getting too close to the water. She knew she couldn't swim. Cops said the banks are soft from the rains right now — probably just gave way right under her and she slipped."

"They don't know that," Francie said, and then regretted it. If the cops hadn't mentioned the possibility that Vi had gone into the water on purpose, that she'd . . . Francie couldn't bear to think about it. But it would be better if the boys never knew.

"Slipped, fell, tripped, does it matter?"

Of course it mattered. And shouldn't he be consoling their sons right now?

"She's *dead,*" she said. "Do you under-*stand* that, Harry? Vi is dead. She's not coming back."

A sob escaped her, an ugly, gulping sound. She hadn't meant to cry — she didn't *want* to cry in front of Harry. He didn't deserve her tears!

"Francie?" Harry said. She could hear the wind in the background. "You okay?"

"I'm *fine,*" she said, rooting through her pocketbook for her handkerchief and wiping her nose savagely. "Have you told the boys?"

"Of course I told the boys. I told them as soon as I heard." Now he sounded affronted. "They're taking it like real soldiers."

A memory of the two of them one long-ago Easter came to mind — Frank was a

140

little man of seven, so proud of his Easter suit, and Charlie was a chubby, disheveled six with a headful of russet curls. The Carotherses had come for dinner, and afterward, as the adults finished off their lemon meringue pie, Charlie had fed Alice an entire chocolate bunny and she'd thrown up all over his pressed white shirt and his little tie. She'd been only four at the time, but she'd already loved Charlie.

Everyone loved Charlie — but none so much as Vi. She'd adored both her boys, but Frank had been the apple of his father's eye and Charlie was often left behind. He was kind like his mother, and generous, and if his father thought him soft, Vi had seen through to the quiet strength inside. He was built to endure, just like she was.

Until she apparently couldn't endure anymore.

"You've got to come," she said. "Decisions have to be made. The" — she had been about to say *mortuary,* but what she really meant was *body,* and that was not a thing she could think about just now — "service," she said instead.

"Yeah." Harry sounded not so much heartbroken as annoyed. "I'll have Eugenia start working on that. I guess I probably need to call Father Fletcher and find out when we can have it."

"No, Harry, she wanted to be buried here. In Reno, with her parents." She waited for it to sink in that Vi could not be buried in the Carothers family plot, not after Harry had taken up with that tramp from last night and asked for a divorce.

"We don't know anyone in Reno!"

"There's cousins, I think," Francie said defensively. "Nieces and nephews." Another thing she needed to do — contact what little was left of Vi's family.

"I wouldn't know about that. We haven't seen them for years."

Because you *didn't want to,* Francie thought bitterly. Vi's remaining relatives were country folk, farmers and laborers, and Harry thought them coarse.

"She sent them birthday cards and Christmas cards and presents." Francie knew, because she'd shopped with Vi for gifts for her nieces' and nephews' weddings, practical things like everyday dishes and stewpots. A check for every child who graduated from high school.

"Well, that's Vi. Give away the shirt off her back."

"The point is, Harry, that Vi wants to be buried here, and that means we need to find a mortuary and contact the cemetery and plan a luncheon and —"

"How the hell is Eugenia supposed to do all that? And who's going to run the office while she does?"

Red spots were floating in front of Francie's eyes. She squeezed the telephone receiver so hard she was sure it would break. "Since you are still her legal husband, I believe the responsibility falls to *you,* Harry."

"For the love of Christ!" Something clanged in the background, and a man let loose a colorful string of curses. "Sorry, some idiot just dropped a pallet. Francie, we opened *today.* I've got shows back-to-back through the weekend. Hundreds of people are paying three dollars and fifty cents each to see a mushroom cloud, and I've got reporters here from three states. I had to get a goddamn cowboy to drive an iron grill big enough to roast two pigs on a flatbed truck into the desert for this day. There is no way I can do what you're asking, not this week."

After a brief silence he added, in a calmer tone, "It's not that I don't want to, you know that. I'd be there if there was any possible way. Vi would understand."

It was that last bit that made something snap inside Francie. Because Vi *would* have

143

understood. She always did, when it came to Harry — right up until he asked for a divorce. She'd refused him for months until she suddenly changed her mind for reasons known only to her. Vi had excused every forgotten anniversary, every time his car smelled like another woman's perfume, every maudlin promise to do better after every single transgression. And all it had done was embolden Harry to commit more and more brazen acts.

"She might," she snarled, "but *I* don't. I will never understand how you could have ended up with her and not count your lucky stars every day of your life. But if you don't have the decency to give your own *wife* the farewell she deserves, I will. I'll take care of everything, and I'll have the bills sent to you. We'll do it on Tuesday, so you can have your precious grand opening weekend and even a day to travel. All you need to do is show up. And trust me when I say, Harry, that if you *don't* show up, then I'll never speak to you again — I'll curse you every day of my life."

"Calm down, Francie, you sound like you're about to have a coronary. Jesus H. Fine. Leave messages at the hotel, okay? And look, I'll send Charlie to pick up her things, have him give you a hand. We can

144

do without him here. Whatever needs to be decided, Charlie can take care of it. He can be there tomorrow."

This was the best offer Francie was going to get. "Have him come here to the hotel once he gets settled. I'll let them know we're expecting him. I trust you have the address where we're staying — seeing as you booked both Vi and *Willy* into the same place."

She'd forgotten that trump card until just now, because who calls a newly widowed man expecting to have to shame him to decency? The silence following her last remark confirmed that Harry had been hoping Willy's identity would stay his secret.

"That wasn't supposed to happen," he said defensively. "I found that place for *Vi,* the nicest place in town. But she kept refusing to go, she said she'd never give me a divorce and meanwhile I've got Willy hounding me to send her so she and I can . . . and anyway I can't help it if Vi suddenly changed her mind and wouldn't listen to reason, I told her wait a month or two, what's the rush all of a sudden — you think I *wanted* those two to run into each other?"

"Why is it," Francie asked coldly, "that no matter what you've done, you always have to be the victim? Why is nothing ever your fault? Listen to yourself. You're the one who made a laughingstock of her, but you're blaming your *wife,* the woman who vowed to stay by your side through sickness and *health,* for —"

"I'd love to do this all day," Harry bellowed over the noise in the background, "but as much as I enjoying you taking your misery out on me, I've got a job to do so I can *pay* for all of this. Look, once you settle down, you'll see I don't have a choice. And I appreciate what you're doing, Francie, I really do. She would have done it for you."

He hung up before Francie could respond. What would she have said, anyway? Of course Francie would have done anything for Vi; neither of them had ever needed to ask.

CHAPTER 18
VIRGIE

Virgie was the one who answered the door when the first of the reporters arrived, but after that her mother took over and she was ordered down to the end of the circular drive to direct traffic. Guests — coming or going — were to be told not to speak to reporters and to be reminded, if necessary, that discretion was guaranteed to *all* guests at the Holiday Ranch. And reporters were to be told that they were not to park on private property, and that none of the staff had any comment.

After the first newsman — the crime reporter from the *Evening Gazette* — was shown the door; the rest had to content themselves with standing around on the sidewalk. Virgie's mother assured the staff that they'd be gone by the next day, when some other story caught their attention, but for now they were to be ignored and endured. A cameraman from the *Nevada Ap-*

peal tried to sneak past Virgie to get a better shot, but when she told him her mother would call the police, he retreated.

None of them seemed interested in asking Virgie what she knew, which showed how dumb they were, because she could have told them a *lot*. Still, when a short, thickset man in a white shirt sidled up to her, she checked the name tag on her smock to make sure it was straight and tried to look extra serious.

"Say there — what's going on here?" he said. He took a cigarette from his pocket and struck a match on his teeth. Virgie tried not to look impressed.

"Police business," she said curtly.

"Well, obviously." He scratched his head. "But what happened? Robbery?"

Virgie took a closer look — the man had no notebook, no camera, nothing but a cheap wristwatch and a signet ring shaped like a horse's head. "I'm not at liberty to say."

"Guest drowned," the fellow from the *Gazette* said. "One of the divorce gals."

"Drowned?" the stranger repeated. "What was her name?"

The cameraman glared at Virgie. "*She* knows, I'd wager," he said. "But she's not talking."

Virgie didn't like the way the stranger was looking at her. "Maybe I do, and maybe I don't, but I couldn't tell you anyway. All guest information is confidential."

The reporter snorted. "Older lady. There's a rumor she jumped," he told the man. "Cops aren't saying if she left a note."

Virgie felt her neck grow warm. She was pretty sure her mother wouldn't want them talking about notes. There had been a suicide at the ranch years ago, when Virgie was too young to remember — a lady whose six weeks were almost up was found in the old stable that Clyde used as a toolshed. Somehow she'd gotten the door open (likely, Clyde left it unlocked) and driven her car in late one night. She closed the door and got back in her car with the motor running, and Clyde found her the next morning. The papers ran a story featuring photos of the car being towed out of the shed, and bookings were down for months afterward. Virgie certainly wasn't about to tell the reporters any of that.

The stranger flicked ash onto the lawn. "Damn shame. How are the rest of the gals taking it? Something like that could really shake a person up."

"We're *not talking* about it," Virgie said. Honestly, sometimes she could see why her mother was so strict. "So that they *don't* get shook up."

"Yeah, I get it." The stranger dropped his butt onto the sidewalk and ground it out with his shoe. Now somebody was going to have to pick it up. "I guess you just never know what love will drive a person to do."

CHAPTER 19
JUNE

June had bathed Patty and was dressing her for lunch. She hoped it would be served on time despite the morning's excitement, since Patty hadn't had anything but the toast Mrs. Swanson had made for her hours ago. She was almost ready to go when Francie knocked on the door.

"I'm sorry to bother you, June," she said. She looked terrible — there were dark circles under her eyes, and she'd obviously been crying.

"Please — come in."

"Oh, look at you, sweetheart — aren't you a sight for sore eyes," Francie told Patty. She sat on the edge of the chaise and opened her arms, and after a moment's hesitation, Patty clambered up into her lap.

June was surprised, but she supposed that she'd better get used to Patty being with strangers, since she'd have to find a job pronto now that her benefactor was dead.

The shock of poor Vi's death was bad enough, but the knowledge that she was back to square one, broke and alone in a strange city, was overwhelming.

"Mrs. Meeker —"

"Francie. Please, June."

"Francie." It felt awkward to be addressing a woman her mother's age this way. Especially given what she needed to say. "I don't mean to add to your hardship, especially at a time like this, and I'll be . . . that is to say, I just — Patty and I just —"

"Whatever is wrong, dear?"

"It's just that I haven't had time to find a place to stay yet and I was wondering, if it wasn't too inconvenient, if Mrs. Swanson wouldn't mind, if I could stay just until tomorrow morning? Because I can spend the afternoon looking for a new place. With any luck I'll find a job too, and I've got enough to put a deposit on a room."

"My goodness, June, don't be ridiculous! The room is paid for, and I won't have that wretched Harry getting one cent in refund, so there's no reason for you to leave. I'm sure Vi would have wanted you to stay."

"But — ma'am — I couldn't," June said, shamefaced. She'd seen the rate card in the drawer of the desk — a single night in the suite cost twenty-two dollars. "There's plenty of perfectly nice places that don't cost near as much. I might even be able to get board if I can find a position with a family. And I don't want to be a burden while . . . while Mrs. Carothers's family is here."

She'd been worrying about that all morning — that Vi's family would arrive and demand to know why June was staying in her room. That they might actually think she had taken advantage. It would be so hard to explain — why would they ever believe that Vi would invite a perfect stranger in?

Francie was regarding her oddly. Had she said something wrong?

"June —"

"I'm sorry, Francie, I know it didn't come out right. You and Vi did so much for me already. Now you've got bigger things to worry about and I don't want to be in the way."

"But that's just it. I've just had an idea. June . . . didn't you say you have secretarial experience?"

That wasn't the question she'd expected to hear. "I typed and filed for my uncle's business when I was in high school, and I started secretarial school," she admitted. "But I dropped out when I got married.

153

Stan didn't like me working and besides, I was awful sick when I was expecting."

"It doesn't even matter. You're smart and quick and I can help out too. June, I'd like to hire you to arrange Vi's funeral and help me with her affairs." Francie became more animated. "There's so much to do! She wants to be buried here in Reno, you see, and we have to contact all her family and her friends to let them know. We'll have to find them rooms — the ones who can come — and we'll need to plan a luncheon. I told Harry we'd have the service on Tuesday, which gives us —" she glanced down at her watch and shook her head. "Honestly, I'll never pull it off alone. I'll pay you, of course, and we can get set up right here in the suite, and perhaps we can ask Mrs. Oglesby to watch Patty again. Please, say you will, or I don't know what I'll do."

June looked closely at Francie to see if she was lying — not about Vi's wishes but about needing her help. It had been very difficult for June to accept the generosity Francie and Vi had already shown her, and she never would have agreed to it if it weren't for Patty — but she wasn't about to get into the habit of accepting charity.

"I'm sure you could hire someone better," she hedged. "I bet there's lots of girls who could help."

"But I don't want anyone else. Don't you see? I've just lost my best friend — I can't bear to see strangers going through her things. And even though we only just met yesterday, I feel like — well, you're kind, and good, and I could use a friend."

June could see that Francie was close to tears again. Hastily, she agreed. "I'd love to help, and I'll work as hard as I can, I promise."

"Oh, good." Francie visibly relaxed. She kissed the top of Patty's head and gently set her down. "Let's get this little one fed and see if Mrs. Oglesby can watch her, and then we'll get started. We'll need to make arrangements with the mortuary right away. And we must call to put a notice in the paper — here and back in San Francisco. And of course we need to start making calls to her family."

"It'll be all right," June said, wishing she had more to offer than this tired lie.

CHAPTER 20

After getting Patty settled with Mrs.
Oglesby, who assured her that she welcomed
the chance to "do something other than
waiting around feeling miserable," June
helped Francie rearrange the living room so
that the coffee table was next to the writing
desk, so the two of them could work side by
side. Francie had found Vi's address book
in her purse, and she laid it next to her
daybook and her checkbook, and began
making a list while June copied down the
phone numbers of florists and mortuaries
from the phone book.

While Francie started making calls, June
made a neat list of the names and phone
numbers of every entry in June's address
book that wasn't a business, like her hairdresser and dentist and window washer and
the like. She divided them into family, local
and out-of-town friends as best she could,
marking those she was unsure of for Fran-

cie to review.

June listened to Francie talk on the phone while she worked, marveling at her confidence. June had never heard a woman speak with as much authority as Francie did. She didn't hesitate to ask for clarification or object when she was given the runaround, whether she was speaking to a funeral director, a church secretary, or the cemetery manager.

When the funeral director balked at speaking to someone who wasn't immediate family, Francie had asked him if he wanted her business or if she should call someone else. She'd told the cemetery manager she'd pay overtime if necessary but the flowers *would* be planted around Vi's parents' graves by the morning of the funeral. And when she read from the obituary she'd composed, she included herself — "Frances Meeker, friend of many years" — among those left behind.

June was torn between intimidation and admiration. Her own mother had grown up in poverty and quit school in third grade, and she'd always been ashamed of her lack of education, her bad teeth, the hardships of trying to get by, especially after June's father died. June had seen her mother reduced to tears when a traveling salesman looked around their humble living room and left without even opening his sample case. She'd been too afraid of telling the doctor about her pains until it was too late.

It was a priest who finally dented Francie's composure. She had called two Catholic churches and been told by the administrative staff of each that a funeral Mass could not be arranged until the proper documents were received from Vi's parish in San Francisco, as the church she'd attended as a child had burned down and all the sacramental records were lost. The parish priest himself answered the telephone at the third church Francie called. After listening to Francie explain the situation, he hinted that the process could be expedited should Francie make a generous donation to the parish fund.

"Are you suggesting, Father, that my friend, a pious woman who has lived a life of faithful service, who has made countless donations to dozens of charitable organizations, not to mention the church she has attended for the last three decades, must *pay* for the privilege of her own funeral Mass?"

June watched Francie's expression grow thunderous; the priest's response obviously didn't satisfy her, because she barked, "I've heard enough, thank you," and slammed the receiver down in the cradle.

"This is ridiculous," she fumed. "For all the money Vi's given the Church — you know what, come to think of it, maybe I should just call her priest back home and see what he can do."

Armed with the phone number June had found in Vi's address book for the parish office, Francie spent the next twenty minutes wheedling and pressing her case until Vi's favorite priest, Father Fletcher, agreed to make the trip to Reno on Tuesday.

"There's only one problem," Francie explained after she hung up. "There isn't time for him to go through the proper channels to make arrangements with a church in Reno. But he's willing to perform a funeral liturgy as part of the graveside service. He says a Mass isn't required — I hope Vi won't mind."

"I'm sure she wouldn't," June said, "especially since the *Lord* won't mind."

"I suppose you're right," Francie said. "Don't be scandalized, June, but Arthur is an atheist, and I must admit I never particularly enjoyed going to church, so after the children were all baptized I got out of the habit. Vi used to try to convince me to go with her — but I never understood why I'd want to get up before dawn just to listen to some priest drone on and on in Latin with his back to us."

"You're a good friend, Francie."

"You think so?" Francie smiled wistfully. "There were plenty of times when we quarreled, you know. Usually over silly stuff. I hate to be proved wrong, I'm afraid, and I let my pride get in the way much too often — but Vi never stayed mad at me for long."

"I've never had a friend like that. Not since grammar school, anyway. Stan didn't even like for me to socialize with the neighbors."

"Well, maybe that should go on your list. Make some friends — have a little fun. You deserve it, June."

"I'd . . . like that," June said quietly.

"Well, I think we've done enough for today — this list you made me is starting to swim before my eyes. I'll start calling first thing in the morning; there's no reason you should have to talk to perfect strangers. I've met most of her family and her good friends from college, and it's best they hear the news from a friend, since Harry refuses to do it."

"There's an awful lot of them," June ventured. There were over forty names on the list. "Are you going to call them all?"

"No, I don't think so. Vi wouldn't have wanted a fuss — I'll just call the ones I've heard her mention." She stood and stretched, massaging the tendons in her neck. "We've still got a couple of hours of daylight — let's drive out to the cemetery, shall we? Mrs. Swanson offered me the use of her car until Arthur gets here. I'd like to take a look at her parents' headstone, since we'll need to order one for Vi, and also see what kind of shape the plot is in. And we also need to figure out where to set up chairs and . . ."

Her voice trailed off as she picked up Vi's address book and flipped through until she found the entry she wanted. "We can drive by her parents' house while we're out that way — she loved that place. Other than college, she never lived anywhere else before she married Harry."

"Who lives there now?"

"Honestly, I'm not sure that anyone does . . . she's had caretakers staying there for years. She let them live there for free in exchange for keeping up the place, but I think the last one moved away a while back." Francie sighed. "Vi had always hoped one of her boys might like to have the house, but now that they're working for Harry, I doubt they'll ever want to leave San Francisco."

"I bet it's beautiful," June said. Everything

about Vi had been so elegant, from the way she moved to her wardrobe and her fine leather luggage; it was easy to imagine her growing up in one of the stately mansions across the river.

"Oh, honey, that house wasn't anything fancy. She didn't come from any money at all, you know. Her father delivered ice for a living, back before people had electric refrigerators. Vi's mother once told her that they never had any more children because they took one look at her and knew she was perfect, but her father used to say that one child was all that house had room for."

"Sounds like how I grew up," June said. "I shared a room with my grandmother, and my brothers slept on the porch except when it got too cold and then they slept in the barn."

"You and Vi had that in common." Francie smiled. "Both of you had a hard time of it coming up — and it only made you sweeter."

June smiled, but Francie's compliment had made her uneasy. Because if Vi had been able to improve her life, to put the hardships of her past behind her and go to college and have everything money could buy — why had June made such a mess of hers?

CHAPTER 21
FRANCIE

They drove north in Mrs. Swanson's gleaming sedan, a deep red Chevrolet Fleetmaster with the Holiday Ranch logo painted on the passenger door. As they left the city behind, the land changed to gentle rolling hills covered in parched-looking grasses and tough little bushes and the occasional tree, crisscrossed here and there with rocky trails — the very same trails Vi had spoken so fondly of hiking as a child. The vegetation here looked as if it had to work hard to survive, Francie thought, pleased with the notion, because it reminded her of Vi. You'd never know it to look at her, but Vi had had a sturdiness to her that had enabled her to endure all those years of disappointment.

Which made her final act even more devastating. *Why, Vi?* How Francie wished they could have talked about it, that Vi had shared what had caused her to give up, just as she finally had the chance to start over.

"Oh, look at that," June said, pointing off to the left. "I see the cemetery. What a lovely setting!"

It was set into a hillside, with evergreens and shade trees and a grassy lawn that looked like an emerald pool against the backdrop of the golden hills. Here and there, flowers left by loved ones provided spots of color.

They drove through the gates and made a slow tour, finding a caretaker loading a lawn mower into his truck.

"Excuse me," Francie said, rolling down her window. The gentleman looked too old to be handling the heavy equipment, but his sun-browned face and strong, muscled forearms spoke of a life of hard work.

"Somethin' I can help you with?"

"My friend passed yesterday unexpectedly, and she'll be buried here with her parents. I was just hoping to take a look at the plot."

"I'm sorry for your loss. I been working here since thirty-nine, so I reckon I know every soul in the place. What's her family name?"

"Buckley. Her mother was Brigid. I'm sorry, I don't recall her father's name."

"Thomas! Old Tom and Brigid, I know them well." The old man smiled, his grin splitting a nest of wrinkles. "Don't tell anyone, but sometimes I talk to 'em. Glad to show you, just follow me."

"You wouldn't have happened to know them before they passed, would you? They lived very near here, at 8 Ely Road. They had just the one daughter — she used to play here as a child."

"Sorry, ma'am, I only moved here when I retired from the railroad. But you can see their house from here — it's sure to be one of those." He pointed up to three little houses perched on the hill, one of them nothing but a leaning collection of boards that looked as if it was going to collapse.

Francie thanked him, and he got into his truck and drove slowly up toward a far corner of the cemetery, pointing toward a pair of tall pines. He gave the horn a tap and waved before driving away.

Francie parked, and the two of them got out. There were only a handful of graves between the road and the edge of the cemetery here, and it took no time at all to find Vi's parents'. Their gravestone was modest, laid flat to the ground, with only their names and dates and a simple cross. Weeds grew around it, and pine needles had fallen on its surface.

"Which side is hers, do you think?" June asked.

"I'm not sure. But we'll find out tomorrow. And it will be easy to set up chairs over here. I don't think we'll need more than a dozen, for the older folks — everyone else can stand."

"And her priest can stand right here," June said. "That way the hill will be behind him, and the trees — and we have them put the flowers on stands right back here in a little half circle around her folks' grave."

"That's perfect, June — that's just the sort of help I need. I knew you'd have clever ideas."

June beamed; it wasn't surprising to see what a little praise did for her. Poor thing probably hadn't heard many kind words in recent years.

And it was good to have her company; without it, Francie knew she would have given in to the despair that pressed in on her. *Keep busy,* she reminded herself. *Don't think, just do.* Otherwise she'd never get through the next few days.

"Let's go see the house — we'll need to get back soon if we don't want to miss dinner."

They got back in the car and drove out of the cemetery, then doubled back after they missed the turnoff to Ely Road. The sign, a hand-painted wooden affair, had been hit by a car at some point and leaned sideways.

"I bet it's that one," June said, pointing. "It's the prettiest. Oh, look at the garden!"

Garden was perhaps too grand a word for the weed-choked beds in front of the house, but overgrown geraniums burst with red and pink blooms amid purple allium and pink coneflowers and others that Francie didn't recognize.

"This is it," she confirmed. "See, there's the number on the porch."

"Isn't it darling! I can't believe nobody's been taking care of it."

June was right; the white paint looked fresh, the roof solid, the porch boards sturdy. White curtains hung in the windows, blocking the view inside.

They got out and walked up a stone path to the front of the house, pausing at the flowerbeds.

"Vi loved to garden," Francie said. "It was one thing she hated about her house in San Francisco — other than the window boxes and the tiny yard in back, she had nowhere to plant."

"These have been here for years," June said, bending to snap a spent bloom. "Someone must have given them water now and

167

then, even if they didn't do anything else. But they just need to be deadheaded and trimmed, and the weeds dug out, and they'd be lovely."

"I wish we could get in," Francie said.

June walked up the porch stairs and looked under the mat, and behind the mailbox, and finally she climbed up on the rail and felt around the top of the porchlight.

"Good heavens, you're going to break your neck!"

June held out a key triumphantly and jumped lightly down. "Same place my aunt kept hers! Where I grew up, everyone kept a spare key out in case a neighbor needed to get in."

"You'd never do that in San Francisco," Francie marveled. "Someone would come along and rob you blind."

"Well, there's probably not a whole lot to steal here," June said.

She handed the key to Francie, who fitted it into the lock. Before she opened the door, she had the urge to say something — a prayer, maybe — as though Vi's parents' spirits might be waiting inside.

But it was even better than that. The room was bare save a broom leaning against the wall and an upright piano covered with a sheet — the piano Vi's mother had scrimped and saved for, the one she'd practiced on all through her childhood. Windows on three sides filled the room with light, and the wooden floors were inlaid with a pretty design. The curtains were dusty, but they were trimmed with a sweet band of lace, and there were built-ins with carved details and cut-glass knobs. The wide doorway to the rest of the house was arched, and the old plaster was carefully patched and painted. For such a modest house, someone — Vi's father, no doubt — had worked hard to make it as nice as possible.

"I love it," June said. "Look at the sweet little hutch! And oh — the pretty glass shades on the light! The sofa would go here, and a chair for reading under the window here and — oh, the floors are so pretty where they peek out from under these rugs." She walked over to the piano and lifted the lid and ran her finger lightly along the keys. "It's in tune! Someone must have played it not too long ago."

"Do you play, June?"

"Oh, no, but I used to sing at church every Sunday when I was in high school, and my best friend played the piano."

They explored the rest of the house, the two tiny bedrooms — Francie was certain the first had been Vi's, since she'd always talked about the birds that nested in the tree outside the window — and a small bath with the fixtures in perfect working order.

The kitchen was laid with black and white tile on the floor, and a screen door opened onto a patio with weeds coming up between the stones, littered with apples that had fallen from a gnarled old tree. The cupboards had glass doors and the backs were papered in a faded pattern of roses.

June touched a square of marble set into the scrubbed wood counters next to the sink. "For making pie crust!" she exclaimed delightedly. "My mama would have loved that. And you could put an African violet on this little shelf where it gets the sun and —"

She suddenly stopped and turned to Francie, eyes shining. "What if — oh, maybe this is a crazy idea but — what if we had the luncheon here, after the service?"

"In this house?"

"Yes! We'd just have to rent some tables and chairs, but as long as the icebox and the stove work, we could cook everything here, and —"

"June," Francie said, laughing, "we're not going to cook a thing ourselves. We'll hire caterers."

170

June blushed. "Oh. Of course. But they could set it all up in here, and as long as the weather is nice people could go out on the patio or sit in the front room, so there would be plenty of room. Why, people could practically walk here from the cemetery!"

"I don't know, June. It would be hard to get everything ready by Tuesday — it would be so much easier just to hold it at a hall."

"But that's why you hired me! To take care of everything. Francie, I know you want this to be special for Vi. And if she loved this place as much as you say . . ."

She *had* — that was the thing that made Francie even consider the outlandish suggestion. It would be taking a gamble to let June, who had plenty of enthusiasm but so little experience, take on a project like this — but if it worked, it would be the best possible send-off for her dear friend.

"It's certainly — it's a wonderful idea," Francie found herself saying. "Oh, what are we thinking? Do you really think we can pull this off?"

"I *know* we can. Mrs. Oglesby told me she'd take Patty every single day if I let her, she misses her own grandchildren so, and Patty loves her. So I have all the time in the world. And I'll work hard — I'm a hard worker, Francie, you'll see."

Francie took her hand. "I have no doubt of that. It's just, Arthur and the kids are coming, and Vi's boys —"

"Maybe they'll want to help! I know when my mama passed, getting everything done for her funeral was the only thing that saved me. Otherwise I don't think I'd have gotten out of bed, I was so sad."

The kids, helping? Francie had her doubts. Even though they arranged events for a living, Frank and Charlie wouldn't know the first thing about planning something like this. And Jimmy wouldn't come until the very last minute, he was so busy at the bank. Alice would help, of course, but someone would have to look after Arthur, and —

"Oh, I hope I don't regret this," Francie said. "But yes. Yes! Let's make this the most wonderful day for Vi. I mean, I know it will be sad — everyone will be sad — but at least they'll remember Vi exactly the way she would have wanted."

"Thank you for trusting me, Francie," June said. "I won't let you down."

CHAPTER 22

Back at the hotel, the reporters who'd been hanging around the drive had finally given up and left. June collected Patty from Mrs. Oglesby's room and then the three of them went down to dinner. As they were eating, Francie took a chance and confided her plan to June.

"I'm going to go talk to her, somewhere in public where she'll be less likely to make a scene. I simply won't have her in this hotel — or anywhere near Vi's family and friends. If she has any decency at all —" Francie caught herself. What were the odds of that? A girl who'd take up with another woman's husband when they were still living under the same roof wasn't likely to care. "Or if she has any hope of keeping the entire world from knowing just how brazen she is, she'll go quietly and wait a few months before they even think of announcing an engagement. There's plenty of places she can stay outside city limits where she can still meet the residency requirement. There's the Del Monte, the Flying M E, plenty of them — and I'll make sure Harry pays every cent."

June looked worried. "It's awful, what she's done," she agreed, "but what if she doesn't care? We can't *make* her leave."

Francie shrugged. She knew this wasn't true — there was always money, and money always worked — but she wanted the satisfaction of *shaming* Wilhelmina Carroll. She wanted that strident little harlot to feel as small as Vi must have felt when Harry told her he was really doing it this time, that he was leaving her for good. To Francie, Harry was no great loss; but Vi'd had her reasons to stay and that was good enough for her.

She didn't tell June, but she had a larger goal in mind. It was a long shot — but Francie was willing to give it a try. If Willy refused, as Francie suspected she might, then Francie would make sure everybody knew — first thing after the funeral, she'd seed the rumor among everyone who mattered in San Francisco — and once it became a great enough scandal, Harry would come to his senses, because his business relied almost entirely on his reputation. He was a scoundrel — but a scoundrel with an eye firmly, always, on the bottom line. He displayed his Chamber of Commerce citations above his desk and lunched with members of the city council and gave money to their campaigns, all to keep business flowing his way. In fact, the one thing Harry might love more than chasing skirts was money, and he wouldn't put up with anything that could set him back.

And then *Willy* would be the one left to suffer. Harry might not leave her right away, but his wandering eye would soon land on a girl just as pretty, who didn't have the added complication of attracting the wrong kind of attention. And then he'd toss her aside just as he'd done to Vi.

"It's a free country," she conceded, "and Harry's money probably spends anywhere in town. But I'm not going to force her — if she leaves, she's going to do it on her own. And if she doesn't, I'll make sure she pays."

"But how are you going to do that?"

"Trust me," Francie said. "A woman like that always forgets that one reaps what one sows."

CHAPTER 23

Francie waited until after nine o'clock, when the guests who were staying in had retired to their rooms and the ones who were going out had already left. Among the evening outings on the schedule for the week that had been distributed to the rooms were bingo at the Nevada Club, dancing at the Poodle Dog, and a ladies-only craps lesson at Harrah's.

Francie had taken pains to get her information from a reliable source — not Mrs. Swanson, who was as tight-lipped as they come. Instead, after dinner, Francie had folded a crisp five-dollar bill so that it fit in the palm of her hand and gone looking for Clyde. She'd found him in the lounge, changing a light bulb.

"Mrs. Meeker," he said, climbing down his ladder. He took off his hat. "I'm so sorry about Mrs. Carothers. What a shame, what a terrible shame."

"Thank you," Francie said, thinking, *Oh no, a decent man.* How inconvenient to find one when she wasn't looking. "See here . . . there is no delicate way to say this, but her family will be arriving in town for her funeral, and I very much want there to be no distractions."

"Yes, ma'am," Clyde said.

"There is a young lady staying here, who has an acquaintance with Mr. Carothers, Vi's husband. An . . . unfortunate acquaintance, one that could be quite upsetting to her children, if the lady in question were to mingle with the other guests. Do you see what I mean?"

Francie could tell from the way the tips of his ears went pink that he did. "Yes, ma'am."

"So what I would like to ask," Francie said, showing him the bill in her hand, "is where I might find this young woman, so we can have a conversation about how this unpleasantness can be avoided. It's Miss Wilhelmina Carroll, though I would appreciate if you would keep that information to yourself. Do you happen to know where she might be this evening?"

Clyde stared at the bill but made no move to take it; in fact, he looked slightly wounded. "She goes to Gwin's most every night," he said, "unless her friend comes to see her. Then he takes her out and she comes home very late."

Why, the *nerve* of that Harry! He couldn't even go a few weeks without seeing his little tramp. The whole time he'd supposedly been in Las Vegas setting up the nuclear tour, he'd been sneaking up here! What sorry excuse had he given the boys?

"When was the last time this *friend* came calling?"

Clyde scratched his ear and looked at the ceiling. The pink had spread from his ears to his cheeks. "Well, last Friday. Reason I remember is, he was keen on putting some money on the fight, asked me where he should go."

"Last Friday? You're sure?"

"Oh, yes, ma'am. I sent him down to Harold's Club."

Last Friday, Harry could not have been in Reno, because he was home with Vi. He'd returned from Las Vegas to entertain some livestock men who wanted to hold an exposition at the Cow Palace Expo. Apparently, they were conservative sorts who took a dim view of divorce, so Harry had insisted that Vi accompany him to dinner. *You're still my wife,* he'd told her.

"Just exactly what did this 'friend' look like?"

178

"Uh, six-one, six-two, dark hair, and one of those little moustaches."

"And you're sure he was visiting Willy," Francie said, pressing the bill into his hand.

Harry was five-foot-nine with receding gray hair — Clyde might have just handed her all the ammunition she needed.

CHAPTER 24

Obviously, it would be unseemly for a woman in mourning to frequent a tavern — but Francie wasn't about to put off this mission, not with family arriving tomorrow. This would be her one chance.

She did assemble a disguise of sorts, however. She'd packed a pair of blue jeans and a plaid shirt with a Western yoke that she'd bought for her stay, thinking she might go on a dude ranch outing. She tied a checked kerchief around her neck, and as she examined her reflection in the mirror, she had to admit she liked the way the getup looked on her. The last touch was the cowboy hat she'd bought on a whim; she put it on so that the brim shadowed her face. With any luck, no one would connect her to the woman who'd come to town yesterday in a Claire McCardell suit.

She checked the hall before leaving her room. No one was about, and Francie congratulated herself on leaving without being noticed.

CHAPTER 25
VIRGIE

Virgie was hiding in the niche under the
stairs, hoping to spot June leaving and follow her to see where she went, and writing
in her notebook.

Tabby, I think Mrs. S knows I have been
following her. I don't know when she saw
me but maybe it was this afternoon when
she came home and went up to Mrs. O's
room to get Patty. (If Patty is her real
name!!!) I need to not use the supply
closet for a while anyway because Clyde
saw me coming out of it the other day and
asked me what I was doing.

I don't think there is any way she could
know it was me that took the ring but the
only people that ever went in that suite
besides her are Mrs. M and me and the
maids. She might think it was Flossie or
Ruth but that would be terrible because
Mother might fire them so I would have to

tell Mother and then I'd be in so much trouble! Anyway so I think maybe Mrs. S is waiting to see which of us it is. She is a good actor she acts like nothing is wrong but why would she stay here now that Mrs. C is dead other than she wants to get it back. Also Mother says the room is all paid for already and I think it is awful how she is freeloading off a dead woman but Mrs. M doesn't seem to mind even though Mrs. C was her best friend.

As the hour grew late, Virgie had been about to give up when she saw Mrs. Meeker coming down the hall, dressed for some reason like a cowgirl.

A sudden, terrible thought occurred to Virgie — what if Mrs. Meeker had been in on it all along? What if she was the one who'd planned the theft and had brought June in on the scheme only when she couldn't find another way to get rid of her?

And what if Mrs. Meeker was now *setting her up*? She could have had Mrs. Samples steal the ring with a promise that she would fence it and share the money. When Mrs. Carothers discovered it missing, Mrs. Meeker would have been furious — and suspicious. She might think that Mrs. Samples had sold it already and kept all the money — but then why wouldn't she have simply disappeared with it? So maybe Mrs. Meeker *did* believe her, and now the two of them were trying to figure out who else might have taken it. And since Mrs. Samples obviously suspected Virgie, that would spell trouble for her. She would have to watch her back even more carefully.

But there was also the matter of the stranger who'd been nosing around when the reporters had come. Virgie wasn't positive, but she thought she'd seen him again this morning, loitering out back near the shed. Whoever it was, he'd had the same build and moustache as the stranger and had taken off running through the trees when Clyde came around the corner in the truck. If he *was* their accomplice, there were a few ways he could fit into their scheme. Maybe he was a third partner, or maybe he was their fence, or maybe even a hit man they'd hired to polish off Mrs. Carothers!

But something must have gone wrong, or he wouldn't have been sneaking around the house asking questions. Maybe Mrs. Samples had cut him out of her plans when she decided to keep all the money for herself. Maybe he didn't know them at all but had heard them talking about their plans and decided to steal the ring from *them* — or threaten to tell the cops unless they cut him in.

These thoughts raced through Virgie's mind as Mrs. Meeker walked through the lobby and out the front door. Virgie waited a few moments before she followed, staying away from the street lights until she reached the river path — the same path where Mrs. Carothers had probably met her end. She kept considerable distance between herself and Mrs. Meeker until they passed the stone arch; after that the path rose up on the bank at the edge of the trees and offered a person cover, if they happened to want to go unnoticed.

CHAPTER 26
FRANCIE

Gwin's was even more crowded tonight than it had been last night, though if one was just passing time until one's divorce came through, Francie supposed one night was like any other.

The burly man sitting on a stool inside the door recognized her. "Hello again," he said affably. "Where's your friend?"

Francie realized he was talking about Vi and stammered a response. It didn't seem possible that Vi had just been here, dancing and laughing like she hadn't a care in the world — and now she was gone.

"Have a nice time tonight," the man said. "It's Antsville in there!"

Francie spotted Willy sitting by herself at a table in front of the piano, watching the pianist with her chin in her hands. The drink in front of her had barely been touched — but there was no way to tell how many she'd already had.

Francie found a seat at the bar and ordered a sidecar. The pianist was playing the last notes of "My Baby Just Cares for Me," ending with an extravagant arpeggio and a saucy wave at the crowd, to much cheering. She leaned in to the microphone and thanked everyone.

"And now for something special," she said, absently running her fingers along the upper keys. "All the way from San Francisco, California" — she pronounced it Cali-FOR-NI-YAY — "Miss Willy Carroll, here to sing the blues for you!"

The crowd cheered, though they probably would have cheered anyone at that point, considering how drunk many of them were. Willy approached the piano and took the microphone from its stand, blowing kisses, to even more cheering. As the pianist played the lead-in, Willy took her time arranging herself with one bare arm stretched provocatively on the worn wooden piano as though it were an ebony grand in the finest club in New York City. She tossed her blond curls and closed her eyes and set her lips in a pout. When the pianist launched into "Skylark," Willy opened her eyes and came to life.

Willy with a microphone in her hand was not the same brassy, hard-edged girl they'd met the other night. She played to the entire room, swaying to the music, casting her seductive gaze from one patron to another. And her voice! Smooth and languid, it compelled the audience to pay attention, conversations interrupted and drinks set down. Willy's range spanned octaves, from a throaty alto to the highest notes without breaking. When she reached the end of the song she held the final note and threw her head back, exposing her long, white throat as the audience whooped and cheered.

To say that the crowd loved her would be like saying that a dog likes a steak. They cheered and stomped and called for more, but Willy took her bow and applauded the pianist, who waved once more and then got up and slipped out the back door, leaving Willy to soak up the wolf whistles and demands for more.

When the applause finally died down, Willy headed straight for the bar and slid onto the stool next to Francie. If she was surprised to see her, she didn't show it.

"Hello, Francie. How did you like my song?"

Francie glared — Willy hadn't even acknowledged Vi's death. "I didn't know vipers could sing."

"Want another drink?" Willy said, ignoring the comment. "Shirley'll make you whatever you like, since you're with me. I'm good for business."

"I wouldn't touch anything that came from you," Francie snarled. "Any more than I'd drink the blood on your hands."

"Oh my," Willy murmured as the bartender made her way over. "Such drama. Well, I'll go ahead and order for you in case you change your mind. How about a bottle of your best champagne, Shirl?"

The bartender laughed. "I don't know if Rita would be too happy with me comping you an entire bottle."

"All right, make it your second best," Willy said, taking her cigarettes from a pocket hidden in the folds of her full skirt. "Though given how many people I bring in the door, she shouldn't complain. Actually, if Rita doesn't want to buy us a drink, I'm sure those fellows will."

She nodded at a nearby table as she lit her cigarette, and the rowdy trio of men waved and whistled.

"Now you're talking," the bartender said. "Maybe I'll charge them double and keep the difference."

"That's the way to think," Willy said with a wink.

Throughout this exchange, Francie

fumed. The moment Shirley walked away, she leaned in close and muttered, "That'll be the last time you sing in this bar. No, strike that — the last time you set foot in this bar. Or anywhere in this town. I'll expect you to be on the first train out tomorrow morning."

Willy regarded her with amusement, raising an eyebrow that had been plucked into a narrow arch. Wings of eyeliner tipped up at the outer corners of her eyes, the lids shimmering silver. Her thin lips had been lined and painted to appear fuller and she wore a beaded choker that drew the eye away from the softness in her chin. This was a girl who knew how to make the best of what God had given her.

"Where's your little friend tonight? Home washing her hair?"

"Leave her out of this," Francie snapped. "This is between me and you."

"Oh dear." Willy feigned dismay. "Harry's going to be terribly disappointed to hear that — he thought he was my only beau."

"How can you joke about this?" Francie snapped. "Harry's *wife* — the one you stole him from — is *dead.* Isn't that enough for you? Do you have to make a mockery of her too?"

Willy put a hand to her chest. "Are we

talking about the same woman? Violet Carothers née Buckley? Let me tell you, if she *did* kill herself — and you can't convince me she didn't simply fall in after all the booze she was putting away last night — it wasn't over a broken heart. The minute Harry rescued her from this backward little town and married her, she showed her true colors. She never really loved him, and she's been making his life hell for years."

"Oh, no no no," Francie said. The bartender had come back with the champagne and a couple of flutes, which she plunked down and left. "You don't know anything about Vi. I'm her best friend, I lived across the street from her for almost thirty years. I've been there to pick up the pieces every time Harry strayed. Which, believe me, was often enough to make your head spin — you're just the latest flashy little piece of trash to catch his eye. He'll be done with you too before long, no matter what he's told you."

"You think so?" Willy said in a bored tone. "I'm not so sure. He wants to marry me the minute I get my papers. He said I can pick any chapel in Reno and he'll marry me again in California — and we're going to have our reception at the Palace."

"And you really think that's going to happen now? Harry's an idiot, but he isn't *stupid.* His business is built on reputation and word of mouth. Even someone as soulless as Harry knows that throwing a huge gaudy wedding right after his wife died will cause an uproar. I'd be surprised if he didn't keep you hidden away until a decent amount of time has passed."

"You seem awfully concerned about my reputation all of a sudden," Willy said. "So why don't you get it off your chest? Go ahead, tell everyone you know about how Harry treated poor Vi. Maybe they'll believe you. Better yet, maybe they'll tell everyone *they* know. Only, when it comes out that he gave her everything she wanted, that she had a monthly allowance more than most men earn in a year, that she would have gotten a house worth ninety thousand dollars in the divorce — how sympathetic do you really think they'll be? Oh, and I know all about her lawyer. Harry showed me the letters he's been sending. I have to hand it to her, she hired a shark."

"She had to. Harry wouldn't have given her a cent if he could avoid it."

"Harry knows how to present this in the news," Willy went on, as though Francie hadn't spoken. "He has the best publicists working for him, remember? If he has to give interviews, he'll say that she shut him out years ago and barely spoke to him anymore, but out of respect and genuine affection, he did his best to save the marriage. And then she thanked him by trying to rob him blind. There are those who will see her terrible accident as just desserts, don't you think?"

"Vi never cared a whit about money!"

Willy shrugged. "Then spread the word. Make me out to be Harry's little whore, if you want. Heck, you can start tonight. I bet at least a dozen of the women in this room are from San Francisco, wouldn't you think? If they tell everyone they know, it'll spread faster than a front-page headline in the *Examiner.*"

"Are you really as stupid as you look?" Francie demanded, shaking with rage.

"There's a saying in show business," Willy said mildly. "There's no such thing as bad publicity. Have you heard that before?"

"Harry's not in *show business,*" Francie retorted. "He's a promoter who needs to get people to come to his events, and he succeeds because of a reputation that took him years to build. Trust me, he's not going to risk that."

"I wasn't talking about Harry," Willy said witheringly, gathering her cigarettes and her little beaded purse. "I was talking about *me*. Do you really think I'm content to sing in joints like this? I've got *plans*. Harry's already booked me into Bruno's for a two-week gig this fall, and I don't care what anyone says about me as long as it gets them in that club. So do your worst — give me a secret baby if you want, or late-night orgies, or an affair with a mob boss. All you'll be doing is putting money in my piggy bank."

The pianist chose that moment to return from her smoke break and join them at the bar. Willy stood and gave Francie a regal nod. "Francie, please meet my accompanist, Helen. Sorry girls, I've got to take care of my vocal cords. Enjoy the champagne."

"It's nice to meet you, Francie," Helen said, watching Willy stomp away.

"Is she always so impossible?"

"Always," Helen said, reaching for the bottle. "I'm not going to say no to Pol Roger. Shall I pour?"

"If you want — but I think I might just go."

"Oh no, did Willy say something to you?"

Francie truly looked at Helen for the first time. She was in her forties, with cheekbones like Lauren Bacall's and a streak of white in her dark hair near her temple, and she was wearing tuxedo pants and a man's silk smoking jacket. "I'm not going to let that little strumpet think she can scare me."

"Mee-*yow*," Helen said admiringly. "Kitty's got claws, is that it? Don't worry, you're not the first gal she's rubbed the wrong way. I think Rita keeps Willy around because she makes things interesting. She's either got the crowd hanging on to her every note or she's starting fights. Tell you what, have a drink with me, and if she comes back, you can throw it in her face."

"You're not friends?" Francie asked, as Helen poured nearly to the top of the flutes. Before answering, she took a long sip.

"Depends on the day," Helen said.

"Well, today isn't the day I'd pick to get close to her."

"What did she do to you, anyway? Go after your husband?"

Francie sipped her own champagne to buy herself time. Telling a perfect stranger the story would be foolhardy — but if she didn't tell someone, she was going to lose her mind. There was June, of course, but she was such a gentle soul, Francie avoided sharing her darkest thoughts with her.

"Not *my* husband," she said. "You know the woman who drowned last night?"

"*No*," Helen said, shocked.

"She was my best friend. We came here

together to get our divorces — in her case, because her husband took up with that — that —"

"I'm *so* sorry," Helen said. "I can't even imagine. But it was an accident, wasn't it?"

"Nobody knows."

"And . . . why is Willy buying you champagne? I mean, only if you feel like telling me. Hell, if I was you, I'd probably have made it through that bottle already."

Francie shook her head miserably. "Believe it or not, Vi's husband put her in the same hotel as Willy — the Holiday Ranch up the road — and I made the mistake of coming here thinking I could shame her into moving somewhere else. I ended up begging her to simply not ruin the funeral."

"Your friend is being buried *here*?"

"She grew up here," Francie said, "in a little house overlooking Lourdes Cemetery, where her parents are buried."

Without really meaning to, she launched into an account of their day, explaining how June had come to be involved, how the house had turned out to be a little gem, how her family and Vi's would start arriving tomorrow. "I don't know if I can even look Harry in the face without wanting to kill him."

"Listen, I understand why you'd hate

196

Willy, and I'm not going to tell anyone if you want to toss her in the river too. Only, maybe it would help if you know that she's way more bark than she is bite."

"She doesn't get to play victim," Francie said. "Not when she's getting everything she wants by taking it from someone else."

"Don't be so sure," Helen said, topping off Francie's champagne. "Here, drink up, it'll make you feel better."

"Don't be so sure what?"

"Don't be so sure Willy's getting everything she wants. She's out back there right now, talking to a girl who you don't talk to unless you've got a particular kind of problem, if you see what I mean."

Interesting. Francie thought that over while she drank. "Pregnant?" she guessed.

"That — or VD. There's a doctor that girls around here go to — one of the waitresses just had a little problem taken care of."

"In that case, I hope it's gonorrhea *and* twins, and Harry refuses to raise them. *And* that she gets run over by a truck on the way to the county welfare office."

Helen laughed. "Sorry," she said, "but you're funny, you know that?"

"Really? I don't think anyone's ever said that about me before. Well, I'll return the compliment — you're very talented."

"Thanks, doll. It pays the bills — most of the time."

"How did you get into this line of work?"

"I came here two years ago for my own divorce. Would you believe I used to give lessons to schoolchildren in Modesto? When the checks from my husband stopped showing up before my six weeks were even up, I started picking up a few gigs out of desperation. By the time I got my papers, I'd decided that I liked the night life better than nagging twelve-year-olds to practice."

"Where else do you play?"

"Anywhere they'll have me. Clubs, parties sometimes, weddings. Got on at Harrah's one time, that was a good gig. I've done the Prospector, Harold's . . . they call me if they need me to back up an act at the last minute, which pays pretty well. And then there are the little clubs. They don't pay squat, but you drink for free." She smiled. "And sometimes I get lucky and make a friend."

"It sounds like an exciting life."

"Oh, I don't know. There's a reason I'm playing this dump instead of Vegas — I'm not exactly Liberace, if you catch my drift."

"Nonsense," Francie said. "You're talented. That and hard work will take you far."

Helen laughed. "Maybe in your world. But

there's plenty of musicians with just enough talent to be dangerous."

"Listen," Francie said, an idea coming to her. "Would you consider playing after Vi's burial? We're not having a Mass — only a graveside service — and then we're serving a light lunch at the house I was telling you about, the one she grew up in."

"I've never played a wake," Helen said dubiously. "I don't think it's done."

"Maybe not, but if people are scandalized by a little piano music, they don't have to come. Vi would like it, and that's good enough for me."

"You knew her well enough to know that? Do you know what songs she liked? Is there even a piano there?"

"There is, as a matter of fact — nothing too fancy, but it seems to be in tune. I mean, I'm no expert, but it sounded good to me. And as far as the music, there's sheet music in the bench that was hers and really, she loved all kinds of music, I'm sure you can choose what would be best. And yes . . . yes, I believe I knew Vi better than anyone in the world."

"Well, I tune pianos," Helen said. "I can come take a look, go over the music, if you're serious. What day is the service?"

"Tuesday," Francie said. "It's three days

away. It will start at eleven and then everyone will proceed to the house. Can you come by tomorrow at ten o'clock and take a look?"

"Honey, I'm usually just getting out of bed at ten o'clock," Helen said, draining her glass and getting up from her barstool. "But for you I'll make an exception. Leave the address with Shirley and she'll get it to me. Got to run — if I don't earn my keep, I'll have to start buying my own drinks."

CHAPTER 27
VIRGIE

Outside, from the vantage point of a low branch of a carrotwood tree that grew next to the tavern, Virgie watched the piano player begin to play a new set as Mrs. Meeker wrote something on a cocktail napkin and gave it to the bartender.

Virgie knew she should be getting back. Many nights before her mother went to bed, she came into Virgie's room and sat on the side of her bed. Virgie would put down her book or her diary or her sketchpad and wait — one of these nights, she was sure that her mother would tell her the story she'd been waiting her whole life to hear, the one she said Virgie wasn't old enough to hear yet. Who her father was . . . and why he left.

Mostly, though, her mother just made small talk about the guests or her chores for the next day, as though Virgie wasn't even there. But sometimes she'd run her fingers through Virgie's hair — she'd pretend to be impatient, saying for the hundredth time that Virgie should stop chewing on the ends, that she'd look so much nicer with a shorter cut, but eventually she'd fall silent and just gently rub Virgie's back, and Virgie would close her eyes and drift off to sleep.

Virgie was fearful of her punishment if her mother discovered she had snuck out. But even more important, she didn't want to miss the sweet, peculiar time when her mother behaved like someone else's mother entirely.

Dear Tabby,

I followed Mrs. M to Gwin's tonight which Mother says is a rough place the ladies should stay clear of but lots of the ladies go there. W says in most places like in San Francisco ladies don't go to places like that unless a Man is with them but I think it's good if they can go wherever they want because that is why they are getting divorces in the first place is because they are tired of getting told what to do all the time is what Mother says. So I asked her did my father tell you what to do and is that why you got a divorce and she got mad and said I knew better than to ask her a question like that.

Oh and W was at Gwin's too, I climbed the tree on the side so I could see in the window and in the parking lot too. W was right under that tree for a while, she was telling some other Ladies that she can't wait to go back to a Real city and I don't know why she doesn't think Reno is real when I heard on the news we are getting our own television station next year.

Anyway I don't know why Mrs. M was there, also she was dressed in Blue Jeans and a cowboy shirt for some reason which I wouldn't think a lady like her would wear. By the time I figured out how to look in the window she was drinking a whole bottle of champagne by herself!! But then the piano player sat down next to her whose name I can't remember who played here one time at Christmas who could play any song you could think of. I asked her did she know Praise the Lord and Pass the Amyunition which I thought would trick her but she played it two times in two different keys.

Mother told me Mrs. S is helping plan Mrs. C's funeral that they are having on Tuesday and we are going even though we only met her one time. Why they are having the funeral here Mother says she doesn't know but Mrs. C's son called to say he is coming to get her things and when he finds out that ring is gone I think he will be very interested in what Mrs. S is doing living in her room. If he seems Honest and trustworthy I will give him his mother's ring back but only after I tell him what I saw so he can tell the police because they will believe him because he is an adult.

W said she would pay me three dollars to take a note to Dr. P. I looked and all it said was one word CLAP but when I showed it to Dr. P's office lady she wrote me a note to give W but she put it in an envelope and sealed it shut so I don't know what it said, but W gave me the money anyway plus a quarter for being so quick about it. Also Mrs. T got her divorce papers and she is leaving tomorrow and she gave me a dollar too just because she said I made the time go quicker. But I'm glad she's leaving because she always took all the marmalade and Mother wouldn't let me put out extra.

$18.72
+ $4.25
= $22.97

When Francie got back to her room she took off the shirt and the blue jeans and put them away. She pulled on her nightgown and was just about to get into bed with the novel she had bought for the trip when the phone rang.

"Hello?"

"It's me, Mother, how are you?"

Nothing could be more welcome than Alice's dear voice. "Oh, sweetheart, did Daddy tell you?"

"Yes, and I've been crying buckets. I can't believe it! Is it true, did she really . . . I mean, was she that unhappy?"

Francie flinched — this was the same question she had been trying not to ask herself. "The police seem to think it was an accident. You know Vi never learned to swim."

"But how? How could she just accidentally *fall* into the river? And Daddy said it was the middle of the night — why on *earth* would she go outside in the middle of the night? You *know* how careful she was."

It was true — ever since the Lindbergh child had been kidnapped and killed, Vi always checked all the doors in the house after the boys left for school and again after dinner to make sure they were locked. It had started when the boys were little, and during their high school years they were constantly locking themselves out of the house and coming to Francie, who had a spare key.

Oh, dear Vi.

"We were at dinner until rather late," Francie said, twisting the threads of the lie she'd been telling herself in the deepest hours of the night, when she couldn't stop imagining Vi staring out at the rushing waters and making an unthinkable decision. "And, I do hate to tell you this, sweetheart, but we had been drinking. Too much, I daresay."

"But Vi never drinks more than a sip or two!"

"Yes, but . . . oh, Alice, I have so much to tell you. You see, we met a young woman on the train, a poor little thing even younger than you, and her husband beat her and she'd run away to get her divorce in Reno with almost nothing but the clothes on her back and her little girl, and you know how Vi is" — another wince as she realized her error, but she wasn't ready to talk about her in the past tense, not yet — "she invited June to stay in her suite because there was an extra room and she hadn't anywhere else to go. And it was my idea to have a celebration of sorts the first night, to pick up our spirits, and we went to the Sky Room and it *was* grand." But they'd all been pretending, hadn't they? Forcing cheer for each other's sakes, finishing the bottle that had failed to lift their heavy hearts.

"Oh, Mother," Alice said sadly. "That was kind of you, but I can't imagine any of you felt like celebrating."

"No, I suppose we didn't."

"Mother, don't cry. At least wait until I get there tomorrow and we can be sad together."

"You're coming with Daddy?" A tiny burst of joy broke the surface of Francie's heart.

"I am . . ." There was something off in Alice's tone.

"You don't have to, not for me. If you want to wait and come with Margie and Jimmy, I'll be fine, I promise. The service won't be until Tuesday anyway."

"It's not that, Mother. I *want* to be there

with you — I want to help. But there's something I need to tell you. Only, I don't want to make you feel any worse."

Francie's heart shifted in the particular way it always did when Alice was involved, fear balanced by fierce protectiveness. "What's wrong — are you having trouble with your ankle again?"

"No, no, I'm fine — fit as a fiddle. It's just . . . oh, Mother, I don't know how to tell you. Promise you won't be furious. Daddy didn't want me to tell you but I thought you should know."

"Know *what*?"

"He's bringing Bill. He'll stay in the room, don't worry, no one will know, you won't have to see him. It's just that Daddy's so upset, you should see him, I don't think he slept at all last night. I don't think he can bear to be alone right now."

"I . . . see," Francie said faintly — but she didn't. Arthur wouldn't be alone — he would have *her.* Like always. That was what they had agreed — that they would remain the best of friends. "I didn't know that you knew about him."

Francie couldn't bear to say the name — she wouldn't even know it if she hadn't found that half-written letter in Arthur's briefcase three years ago, the letter that had forced her to confront a subject they'd long ago agreed never to discuss.

"I know you must wish that you had been the one to tell me," Alice said, "and I wouldn't blame you for being angry, but you must forgive me, because it has been awful for me to know about Bill and not be able to say anything to you."

"How long?"

Alice was silent for a moment before admitting, "Almost a year. It was Daddy's birthday last year and I went around to the office to surprise him and take him to lunch, but he wasn't there, even though his car was in the lot, and his secretary said he'd gone to get a coffee. But he hadn't, because on the way to the coffee shop I ran into him with a stranger, coming out of a theater. You know . . . *that* kind of theater."

Now it was Francie's turn to be at a loss for words. That had been her one request of Arthur: never let the children know, at least not until the divorce was well behind them and everyone had grown accustomed to the idea. She wasn't naïve; she knew they wouldn't be able to keep it from the kids forever, not with Arthur living with . . . him. But as long as no one knew, Francie had been able to pretend that he didn't exist.

"Well," she said. And because she couldn't

think of anything else to say, she said it again. "Well."

"I know it's awful for you. It took me forever to get used to the idea. But Bill is very nice," Alice said. "I just wanted you to know that. And they're very careful, I promise. Daddy says we can drop Bill off a few blocks from the hotel so no one will even see them together."

"Alice," Francie said, recovering herself, "how did you . . . I mean, we've never discussed anything of the sort — of course, people are so *open* about things these days — but it must have been shocking all the same —"

"Mother, it's all right. Daddy's a homosexual — you can say it."

Francie pursed her lips in distaste. "You don't have to sound so happy about it. And I certainly hope you haven't told anyone else!"

"I'm not happy about it, Mother, how could I be? In truth I'd rather not think about either of my parents . . . you know, *that* way. But it's not like he died or something. And there's loads of homosexuals in the city these days, so at least no one will make trouble with him if he's careful. Really, it could be so much worse — they're sending plainclothes police into gay bars in

New York City to arrest men. Can you imagine?"

Francie could, as a matter of fact. She'd spent many anxious hours worried that Arthur would be in the wrong place at the wrong time, that he'd be careless, that he'd be beaten by an angry mob.

And there was something else: she felt guilty. Which was ridiculous, because it was hardly her fault, but it wasn't just her who was made to suffer because Arthur was queer — it was the children too. How could Margie ever explain it to her children? What if Jimmy's boss found out? And she couldn't even be angry at Arthur for choosing to be so self-indulgent and reckless, because according to an article she'd found in a medical journal that she'd furtively read in the library, as many as one man in ten were homosexuals, and most of them were *born* that way.

"I'm sorry that your father is like this," she said stiffly. "Obviously, if I'd had any idea, before we married —"

"Mother! Please don't say it. If you hadn't met Daddy, you wouldn't have any of us."

"I didn't say I wished I'd never met him. Only that he was — different. Normal."

There was a pause, and then Alice said quietly, "Normal? Just like you've always wished *I* was normal?"

"Alice! It's hardly the same thing —"

"Isn't it? All my life you've never let me forget that I was different. Do you wish you hadn't had me either?"

"Stop it! Alice, it isn't the same at all, and you know it," Francie said, wondering how this conversation had gone so far off the rails. "You're just upset and you're looking for someone to take it out on. But if you must blame someone, blame your father — *I'm* not the one who's behaving scandalously when Vi isn't even in the ground yet!"

There was a long silence, and then Alice said, "Anyway, we should be there by noon."

"Good. Then we can have a nice lunch," Francie said, anxious to put the ugliness behind them. "And I'm sorry for . . . whatever I said to make you so upset."

"I'm *not* upset," Alice huffed — and hung up without another word.

CHAPTER 29

Francie got to the little house early the next morning. She hadn't slept well, and there was only so much coffee she could drink in the dining room, especially since she had become something of a curiosity to the other guests because of her friendship with the woman who had drowned. She was wearing her bottle-green shirtwaist, the only dress she'd brought besides yesterday's navy suit that seemed suitable for mourning, but she wished she were back in last night's blue jeans.

She'd never gone out in public in them before, but she'd taken to wearing them around the house. It was so much easier to do housework when one didn't have to worry about dirtying one's skirts. Plenty of younger women had begun wearing trousers — *Harper's Bazaar* had even done a feature and the department store windows were full of them — but among Francie's friends, it was still considered poor form.

She went through the house again, savoring the chance to try to see it through Vi's eyes. She imagined her iron bed made up with quilts, her closet filled with dresses her mother had sewn for her. She wondered if there were any keepsakes stored in the attic. There would be time to check later, as long as Harry didn't get in the way. Francie wondered if Harry even remembered the house. He'd probably sell it just as soon as he could, so she'd have to get there first. *Don't worry, Vi,* she silently promised; she'd make sure to save anything Vi would have wanted the boys to have, even if she had to steal it and sneak it home.

The house had been scrubbed before the last tenant left, but a layer of dust had settled on everything. The dishes and glasses in the cupboards were mismatched and many of them were chipped; she'd have to remember to tell June to order some from the rental place. In a kitchen drawer she found a much-washed tea towel clumsily embroidered with Vi's initials. She pressed it to her face, imagining Vi as a girl sewing at her mother's knee, and then she stuffed it into her purse.

She was checking the built-in cupboards to see if anything had been left behind when there was a knock at the door.

"Come in!" Francie called.

Helen let herself in, looking around curiously. "Sweet little place, isn't it? Oh, look at that."

She went straight to the piano and ran a hand along the plain-finished cherry cabinet before lifting the dust cover. "A Price and Teeple! And in such good shape too. They don't make them like this anymore, do they?"

The piano seemed bulky and inelegant to Francie, its only decoration a series of square wooden adornments at the juncture of the panels. At home in her dining room was an intricately carved Brazilian rosewood Steinway that she had inherited from her grandmother; the man who came to tune it every year was outraged that such a fine instrument was almost never played. She'd tried — Margie and Alice both had lessons, but neither took to it.

"It's rather . . . plain, don't you think?"

Helen looked at her incredulously. "This is quarter-sawn oak. Look at the grain! And the fittings — pure copper. Someone should polish them."

She played an experimental arpeggio; as the notes hung in the air, she sighed with pleasure. "Do you mind?"

"Not at all."

Helen sat down on the bench, tapped the foot pedals, adjusted her skirt, and played a mournful phrase, a simple series of notes that was vaguely familiar.

"What is that?" Francie asked.

"Grieg's Piano Concerto in A Minor," Helen said with her eyes closed.

She played the same phrase once more, and while the last note hung in the air, she took a deep breath and lifted her hands from the keys, sitting motionless until it faded completely.

And then her hands touched down and she began to play — for real this time, as though, once introduced, she and the piano had discovered that they were related. She bent her head low over the instrument, eyes still closed, playing by feel; her hands danced and flew as though they were disconnected from her body. The phrase repeated itself as though it were chasing its tail, a trill of high notes followed by an echo from the bass, the notes thundering through the floor and up through Francie's feet until she could feel the piece all through her body.

This was nothing like the music Helen had played last night. It seeped inside Francie and reflected back the feelings she'd worked so hard to keep hidden, echoing the mournful theme, building to a frenetic crescendo only to fall back in a receding wave of minor-key chords in the lower registers, then built again. Over and over the music repeated the simple theme, but it was different each time, as though filtered through a range of emotions, as if the composer had been arguing with himself one moment and berating himself the next, then comforting and threatening and — and oh, there was joy, trickling in and then out again, but there nonetheless.

And then, abruptly, the music stopped.

Helen remained still for a moment, her fingers resting lightly on the keys. When she turned to face Francie, swinging her legs around the stool, she was wearing a mischievous grin. "Don't ever let anyone sell this piano," she said, "or its soul will hunt you down."

"It's not mine to sell," Francie said. "Why did you stop?"

"Well, that's not what we're here to do, now, is it? It's hardly funeral music — at least, not the type your average crowd of mourners would appreciate. So where's this sheet music you were talking about?"

"It's, ah, underneath you. In the bench."

Helen lifted her bottom from the seat and pulled out the sheaf. She handed half of it to Francie.

"Best thing to do, probably, is pick a dozen or so of her favorites. Folks'll end up asking for things once we get going — they always do."

"At a funeral?" Francie asked dubiously. "You really think so?"

"Well, we'll see, but I expect people want music that reflects how they feel." Helen started flipping slowly through the stack. "Like at Gwin's last night. Willy picked 'Skylark' because most of the women there, no matter how hard they try to pretend otherwise, their hearts are broken."

"Then you choose," Francie said impulsively. "You're the expert. Though I suppose her boys should have their say . . ."

"I'll be glad to pick," Helen said, plucking a sheet out and setting it on the bench next to her. "Don't worry about her boys. Who knows a woman's heart best? Not her husband . . . not her sons. It takes another woman to know what she's keeping for herself, the thoughts she doesn't share. Don't you agree?"

"Sure — I suppose," Francie said. "I mean, no, actually. I think my husband knows me better than anyone. I used to tell him everything."

Helen gave Francie an intent look. "And

yet, here you are in Reno. And somehow I doubt you're here for the gambling."

What kind of comment was that? Francie wondered if she'd made a mistake. Last night, asking Helen to play had seemed like a marvelous inspiration, but now that she was here in Vi's house, she seemed a little too familiar, asking questions that were none of her business.

Francie leaned over and took the stack of music and thrust it into Helen's hands. "I'm sure whatever you pick will be fine. I should go now."

Helen accepted the stack, smirking. "I'll give you a chance to approve," she said. "Give me a call and I'll come by. Or if you're feeling adventurous, come on over. I'll be around until at least four in the afternoon."

"Thank you," Francie said stiffly. Helen had started to make her feel distinctly uncomfortable. "And there is the matter of your payment. What do you ordinarily charge for an event like this one?"

"Tell you what," Helen said, lifting her skirt and throwing her leg over the bench instead of simply walking around it. "Why don't you see how I do and then you can decide what I'm worth."

And with that highly unsatisfying answer,

Helen strode to the door, letting the screen door slam behind her and leaving Francie wondering what Vi would make of her.

CHAPTER 30

Charlie had left a message at the desk that
he'd gotten a late start and wouldn't arrive
until the afternoon. Francie was writing a
note to leave for him, in case he arrived
while she and June were out, when a voice
cried, "Mother!"

She spun around and held out her arms
as Alice hurried toward her in the uneven,
wobbling gait caused by the orthopedic shoe
with the four-inch sole that compensated
for her shortened leg and deformed ankle.

"Darling!" she whispered, closing her eyes
and burying her face in Alice's soft auburn
bob. "I'm so sorry we quarreled earlier."

"Me too. I've just been so upset about Vi
— but I didn't mean to take it out on you."
She pulled away and tried to smile, her eyes
red from crying. "Daddy wanted to know if
we could have dinner — just the three of
us," she added hastily. "He got us rooms at
the Mapes and he's there checking in now.

He said to call when I want to be picked up."

"That sounds nice," Francie said. Maybe dinner with Arthur was a good idea, if only to prove to Alice that they could still treat each other civilly. "June and I are going to the mortuary to pick out a casket and discuss the burial — I was hoping Charlie would be here in time. It does seem that he and Frank should have some say in all this."

"Are Frank and Harry coming this afternoon too?"

"No, I'm afraid not," Francie said, and sighed. "When I spoke to Harry, he behaved as though Vi's death was a terrible imposition. And I haven't heard from Frank, but I suspect he'll come with his father. I can't help thinking the only reason Harry sent Charlie —"

"— is because he still acts like Charlie is ten years old and being picked last for gym. Well, it's true, Mother, don't make a face."

Alice certainly knew about getting picked last — during her childhood she'd endured snubs and being passed over, and it wasn't just in gym class, either. Some people seemed to look at her leg and special shoe and see a mental deficit. Francie had spent most of Alice's school years demanding that her daughter be given the same attention as everyone else . . . and academically, at least, she had succeeded.

Charlie hadn't been so lucky. Vi, who would have moved the world for her younger son, could do nothing to convince Harry, who considered Charlie a do-nothing dreamer despite his valiant efforts to please his father. When Charlie returned from the war and joined the company, he initiated an overhaul of the books that saved the company thousands, and still Harry had continued to take only Frank with him on sales calls, leaving Charlie at home.

"I wasn't going to argue."

"I'll be glad to see Charlie — Harry has been keeping him so busy that he's barely been home in weeks. I hope he's finished *The Disenchanted* — I can't wait to find out if he thinks it's as good as Schulberg's other work."

Francie felt that old, familiar pang. Charlie and Alice had grown up best friends and stayed close through the years. If things had been different . . . how lovely it would have been for the two of them to have found love together. Instead, the series of girlfriends Charlie'd had tended to be extremely jealous of the childhood friend he spoke of so often — until they met her; then their envy turned to pity, and they tried to befriend her. Alice was always perfectly sweet about it too and never gave up hoping that each new one would make Charlie happy.

"Let's go up and introduce you to June. I just know you'll like her; she's been so helpful to me."

"Oh, Mother, I'd be jealous of your new friend if she didn't need your help as much as you need hers. It must be awful, what she's been through . . . Perhaps I could help too?"

"Absolutely. Oh, look — here's someone else you must meet."

Virgie had been walking down the steps with a book open in her hands, her eyes on the page.

"Who does she remind you of?" Francie winked.

Alice laughed delightedly. "Remember when Charlie ran into that tree and got a black eye? And Harry wouldn't let him go to the library for a month?"

"Virgie," Francie called. "Come here, sweetheart, I'd like to introduce you to my daughter."

Virgie looked up, her face registering surprise. "Good morning, Mrs. Meeker. How are you today?"

"May I present my daughter, Alice Meeker? Alice, this is Virginia Swanson, daughter and assistant to the owner of this lovely hotel. She's a very clever girl."

"How do you do?" Virgie said, offering her hand.

"Very well, thank you. It's a pleasure to meet another book enthusiast, Virginia," Alice said. "May I ask what you're reading?"

Virgie showed her the cover of her book.

"*The Sign of the Twisted Candles.* Oh, I *love* Nancy Drew!" Alice exclaimed. "Would you believe I've got nearly the entire set? They're quite antique, of course — nearly as old as me."

Virgie regarded her unblinkingly. "You're not old," she said seriously. "You're lucky to have them. I have to buy them one at a time when I can afford them. I can get them from the library too, but the best ones are always checked out and I need them for reference. I'm going to be a sleuth myself, see."

"What a marvelous idea," Alice said. She had always been good with children; for a while she'd tutored students from the local elementary school. "It's a fascinating career choice."

"Mother says girls should be able to do whatever job they want. And detective is a good job because you just have to get a certificate and then you can open up your own office. I'm going to have mine on

226

Court Street, with a view of the river."

"I'll be sure to look you up if I ever need a mystery solved."

"What happened to your leg?" Virgie asked. "Does it hurt?"

Francie winced; the child meant no harm, but hadn't her mother taught her not to ask people rude questions? Twelve was certainly old enough to learn that lesson.

But Alice didn't seem to mind. "I was born this way," she said. "My right leg is shorter than my left. My father says that I'm one in a million. And it doesn't hurt a bit, not when I wear my special shoe. See? It helps me walk better so I don't end up hurting the other one."

"Interesting," Virgie said.

"Virgie, sweetheart, I'm afraid we need to be on our way. We're going to collect Mrs. Samples from upstairs and have lunch. Would you care to join us?"

"I can't," Virgie said. "Mother's finishing the activities program for next week and I have to deliver them to all the rooms."

"Important hotel business," Alice said gravely. "What sort of activities are coming up?"

"Well, Mother lists the movies and shows, and Clyde drives the ladies if he's not busy doing something else. On Tuesday night there's dancing with the Three Sharps at Buddy Baer's. Wednesday night is the ring toss, Thursday there's a matinee of *The Nevadan* at the Granada, and Saturday Harrah's is hosting a slots tournament."

"What on earth is the ring toss?" Alice asked. "It sounds like a carnival game."

"No, it's a tradition here at the Holiday Ranch," Virgie said. "Once a month, interested ladies meet in the lobby at nine o'clock, and a chartered bus takes them down to the Virginia Street Bridge. Whoever wants to can throw their wedding ring into the river, and afterward everyone goes out for pie and coffee."

"My goodness," Alice said, raising an eyebrow. "How . . . dramatic. Are you planning to participate, Mother?"

"Much as I'd love to, I don't think so," Francie said, holding up her hand to show her diamond band. "At least, not until I have the diamonds removed and made into something else. They're quite nice — it would be a shame to send them to the bottom of the river."

"You don't have to use your real one, ma'am," Virgie said. "Lots of ladies use fake ones. And we do it every month during the full moon, so you can do it next month if you want."

"Well, then — you'll be the first to know should I decide to join in."

"Thank you, ma'am. Good day, Miss."

"What a delightful girl," Alice said as Virgie walked away, absorbed once more in her book. "And what an intriguing practice. But it's also quite sad, don't you think? When I get married, I don't believe I'll ever take my ring off."

Francie was glad Alice couldn't see her expression. As much as she tried to mask it, Francie knew that every dashed hope for Alice showed on her face.

Sometimes she wondered what the harm was, in letting Alice dream of the things normal girls did . . . but Francie had lived long enough to know far too much disappointment. Better to be content with what life brings than to upset the balance by seeking more.

CHAPTER 31

Francie opened all the windows in her room so that they could enjoy the breeze and called June's room to ask if she might bring Alice by to meet her.

"She sounded a bit flustered," Francie said when she hung up. "Since I've abandoned her today, she's trying to get everything done by herself. Let's give her a few minutes to finish whatever she was doing."

They relaxed in the comfortable armchairs, much as Francie and Vi had on the day they arrived. Could it really just be two days earlier that they arrived in town? That meant that Vi had been gone for an entire day already. Was this how it was going to be from now on — measuring the days since she'd lost Vi? Soon she would be marking the time by months — even years. How long until it didn't hurt so much?

"So tell me more about this girl who made such an impression on you and Auntie Vi,"

Alice said.

"She's lovely, but we took her under our wing because she was so obviously in need," Francie said, remembering Alice's earlier comment about being jealous. "She had bruises from her husband's . . . rough treatment. And she has next to nothing, not even a decent dress to travel in."

"Fleeing with her child," Alice said. "It's just unthinkable that she has no one to turn to."

"Once she has her divorce, she'll be much better off," Francie said. "Her ex-husband will have to go through the courts to win the right to see the child."

"Then you must see that it happens."

Francie smiled at Alice's serious tone. "I will, darling — you can count on it. You should have seen Vi; she was so taken with June's little girl. You know she wanted grandchildren so badly. It's one of the things I understand the least, to be honest. Ever since Margie and Roy started having kids, she's been waiting for her turn to be a grandmother. You should have seen her when we went to buy a gift for Dorrie — she was wild for all the tiny bonnets, the little socks."

"I just wish I understood. Mother, do you remember, when we were saying goodbye?

And Auntie Vi touched my face?"

"I do."

"She whispered something to me. I wasn't sure I'd heard her right, and the next moment the driver came inside, and everything got very confused, but I swear she said 'You've always been my favorite.' " Alice was blushing furiously. "I know she loves all of us, Margie and Jimmy, and Roy and Evelyn too, but . . . I couldn't help the feeling that she was telling me goodbye."

"That just about breaks my heart." Francie took Alice's hands; she was wearing the little pearl ring Vi had given her for her fifteenth birthday.

"Before I call Daddy to pick me up, Mother . . . there is something I wanted to tell you. I know it isn't the best time, and I *had* hoped — I'd planned to tell you when you got back home, but now that I'm here — and Daddy is here too —"

"Whatever it is, you can tell me," Francie said, but at the excited look on her daughter's face, fear rose up inside her. She couldn't bear to see Alice go through another disappointment. She should have known something was going on; she should have nipped it in the bud. Memories of that horrible afternoon when Alice had sobbed for hours were almost more than her poor heart could stand.

But she would never shirk a mother's duty. "I want you to know — if things don't . . . work out the way you hope, I'll be right there for you. We all have to lean on each other from time to time, and I've certainly leaned on you much too often."

"Oh, but it's nothing like that," Alice said, surprised.

"It's just that I've noticed you've been . . . your head in the clouds, missing dinner, coming home late after that class."

Alice's expression shifted; she gave Francie a funny little smile. "Oh, *that.* Well, you're right — I *have* had something on my mind. But it can wait. No, this is about — well, about Daddy, and Bill."

Oh, dear. Francie didn't know whether to feel relief or dread. She should have known that this talk would take place at some point. She'd had a conversation years ago with each of her girls about the prospect of womanhood arriving, how the initial excitement would give way to the tiresome monthly inconvenience. With Margie, she'd stressed the sacred joy of one's body preparing to give birth to babies conceived in marriage to a wonderful man.

But with Alice she had no such promises to make. Alice's womb would remain empty month after month, year after year, until someday it would begin to fail as Francie's own had recently, the body putting a stop to the possibilities that most women were quite ready to bid farewell to anyway. And so she'd consulted a medical textbook and done the best she could, focusing on the drawings of the female sexual organs in their curious arrangement, using the story of Alice's own birth to describe the mechanics of the process. Alice, always so serious about her studies, listened attentively and was especially thoughtful and quiet in the days after.

What had Alice made of meeting Arthur's friend outside that squalid theater? Francie wondered if Alice had heard about the congress between two such men through some other source — a book, perhaps, or an overheard conversation? It seemed unlikely. (And how awful for Arthur, Francie couldn't help thinking, imagining her shy, thoughtful husband attempting to explain his presence there.)

"Do you understand," she said carefully, "the, erm, nature of Daddy's friendship with Bill? The reason that they will be living together in Daddy's apartment?"

"Well, yes, of course," Alice said. "They're quite in love. Daddy says you've known about it for a long time, that you gave him your blessing."

"Oh." Had she? Not exactly . . . *blessing* was perhaps too strong a word. *I suppose there's nothing to be done* had been her sad conclusion, and Arthur had nodded just as regretfully.

"And what I didn't tell you — after that first time, when I met Bill, and he was so very nice, Daddy asked if I would come to dinner. With the two of them. I don't think he meant to — Mother, I know he would never want to hurt you. But I think it was the relief of someone knowing — of *me* knowing, and whatever fears Daddy had about me and Margie and Jimmy, how we would react, whether we'd still want to see him — I could see how happy it made him that I didn't act horrified. I mean, I was very uncomfortable, Mother, you must imagine, but he looked so shamed, and I couldn't bear it — and I said yes. I had dinner at the apartment the next week."

Francie said nothing, imagining the three of them at the table, making small talk, breaking bread. Arthur was a gifted host, and a meticulous one — in all the years they'd entertained together, it was Arthur who set the table with their wedding china and crystal, who created careful seating plans to encourage lively conversation, who remembered to decant the wine and order the flowers and select which records to play.

Francie suddenly remembered Alice insisting on going to the first session of a new class despite a rainstorm, declining the ride that Francie had offered, saying she didn't want to be the only girl dropped off by her mother.

"That's when I started going to the class at the School of Fine Arts," Alice said. "Except I didn't."

"But you bought the supplies," Francie protested.

"Window dressing," Alice said. "To fool you. I'm so sorry, Mother, I know it was wrong. After that first time, I just pretended I'd signed up for more sessions, and each week I was actually going over to the apartment. It just made Daddy so happy. And Bill too — I could see how good they are for each other."

"But why didn't you tell me?"

Alice regarded her sadly. "If I had . . . do you really think you would have allowed me to keep going?"

"I — maybe," Francie said, though of course the answer was no. She was beginning to feel angry. She thought of the care she took to guard Arthur's secret, when he was keeping yet another from her — one that involved their *daughter.* "At least I wouldn't have been made a fool of. What did you think, when you came home from one of these evenings — 'Oh, poor Mother, toiling along in this sham of a marriage'?"

"No! I never — Daddy said that he would never leave you, that he'd been as loyal to you as he knew how. All he wanted was someone to . . . to witness this other life of his, to give him permission to be happy."

"Well, it's wonderful that *he* got to be happy," Francie fumed. "That he and Bill get to have their little love nest where they can pretend the outside world doesn't matter. But it does, Alice, you know that. You know that better than anyone."

She wouldn't forgive him, she decided. When this week was over, she'd tell Arthur that once she returned to San Francisco, he was to call before visiting, he was to behave like any other guest in her home. He wouldn't be allowed to risk her honor and invite scandal without paying for the privilege.

"I was thinking — I was hoping — that maybe Bill could come to dinner tonight," Alice continued doggedly. "No one will think a thing of it, not with us there. He could be Daddy's brother, or colleague, or

—You could get to know him, just a little at first. And you could leave if it became too much."

"I'm afraid that won't be possible," Francie said stiffly. "I'm grieving the loss of my best friend. I shouldn't have to deal with that as well, not now."

"All right," Alice said sadly. "I'll let Daddy know. But I wish you'd change your mind."

"You said there was something else you were going to tell me. I think, given the circumstances, that it shouldn't wait. After what you've already told me, I won't be able to think of anything else if I don't have at least a clue."

Alice smiled shyly. "Well, all right, Mother, but only because I'm fearful it will come flying out of me — it's been so hard to keep it to myself. I've met someone."

So it was true — Francie's greatest fear for her daughter. She hadn't learned from the last time after all. "You've met someone," she echoed. "Would this be a beau?"

"Yes," Alice said, beaming.

"And does he . . . know how you feel?"

"I certainly hope so. I know he feels the same way about me. He told me so."

Francie's stomach twisted. The last time, Alice had thrown caution to the wind; she was too naïve to understand the intricate

238

dance of courtship — or the special dangers that attended a lonely girl from a wealthy family. And see how that had ended up?

"Alice, darling, whatever conversations you've had, or think you've had, it would be a good idea to stop and take your time. You're . . . new to this sort of thing, and rather naïve, there's no shame in admitting it. The world isn't always as safe as we'd like it to be; there are unscrupulous — there are terrible —"

"Mother," Alice interrupted her. "This isn't like that. It isn't like last time. I'm not a little girl anymore."

"You weren't a little girl then," Francie said. "You were nineteen."

"I thought you'd be happy for me," Alice said, digging in her purse for her handkerchief. "I thought you'd understand."

"Oh, sweetheart, I *am* happy for you — or at least I would be, if I could be sure that this wasn't — that he isn't —"

As Francie floundered for the right words, Alice dabbed furiously at her eyes, then took a deep breath. "I think it's best we talk about this another time. I shouldn't have brought it up now, I don't know what I was thinking. Losing Auntie Vi like this . . . I think I'm still in shock. I just can't believe it's true."

"Of course, Alice, that would make perfect sense," Francie said, trying to ignore the feeling of relief that Alice had let it go — this time. If this was anything like Gerald, Alice wouldn't let it go for long — but at least Francie had a little time to plan her response. And, perhaps, to sniff around and find out a little more. She'd ask Margie if Alice had confided any more details to her.

Though it was more likely to be her father that Alice took her problems to. Unlike Francie, Arthur listened without judgment, offered comfort before solutions. Francie couldn't help the way she was built; she couldn't stand not to act, especially if her children were making a mistake.

But she couldn't very well talk to Arthur about this now — not when he'd swanned into town with his *friend* in tow, for anyone to see. For the love of God, she hoped at least Arthur had been smart enough to reserve two rooms. Love made people careless — just look at Alice. Just look at *her*! All those years ago she'd watched Arthur across the room at that party and decided he was the one, and thrown herself into the courtship and soon after, marriage, without ever stopping to notice the little signs. Because they had been there — if only she'd been more careful.

But if there hadn't been Arthur, there wouldn't have been the children, the beautiful home filled with laughter and comfort; there would never have been *Vi*. It seemed so cruel — Francie wouldn't trade the life she'd made for the world, but in the moment, it seemed she was losing everyone she loved the most.

"Well, then," Alice said briskly. "Shall we go? As you said, there's lots to be done."

"Yes, you're right." But Francie didn't want to end the conversation this way, with Alice upset. "Darling, I'm just so grateful you're here."

She folded Alice into her arms and kissed her cheek.

But for the first time she could remember, Alice pulled away.

CHAPTER 32
JUNE

When they knocked on her door, June took a last look around the room. She had dropped Patty off with Mrs. Oglesby after breakfast and started working on her list of tasks, but when Francie called to say she was bringing her daughter by, she'd rushed to change into a simple leaf-green suit she'd found among Vi's things, grateful that Francie had encouraged her to wear any of Vi's clothes that she fancied. The maid had been there earlier to change the linens, but a full cleaning was provided only once a week, so June ran around the suite making sure everything was in its place.

She opened the door and there was Francie, along with a slim, auburn-haired girl who had Francie's smile and her soft brown eyes, plus a sculpted jaw and narrow nose that must have come from her father. The girl seemed startled, taking a step back with a little gasp.

"I'm sorry," she said, with her hand at her throat. "It's just . . . I'm sorry. I'm Alice. It's very nice to meet you."

"I'm June Samples. It is a pleasure to make your acquaintance, though I wish it was under different circumstances." It didn't come out quite the way she'd practiced — she rushed through the words and garbled them a bit. "Please, come in," she added belatedly.

Alice walked with a limp, twisting her hips and seeming to drag her foot. June had known a boy who walked like that during school; the other children had teased him, but he'd continued all the way through high school while his brothers left after fifth grade to work on the farm. The last she'd heard, he'd gotten a degree from UC Davis and owned an insurance office in Dixon.

"June . . ." Alice said. "I'm sorry I seemed startled when I first saw you. It's just . . . that suit. Vi wore it one of the last times I saw her."

"I'm sorry!" June exclaimed, horrified. Why hadn't she thought? She shouldn't have changed — how presumptuous Alice must think her!

"Oh no, please, I didn't mean to make you feel uncomfortable."

"June brought very little with her," Francie said diplomatically. "It seemed sensible for her to wear Vi's clothes until she had a chance to get some new things."

"Of course, that's such a wise idea," Alice said kindly. "But I wonder . . . with Charlie coming today . . ."

"Oh dear, you're right," Francie said. "I should have thought. There's just been so much to attend to —"

"I'll go and change right now," June said. How awful it would be, for the poor man to see her wearing his mother's clothes. "I'll put on my old poplin."

"Wait, I have an idea," Francie said. "Now that Alice is here — Alice, darling, could you take June shopping? She needs a few new dresses and perhaps a pair of heels — you weren't anticipating being dragged around with us, were you, dear? And that way I can be here when Charlie calls. Taxis come right to the front door, and I'm sure we can ask Mrs. Swanson for a recommendation for a good place to shop."

"But — I can't . . ." June stammered. She *did* need new clothes, but she had been planning to wait until Francie paid her, and then see if there was an inexpensive seamstress or perhaps even a secondhand shop where she could find something cheap. And her shoes . . . she felt her face heat in shame.

They were scuffed beyond repair and the soles were nearly worn through, but a good pair of shoes would cost at least three dollars. If only she were alone with Francie, she could confide in her. But she couldn't bear the pity of a stranger.

Realization dawned on Francie's face. "I believe I told you that June has been kind enough to agree to arrange everything this week," she said to Alice, "and she'll need an appropriate wardrobe for calling on everyone she needs to see, the mortuary and the florist and so forth. Not to mention receiving the family, and Vi's friends when they start to arrive. So these would obviously be *business* expenses — have the bills sent home, sweetheart, and June, dear, perhaps you'd be so kind as to file the receipts for the accountant."

Alice smiled. "That makes perfect sense, Mother. June, how clever you must be — I'm completely hopeless with paperwork. This is exciting. I haven't been shopping with anyone but my sister or my mother in a very long time."

"I don't know what to say," June fretted. "You've already been so generous, Francie, letting me stay here and all. Besides, you hired me to help — not to go shopping when we have so much to do before Tuesday."

"It won't take any time at all," Francie said firmly. "Alice is a very sensible girl, and she has a splendid eye for fashion."

"Do you have dinner plans, June?"

"Yes, I'll be eating here with Patty — I like to spend the evenings with her when we're apart during the day."

"Of course. Well, this is all working out well," Alice said. "We'll be back in time to reunite June with Patty, and to change before dinner. I'll tell Daddy to make reservations and then he and Bill can pick us up on the way."

"Alice . . ." Francie said warningly.

Some unnamed tension stretched between them, and June looked at the floor, embarrassed at being a witness to their disagreement, whatever it was. As she followed Alice to the door, she wondered why love had to be so complicated.

CHAPTER 33
VIRGIE

Virgie watched Mrs. Samples leaving in the company of Mrs. Meeker's daughter. Somehow Mrs. Samples had already wormed her way into Alice's good graces. How did she do it? One after another, everyone seemed to be falling for her act.

Except for Virgie. If she had to solve this case all by herself, she would, but it would be a lot easier if Mrs. Samples wasn't such a good liar. But that was what made a criminal successful, according to George Barton — lying consistently. He said most crooks got caught when they forgot what they had told to whom and started making mistakes. (Mr. Barton's books on detection had taught Virgie a great deal, even though they were much harder to understand than her Nancy Drew books. The good thing about them was that they were old, and sometimes Flossie and Ruth found them at garage sales and gave them to her as presents. One of these days, Virgie was going to read every single one.)

Virgie made her way to Willy's room, dropping off the week's activities list as she went. Her mother had made them up just this morning, and Virgie had been afraid she'd left the master of her own flyer in the mimeograph machine; her mother wouldn't approve of the ring business. But her mother had been too distracted to do much of anything besides get the machine set up and tell Virgie to run it. The police visit had upset her; she was convinced people might cancel their reservations if they heard about it.

When Virgie knocked, Willy called for her to come in. As usual, Willy had the shades drawn and the draperies closed, and it took a moment for Virgie's eyes to adjust. On the little table in front of the fireplace was a plate covered in crumbs, in defiance of the rules. A pile of clothes lay on the bed, tried on and discarded from the looks of it.

"My, my, look what the cat dragged in," Willy said. She was curled up in the armchair with her legs tucked under her, a stack of magazines on the floor, an ashtray overflowing with butts on the little table. Her hair was up in curlers, and her face was scrubbed clean. Despite looking far health-

248

ier today, she seemed down in the dumps.

"I brought you the activity calendar for next week," Virgie said, digging one from the big pocket in her smock and handing it to Willy, who didn't bother to look at it before setting it aside.

"Do you have . . . ?"

"Right here," Virgie said, taking the small brown paper bag from her smock. Dr. Peabody's nurse had stapled the bag shut twice, so there had been no way to see what was inside, but from the heft and rattle it was obviously some kind of pills. Virgie was no closer to understanding what Willy had communicated with her brief note.

Willy took the bag and opened it right in front of Virgie. "Ah, perfect," she said. "Be a love and get me some water, won't you?"

Virgie filled a drinking glass in the bathroom and brought it to Willy, who shook out a pill from the bottle and swallowed. She dug a small piece of paper from the bag and read it, then groaned. "Seven days," she muttered. "Unbelievable."

"What's seven days?"

"Never you mind that. Let's just say the timing isn't exactly ideal." She took a cigarette from her pack and struck a match on a small gold box. "This hasn't been much of a week, has it, Virgie?"

"Well, not for Mrs. Carothers, anyway," Virgie said.

Willy was lifting her cigarette to her lips to light it, but instead she suddenly started coughing, and had to take several sips of water to clear her throat. "No, I suppose not," she said. "So what's your theory, Virgie? Did she do herself in? Or was it an accident?"

"I don't know. But Mother says you'd have to be awful drunk or awful clumsy to fall in along here since the path doesn't go all the way to the edge. So if it *was* an accident, she would have had to walk quite a ways."

"Sounds like a good point. Well, I guess we'll never know, will we? Since the dead don't have a lot to say, and they probably don't care much anyway."

"Shakespeare said that death pays all debts."

"Is that so? You're a walking encyclopedia, you know that?"

Virgie was pleased at the compliment; she wasn't sure exactly what the quotation meant, but Mr. Barton put it in the front of one of his books.

This seemed like a good moment for the favor she wanted to ask for. "Remember you were saying you were going to help me with

250

my pitch? The next ring toss is Wednesday, and I wanted to see if I could sell some rings this weekend."

"That's the spirit," Willy said, perking up. "Then we'd better get to work, hadn't we?"

She picked up the activity calendar off the floor. "Did you make this? It's very nice handwriting."

"No, Mother did," Virgie conceded. "My teacher from last year says I need improvement. Which is dumb because I'm going to be a detective, so who cares how I write?"

Willy made a tsking sound. "That's no way to think. If you want to get ahead in this life, you have to be improving yourself all the time, and not just the things you're already good at."

"Ha," Virgie said. "That's easy for you to say — you're good at everything. Except cleaning. You're not very good at cleaning, but that's probably because you don't try."

Willy laughed. "You have a point there. But you're wrong about me being good at everything. Want to know a secret? Something no one else knows about me?"

Virgie did, very much, but she tried not to let it show. "I guess."

"When I was your age, I wasn't good at much of anything. I talked with a lisp, and kids at school made fun of me, so I just kept quiet all the time. I didn't have any friends and teachers thought I was stupid."

"What's a lisp?"

"It's where you can't say your *s*'s," Willy said. "Like thith. *The thell thea thell by the thea thore.*"

"Oh. But how did you stop?"

"Well . . . now *that* is a rather long story for another time. But the most important part is that I started singing as a way to practice making the *s* sound correctly. When I sang, I didn't feel as embarrassed, so I started singing all the time, and before long I joined the choir and . . . well, some other things happened, but the long and short of it is that I never would have become a singer if I didn't work hard to change something about myself.

"So you can let this teacher tell you that you need improvement . . . or you can decide that you're going to have the very best *Virgie* handwriting that the world has ever seen. Here, write something for me." She shoved the calendar back at Virgie.

"What should I write?"

"I don't know . . . you decide."

Very carefully, Virgie started writing. It was exciting to think that she could change an important part of herself just by trying. What if, in this very moment, she was becoming someone new? Someone even better?

When she was finished, she slid the paper back across the table.

"Well, well," Willy said. " 'Virginia T. Swanson, Private Detective.' What's the *T* for?"

"Tabitha," Virgie said shyly. "Tabby for short. It's not my real middle name — it's Katherine, after my grandmother. But I'm actually thinking of changing my name to Tabby when I grow up."

"Whatever for?"

"I *hate* my name," Virgie said. "It's ugly."

Willy laughed. "It is not. And I'll bet you ten bucks you'll change your mind. Anyway, I think you're on the right track. Now, what do you want to say about your rings? Why would I want to buy one from you?"

"They're cheap, and they come in silver or gold, and you don't have to throw your real one in the river."

"Hmm. Well, that gets the point across. But let's see if we can come up with a bit more pizzazz, shall we?"

CHAPTER 34
FRANCIE

Charlie called at three o'clock to say he'd arrived and checked in.

"You'll come to dinner tonight, won't you? Arthur is making reservations." Since Alice had managed to railroad her into dining with Bill, Francie's only hope was to invite other people so that she could be seated far enough away that conversation would be impossible.

"I think I'll stay in tonight; it was a long drive. But, Auntie Francie . . ."

"Charlie, you are twenty-seven years old," Francie said tiredly. "I think it's time you simply call me Francie."

"All right. Francie . . . may I speak to you privately? Just the two of us? I'd prefer to do it in person. Before dinner, if it can be arranged."

"Of course, dear." Francie had been expecting this, girding herself for it. With Vi gone, and Charlie excluded from the tight bond between Frank and Harry, she would need to serve as a surrogate mother. "Gentleman are only allowed in the parlor here, however. But it's a fine day to sit outside."

"Good. I'll have the car brought around."

Francie was waiting on the front porch when he arrived twenty minutes later at the wheel of a pickup truck, looking more like a delivery man than the son of a wealthy business owner. He was dressed in work pants and an old shirt, for which he apologized right away.

"I'm sorry, Auntie — er, Francie. I had to return some scaffolding this morning."

"I'm not worried about that," Francie said fondly. Because he pitched in with the physical labor on the job sites, Charlie was often mistaken for one of the tradesmen Harry hired, but he didn't seem to mind. He took after Vi that way, preferring to stay out of the limelight. "So what did you want to talk to me about?"

Charlie seemed to deliberate a moment before asking, "Did my mother seem different to you, in the last few weeks?"

"Different . . . ?" Francie suspected she knew what Charlie was asking, but she had nothing to offer him. Vi had been distracted, sure, and maybe a little more melancholy than usual, but if there had been clues that she was planning to take her life, Francie had missed them. "Honestly, no — other than changing her mind about the divorce."

"What do you mean? I thought they just decided to divorce, right before she came here."

Had he and Frank really not known? "Your father asked for a divorce quite some time ago," she said gently. "Last fall, right before Thanksgiving. But your mother refused. She . . . felt strongly about divorce, as you may know."

Charlie's jaw tightened. "Yes. I do."

"Your father kept asking for a while, but — well, you know your mother — she could be stubborn about things, and he finally gave up." At least, that's what Vi had told her. Francie thought back to Christmas, Vi's usual frenzy of decorating and baking and shopping. She'd occasionally mentioned Harry's latest mistress, but it was with exasperation, not despair. Unless . . . was it possible Francie had misread her feelings? "And then one day she simply changed her mind — came to me and said she didn't want to wait, she had called the hotel he'd originally booked her in and told them she was coming. And then, as you know, I decided to join her."

"Did she seem — upset? When she told you?"

"No, actually. She seemed . . . relieved. It cheered her, I think. She immediately started arranging everything, asking other volunteers to cover her shifts at St. Vincent de Paul, finding someone to take care of the dog, that sort of thing."

Charlie looked perplexed. "And you just decided to . . . get divorced too? Just like that? I know it's rude of me to ask, Auntie Francie, but I just don't understand —"

"I'm not sure I understand it myself," Francie admitted. "Oh, things haven't been right between Arthur and me for years — you're old enough hear that, aren't you, Charlie? — but it wasn't until Vi made her decision that I realized I could do the same. Before that I felt like . . . like the moment I said 'I do' to Arthur, it committed me to a certain life, that all the other choices I might have made were lost."

"I know how that feels," Charlie said heavily. "Once I went to work for Dad, all my other plans just kind of faded away."

"Charlie . . . maybe you should let your mother's courage serve as your inspiration," Francie said gently.

"Yeah, and kill myself, like she did? Instead of letting any of us say goodbye?"

Charlie's anger died as quickly as it had flashed. "I'm sorry, I don't mean that. I just can't believe she left us that way."

"I'd give anything to have her back too, you must know that. And we don't know that she took her own life, Charlie. The police haven't ruled it a suicide — in fact, they seem more inclined to view it as an accident. You mustn't ever think she wanted to leave you and your brother." *Or me,* the voice inside her clamored. *How could you do that to me, Vi? What am I supposed to do without you?*

" 'We don't know,' " he echoed dully. "I suppose I should try to remember that. It's pointless, isn't it, wondering why."

"I wouldn't say —"

"It's all right, Auntie Francie. I suppose the best thing to do is just get this over with, put one foot in front of the other. Dad sent me with a list. I might as well get started."

"A list?"

"Yes, a to-do list. I've booked rooms for Dad and Frank at the Mapes too. And then Dad wanted me to deal with this situation with Mom's room. I don't want to leave this young woman with nowhere to go, obviously, but Dad doesn't want a stranger involved with Mom's funeral. He suggested, well, a sum of money to help her get settled

258

elsewhere." Charlie's was absently twisting his shirttail just as he'd done when he was a little boy, a sign of his discomfort with his father's request. "And then there's the matter of Dad's, um, girlfriend. There was some sort of mix-up that ended up with her staying in this same hotel, and he wants her moved somewhere else."

Francie snorted — she couldn't help it. She could just hear Harry dictating this unpleasant list to his younger son, rather than deal with any of it himself.

"Francie . . ." Charlie plowed on, "Dad wanted me to ask you to reconsider — he said it would be so much easier for everyone if you'd let him bring her back to San Francisco and bury her there. He said that he'd pay for everything."

"Charlie William Carothers," Francie exploded, unable to contain herself. "Your father may have sent you to do his dirty work, but I will *not* allow that to happen! Your mother made it very clear that she wanted to be buried right here where she grew up. It was, as far as I can tell, her *only* request."

Charlie was silent a moment, emotions battling in his eyes. When he spoke, his voice was filled with pain. "She really told you that?"

"She did," Francie said, a bit more calmly. "The night we arrived, at dinner. She was very clear about it, said her father had bought her plot years ago, right next to theirs."

"Because she never told me. She hardly ever talked about her past at all." His voice thickened. "Mom told stories about Reno to me and Frank sometimes, when we were little. She made it sound . . . She talked about the snow and playing in the cemetery and riding in the back of the neighbor's truck to school, but she never brought us here. And when we got older she never talked about it at all."

Francie wished she hadn't come down on him quite so hard. "I think that maybe, as your father became more successful, and the demands on her to occupy a particular place in society — she couldn't very well talk about growing up in a tiny house with a father who delivered ice at a black-tie ball at the Palm Court."

Charlie hung his head in his hands. "And now she's gone," he said raggedly. "Who cares about keeping up appearances now? What good was any of that if she was *that* unhappy —"

His voice broke off, becoming ragged sobs, and Francie — who'd once held him after he broke his arm falling from Alice's bedroom window — pulled him into her arms and held him, letting his tears fall on her blouse and murmuring the kind of things that mothers say. There would be other moments when he'd need her: when he found a girl to marry, when his first child was born, when life's challenges seemed too much, and when he wanted to share his successes. Harry would retreat into his new marriage; there might even be more children, half-siblings that Frank and Charlie would rarely see. He wouldn't be there for Charlie and Frank the way a father should.

But *she* would be there.

"Darling," she said when he pulled away in embarrassment, clearing his throat. "Your mother had a good life, a *happy* life. All she ever wanted was to see you and Frank grow up and take your place in the world. Yes, she had her problems — like any of us. Her marriage to your father wasn't perfect. But she loved her charity work, she loved her home." *And me — she loved me,* Francie reminded herself, because she'd given herself this same speech last night when she couldn't sleep, when missing Vi felt as if it would smother the breath from her. "She talked about you and your brother all the time — she was so proud of you two! If she was here she'd be quite impatient with us for moping, she would want you to do whatever makes you happy, to find a nice girl and get married and have a baby. A *lot* of babies, if I know your mother."

Charlie smiled — a very sad, fleeting smile, but it was something.

"And . . . if it helps, she *did* talk about Reno, to me. Not often. Usually in the winter, when we walked up to the top of Russian Hill to see the sun turn red over the ocean, and she'd tell me about the seasons changing — how she missed that. She told me how her mother used to save the prettiest leaves from the yard, and she and Vi would string them on thread and hang them in the kitchen as decorations. And how they would search for the first daffodil shoots in the spring."

"Thank you, Francie," Charlie said haltingly. "I *do* want to know, whatever you can tell me. It helps."

"Charlie, you *do* know that your mother never sold the house? The one she grew up in?"

"I thought they sold it years ago. I remember her talking about it with Dad."

"Your father wanted to, but your mother refused. He gave in when she promised it wouldn't cost him anything, that she'd hire caretakers to maintain it in exchange for living there for free. I think . . . I think she thought that someday you or Frank might like to have the house, even if it was just for vacations."

"Hell *yes,* I want it!" Charlie exclaimed. "Are you kidding? Do you think any of her old stuff is still there?"

There he went, looking for clues. It broke Francie's heart. "I don't think so. I actually saw the house myself for the first time yesterday. June and I drove out and she found the spare key and — well, June had the idea to have the wake there. Since the cemetery is right next door, it couldn't be more convenient." She took his hand, suddenly unsure. "Maybe it was wrong of us to make those plans without consulting you and Frank. There's still time — if you would rather have it elsewhere, the funeral director is quite accommodating. I'm sure he'll be glad to help with the arrangements."

"No," Charlie said, squeezing her hand. "That was a great idea. I think Mom would like it. Could you show me?"

"Yes, of course. We can go out there tomorrow morning. There's still a lot to do — we need to choose the casket, and there's the matter of a headstone. We're still trying to get in touch with some of Vi's distant relatives and your parents' friends who haven't heard. June will need an estimate for the caterers. Oh, and we'll need to find a valet because there's no parking at the house, just the field next to it. And I think June's made an appointment with the florist for tomorrow too — unless you'd like to make those decisions?"

It was a bit of a dirty trick to play on the poor boy, but by overwhelming him with the details she was counting on Charlie to realize that he couldn't simply send June packing as his father wanted him to do.

"Oh. That's — no, I don't think I should interfere, since you've accomplished so much already. Francie, I didn't realize . . . I had no idea there was so much to do. I should have, though — I deal with those sorts of details every day for our clients, and yet . . ."

"It's all right, dear," Francie said, patting his arm. "You just come along to make the big decisions, and let us handle the rest. You don't need to be worrying about the little things at a time like this."

"Thank you." Charlie looked exhausted. "I honestly don't know what we would do without you. Mom deserves — she deserves —"

He was getting choked up again, so Francie said briskly, "She deserves the best we can do, and she shall have it. Oh, one other thing, we thought we would hire a pianist to play during the luncheon. We found some sheet music in the house that belonged to your mother."

"That's a great idea."

"Good, then I'll just confirm with her, shall I? I can do that this afternoon, before dinner."

"God, it will be good to see Alice."

"Well, you won't have to wait very long," Francie said. "Here she comes now."

CHAPTER 35
JUNE

They were walking across the parking lot, laughing together over something Alice had said, when a tall, curly-haired man in work clothes came running toward them with Francie following behind. He picked Alice up and swung her around before putting her back down, both of them laughing. He made sure she had her balance before he let go. "I'm so glad to see you, you have no idea. Also, you're looking mighty pretty."

Alice rolled her eyes. "Coming from someone who used to call me Caterpillar Face, I'll take that with a grain of salt."

The young man turned to June. "Hello, you must be June. I'm Charlie Carothers. I'm grateful for everything you're doing for my family."

He shook her hand rather formally; his was callused and strong.

"Oh, it's nothing," June stammered, pulling back her hand in embarrassment. "I mean, it's my pleasure. I mean, not my pleasure, obviously, because it's such a terrible thing that happened —"

"June has been such a help to Mother," Alice interrupted, with a wink, saving her from further embarrassment. "And she's terribly clever."

"Francie told me," Charlie said, still watching June. "Obviously, my father will compensate you for your time and effort. Are the accommodations here adequate for you and your daughter?"

June saw Francie exchange a look with Alice, smirking knowingly.

"Oh yes, Mr. Carothers, they're very nice," June said cautiously, wondering if he was being sarcastic. The suite was obviously much more extravagant than they deserved; maybe he was angry that she was still there. Except he seemed so genuinely kind, and he and Alice were obviously close.

"Call me Charlie, please, since we'll be working together on this. Francie has told me how much there is on your to-do list, and I'm ready to roll up my sleeves."

"You should put him to work calling the rest of the people on your list," Francie prompted, seeing how uncertain June was feeling. "Perhaps you could get it for him? He's staying at the Mapes; he can make some calls tonight."

"Oh yes, of course. I'll just run upstairs — I'll be right back."

As June hurried toward the front door, she overheard them talking behind her.

"Pick up your jaw, Charlie," Alice said. "You look like a dog staring in the butcher shop window!"

CHAPTER 36

June folded the list carefully and stuffed it into one of the hotel envelopes, wishing she'd had time to copy it over more neatly, and headed back downstairs.

Charlie was a surprise. Unlike his pale, slender mother, he was a strapping man of well over six feet, with dark curls falling into his eyes and the shadow of a beard. He had big scarred hands like a carpenter, but he'd held hers delicately, as though he was afraid to hurt her.

June wasn't used to talking to men. Since meeting Stan the summer after high school graduation six years ago, she'd learned to say little and keep her eyes on the ground, lest she accidentally spark his temper. Stan didn't tolerate any attention from other men, even someone as harmless as the man behind the butcher counter or one of the deacons at church.

Since spotting him that first night at the

Sky Room, June had been on edge. Too late, she'd realized how he'd tracked her to Reno — she had given the motel her phone number so they could call back and confirm her reservation, and they must have called again the day she left. Stan, discovering her missing, had stayed home from work that day waiting for her to come back — and then, after learning what she'd done, driven to Reno like a bat out of hell.

Still, that didn't explain how he'd known she was at the Sky Room. She'd gone over and over it in her mind but couldn't figure it out. At least he thought she was staying at the Twilight Inn, but once he realized that she had never checked in, it was only a matter of time before he tracked her down. When it came to June, her husband was relentless.

Charlie was the sort of man who made June wonder what she'd ever seen in Stan. He wasn't bad-looking, and he'd turned on the charm at first, and that was all it took — by the time June realized that it had been an act to win her over, they were already married, and she was expecting. So maybe she shouldn't trust her first impressions of people, but Charlie seemed genuinely polite. And funny too, the way he'd treated Alice. June had almost been envious of his atten-

270

tion to Alice, though clearly they were like brother and sister. To think she had been afraid Charlie would be angry to find her still staying in his mother's room! Instead, he'd asked her if it was "adequate" — as if a girl like her could hope for anything half as nice.

The two families had shown her nothing but kindness and generosity — Alice hadn't let her see the bill from the dress shop, but the three dresses, suit, cardigan, and two pairs of shoes had to have cost a fortune. They were trusting her with planning the service, and that trust was even more precious than money. But what would they do if they knew she was a magnet for disaster, that Stan would stop at nothing to get her back? What would *she* do if he tried to disrupt the service or threatened those around her? Was she a terrible person for staying, when they might end up getting pulled into her troubles at a time like this?

Down in the garden, Alice and Charlie were seated on the bench talking animatedly. When Charlie saw June, he jumped up and smiled.

"Here," June said, thrusting the envelope at him. "I've already talked to the ones I've crossed off, and there's a tally at the bottom — I'm sorry it isn't neater."

"I'm sure it's fine," Charlie said, folding the envelope and stuffing it into his shirt pocket. "Thank you. And, June . . . it occurs to me that, with Alice and Francie having dinner with Arthur tonight, you might find yourself without plans, and, well . . . there are apparently several very nice restaurants in town."

Alice rolled her eyes. "You're sure you're not too *tired*? From that long drive?"

Charlie reddened. "No, actually — I seem to have got my second wind."

"Oh, well, in that case — you may as well have dinner with him, June," Alice said. "He can be sweet, though he does require a great deal of patience."

Charlie shot her a scowl before turning back to June. "I only meant so we could discuss plans, of course," he said. "To see how I might help."

"That's very kind," June said, "but I've got to pick up my daughter from her sitter."

"I completely understand," Charlie said. "Forgive my thoughtlessness. Perhaps another time. But tomorrow morning, will you be returning to the house? Because I could meet you there and we could discuss everything. At the house."

"That would be fine," June said. Then she found herself saying, "Mrs. Swanson serves

272

sherry in the lounge every afternoon. I mean, if you would like to talk there for a bit. I don't need to pick Patty up for another hour."

"He'd love to," Alice said. "It'd be just the thing. I'm so sorry I won't be able to join you, but I need to freshen up before dinner."

"Alice, thank you so much for taking me shopping," June said. "It was really too generous."

"You've given us all a respite from our sadness." Alice leaned in and kissed June on the cheek. "I'll see you tomorrow, I'm sure. Good night, Monkey Butt."

Charlie and June watched her go in awkward silence.

"About that," Charlie said. "It's — well, it was a childhood nickname. I don't even remember how it got started."

"It's all right," June said. "My parents used to call me June Bug."

"Somehow, that seems slightly nicer." Charlie cleared his throat and offered his arm. "Shall we, then?"

Inside, the guard looked up from his textbook. "Good evening, Mrs. Samples," he said. "You'll need to sign in your guest."

"Oh — of course." She remembered the way Francie had introduced her to Alice.

"Mickey, may I present Charlie Carothers, Mrs. Carothers's son. And, Charlie, this is Mickey . . . I'm sorry, I don't know your last name."

"It's Walsh, ma'am," Mickey said.

"It is a pleasure to make your acquaintance, Mickey," Charlie said formally, shaking Mickey's hand.

"Nice to meet you, sir. If you could just sign the book . . ."

"Of course." His signature was barely more than a squiggly line that ended in a flourish.

A group of ladies waited in the lobby for Clyde to bring the car around to take them to whatever tonight's activity was. June felt them watching her as she and Charlie passed. *It's because they can't believe a man like him would be with a girl like me,* she thought, automatically looking down in shame — until she remembered that she was wearing a suit that cost fourteen dollars and forty-nine cents and was every bit as nice as anything they were wearing.

Could it really be that easy? she wondered. There had never been a time when she'd been confident in her appearance. Whenever they were in public, her mother had covered her own mouth when she smiled to hide her crooked teeth. Her father had waited at the end of the line to greet the pastor after church, embarrassed by his old suit. June had absorbed their self-consciousness until it was as familiar as her own skin. She'd learned to make herself invisible, accepting her place among the overlooked, even as her brothers had rebelled. Donny and Mike had both dropped out after fifth grade and had trouble with the law before getting jobs at the plant and settling down, but June had graduated high school with good marks and started secretarial school with high hopes, thinking she might finally do something to distinguish herself.

But then Stan Wentlandt, a young sales-man with a company that made siding, had noticed her one sunny day, sitting on the steps of the trade school on their lunch break, and how could she resist? He was the first man ever to see something special when he looked at her, other than her father, who'd died the year before from a heart at-tack. Her mother, struggling to feed the two of them on his meager pension, had been overjoyed that Stan had a good job with a company car, and when Stan proposed after only three months, it felt like luck she didn't deserve.

But the job didn't last — nor did any of the ones that followed, due to Stan's temper, and before long June was an exhausted young mother not so different from her own, once again invisible as she went about her errands, and tried to keep up the house, and coaxed vegetables from the garden to supplement Stan's intermittent paychecks. By the time she'd found the courage to leave him, she had forgotten that she'd ever been anything but invisible.

But here, sitting in a fancy room with a handsome man, wearing beautiful clothes, a tiny spark caught inside June, and she felt the stirrings of hope.

"So," Charlie said, after he'd poured them each a tiny glass of sherry and they'd taken seats in the corner at a little table under a sconce that gave off soft golden light. There was no one else in the lounge, as it was nearly dinnertime. "Francie has told me that you're arranging the food and flowers and everything for the reception?"

"Yes," June said. "I can show you the receipts if you like — I've kept detailed records."

"Oh, that's not necessary. Would you like to tell me what you've got planned?"

"Well, once I saw the cottage, and Francie told me how your mother used to talk about it, it gave me the idea to serve the luncheon in the kitchen and put tables in the front room and open up the patio so people can go outside if they like," she said. "Francie thinks we won't have more than thirty people, since it's so far for people to travel and —" And there had been so little notice, due to the nature of Vi's death — but she could hardly say that to Charlie, could she? "And so I rented these little round tables, and I thought I could set a board on the radiator in the kitchen and cover it with a cloth to make it nice and serve the food there. I found a bolt of the sweetest flowered cotton sateen in a shop downtown and the salesgirl gave me a discount for buying the entire bolt, and I hired a lady to cut and hem it for the tables." The fabric was printed with tiny sprays of violets, a detail that June had thought was perfect at the time, but now she wasn't sure — maybe it wasn't sophisticated enough, or maybe people would be offended that she hadn't gone with plain white.

"I ordered sandwiches and little cakes," she went on. "There's going to be ham and chicken salad and — and another, I can't remember, and they'll deliver two large coffee urns as well. Oh, and I'll make tea the day before for iced tea, and I need to have ice delivered. Did you know your grandfather delivered ice? Oh, what am I saying, of course you did. Virgie found two steel tubs in the basement here, and I cleaned them and they look good as new, and we can use them to ice down bottles of lemonade and ginger ale."

"June," Charlie said, but she didn't dare let him talk until she'd told him everything, because if he criticized her efforts she wasn't sure she'd be able to get it out.

"There's a piano that your mother used to play, and it was actually in tune, and Francie found someone to play during the luncheon. I thought some small bouquets would look nice, to set on the tables. Of course there will be the flowers from the funeral too — I haven't finalized those yet, but maybe you'd like to choose? And people will probably send more, of course, but they might like to see them at the cemetery, on those little stands . . ."

She was aware that she was beginning to prattle, but Charlie was watching her with what looked like consternation, and it made her nervous. Was she making a fool of herself — had she gotten everything terribly wrong? Or worse — did he hate the idea of having the luncheon in the little house when all he'd ever known was luxury?

"June," he said more firmly, interrupting her. "You've put a lot of work into this, it's

obvious. But you needn't have economized. I'm more than happy to pay for the very best you can find."

"But I did," she said, crestfallen. "Find the best, I mean. I asked the hotel owner for the best bakery, the best delicatessen —"

"But you're doing so much yourself," he said. "A caterer could take care of all of it — the tables and linens, the plates and glassware and the food. And they'll send people to help serve — there's no reason you should be worrying about that, plus they'll clean up after. And instead of crowding everyone into the house, why don't we simply rent a tent? I can have my father send one, we use them all the time on the job — there are really nice ones that look elegant and provide protection from the elements."

June *had* thought of hiring caterers — Mrs. Swanson had given her the name of a caterer who did wedding receptions for some of her clients who remarried the minute their divorces went through — but the prices were sky-high. They wanted more than two dollars for a plate of chicken and scalloped potatoes that would cost all of a few cents to make!

"I'll be happy to come with you to the

florist," he said hastily, when she didn't answer immediately. "I know that lilies are traditional, but my mother loved roses — yellow were her favorite. Surely, they can make arrangements that incorporate both. Oh — and has anyone discussed the pall-bearers?"

Pallbearers — June hadn't even thought of that. "Will you and your brother be serving as pallbearers?"

"Absolutely. I suppose it wouldn't do to have my father . . . no, definitely not. Let's see, there's Arthur, and Jimmy — Francie's son — and Margie's husband, Roy."

"I should be writing this down," June said in a panic. "I'll never remember everything."

"Leave it to me," Charlie said. "In fact — you can leave everything to me, if you like. This is what I do for a living, after all — we cater events all the time. Besides, sitting idle will only remind me that . . . well."

But June couldn't leave it to Charlie. Francie had given her the responsibility, the *job,* and without it she couldn't possibly justify the room and the clothes, and the pay Francie had promised her. And besides, she'd worked so hard to try to make it the way Vi would have wanted. How could she explain to Charlie that, though she had known his mother for barely a day, she had come to matter deeply to June? That she felt Vi's loss in her heart?

"But you can't change it," she said miserably. "I mean, I know you can make it fancier, and nicer, but — but she *loved* that house and I know when you see it you'll understand. I found some of her old schoolwork in the back of a cabinet, I saved it for you, and she drew a picture of the view from her room and it's almost the same as it is today, only the tree is taller and . . . and there was a cat. A little striped cat. And the way she was talking about her childhood that last night" — oh God, why had she said that, the last thing he'd want to be reminded of was his mother's *last night* — "you could tell she missed how simple it was here, with the mountains and the fresh air and the garden. If you put up a tent, if you bring in fancy caterers, it will be completely different. It — it might as well be in the city."

"June — June, please don't cry," Charlie said in alarm, offering his handkerchief.

"I'm *not* crying," June said, but she took the handkerchief and swiped angrily at her eyes, ruining the makeup Alice had insisted she let the Elizabeth Arden girl try on her at the store's cosmetics counter.

"I'm sorry I upset you — I'm sorry I stepped on your plans. It was thoughtless. I was only trying to make it easier on you —"

"I don't *want* it to be easier!"

Someone poked their head in the lounge, then quickly disappeared. June was mortified; who else had heard her outburst?

"I don't know how to do easy," she repeated quietly, getting up from her chair. "Nothing is easy. In my life, the only thing that has ever helped was hard work. Good night, Charlie."

Charlie had hastily pushed back his chair. "Please, June, don't leave —"

"I need to get Patty," she said, and ran out of the room.

As she hurried up the stairs without looking back, she felt her face burning. That's what she got for thinking she could pull off mixing with people like the Carotherses; she'd made a fool of herself and made a grieving man feel even worse.

Stupid, stupid, stupid — when would she ever learn?

CHAPTER 37
VIRGIE

Virgie watched Mrs. Samples race up the stairs, leaving Charlie Carothers with a gobsmacked look on his face, before he walked out slowly past the security desk without even saying goodbye to Mickey.

Virgie was standing behind the draperies in the library, where she'd hidden after she'd gone to clear away the sherry things and seen Mrs. Samples and Mrs. Carothers' son talking. She was almost positive they hadn't noticed her, and while she hadn't been close enough to hear everything, she'd seen enough — the way Mrs. Samples leaned toward him, for instance, and kept adjusting her skirt to show off her legs. It was obvious to Virgie that Mrs. Samples was trying to distract him, like Rita Hayworth in *Gilda* — and it was working too, because he couldn't keep his eyes off her.

Virgie knew that men could be dumb; a pretty lady they weren't married to was at the root of many of the divorces that took place in Reno. And Charlie Carothers was rich, despite the old clothes he was wearing and the beat-up truck he drove. Maybe he was an eccentric, like Howard Hughes. No wonder Mrs. Samples was flirting with him — she probably planned to swindle him out of his money!

She waited for the door to close behind him before checking to make sure the way was clear, and then she hurried up the stairs after Mrs. Samples. Instead of going to Mrs. Oglesby's room, Mrs. Samples hurried to her own room and slammed the door behind her.

What was she up to, and why was she in such a hurry? Virgie let herself into the supply closet next door as quietly as she could and pressed her ear to the wall, hoping Mrs. Samples had gone to make a call before she went to get Patty — perhaps to tell her accomplice she'd found a new mark.

Pressing her ear to the wall, she did hear voices, but one of them was a man — in her room!

"It's none of your business," Mrs. Samples was saying. She sounded upset. "Hidden safely away and there's nothing you can do about it!"

"Yes, it *is* my business!" The man was

obviously trying to keep his voice down, so he didn't get caught, but Virgie could tell he was very angry. "You made it my business when you ran. You took off without one goddamn word — what was I supposed to think, June?"

"You need to leave now," Mrs. Samples said, her voice quavering with fear, which surprised Virgie — she would have expected her to be tougher. "Otherwise I'll scream."

The man had to have come in through the window — he never would have gotten past Mickey, who was the most serious of the guards and a medical student too. There was a fire escape that ran the length of the third floor; Virgie had used it herself ever since she'd gotten big enough to climb the magnolia tree whose branches grew close to the fire escape.

She could hear the man crossing the floor to the window. "You know what I want, and I mean to have it," he said. "Remember what happens when you make me mad. I can't be responsible for what I'll do if you don't come to your senses."

Mrs. Samples didn't reply. Moments later Virgie could hear the man moving along the catwalk, the creak of the iron. Soon after she heard the sound of the window being lowered.

And then, crying. It was muffled, and it didn't last long, but Mrs. Samples was obviously rattled.

Virgie sat down on the floor to think, her legs crossed, her back against the wall of the closet. So she'd been right — Mrs. Samples had a partner whom she had double-crossed. He didn't know she no longer had the ring, and she was bluffing — probably trying to buy more time to try to get it back.

But the crying . . .

Virgie had overheard a lot of women cry as she went about her business in the hotel, and she'd become something of an expert on the subject. There were the gusty, ragged sobs that marked the early days of the guests' stays, when they could still barely believe what was happening. Then there were the bitter, angry tears — and sometimes things being thrown against walls — as their fate sank in.

But Mrs. Samples's crying wasn't either of those: she sounded like she'd given up hope, like all was lost. For a second, Virgie felt almost sorry for her.

What if she needed the money for something? Like an operation to save her sister's life — or to pay off her father's gambling debts so he wouldn't get thrown in the lake with his feet in a bucket of concrete?

Or maybe someone had been kidnapped. Back when Virgie used to get in trouble for sneaking out, before she got better at it, her mother had once said, "What if you'd been *kidnapped*?"

At the time, it had seemed ridiculous; her mother should have known that Virgie was way too smart to let something like that happen. But most people went through life not paying attention to what went on around them, which sometimes led to them getting robbed and killed. Her mother, for instance, always had her mind on so many other things, anybody could slap chloroform over her mouth and drag her away.

What would she do then? Virgie wondered. She imagined a note being shoved under her door; it would have letters cut out of the newspaper and pasted together to make words and would say something like *If you ever want to see your mother again, bring $1000 in unmarked bills to the oak tree on the hill at midnight. No coppers!!*

A wave of almost nauseating anxiety passed over Virgie, imagining her mother tied up and terrified in some dark warehouse. Virgie would have to do exactly what the kidnappers said, because her mother would never have the courage or skill to escape. She'd find a way to get the money, even if she had to steal it herself — and then, the minute her mother was safe, she'd hunt the kidnappers down and turn them over to the authorities.

Maybe Mrs. Samples hadn't kidnapped Patty after all. Maybe she actually had *two* kids — twins, even! There was no loyalty among thieves, and if Mrs. Samples was in the habit of double-crossing her accomplices, they might have taken one of her kids to hold for ransom, and then she would have had to steal the ring to get the money to get her back, but she'd trusted the wrong person and now she had to figure out how to keep from getting beat up *and* find the ring *and* sell it so she could pay off the kidnappers, who were probably threatening to take Patty too.

As she got to her feet, Virgie marveled at the mess Mrs. Samples had gotten herself into. People who said crime didn't pay were wrong — every day, creeps with any brains got away with all kinds of things. With her training, Virgie could probably commit all kinds of crimes and never get caught. But given how complicated a life of crime turned out to be, she figured she'd made the correct choice in staying on the right side of the law.

CHAPTER 38
FRANCIE

The directions Helen had given Francie took her over the river and through an industrial area to a neighborhood crammed with square little houses with tiny front lawns. It reminded her of the neighborhoods that had sprung up across the bay from San Francisco to house all the factory and refinery workers in the early part of the century.

Laundry hung on lines in backyards, while men chatted in driveways and children played in the streets. Cooking smells spilled out from open windows, and mothers rang dinner bells calling their kids home. The taxi driver dropped her off in front of a little yellow house with a brown shingle roof and a porch crammed with old chairs and a rusting icebox, and as Francie went hesitantly up the walk, an old dog lifted himself painfully from a blanket near the door and shook, his rheumy eyes watching her warily.

"Are you a good dog?" she asked, stopping at the bottom of the porch steps. "Or are you planning to bite my head off if I come any closer?"

"He's deaf," a voice called from behind the screen door. "And I'm not sure he'd understand you anyway, but he won't bother you. Too old and he's lost too many teeth."

A second later the screen door swung open and there stood Helen, barefoot and wearing a colorful peasant skirt and silver bracelets on both her wrists. In her free hand, she held both the neck of a violin and a lit cigarette.

"Welcome!" she said. "It's the maid's day off, so excuse the state of the house, won't you?"

Francie laughed uneasily at the joke, picking her way across the porch boards that groaned beneath her feet. As she pressed past Helen, she caught the scents of sandalwood, sweat, and liquor.

"You play the violin too?" Francie asked, taking in the living room. It was tidier than the outside — or at least cleaner. Someone kept the floors swept and the place dusted, but the room was jammed with furniture and books stacked on tables and paintings leaning against the walls — and a beautiful, polished black piano.

"Fiddle, actually — I've joined a little bluegrass group. Just for fun — I'm no good at all, not yet, anyway. Get you a drink?"

"Maybe a little of whatever you're having — pour light, though, because I've got dinner with my soon-to-be ex-husband tonight and I need to keep my wits about me."

Helen threw back her head and laughed. She'd worn her hair loose today, and it cascaded down her back, streaked here and there with silver. She had the sinewy arms of a washerwoman and no hips at all, but her kohl-rimmed eyes sparkled with life and her smile was hard to look away from, the end of her cigarette stained the same red as her lips.

"I hear you — the last time I got drunk around my ex-husband, I ended up knocked up and he stole my car. Take a seat there on the settee — I don't let Rex up there, so you won't get fur on your clothes."

"How long have you been divorced, again? I know you told me the other night, but it was a bit . . ."

"Yeah, Gwin's isn't good for your memory. Two years, give or take."

"So you've got a child at home?"

"Oh no, honey, I took care of that. My first two are my pride and joy, but they're grown and on their own and now I do

291

whatever I want."

Helen winked and handed Francie a tumbler with an inch of amber liquid in the bottom. "That's the last of the good stuff, so enjoy. I'm going to have to beat someone else at poker before I'll be drinking top shelf again."

Francie took a sip and nearly spit it out. "It's . . . strong," she said, her eyes watering.

"That's twenty-five-year-old scotch," Helen said, swinging a leg over the piano bench as though she was mounting a horse. "As my father used to say, it'll put hair on your chest. Okay, I've gone through the music and I think we'll have a nice variety. I kept everything that was in a minor key because, you know, people like the sad stuff for funerals, but I threw in some of the others that I thought might work. Like this."

She began to play, a lilting piece that started in the upper registers before being joined by a theme that echoed the first, her fingers dancing across the keys. She made it look as easy as dusting a shelf, humming to herself here and there, and then she stopped abruptly and looked over her shoulder.

"Like that? Or too cheerful?"

"Oh, no . . . I think it's lovely. If we have too much sad music, everyone might spend the whole day crying." Vi would hate that, Francie thought. "Did you happen to see the Schumann Arabesque in there? That was Vi's favorite. She used to come over and ask my daughter Alice to play it for her, but I'm afraid Alice doesn't have half your talent."

Helen shuffled the pages and held her hands suspended over the keys for a moment, then brought them down gently and began to play.

It was as though someone else entirely was at the keys. The familiar notes glided from the beautiful instrument, melancholy and haunting, and Francie closed her eyes and remembered an afternoon years ago, a few days after Christmas. Vi was hosting a New Year's Eve party and had come to borrow two of Francie's silver trays, but when Francie told her Arthur had taken the children skating, she accepted a glass of mulled wine and they curled up in front of the Christmas tree, the room dark except for its twinkling lights. The Arabesque had come on the radio — Gina Bachauer had recorded it in Philadelphia — and Vi had exclaimed, "An angel must be playing it just for me!"

But how could Helen have known? Because she played as if Vi was whispering in her ear, sharing her wishes and dreams.

When the music finally ended, she held very still until the notes faded completely away.

Then she turned to Francie with a smile. "Would you mind turning the pages for me on this next one?"

"Sure," Francie said. "I used to do it for Alice. I'm not the best at reading music, but —"

"You don't have to be," Helen said. "I'll let you know when it's time."

Francie set down her glass and took her place next to Helen on the bench, her ample hip against Helen's slender one, fine linen against India cotton. As Helen began to play again, Francie could feel the music rising through the bench and into her body. She breathed Helen's scent and felt her foot shifting on the pedals, and she had to concentrate to keep her place.

When Helen nodded, Francie had to reach across her to turn the page, and Helen's breath raised the fine hairs on her bare arm. Francie had the peculiar feeling that her body had aligned with the music, that her heart was beating in time. She almost didn't notice when Helen trailed off, her left hand playing the last few bars as she turned to Francie.

"What's wrong?" Francie asked. "You were playing so beautifully . . ."

"Nothing's wrong," Helen said softly. "Nothing at all."

And then she leaned in and kissed Francie on the lips.

Her breath was sweet with liquor, and her lips were soft and warm, and for a split second the shock of the moment kept Francie immobilized — and then she leapt off the bench, nearly falling as she backed away. She touched her lips, the kiss lingering there like a burn.

Helen got up too, her face stricken, the sheets of music falling to the floor. She bent to gather them, stacking them haphazardly, then dropped them on the bench where they slid to the floor again.

"I'm sorry," she said, "I thought — you must think I'm —"

"I didn't think anything at all!" Francie said, though that wasn't true. She realized she'd been watching Helen from the moment she saw her playing at Gwin's; there was something about her that had made Francie want to know her, to learn her secrets. She wasn't like anyone else Francie had ever met — with her bare feet, her long unruly hair, this little house that she lived in with no one but an old dog for company — but how could she have thought that Francie was . . .

"Are you a lesbian?" she asked dumbly.

Helen laughed, but this time it was rueful and awkward. "I suppose," she said, "though I've known my share of men too. Honestly, I wasn't thinking about, well, the fact that you're . . . oh, what a mess. I'm terribly sorry, I truly am. I obviously made a mistake and I hope you'll forgive me, but if you want to fire me I would understand."

"Fire you?"

"Find someone else to play for the service." Helen crouched down and gathered the sheets again, taking more care this time, stacking them and squaring the edges on the surface of the bench.

"No — wait." Francie's mind was spinning with thoughts that barely made sense. "I'll never find anyone else, so please, let's just pretend that didn't happen." But a moment later she couldn't help asking, "Whyever would you think that I — I mean, what gave you the notion — am I that plain?"

"Plain?" Helen echoed. "Good God, no. In fact, if I wasn't afraid you'd be insulted, I'd tell you that you're just my type. But I never would have — look, I know how it is. I'm not crazy. It's not like a girl like me can exactly take out a personal ad. Though . . . some do."

Francie's only interaction with lesbians

296

had been coming home late at night from dinner in North Beach and seeing women drunkenly sharing a cigarette under the awning of Mona's 440 Club. "Well. Like I said, it's best if we put that behind us. You do play beautifully and I'm sure that Vi's sons will be very pleased. I'll bring a check, and if you could leave the music afterward, I'll make sure to pass it along to them in case they'd like it as a keepsake."

She was already backing toward the door, avoiding looking at Helen. "Well, good night, then," she said, and let herself out the screen door.

The old dog lifted his chin off his paws as she stepped over him, then rolled onto his side. Having vetted her once, the gesture seemed to say, he'd found her barely worth the trouble.

CHAPTER 39
ALICE

Alice was nervous. She'd been the first to arrive for dinner — ten minutes early, a longtime habit — and now, seated at a wooden table in view of the bar, she was certain she'd made a mistake. Her father told her he had chosen Casale's Halfway Club on the recommendation of the concierge, but Alice knew the real reason had to be that it was far from the city center, which would provide the illusion of anonymity. She was actually surprised he'd put the reservation in his real name.

Alice had deliberately come alone in a taxi, so her mother wouldn't feel like a fourth wheel when she arrived. The place was a bit rustic — apparently, they were known for their ravioli and spaghetti, but the place had the air of a tavern, with a long bar down the center and scuffed wooden floors and checkered cloths on the tables. They would all be overdressed. Why, why had she thought that now was the time for her mother to meet Bill?

It had to happen eventually — really, why her mother seemed to think otherwise was beyond her — and with everyone together far from home, unlikely to run into people they knew, Alice had seized on the opportunity. But with emotions running high from Auntie Vi's death, bringing Bill had been a brazen choice for her father.

Though the alternative was unthinkable as well. Alice suspected that she alone understood how devastated her father was by Vi's death. Because she'd been a sensitive child, and sequestered by her mother's good intentions, she'd learned to read people at an early age. She'd noticed how Vi and her father seemed to always seek each other out at parties, and they were always going to art exhibits at the Modern that neither her mother nor Harry cared a whit about. There was nothing flirtatious about their friendship and, as far as Alice could tell, it had never engendered the least bit of jealousy on the part of either's spouse.

But Vi was more than a pal for her father — she was a kindred spirit and, she suspected, one who knew all about Arthur's secret life without being told. (For that matter, Alice believed Vi probably knew more about *everyone's* secret life — including her own — than she ever let on.)

So it was impossible to imagine her father surviving this loss without someone to lean on, and since that person was now Bill, she couldn't fault her father for bringing him. Bill wouldn't attend the funeral or the reception, of course, but he'd be there when Arthur returned to their room, exhausted by grief and socializing.

Bill always did whatever Arthur thought best — after five years, the pair were still utterly, almost ridiculously smitten. Seeing them together sometimes made Alice ache — for Vi, for her mother, for anyone who had never known love like that.

She checked her watch — it was already nine minutes past the hour, and where was everyone? The waiter had come by twice to ask if Alice wanted a drink, and the second time she'd ordered a Manhattan just to placate him.

There she was — finally, her mother came through the door, looking harried, ignoring the waiter when she spotted Alice, so that the poor man had to follow behind her.

"Alice! Darling, where on earth is your father? He's *late.*" She allowed the waiter to pull out her chair and plopped unceremoniously into it.

"I don't know, Mother, it's not my job to —"

But that was the precise moment when they made their entrance, her father looking furtive and even sheepish, and Bill beaming. Sweet, optimistic Bill, who'd listened to all of Alice's stories about the family, seemed to think this was an occasion to be celebrated, not endured.

Her mother followed Alice's gaze, and her slightly harried expression seemed to collapse inward, giving way to something akin to fear.

"Alice," she said, seizing her hand, "I'm afraid this was a mistake. I've had a very upsetting afternoon. I'm not sure —"

"Just *relax,*" Alice said. "It's only dinner. You can do this, for me."

For me? Had she really just said that? Her parents should have made this happen. Alice shouldn't have had to orchestrate this meeting, but since she'd been forced to live at home with them well past the age when most young people struck out on their own, she'd ended up in the role of peacekeeper.

"Dad!" she exclaimed, with brittle cheer. "And Bill!"

Arthur bent to kiss her cheek, then started to do the same to Francie, until he caught her expression. "Good evening, Francie.

301

You're looking lovely tonight."

"Hello, Arthur," her mother said coldly.

Alice poked a knuckle into her father's rib, since he'd made no move to introduce Bill, who was hanging back awkwardly.

"Oh! This is Bill," he said, with a little too much enthusiasm. "Bill Fitzhugh. Bill, this is Francie Meeker, my wife."

"Former wife," her mother snapped. "It's nice to make your acquaintance. Do sit."

Alice rolled her eyes; her mother was obviously intent on making everyone miserable all evening. If only Vi had been here, she would have teased and goaded her mother into behaving. Vi had always been able to bring out the best in her.

Her father and Bill seemed unable to decide who should sit where, and — worse — the waiter had arrived with Alice's drink and narrowly avoided spilling it when Bill backed up.

"Daddy," Alice said, "sit by Mother, please, and Bill, why don't you sit next to me?"

Bill shot her a grateful look and sat like a chastened schoolboy. Once everyone was seated, and a round of drinks was ordered — her mother for some reason ordering a double Old Fitzgerald, neat — Bill launched into a speech he appeared to have prepared for the occasion.

"Francie — may I call you Francie? — I must say that I've been looking forward to meeting you for some time. It has been a privilege to get to know Alice. She is such a delightful girl, so I've known that her mother must be quite special as well. You really must be so proud of her. And your other children, though I have not yet been lucky enough to meet them, I'm sure they are quite accomplished, like their mother."

Oh, Bill, Alice thought, wishing he'd discussed this with her first. Before she could intercede, her mother gathered herself and regarded him frostily.

"My children are perfectly ordinary," she said. "*I* am perfectly ordinary. It is only Arthur who has chosen to distinguish himself. But then again, you must know all about that, since you *live* with him."

"Mother!" Alice exclaimed, digging her nails into her mother's arm. "That's quite enough." She turned to her father. "I'm sure mother would love to hear about the new apartment. The style is Beaux arts, isn't it?"

"Indeed it is, Alice." Her father launched into one of his scholarly diatribes; architecture was one of his passions. While he was explaining how the building's framing had survived the 1906 earthquake, the drinks arrived; her mother managed to down most of hers in her first gulp.

On one level, the evening proceeded in a perfectly conventional fashion. Menus were brought; the waiter, perhaps sensing the tension, if not its cause, made himself scarce until he was summoned. Francie grilled him relentlessly, asking about nearly every dish on the menu before settling, as Alice had known she would, on the plain broiled chicken. She was well into her second cocktail by the time the rest of them had finished their first.

Alice did her best to sustain the conversation. It was like the first time she'd gone out with the driving instructor her mother had hired several years ago, when he'd driven her out to Lands End, where they had the road to themselves, and shown her the gears, the brake, and the gas pedal and explained that they all had to work in tandem. In the same way now, she steered her father and restrained her mother and coaxed Bill to participate and was too exhausted by the effort to add anything to the conversation herself.

The food arrived, and everyone picked at it except Francie, who ignored it and ordered a third cocktail and began interrupting. Alice was trying to tell Bill about the trip they'd taken to Yosemite with the Carotherses, while her mother interjected ("it wasn't Vernal Falls, it was Bridal Veil," and "Frank was the one who found that poor squirrel and he only let your brother take it because it was dead") — until finally Alice couldn't tolerate it for one more second.

She laid her silverware on the edge of her plate and cleared her throat to get everyone's attention. "There's something I would like to say."

Everyone turned to her in surprise.

"I'm going to be married."

For a moment, no one said anything, and then Bill applauded — once, twice, until he realized that no one else seemed happy.

"What on *earth* are you *talking* about, Alice?" her mother huffed. "Please don't be ridiculous."

"I'm not being ridiculous, Mother. I'm twenty-five years old, and I'm in love, and I've already said yes. Reggie wanted to ask Father for my hand, but I told him not to bother."

"Well, I think it's a splendid match!" Bill said. He'd had several cocktails himself, which seemed to make him all the sunnier.

"Thank you, Bill," Alice said. For some reason, she was feeling very calm — even detached, as though she were watching this strange evening play out from across the room. "We're hoping you'll do one of the readings at the wedding."

Bill put his hand over his heart. "It would be my *honor.*"

"Arthur," her mother said accusingly, "did you *know* about this? Have you been *encouraging* it?"

Diners at neighboring tables looked over, her voice having risen above the conversations around them. Her father winced. "I've met him," he said. "I don't see how that counts as encouraging it."

"Well, that's just fine!" Francie said, throwing her napkin onto her plate. "So I'm the last to know!"

Their waiter hurried over as she started trying to get up from her chair, too drunk to release her purse, whose strap had gotten stuck under one of the chair legs.

"Madam," said the waiter, "would you like to get some air?"

"I'll take her," Alice said. Meanwhile, both her father and Bill — old-school gentlemen both — had stood.

Alice grabbed her cane and limped around the table and took her mother's arm.

"Is she . . . all right?" the waiter asked Alice, and took her mother's other arm. The restaurant had fallen silent, the other diners riveted by the spectacle unfolding in front of them.

"Stop it," her mother said, swatting at the waiter. "She can walk just fine. She's *fine,* I tell you — she can do anything any other child can do."

"Mother," Alice pleaded. "He's only trying to help. Let's get you outside, shall we? Get you some fresh air?"

"You have every right to be here," her mother said to Alice, slurring the words. Her makeup had settled into the lines around her mouth and eyes, and her collar had escaped her jacket. "You're just as good as them, you know."

Somehow, this was the most horrifying thing of all. Anyone with eyes could see that Alice was a cripple. But the fact that her mother still needed to belabor the fact after all these years twisted Alice's pity into rage.

"*You* don't believe that," she retorted. "If you really believed I was as good as everyone else, you wouldn't have kept me locked in the house all these years!"

"Alice, sweetest" — her father was trying to get between them, attempting to pry Alice's fingers from her mother's arm — "let me take it from here, shall we? I'll just — Francie, please don't — *ow!*"

"Go sit down with your queen boyfriend!" her mother barked.

Her father retreated, muttering under his breath, while Bill seemed immobilized by shock. Their waiter was conferring with one of the other servers, while a third had hurried to the house phone and was probably calling the police.

But Alice didn't care. "Mother, that was a *horrid* thing to say!"

"Well, it's true. What am I supposed to do, pretend not to care while they bring scandal on the rest of us? I won't sit quietly by anymore — it's *unnatural.*"

"All I wanted," Alice said in a quavering voice, "was one lousy civilized evening with the people I love, now that we've lost Vi. What do you think *she* would think of the way you're behaving? You should be ashamed of yourself."

Alice picked up her purse and, wishing she could storm out, had to settle for limping her way past the other tables toward the exit.

Behind her, she heard a crash, a breaking of glass and crockery, and then — in her mother's strident voice — "God*damn* you, get your hands off me!"

But Alice didn't turn around — she didn't even slow down. This was a mess of her parents' own making, and they were going to have to clean it up themselves. Because Alice, after a quarter century under her parents' roof, had finally found other fish to fry.

CHAPTER 40
WILLY

Willy had never been to the bar at the Horseshoe Club before; Harry had promised to take her when he came to town, but in the three weeks that she'd been stuck in Reno, that had happened exactly zero times. So when Charlie Carothers called and asked to meet, she'd named the Horseshoe and gotten there early and ordered a bottle of champagne to boot, since her last bottle of champagne had been wasted on that stupid fat cow Francie Meeker.

But by the time he arrived, ten minutes late and looking none too happy to be there, Willy had barely touched the glass the waiter had poured for her. She was too nervous — whatever Harry's youngest son had to say to her, it couldn't possibly be good.

She knew it was Charlie the moment he walked in and scanned the room, and despite the crowd of swankily dressed people, he zeroed in on her instantly. Though Willy supposed it wouldn't have been very difficult to spot her, since the only other women present were with other men or were prostitutes making time at the bar.

Willy *had* been propositioned by a man at Dunc's the first week she was in Reno. Since then, she'd avoided going to establishments like that alone. That was the great thing about Gwin's — there were always far more women than men, which tended to keep the fellows in line, and those who *did* exceed the bounds of decency were generally so drunk that they were easily managed.

"Miss Carroll?" Charlie asked politely when he reached her table.

"Yes, it's very nice to meet you. Do sit down," she said. "I took the liberty of ordering. I hope you like champagne."

Charlie barely glanced at the bottle sweating in the silver bucket as a waiter appeared. "I like it fine. On second thought," he said to the waiter, "bring me a tonic water, please. And a couple aspirin, if you've got 'em."

"Very good, sir," the waiter said, removing the second champagne flute from the table.

Willy wondered if Charlie was hungover. Harry was fond of the bottle himself, and it amused him to see her tipsy — or maybe he just knew it increased his chances of getting her into bed. She'd had to work harder, lately, to show enough enthusiasm; until the ring was on her finger, she needed to remind him what he was buying. Too little, and Harry became petulant and glum and the just-because gifts dried up. But too much, and a man like Harry would begin to think he'd aimed too low and start looking around.

"It's so nice to finally meet one of Harry's sons," she said after the waiter left. She'd dressed with care for the meeting, borrowing a yellow cotton batiste dress with a sweetheart neckline from the girl in the next room, adding pearls that looked real enough and only a bit of rouge and eyebrow pencil. And false lashes, but that was because her real ones had become a bit stumpy and thin from the glue, and she couldn't exactly go without while she waited for them to grow back in. "He talks about you all the time."

"Is that right."

"And I want to extend my most heartfelt condolences on the loss of your mother," Willy continued, putting her hand over her heart to show how sad it made her. And it *was* sad — terrible, really, despite what she'd said to that awful woman the other night — but Willy had her own burdens and found it hard to feel *too* sorry for a grown man who hadn't had to work for anything in his life. Harry paid his sons a scandalous amount of money considering how little experience they had — especially Charlie, who was apparently no good at sales, so Harry just had him supervise the tradesmen.

"I appreciate that," Charlie said. The waiter returned with his tonic, along with a little plate of lemon and lime slices that Charlie ignored, though he plucked the aspirin tablets from the edge of the plate and dry-swallowed them. "Sorry, the altitude's given me a headache."

Now that they were face-to-face, Willy wished he'd just get on with it. She was expecting indignation and rebuke and possibly even threats, but she meant to gain the upper hand, as long as she could remain calm and claim the role of the injured party. Any claims Charlie made later to his father wouldn't hold water if Willy could pull this off convincingly — perhaps even cry.

"I know this must be difficult to understand," she said, letting her eyelids flutter down, folding her hands primly in her lap. "The age difference between me and your father. I'd be terribly upset if my own father — may he rest in peace — had dated someone so much younger after my mother passed."

"Well, technically, he began dating you well *before* she passed." Charlie made this observation tonelessly. "But go on."

"What I was going to say is that what Harry and I have is based on so much more than age. Or status or wealth, for that matter. He's such a kindhearted man, always thinking of his family, his employees, even strangers. Why, just last week he told me he'd found a little cat that had stowed away in the back of the truck, and he gave it water and part of his sandwich and let it ride in the cab all the way back to the hotel that night. The kitchen staff had apparently been feeding it scraps. Can you imagine?"

"I can," Charlie said drily, "since it was, in fact, *me* who found that cat. Dad never drives the truck."

Willy kept her expression steady while she silently cursed Harry — damn it, she should have seen through that one! "I must have misunderstood," she said with a little laugh.

"Mrs. Carroll —"

"Please, call me Willy! We're practically family!"

Charlie narrowed his eyes before continuing. "Willy, then — I think I can save us both some time by coming to the point. You can understand that your presence at the hotel where my mother was staying could create hard feelings among our family and friends. I've taken the liberty of securing you a suite for the duration of your stay in Reno at one of the finest establishments in the county. It offers luxurious accommodations on a par with the Holiday, not to mention a pool, horseback riding, a spa, and two restaurants. I can have a porter come for your things first thing in the morning. I'm also prepared to offer you generous compensation for any expenses you might incur as a result of this inconvenience."

"You're not sending me to the Arrowhead! They had to put one of their horses down from mud fever — the kitchen got shut down by the health department last month."

"I'm not familiar with the Arrowhead, though it sounds like a delightful establishment," Charlie responded coldly. "I was referring to the Double Y. It was profiled in *Collier's,* and the least expensive rooms go for more than a suite at the Holiday. Yours, you'll be happy to know, cost three times as much, and includes daily maid service."

"The Double Y is in Cold Springs," Willy exclaimed. "It's nearly twenty miles away!"

"All the better to enjoy the benefits of fresh air and spring water. And I believe they have a naturalist on staff who gives lectures and guided hikes."

Willy tasted the bitterness of her anger, but it was tinged with hurt. She didn't want to admit it, even to herself, but there had been a part of her that had been hoping that — well, it was ridiculous to think of now, since Charlie was obviously never going to warm to her and his elder brother was probably worse — but that in Harry's sons she might find a sort of family. That she'd become friends with their girlfriends, maybe serve as attendants at their weddings — hold their babies in the baptism photos. Not that she'd ever believed they'd accept her as a stepmother — she was only six months older than Frank — but that in time they might come to think of each other fondly.

But Harry's kids were so opposed to their father finding love again that Charlie had made this ridiculous end run on the eve of Harry's arrival in town.

"Your father is going to be beside himself when he finds out you tried to bribe me," she said.

"I have a check for you in my pocket," Charlie said, his tone hardening. "You may be interested to know that the signature on it is my father's."

That gave Willy pause. "That doesn't

316

mean anything," she hedged. "You could have forged it. You probably write checks on his account for work all the time."

"Not with your name on the 'pay to' line. It's in his handwriting, you can check. Believe me, I wish Dad wasn't too cowardly to do this himself, but I promise you that I am following his instructions to the letter. That last of which, I'm sorry to report, was to cancel your reservation at the Holiday as of check-out time tomorrow — I took care of that earlier today, in fact."

"You can't do that!" Willy said, fury creating spots in her vision. Why, it was all Harry's idea to send her there in the first place! She'd canceled a lucrative — well, a *paying,* anyway — engagement at a club in San Francisco to come! "I can't possibly get ready to move in so little time. I've had my clothes cleaned and pressed — I'm not about to jam them in a trunk again! I've made *friends* here!"

"You can take that all up with Dad tomorrow," Charlie said, reaching in his pocket and taking out the check. "Or since you two apparently speak on the phone regularly, perhaps you can discuss it with him tonight. I'm afraid I need to be going, at any rate."

He held out the check. Willy squinted at it — then tried to hide her astonishment at the amount. On the face of it, the number was good news, except that it signaled a cooling of Harry's feelings for her — one that might lead to him postponing or even canceling their engagement.

But if Charlie was really forcing her out of the Holiday, she was going to need those funds fast. She'd rather go back to waitressing in a cocktail lounge than be stuck out in the boonies mucking out stables for entertainment.

She reached for the check, but Charlie didn't let go.

"There's one last thing — I must advise you to keep out of sight this week while we are gathering to bury my mother. Everyone will be leaving next Wednesday, the end of the week at the latest, so you can resume your . . . *routine* then without worry. On behalf of our entire family, I gratefully accept your condolences, and will make sure they are communicated to my father."

"There is no way on earth that Harry told you to order me to stay away."

"No, you're right. I was counting on common decency to be enough to convince you."

Willy gave a hard tug, and the corner of the check tore off in Charlie's thumb and finger. He looked at it with distaste and flicked the little piece of paper onto the tablecloth.

"Oh dear, look at that," Willy said, folding the check and tucking it into her handbag, then rising from the table. "A bit careless of you, wasn't it? Let's hope you learn to hold on to your father's money better in the future."

CHAPTER 41
CHARLIE

It could have gone worse, Charlie told himself as he walked out. The woman was utterly shameless — obviously didn't care about anything but herself, and whatever she was able to wring from his father — but at least she'd taken the money. He'd been planning to put her in a taxi, but let her find her way home herself — car fare would barely make a dent in that check.

After the conversation in the bar, feeling slightly nauseated from the smoke and Willy's overwhelming perfume, Charlie decided a walk would do him good. The Mapes was only a few blocks away, but he walked toward the river and headed east on the riverside path, which narrowed into a dirt trail as he got farther from the center of town.

His father thought every problem could be solved by money, a philosophy that Charlie had to admit had served him well in business. After a competing company started undercutting their bids a few years back, Harry had taken losses underbidding every job until the other guys were forced to close up shop. No one had dared go up against HFC Events Management since, and Harry had slowly raised their fees until this year marked their highest revenues yet.

Charlie assumed that his father had also been ready to give his mother whatever she asked, to get out of the marriage — money, the house, a chunk of his investments. Now, of course, Harry wouldn't have to part with any of it — at least, none but whatever it cost to maintain his new bride, who was probably already planning to move into the family home.

Which was fine with him. Charlie had no desire to move back to Nob Hill. San Francisco had lost its allure for him lately: too crowded, too busy, too much traffic. In the past few months he'd been thinking more and more often about leaving the company, maybe starting something of his own — far from San Francisco, so he'd never have to compete with Harry and Frank. He knew his mother would have been devastated, but now that she was gone . . . well, now wasn't the time to be thinking about big changes. He just had to get through the next few days, the funeral. Then he'd see if his father would let him take a little time off. Harry and Frank had the nuclear tourism project well in hand; assuming the grand opening went off without a hitch, they'd be able to hand it off to the Moser brothers and all that would remain would be to collect their fees.

The path sloped gently down, closer to the river's edge. He'd have to turn around soon; up ahead there were no streetlamps to light the way. He paused to light a cigarette, listening to the buzzing of insects and the splash of frogs in the cattails along the bank.

Then he heard another sound behind him — footsteps, approaching fast. He turned in time to see a figure with a knit cap pulled low over his forehead — and then something hit him hard in the side of the head.

Next thing he knew he was lying on the ground, being kicked in the stomach. Charlie curled into a ball and then, as kicks landed on his knees and shins, managed to grab the stranger's foot. He yanked as hard as he could, and the stranger went down, sprawled in the mud. But before Charlie could scramble to his feet, his attacker rolled on top of him and started trying to hold him down and punch him at the same time. He hadn't landed any good blows before Charlie slammed his forehead into the stranger's nose.

The stranger howled, clutching his face as he crawled away. Charlie tried to get up but was hit with a powerful wave of dizziness that laid him flat again.

"Stay away from June!" the man bellowed. "Next time I'll kill you!"

With that, he turned and ran unsteadily back up the path and disappeared.

Charlie lay still, waiting for his head to stop spinning. Gingerly, he touched the side of his head; it was sticky with blood. But there wasn't too much, not enough to need stitches, anyway. The first blow had landed half on his ear and half on his cheekbone, and though it had rattled him, he'd likely end up with no worse than a black eye and a hell of a bruise.

As time passed, Charlie's senses seemed to grow sharper. He could smell the dank, fecund river water, the insects starting up again. Overhead, the stars filled the sky with a brilliance he never got to see in the city.

After a while, he managed to sit up. Needles of pain shot through his skull, and he tasted metal, but at least he didn't pass out. Gingerly he ran his hands over his ribs where the kicks had landed: nothing felt broken. By the time he got to his feet, Charlie was feeling a little sheepish about letting the stranger get the best of him.

Only an idiot would walk alone in a neighborhood like this at night. Charlie was lucky he hadn't been rolled by some thug who'd take his wallet and watch and tip him into the river. Instead, he'd been a victim of mistaken identity. Or mistaken something, anyway . . . the only thing Charlie was guilty of where June was concerned was appreciating those long, slender legs and those riveting green eyes. Well, and maybe the way her cheeks turned pink when she was embarrassed and the dimples that popped up when she smiled.

Damn it.

Charlie started walking back toward town, taking care to stay under the streetlights. He didn't need a second fistfight tonight, not with everything that was happening tomorrow: helping Francie with the funeral plans, then meeting Frank and their father at the hotel, getting them checked in, and going to dinner with them. It exhausted Charlie just thinking about it.

Though there was one bright note . . . in the morning, he was going to see his mother's childhood home. Even if nothing remained but a falling-down shack, it was a part of her that he'd never seen before, a key to the past she'd rarely shared.

And June would be there. In fact, he decided he'd pick her and Francie up at the Holiday, to make up for hurting her feelings earlier. Charlie smiled in the dark. Hell — he'd risk getting the tar beat out of him again for another one of those smiles.

Chapter 42
Virgie

Virgie stayed up much too late writing in her diary. So much had happened, and her head was full of possibilities that made sense only when she wrote them down. She started by making a list of everything that had occurred since her last entry.

1. Went to Dr. P's office with W's note and the money W gave me. His nurse gave me a bottle of pills in a sack and I asked for a receet so W would know I did not cheat her but she said no and also there was no name on the bottle like Mother's pills.

2. I took the pills to W and she took one right away but I still don't know what is wrong with her because she looks Fine. She helped me with the Business and we made a flyer and I copied it during lunch and Mother asked What are you doing and I said don't worry it's for my College savings and

she said okay. I gave out eight of them so far to the ladies who were having lunch and two of them ordered rings!

3. I saw Mrs. S leaving with Mrs. M's daughter A.M. who walks with a limp. She has brown hair and brown eyes and is medium height. Mrs. M seemed happy to see her but then she got a little mad about something and then A.M. and Mrs. S left in a taxi.

4. When A.M. and Mrs. S came back later Mrs. S was wearing a fancy new suit. Also a delivery came from Danforth's which is Very expensive that Clyde took up to Mrs. S's room. (Where is she getting money to pay for all those new clothes or did she con A.M.!!!)

5. A Man came to see Mrs. S. He was tall and had medium-dark Brown hair and I'm not sure what color eyes and was probably the same age as Mr. Raynard at school and he had on gray pants and a shirt with little blue and white squares. The Man's hair was the same color as Mrs. M's but maybe she dies hers but also he looks like her in the face but handsom. MRS. M'S SON???? The Man and Mrs. S went to the Lounge to talk

and I listened behind the Curtains in the library even though it was Dinner Time and I couldn't hear everything they were saying but she was Flirting with him but then she got mad and stomped out of the Lounge and the man drove away in a black truck with HFC and some other stuff on the side like the Lepper and Sons truck with the big blue fosset so maybe he is a plumber or other kind of Repair Man and no relation to Mrs. M, and I went to the Closet next to her room and listened and there was ANOTHER Man in her room and he was her Acomplis! And he was so mad that she wouldn't give him the ring but she didn't tell him it is missing and also she sounded scared.

At that point Virgie had chewed on her pencil for a while, thinking about her various theories about the case. She drew a line down the middle of a fresh page and on the left wrote *Facts* and on the right a question mark.

Facts	?
Mrs. S talked to a Man in the Lounge	Flirting?? Trying to get a Date? Mrs. M's son?
She was upset after	He has a girlfriend or Wife already? He doesn't like her?
There was a man in her room who was mad and asking her where the ring was	Her Acomplis who she double-crossed? Was she trying to hide from him? How did he find her? Climbed up fire escape?
She cried after he left	Scared? He will Kill her??? Needs money for sick relative or Child? He kidnapped her other Child?

After that came more pencil-chewing and thinking until Virgie finally closed the book and put it back in its secure hiding place. For every clue she found, there seemed to be more questions. Though sometimes, that was just the way it went on a case.

As she was sliding the panel back over the

hiding place, Virgie hesitated. She reached for the leatherette case and took out the ring, then got her notebook and opened it to the page where she'd pasted the story about Norma Shearer's engagement ring and examined the photograph. Norma's ring had only one diamond, while Mrs. Carothers's ring was much bigger, with *two* rows of diamonds around the big red stone in the middle. If Norma's ring was worth nineteen thousand dollars, Mrs. Carothers's was probably worth at least twice as much. Thirty-eight thousand dollars! The unbelievable amount of money made Virgie feel faint, so she put the ring back in the case and stuck it back in the hole. She had started to wish she had never taken it at all — if only she'd left it where it was, Mrs. Samples would already be gone, her former accomplice wouldn't have found her and threatened to kill her, and she would have had the money to fix whatever problem had driven her to a life of crime. Now Mrs. Samples was so desperate she was willing to try to con a man whose mother had just died, which seemed pretty low, but Virgie knew that desperate people committed desperate deeds. In a way, they couldn't help it.

There was no way around it — Virgie was

in over her head this time. She stared at the notes she had made, trying to figure out what was most likely to have driven Mrs. Samples to kill an innocent woman. But maybe it wasn't that simple. Maybe, just maybe, Mrs. Carothers had taken the ring off before she died, and left it out where Mrs. Samples just couldn't help herself from taking it. In which case the rumor going around the hotel might actually be true — that Mrs. Carothers had thrown herself into the river because of a broken heart, not because she was murdered.

Virgie needed to talk to someone who knew more about broken hearts and desperate lovers. But there was only one person she could think of who fit the bill. Tomorrow, Virgie would find Willy and ask her — as soon as she got up. Ever since she'd arrived in Reno, Willy had never shown her face before noon.

But that left the problem of Mrs. Samples's former accomplice. Virgie would never forgive herself if he killed Mrs. Samples in cold blood and she hadn't even tried to stop him. Warning Mrs. Samples would do no good — she was a con artist *and* a desperate woman, and Virgie was well aware from reading George Barton that that meant she was capable of just about anything except caution.

If Virgie told her mother, she would likely kick Mrs. Samples out.

If she went to the cops, they'd never believe her just because she was a kid — and she didn't have a criminal defense lawyer for a father like Nancy Drew who could get the authorities to listen to her.

She couldn't even tell Willy — not all of it, anyway. Willy was too much of a gossip, and Virgie was going to have to be very careful not to give away any details that could cause even more trouble if she blabbed to the wrong person.

It was out of Virgie's hands: if Mrs. Samples was dead set on pursuing her reckless scheme, no one could stop her. All Virgie could do was try to keep an eye on her and make sure she didn't make any dumb mistakes that would get her killed or Patty kidnapped.

Virgie's eyes fell on the copy of George Barton's *Inside the Mind of a Master Criminal* on her desk, and it occurred to her that there was one thing she could do. She'd been rereading the chapter on the Lindbergh baby's kidnapper, in which Barton mentioned a "copycat" criminal who, a year after the famous case, struck it rich by nabbing a rich housewife and sending a ransom note composed of letters cut from the newspaper and pasted on a plain piece of stationery. The ransom was paid and the kidnapper was never found because there were no fingerprints and no clues to be had from handwriting or the typewriter used.

Maybe there was a way to warn the cops after all.

CHAPTER 43
WILLY

At 9:20 the next morning, Willy was in the
lobby with a brand-new checkbook in her
hand, but Mrs. Swanson wasn't at her desk.
Willy found Virgie stuffing an envelope into
the slot of the bronze postbox down the hall.

"What do you have there, honey, an ap-
plication to the FBI?"

Virgie whirled around, startled. When she
saw it was Willy, she scowled and said, "You
shouldn't go sneaking up on people like
that!"

"Sorry," Willy said, "but I wasn't *sneaking*. I was looking for your mother."

"She's in the kitchen." Virgie gave the letter a final shove, and it popped through.
"And it's just something a guest wanted me
to mail."

"Ah." The kid was obviously lying, but
Willy didn't have time to shoot the breeze
just now. "Well, have a good day."

"I sold two rings," Virgie said. "One silver

and one gold."

"What did I tell you?" Willy said, already on the move. "It's all in the pitch."

Virgie hurried after her. "Can I talk to you about something?"

"Sure, sweets, but come find me a little later, all right? I need to take care of something now."

She found Mrs. Swanson with a clipboard, counting cans in the larder. She held up a finger, and Willy waited while she wrote something down.

"Good morning, Mrs. Carroll," she said. "May I help you?"

"Yes. I'd like to pay my room bill."

Mrs. Swanson considered her coolly, her gray eyes giving nothing away. "Perhaps I misunderstood, but a representative of your gentleman friend called yesterday to tell me that your plans had changed and that you would be leaving us."

"Well, my plans have changed *back*," Willy said. She tore off the top check and handed it over. "Please fill that in with whatever I owe. And from now on, please consult only me regarding any future charges."

Mrs. Swanson glanced at the check. "I'll be happy to do so. The only problem that I see is that your check is from a newly established account. In a case like that, I insist on holding it until it clears . . ."

Willy rolled her eyes and took off the ruby bracelet Harry had given her for Valentine's Day. "Look, this bracelet's worth over three hundred dollars. How about you hang on to it until then? I'm not going anywhere, but if it makes you feel better —"

"That won't be necessary." Mrs. Swanson gave her a rare smile — it disappeared almost as quickly as it flashed across her face. "My daughter seems to be quite taken with you. I suppose that's the only character reference I need."

"Oh." Willy wished she could start the conversation over. She hadn't slept well, and she hadn't had her coffee, and she hadn't meant to be so rude. "Well, thank you very much. You've got a real little firecracker in that kid."

"Don't I know it," Mrs. Swanson said. "Now, why don't we go into my office and take care of this like civilized ladies."

336

CHAPTER 44
JUNE

June paced the lobby, fretting. Francie had called to say that she wasn't feeling well and June should go on to the house without her, but Clyde had gone into town to buy a part for the boiler, Mrs. Swanson was busy with the breakfast service, and June couldn't call a taxi because Francie still hadn't paid her and she wasn't sure she had enough money of her own left to cover the fare. Meanwhile, precious minutes were passing and she still had so much to do at the house before the rented tables and chairs arrived this afternoon.

Alice came into the lobby carrying a huge bunch of tulips in a cut-glass vase.

"Oh, Alice," June said, "I'm so glad to see you."

"You too! Though . . . given your outfit, I think we may have to go shopping again."

June touched the scarf she'd used to tie back her hair, embarrassed by her worn day dress and old shoes. "This is just for working at the house. I didn't dare wear any of my new things — I'll be on my hands and knees scrubbing and they'd be ruined. Those tulips are beautiful."

"Oh, these." Alice looked down at the pink and white blooms. "They're for my mother, but . . . I don't really want to deliver them myself. We had words last night at dinner and I think we both might need a little time to cool off."

"My mother and I used to argue all the time," June said. "I loved her more than anyone in the world, but sometimes we just set each other off."

"Us too," Alice said. "Honestly, I think I'm just too old to be living at home. Sometimes I think she forgets I'm twenty-five years old. And about last night, I *know* I'm right but . . . I could have been more sensitive about her feelings."

"Do you want me to run the tulips up to her room?"

"Actually, I think I'll just leave them at the front desk. Do you suppose there is anyone around who can take them?"

"Mrs. Swanson's out back with a laundry delivery," a voice said. Willy Carroll strolled in wearing big black sunglasses and candy-apple-red lipstick. "Good morning, June.

Lovely outfit."

"Oh, it's you," June said flatly, not even bothering to pretend to be polite.

"Who's your friend?"

Willy had some nerve to stand there in her tight sweater and floozy shoes, June thought, waiting to be introduced. If Francie knew, she'd be furious.

"This is Alice Meeker. Alice, this is Wilhelmina Carroll."

Alice looked taken aback. "Willy Carroll . . . you're Mr. Carothers's —"

"— friend. His very *good* friend," Willy cut in. "I'm sorry about Mrs. Carothers, I truly am. I know your mother is furious with me, but maybe you can make her see reason. I'm just marking time here in Reno like everyone else, trying to put a bad marriage behind me."

Alice drew herself to her full height, glaring down her nose at Willy. "I will *not* speak to my mother about you — I don't know how you can even suggest such a thing. If you had any decency at all you'd stay out of sight while the rest of us are grieving."

"Fine, I'll stay out of the way, but you've got me all wrong." Willy minced out of the room, her full skirt swirling around her shapely legs.

"What a horrible woman," Alice said.

"And yet I can't say I'm all that surprised. Discretion unfortunately is not among Harry's best qualities." Almost as an afterthought, Alice added, "Though what if she tries to come to the service? Poor Charlie and Frank."

June was tempted to suggest that they could just pay someone to keep Willy away, since Charlie seemed to believe everything could be solved with money. But before she had the chance, Alice said, "Speak of the devil — look who's coming up the drive! And — oh my gracious, what on earth —"

Charlie bounded up the porch steps, taking them two at a time. He was dressed in the same old pants as the day he'd arrived and another faded plaid shirt — but the left side of his face was bruised and bandaged, the eye purpled and swollen nearly shut.

"Before the two of you say anything," he said, "it looks much worse than it actually is."

"What *happened* to you?"

Charlie kissed Alice on the cheek. "We got fine weather again today," he said. "Blue skies and a nice breeze. Are those flowers for me? You're too kind, Alley Cat."

"Don't change the subject," Alice said in an exasperated tone. "You obviously got in a fight. What were you thinking?"

"Well, I didn't *start* the fight." Charlie shrugged. "I only defended myself — and not very well."

"Were you robbed?" Despite the awful things Charlie had said, June felt terrible for him — she had heard that grifters cased the casinos and lurked in alleys, looking for drunk out-of-towners to separate from their money. "I hope they didn't get away with much."

"I didn't lose anything but my pride," Charlie said.

"Oh, Charlie." Alice sighed. "You're impossible. What are you doing here, anyway? You should be lying down with ice on that."

"I've come to give June a hand out at the house. She's already put in a lot of work getting it ready for the service, and she shouldn't have to do it all herself. Care to join us?"

Alice looked from one to the other with a shrewd little smile. "No, you two go on ahead. I've got Dad's car, and I need to return it to him. Besides, I've got to get back to the hotel for . . . a thing I need to do."

"What sort of thing?"

"None of your business," Alice said. "When are Frank and your father getting in?"

"Three. So we've got no time to waste —

June's going to have me on my hands and knees with a toothbrush, just like when I was in the marines."

June blushed, wanting to tell him not to bother, but she couldn't very well do so in front of Alice. Besides, she needed a ride.

"Make sure to keep an eye on him," Alice told June. "He's lazy — he used to always try to get me to do his chores when we were children. What are you doing tonight, Charlie?"

"I was supposed to have dinner with Dad and Frank," he replied, his smile fading. "But Dad called this morning to say something had come up, so the three of us are meeting up for drinks earlier instead. He's being pretty vague."

"Well, that's understandable," Alice said kindly. "I'm sure this is very upsetting for him. Please give him and Frank my regards, and perhaps I'll see all of you later."

June waited until Alice was out of earshot to say, "I told you I could handle the cleaning myself."

"You did — after I made a perfect ass of myself. I was thinking I could apologize on the way, since you look like you're itching to get started."

June wavered. Charlie actually looked contrite — and she had to give him credit for coming despite his injuries. "Oh, all right."

Charlie picked up the bucket of supplies. "Your coach awaits. Now, shall we go and get started? I have a feeling you have pretty high standards."

June followed him to the truck parked in the drive and allowed him to help her in. As she squeezed into the passenger seat, she caught his scent of soap and tobacco, a good, honest manly smell that made her feel a little dizzy.

Stop it, she scolded herself. Even if she had forgiven him, she needed to keep the focus on the task at hand. After all, Charlie would be seeing his mother's house for the first time, and it was bound to be an emotional experience.

He got in gingerly, wincing as he slid into the seat.

"You're sure you're all right?"

"Nothing that a Bloody Mary wouldn't fix," he said through gritted teeth. "But it's going to be a long day, so I need to keep my wits about me. After we finish your chores, I've got to clean myself up before I meet my father and brother at the hotel, and then . . ." He glanced over at her as he drove. "Were you going to give me directions, by the way? Or should I just drive around aimlessly and hope we happen upon the house?"

"Oh!" June said, reddening. "I'm sorry — you should have turned back there."

Charlie grinned as he made a U-turn. "I won't make a comment about women and directions," he said. "But you just confirmed one of my father's theories."

"You'll just stay on this road for about two miles," June said, ignoring the crack. "We might get stuck behind a tractor."

"Doesn't bother me . . . just tell me when to turn."

June fell silent, watching the lovely landscape roll by, the gentle hills painted in green and gold, wildflowers adding splashes of color. The truck was well maintained and the ride was smooth, a far cry from the rusty old sedan that Stan drove.

Thinking of Stan brought back the fear June had been struggling to ignore since he'd broken into her room last night. She'd locked the window tightly, even though it made her room stuffy, and got up to check it twice in the middle of the night. Stan wouldn't be getting in through the window again unless he broke the glass, in which case June was fully prepared to grab Patty and run into the hall screaming at the top of her lungs. Patty had been sleeping in

June's bed anyway; it almost seemed a shame, since there was another very nice bed in the other room, one she could have had all to herself — and who knew when Patty would see such luxury again?

"Penny for your thoughts," Charlie said, putting on the brakes as several fat geese waddled across the street.

"Oh, I wasn't thinking anything," she lied. "Just enjoying the view. Look at those calves — they can't be more than a few weeks old!"

But Charlie didn't look, at least not at the cows. Instead he fixed her with a thoughtful gaze before coasting slowly to the side of the road and turning off the ignition. "All right, how about this. I'll pay you a penny to listen to *my* thoughts. Sound like a deal?"

"I'm not sure I have a choice, seeing as I'm stuck in this truck with you."

"Yes. Well . . . this fellow I met last night, the one who gave me these souvenirs on my face? It was the strangest thing . . . he asked after you."

June snapped to attention. "Me?"

"Yeah. Well, more precisely, he told me to stay away from you. You could almost call it a threat, seeing as how he used his boots to get the message to my ribs."

"Oh, no," June said faintly. "I'm so sorry. It's all my fault."

She shouldn't be surprised — if Stan had seen her talking to Charlie, he would be furious. She buried her face in her hands, wondering if she'd been stupid to leave Patty with Mrs. Oglesby — but it seemed like the safest place for her to be. After all, even if Stan forced his way into the hotel somehow, he couldn't exactly go door to door searching for Patty.

"It's *his* fault — you didn't have anything to do with it. I'm going to go out on a limb and guess that this guy doesn't want a divorce as much as you do. Now, I can't say I blame any man for kicking himself for letting a girl like you get away — but I draw the line at him kicking anyone else, especially you. Let him come after me again — I'll be ready next time. But June . . . don't you think you should go to the police?"

"I can't," she whispered. She didn't dare look at Charlie, at the injuries he'd gotten because of her. As jealous and mercurial as Stan was, Charlie was lucky to be alive — especially because Stan owned a gun.

"Why not?"

"Because . . ." June shrugged helplessly. There was hardly any point trying to keep it to herself now. "All right, I'll tell you. But you must promise not to tell Francie. Or anyone else. And you absolutely can't tell the police."

"That doesn't make any sense," Charlie said. "But all right, I promise."

"Stan is my husband. We've been married for almost five years. He didn't lay a finger on me for the first year."

"Give the man a medal," Charlie muttered.

"After the first time he hit me, it didn't happen again for a long time. I was pregnant, and then Patty was born, and . . . Stan lost his job, he had trouble with his boss. Things were hard, and . . . well." She shrugged. "It wasn't so bad, really. Lots of women have it worse. My uncle used to hit my aunt, half the women in the neighborhood used to show up at my grandmother's house when it happened, because my aunt wouldn't tell her. Besides, I know how to calm Stan down, most of the time. It's just — a couple of months ago he came home late, he'd been drinking, and he started in on me the minute he came through the door. Patty came in the kitchen because the noise woke her up, and he didn't see her and . . . he threw a plate and scared her to bits. I couldn't let it happen again. After that . . . I had to get her out of there. Away from *him*."

June didn't dare look at Charlie. She'd

never told another soul the truth, though she was pretty sure Francie and Vi weren't the first to have guessed. As hard as she tried to cover the bruises, when she looked in the mirror, she could see that something had changed; her eyes looked haunted, and worry had etched lines into her skin.

"I thought I was careful when I ran away," she went on, "but I made a mistake, a bad one, and Stan followed us here. I think he's been spying on me — he must have seen me in the garden with you. He probably paid off one of the staff to tell him what room I'm in." Stan could be charming; he'd probably convinced the security guard he only wanted to sneak in to surprise his girlfriend. "And now that I think about it, he must have paid someone to tell him where we went to dinner that first night, because he showed up and made a scene with the maître d'. He didn't see me and I didn't tell Francie and your mother who he was; I was too ashamed."

"But how did he know where you were staying? Francie told me you had reservations somewhere else before you met them."

"You don't know Stan. He's the kind of man who would go from one place to the next until he found me. Once he realized I wasn't at the Twilight Inn, he probably just asked them where else women stay when they come for a divorce. There's only a handful of ladies' hotels unless you go outside the city limits, so it wouldn't have taken long to try them all. I've been traveling under my maiden name, but he has a picture of me in his wallet."

"That's a lot of trouble to go to, to hunt you down like this. Doesn't he have a job? Responsibilities?"

"He wouldn't care," June said with feeling. "He thinks of me as his property, you see. He'd be furious that I dared to leave. And he won't stop until . . . he won't stop. I'm just hoping I can avoid him until I get my divorce, and then Patty and I can leave and go somewhere he'll never find us."

Why was she telling Charlie all this? He was barely more than a stranger . . . but he made her feel as if he truly cared. And it felt so good to tell someone, after years of being trapped in her marriage, trying to hide the evidence of her husband's anger under her clothes, making excuses whenever she hurt too much to go to church or a meeting at school.

"June — you can't keep living like this. Fearing for your life."

"I don't have a choice. Stan wants me back, and he'll just keep after me until I

349

give up and go with him. And if I go to the police, he'll find a way to take Patty away from me. I know that sounds crazy, but you don't know him. He'll take her just because he knows it would kill me. I can't lose her, Charlie . . . I can't."

"The police will lock him up," Charlie said, barely concealing his anger. "A man like that shouldn't be out on the streets — there are laws against the things he's done to you."

June was already shaking her head. "He's smart. He knows how to talk to them. My neighbors called the police out twice, but Stan . . . by the time they left, they were cracking jokes and shaking his hand. When I had to go to the hospital because he hit me so hard I needed stitches, he told them the old hen house collapsed while I was out hanging the wash, and he acted so worried about me, pestering them to let him see me, to see for himself that I was all right. He had every last one of them fooled, even the nurses. And the thing was . . . I think he fooled himself too. He was sorry — he's always sorry, and he tells me it'll be different, and I think he believes it when he says it."

A single tear had escaped and was sliding down her cheek. Charlie leaned over and brushed it away with his thumb, so tenderly that June wanted to rest her cheek on his hand, to allow him to comfort her. But comfort wouldn't keep Patty safe.

"June. If it isn't safe for you here, then we need to take you somewhere else. I know lawyers — judges. Let me take you back to San Francisco. You'll be safe there while we build a case against him."

"You can't go anywhere — you're here for your mother's funeral!"

Charlie shook his head impatiently. "Then you and Patty go on ahead without me. I'll have someone meet your train and take you somewhere safe."

"I'm not going anywhere," June said. "Not until after. Your mother was kind to me, Charlie, when she had no reason in the world to be. She took me in and made me feel like — like I mattered. Besides, a few more days won't make a difference. Patty is safe during the day, because she stays with another guest at the hotel and nobody knows about it but Francie, and certainly not the guards. At night she's with me and I'm going to keep the window locked. Francie is paying me enough that I can go anywhere I want once I'm divorced. I haven't decided yet, but I've got family in Oregon — and one of my cousins is a deputy there. They'd look after us."

"At least let me move you to my hotel. He won't know — we can get you a suite on the high rollers' floor, where there's security around the clock."

"Charlie, that's very kind, but no. The best thing you can do for me right now is drive me to the house and let me get to work. I appreciate your help, and your kindness, but I'm not some naïve little girl. I've been looking out for Patty her whole life, and I'm not going to let anything happen to her."

"My mother would never forgive me if I let something happen to *you*," Charlie said, but he knew he was beat.

"I promise I'll be fine," June said, relenting as he turned the key in the ignition and eased back onto the road. "I'm sure your mother would be proud of you for offering to help. But right now I just want her to have the best memorial service possible, the one she would have wanted."

"I'll say one thing," Charlie said. "You're as stubborn as she was. I can see why the two of you hit it off."

June lay her head back against the seat, feeling the warmth of the sun on her face. It was only a brief respite from the mistakes of the past and the worries ahead — but for a few glorious moments she forced thoughts of Stan out of her mind and tried to remember what it was like to be just a girl going for a drive with a boy.

CHAPTER 45
FRANCIE

Francie's stomach growled, but the thought of eating nauseated her. She'd tried to get out of bed once already and made it as far as the bathroom, where she drank a glass of tap water before being overcome with dizziness and a pounding headache and crawled back into bed.

Since then she'd been unable to stop thinking about last night. Every time she went over it, she remembered some mortifying new detail. Why on earth had she thought all those cocktails would help? At first, they *had* made it easier to see Arthur with Bill. It had almost been a relief, to find that Bill was perfectly ordinary — nice, and a bit shy. After the second cocktail Francie had felt clever, as if everything that came out of her mouth was witty and people were interested in what she had to say.

But then . . . then it got kind of blurry. The sparkling conversation took a nasty turn as she kept drinking. Arthur had said some things, and so had Alice, and all of a sudden it felt as if they were ganging up on her — *laughing* at her. And they wouldn't *listen* — they didn't seem to understand how mortified she would be when people found out about Arthur, how her friends would talk about her behind her back, how she'd suddenly be left off invitation lists and her name would be a magnet for pity. "Poor Francie," they'd say, until someone made a joke, and then they'd all laugh.

Arthur said he was careful, that no one had to know, but it made Francie dizzy just thinking of how many people he might run into in a week. San Francisco was a small town in some ways, at least for people like them — for Francie's entire married life, she'd moved in the same small circle, shopped in the same markets, and sent her children to the same schools. All it would take was a chance sighting at a gallery, a careless moment in a movie theater when Arthur and Bill thought no one was watching, and her social life might as well be over.

But no, the two of them and even Alice seemed to think that their new life was something to celebrate. Who had given them the right, she wanted to know? She had a vague memory of Arthur driving her home, and having to pull over so that she could get out of the car and . . . oh, it was mortifying to think about. She'd only gotten that drunk twice before in all the years she'd known Arthur, and the first time was actually her first experience with alcohol, at a dance. They'd practically been children! They'd grown up together in a way, learning to make a home and raise a family. She knew every inch of his body, from the delicate shells of his ears to his broad, flat fingernails, to the mole on the small of his back that he hadn't even realized was there until she told him.

And yet last night when he pulled over to the side of the road, he'd stayed in the car with his face averted, to give her privacy while she vomited on the ground. Even in her drunken state she'd noticed and felt deeply ashamed, as though it was a stranger waiting in the car. In a way Arthur and she *were* strangers now, with new identities — one a homosexual, the other a divorcée. But did that make all the years they'd spent together a lie? She couldn't bear it — in fact she'd cried several times this morning thinking about it, making damp spots on the pillowcase.

She remembered a conversation they'd had the week before Arthur had popped the question. The engagement wasn't exactly a surprise; they'd discussed it at length before it happened. Partly, it was because they'd been dating only six months and Arthur had wanted to make sure he wasn't rushing her (he wasn't — nearly every one of Francie's friends was married, and she was ready), and partly because Arthur was methodical about everything he did. Or at least that's what Francie had thought at the time, since all the questions he asked her were practical: where she wanted to live, how many children they would have, whether they would have a dog or a cat, how they would cope with their aging parents. They'd even discussed which newspapers to take and what stationer they would use.

But one evening at dinner at the little neighborhood restaurant that had become their favorite, he brought up a subject they had never discussed before, one for which Francie was not prepared. She had actually thought Arthur might be planning to propose that night and was wearing a new dress she'd bought with her mother only that afternoon.

Arthur waited until Francie had finished eating. He'd barely touched his own dinner, which Francie had chalked up to jitters.

"Francie," he said rather formally, after

the waiter had taken their plates away, "you may have noticed that I'm not the most . . . affectionate man."

"But that's not true!" she said. "You're wonderfully thoughtful — I've kept every one of those lovely letters you wrote me. And you always walk me to the door, and you've sent me so many roses I could fill the back garden with them."

"Ah, yes, well." Arthur dabbed absently at a smudge of sauce on the tablecloth with his napkin. "That sort of thing, yes, of course. And you must know how fond I am of you."

Francie smiled; that was her exceedingly proper boyfriend's way of saying "I love you."

"And I of you, silly."

"But there are other aspects of a marriage . . . *physical* aspects, shall we say . . ."

He trailed off helplessly, and for a horrible moment Francie thought he was trying to ask her if she was a virgin. Of course she was! She'd lived in a sorority at college, then moved back into her room in the house she grew up in with her parents — Francie had known since childhood that she would live at home until she married.

"Arthur, if you are wondering if I am . . . *intact* . . ." She whispered the word, glancing around the room at the other diners to make sure no one could hear.

"Oh no, not at all!" Arthur was aghast. "Francie, I would never think that of you — I hold you in the highest esteem. You're the most wonderful woman I've ever known."

"Well — good, then." Francie wondered if she was expected to ask him about his experiences. It was a conversation many of her girlfriends had with their fiancés, one which many men apparently resisted, though the consensus among her circle was that most men arrived at marriage these days with a fair bit of experience. Some girls even thought it was for the best — better, the thinking went, that *someone* knew what to expect on the wedding night.

"Yes. Well. It's just that, I've noticed, something about me is that I don't have strong appetites in that department. Don't get me wrong, the doc assures me that my health is tip-top, that I should have no trouble fathering children, but I've never been a man who experiences strong urges."

Slowly, Francie was catching on to what Arthur was struggling to say. And it was a wonderful relief! On the few occasions she'd allowed herself to think of the marriage bed, it had been with a good measure of trepidation. All that her mother would say on the subject was that procreation among married couples was blessed by God and therefore nothing to be ashamed of, when the time came — but she offered precious little in the way of details, and since Francie's parents had slept in separate beds for as long as she could remember, Francie was dubious that her mother had much wisdom to offer anyway.

Ever since adolescence, Francie had found that she didn't have the same interest in these matters as her friends did. In fact it was rather a shock the day she and her best friend reclined naked on the floor in front of the mirror in her mother's dressing room with their legs spread, staring in wonder at the mystery between their legs. Her friend had recently begun menstruating and been given a pamphlet published by the Kotex company by her mother, and the pair had pored over the illustrations — but the reality was nothing like she'd envisioned. It was all so . . . unexpectedly pretty, the folds of pink flesh slightly ruffled, like the petals of her mother's prized picotee tulips.

But when Francie had begun dating — and yes, petting, since Francie was a bold and curious girl — she'd been disappointed to find that boys' explorations moved her very little. They squeezed her breasts and pinched her nipples as if they were trying to pick blackberries; they rubbed between her legs as if trying to start a fire with the friction between her cotton panties and her crotch. It was quite underwhelming.

She enjoyed kissing Arthur, loved the soft warmth of his lips, the sweetness from the hard candies he was forever sucking. She liked it when their foreheads touched, when she felt the brush of his eyelashes against her cheek. She loved it when he circled his arms around her and pulled her tighter, burying his face in her hair as though he found comfort there. She *loved* him, with all her heart, and when they held each other, she felt content.

"I, em, also do not have strong urges," she said haltingly. "Not that I would know, of course, but I've never been inclined . . . I haven't especially enjoyed . . ."

Damn this awkwardness between them — it was as though there were no words for the things they were trying to express. Of course Francie knew the crude terms men used as shorthand for depraved acts — she had older brothers, after all — but how was she to reassure Arthur that she would be perfectly happy for things to proceed slowly — even, if possible, antiseptically.

"Well, that's good then," Arthur said, taking her hand. "Isn't it? We'll want children before long . . . but I promise to always be respectful."

"Thank you, Arthur," Francie said, her voice thickened by emotion. "I'm so glad we feel the same way. As long as we're together, I know it will be fine."

And it had been, for the most part. Margie came along almost precisely nine months after their wedding day, Jimmy twenty-four months after that. By the time Alice came, the frequency of their lovemaking had decreased to once every month or two, but they still often held each other as they drifted off to sleep, and Arthur kissed her every morning before he left the house and again first thing when he returned. They rarely quarreled, and Francie secretly thought she was luckier than many of her friends who had to fend off their husbands' advances several times a week.

By the time Alice was in high school, sex took place so rarely that when it did happen, Arthur and Francie were shy with each other, fumbling in the dark. The funny thing was, Francie did remember the very last time. It had been eight years ago, and she remembered the date because it had been their anniversary. They'd ordered wine at dinner, but Arthur, who was getting over a bad cold, drank little, and Francie was tipsy when they got into the taxi to go home. Alice was visiting Margie and Roy in Sacramento, and Francie had felt emboldened walking into the empty house, almost daring when she changed into her satin nightgown. She came to bed and turned off the light and began stroking Arthur's back, and when he didn't respond, she reached lower, under his pajamas — and Arthur had said, "Oh — I didn't realize — give me a moment, darling, will you?" And then it had taken him quite a while, the movement of his fist making the bed shake, until he finally rolled over and climbed on top of her.

So, not a passionate marriage, but she'd always thought it a strong one. Until the day when Arthur finally told her the truth. He'd always been discreet, he said, almost pleadingly, and never allowed any of his infrequent assignations to move beyond a single, anonymous night. There was no question that they'd stay married, and if anything, their friendship grew stronger after Francie got over the initial shock. She refused to think about where Arthur went on those rare nights he stayed out late, and things continued much as they always had — until Arthur met Bill.

Bill was different, he said, almost in apology. Bill was kind, and funny, and thought-ful — he was sure that Francie would quite like him if she'd met him at a party, for instance. In that moment, seeing the light in her husband's eyes, Francie knew that she'd lost part of him forever, but — it seemed strange now to think of it — she had accepted this loss with equanimity. After all, doesn't everyone have to accept disappointments in a long marriage? She certainly didn't have the body she'd been so proud of before bearing children; she no longer paid close attention when Arthur talked about his day.

It wasn't until last night, when she'd actu-ally seen the two men together for the first time, that she understood. Even separated by Alice's preemptive seating arrangement, they had been connected by an invisible thread — when one spoke, the other hung on every word; when the basket of dinner rolls was set in front of Arthur, Bill passed him the butter without being asked. When Bill said something funny, Arthur grinned like a boy. And when Francie and Alice returned from the restroom, the two men were leaning close enough to whisper.

The intimacy between them was some-thing that she and Arthur had never had. Had it been up to her, she would have soldiered on with him for the rest of their lives and never felt that she'd missed anything. But now she felt almost as though she'd been cheated. She wasn't jealous — how could one be jealous of a man like Bill? — but she was left with a hole inside her that was not the precise shape of Arthur's absence.

"There's the cemetery," June said, pointing at the gravestones dotting the gentle hill that rose off to the left. The cemetery was small, a couple acres surrounded by a split-rail fence with a row of mature trees along two sides. "It's really pretty when you get up near the top — you can see out over the whole valley. And the house is just above the far side. If there wasn't a fence, you could drive right up the hill into the back-yard."

Charlie felt a sense of anticipation build-ing inside him. He'd been keeping his expectations deliberately low, reminding himself that many years had passed since his mother had set foot there. Unsupervised caretakers were likely to treat the place poorly, and since it had stood empty the past few years, it was probably choked with weeds, infested with rats, possibly vandal-ized. June had said it was "cute," but she seemed determined to put a bright face on everything. Also, she might be concealing the worst of the damage from him out of concern for his feelings.

The woman in the truck with him caused unexpectedly strong feelings in Charlie. When he'd pulled over to the side of the road to listen to her story, he'd been ready to turn the truck around and go after her worthless husband. Sucker-punching Charlie was bad enough, but any man who struck a woman should, in Charlie's opinion, be made to feel just as powerless, as he was being beaten to within an inch of his life.

But anger at her worthless husband wasn't the only reason Charlie felt protective toward her. There was the matter of how she would provide for herself, raising a child alone with no means of support that Charlie could discern.

On the rare occasions that his mother talked about her childhood in Reno he'd understood her family had been poor, but she described a life full of love and fun — she remembered a swing her father had hung from the tree in the backyard, or a duck she'd been given by the rancher down the road to raise as a pet.

It had been a long time since she'd talked about the past. Now that Charlie knew the truth, he thought he understood her reasons for returning to the place she'd grown up.

"Turn left," June said, "and then see that mailbox up there on the right? Past the little red house? Turn in there but mind the ruts."

Charlie drove carefully, but the truck jounced across the hard earth. At some point, someone had driven after a rain when the ground was wet and left deep gashes in the earth; without them it would have been difficult to tell where the yard ended and the drive began, it was so choked with weeds.

But despite that, the house was every bit as charming as his mother had described. It resembled a child's drawing of a house, a little white box with a triangle of a roof, a door and two windows in the front. The siding had been painted recently enough that it still looked bright and fresh, and the shutters were a sunny yellow. The porch and steps were in good shape, and two brightly colored rag rugs hung over the rail.

He felt June watching him as he parked the truck. He turned to her and smiled. "Shall I assume you were the one who hung the rugs there?"

June blushed. "I took them out to beat them, and I thought a little air wouldn't hurt. Besides, I want to scrub the floors before I put them back down. Do you want to go in?"

That's what they were here for, wasn't it? And yet he could tell June was nervous, gauging his reaction every step of the way.

"I tried to ask the neighbors if they knew anyone who could mow," she said, "but no one was home, so I left a note. Over there, I thought we'd have the cars parked — I hired two fellows recommended by Mrs. Swanson. They'll have to be careful, though, because there's an old foundation under all those weeds."

As she chattered away, leading the way up onto the porch, Charlie tried to imagine his mother sitting there on a summer day sipping lemonade and playing with her cat. He had no pictures of her as a child, but he imagined her as wiry and active, skipping instead of walking, helping her mother without being asked — which was probably a load of crap, but he had nothing but his imagination to go on.

June took a key from her pocket and unlocked the door, then hesitated. "I should give you this," she said. "I found it hidden behind the porchlight. It's yours now."

"You keep it, at least until this is all over with."

June nodded and dropped it back into her

pocket. She opened the door, stepping out of the way so he could enter.

The little front room was as neat as a pin, empty save for an upright piano. Lacy white curtains fluttered in the windows, and a broom and bucket sat in the corner.

"I washed the walls and laundered and pressed the curtains," June said. "Picture this room with little round tables with pretty tablecloths and flowers — the floral arrangements will make a big difference."

"June, it's — it's perfect just as it is," Charlie said. He walked slowly through the room, pausing to open the door of a built-in cabinet, hoping to find . . . what? Anything that his mother had touched — any evidence of her presence: a hairpin, a pencil, a doll. But it was empty, the shelves lined with faded flowery paper.

Past the front room was a hall with two small bedrooms on one side and a bath on the other, and then the kitchen at the back of the house and a screen porch out the back door. That was all.

How odd it must have been for his mother to find herself in the mansion on Nob Hill after she married. His father loved to tell the story of how he'd leveraged himself to buy the house because it came with a title — the Brannan House, named for the man who built it, the founder of the first news-paper in the city. Harry never could resist a brush with fame, no matter how inconsequential.

"I think this was her bedroom," June said, leading him into the smaller of the two rooms. It was empty except for an old iron bed, a small pine desk, and a straight-backed chair next to the window. "See? She would have seen the tree every morning when she woke up."

Charlie put his hand on the bed frame, wishing for some sign from her . . . some signal of her presence. It was silly, of course — Charlie didn't believe in an afterlife, something he'd never admitted to anyone — but he suddenly missed his mother so much it hurt.

"You were with her on her last night," he said haltingly. "I wish I had known . . . I wish I'd had a chance to say goodbye."

June looked stricken. "But then you would have tried to talk her out of it. She had to know that."

He cleared his throat. "I was wondering why, if she knew that she was going to take her life, she didn't want to see this place one last time."

June moved closer to him. "I think I might know. She couldn't be sure what shape the house was in, and it would have broken her heart to see it worn down or abandoned. But she still wanted to come home to die, to be laid to rest with her parents. And she knew that of all the people in the world, Francie was the one she could trust to make sure it was done."

Charlie rubbed his eyes. "Thank God for Francie," he said hoarsely. "Now that I'm beginning to understand just how unhappy my mother was with Dad, I'm glad she had someone to talk to."

"I think Francie was more than just someone to talk to. I think that other than you and your brother, Francie is the person your mother loved most in the world."

"You're a perceptive person, June." Charlie cleared his throat. "Well. We're here to work, aren't we? Put a broom in my hand and show me where to start."

For the next two hours they worked together. There was only one broom, so June swept and Charlie filled a bucket with water and a bit of soap and got on his hands and knees to scrub the floor. When the floors were so clean they gleamed, they brought in the rugs.

Charlie found a toolbox in the shed and nailed down a loose step while June got to work on the kitchen, scrubbing the old counters until they shone. She showed him a window that wouldn't stay open, a door that scraped the floor, a slow-draining sink — and Charlie fixed them all. It felt good to have tools in his hands; when the sink drain ran clear, Charlie felt a greater sense of accomplishment than any day on the job working for his father.

"I'm surprised a fellow like you knows how to do that," June observed, dumping dirty water out the backdoor. "I would have thought your family would hire people to take care of things."

Charlie laughed ruefully. "I'm sure my dad would have preferred that. But he always took me and Frank to work with him in the summers when we weren't in school — he liked to take us to meetings and introduce us as his junior partners. He even had our mom buy us little jackets and ties. Frank loved it — but I was too shy to talk to the clients, and after a while Dad just let me stay back in the shop. We job it all out now, but back then Dad had a warehouse and half a dozen trucks and trailers and all kinds of equipment, and it all had to be maintained and repaired. He had an old man working for him. I never knew his real name but everyone called him China Joe. I'd known him all my life and he let me follow him around, and taught me how to fix things."

"What happened to him?" June asked.

Charlie raised his eyebrows. "I find it interesting that's the detail you're curious about. Wouldn't you rather know about the time I drove a front loader into the side of the building?"

He didn't want to tell her the truth — that China Joe didn't show up for work one day, and rather than send someone to see if he was all right, his father cursed him for laziness. Three days later an old Chinese woman who spoke almost no English came to the warehouse to see his father and managed to communicate that China Joe was dead. His father gave her twenty dollars and sent her on her way.

"I think we've done all we can, don't you?" Charlie said, looking around the house. It smelled of bleach and furniture polish, and there wasn't a speck of dirt anywhere. His father would probably have nothing good to say about having the reception here, but he hoped his mother would have been pleased.

"I still want to wash the porch floor. And weed the garden bed — I'm going to have the gardener from the cemetery put in a few more flowers once he's done planting around the graves."

"June — enough. You've gone over and above what anyone could have asked."

"But it has to be perfect," she said. "I mean, for Vi, first of all, but for you and Frank, and all her friends, everyone she loved who she never got to show this place to. For Francie, because Francie loved her best, and now I've met Alice and I see how much she loved your mother too. I just thought — if I could make it the way she would have wanted — if she is looking down from heaven, I know she is at peace now with the Lord, but still —"

Charlie stopped her by taking her hand. "That's the most pure-hearted thing you could say," he said gruffly, "but I must ask you to stop, or I'll begin blubbering like a baby."

Charlie was doing his best to hold in his grief, but it threatened to force its way to the surface and burst free, and once he started it wouldn't be over until all the pain inside him had poured out. June put her hand on top of his.

"When my mother died, I went to work the day after the funeral and I didn't cry," she said softly. "I was working at a bakery and I had to get up at three o'clock to set the bread to rise, and then it was busy right through until the lunch rush was over, and I went home and did the chores and went to bed that night and I still didn't cry, not for almost two whole weeks. And then one day one of my regular customers came in and handed me a four-leaf clover she'd ironed between two sheets of waxed paper. She said she thought it was a little message from my mother, telling me that she was at peace and to be happy, and I burst out crying and couldn't stop. I went home and cried my eyes out, and there was no bread in the morning, and I nearly got myself fired, but I cried every time I looked at that little clover taped to the window so the sun shone through the paper. I kept it there until the day I got married. Oh, I don't even know why I'm telling you this."

Charlie looked down at their hands joined together. And then he surprised himself by saying, "I got a letter from her doctor."

"Vi's doctor?"

"The day before I got the news that she'd died — the letter took a while to reach me because our mail was forwarded to the hotel in Vegas where Dad and Frank and I were staying." Charlie withdrew his hand and seemed to shrink into himself. "He actually sent it the week before Mom and Francie left for Reno. If only I'd gotten it sooner —

if I'd been home, instead of in the middle of the desert watching bombs go off, maybe I could have done something. I could have stopped her."

"What did the letter say, Charlie?"

"She had cancer. Advanced — by the time the doctor found it, it was too late to save her, but he could have given her a little more time. He wanted her to come in immediately for radiation. He wanted to put her in the hospital, but she told him that she had to think about it. And in the letter, he, he —"

June dug a handkerchief out of her purse and pressed it into his hand, and he swiped at his eyes.

"He said that he'd written to me because my mother told him that she was closest to me. He knew about Dad — I mean, that he'd asked for a divorce, not that Mom had decided to give it to him. The doctor thought she was concerned that Dad wouldn't pay, and he wanted me to talk to her, to convince her to take the treatment. He said if it had been him, he would have wanted all the time he could have with his family."

"Oh, Charlie — I'm so sorry," June said. "But you couldn't have known, and she made her decision . . . at least, that's how it seems to me."

Charlie lifted his head and looked at her bleakly. "So you think she decided to give Dad his divorce, knowing she was going to come here and — and take her own life? I know it's hard to draw any other conclusion, but, June, my mother was Catholic. She went to Mass every weekday morning, even though Dad never went and Frank and I stopped going in high school. It *meant* something to her."

"And suicide is a sin," June said. "Is that what you're thinking?"

He nodded miserably. "I could understand her going against Dad. But what I can't understand is her turning against God. She prayed every night of her life. And if she lost faith in Him in the end . . . then that would mean that she died truly alone. And — June, I don't think I could bear it."

"No, wait, Charlie," June said. "I admit I didn't know her, not really, but — but I *saw* her, that night. I think I truly saw who she was. And maybe she was questioning — who wouldn't? But she seemed strong. At dinner, we got to talking about what we would do differently, after — you know — once our divorces were final. And Francie said she would dye her hair red, and we laughed, but then your mother said — she

378

said she'd done all she needed to do. And, Charlie, I could tell that she meant it. I think she'd made her peace and was saying goodbye, in her way, to her best friend. I don't think she was scared at all, or that her faith had failed her. I think she'd made the best decision she knew how."

Charlie considered June's words. "I want to believe that."

"I don't know, but if it was me, I wouldn't want Patty to see me sick and in pain — I wouldn't want her to remember me that way. I think Vi was brave. I think she knew what she was doing."

"Maybe you're right." Charlie sighed. "I guess we'll never really know. The police are ruling it an accident. I haven't told anyone about the letter — anyone but you. Frank, I don't think he'd understand. And there's no point telling Dad."

"If you keep this secret, you'll have to carry it with you always," June said, and Charlie realized that she was speaking from experience. How hard it must have been to see the same neighbors and friends day in and day out, hiding the horror that took place behind the closed doors of the house she shared with her tormentor. "But you don't need to worry about me. I'll never tell a soul."

"I appreciate that," Charlie said. "I'm sorry to have burdened you — especially since you've done so much for our family already."

"Think nothing of it," June said. "Honestly, it's nice to have someone to talk to. I mean, Francie has been wonderful, but she has so much on her mind and — oh! — I'm sorry, of course you do too, I don't know what I'm saying."

"It's all right," Charlie said gently. "But I'm afraid I need to be getting back. My father and brother will be here soon, and we need to stop by the mortuary. That is, if you're still willing to go with me."

June smiled. "Of course. I'm happy to come. I know Francie wanted you to be able to make those decisions."

"Yes. Yes, that would be best, I suppose. I should change clothes before we go."

"Good heavens, me too!" June exclaimed. "Would you mind dropping me off so I can freshen up? I'll be quick about it."

"Absolutely. If you promise not to laugh when you see me in my monkey suit."

"I have a feeling you clean up just fine. Why, to hear your mother talk, you were the handsomest child ever born, other than Frank, of course."

Charlie laughed — couldn't help it. It

seemed impossible to drown in his grief around this girl, with her earnest good intentions and her gentle reassurances — and that silly kerchief knotted around her hair, the blond curls peeking out from underneath.

"You really are something, June Samples," he said, taking the bucket from her and offering her his arm to escort her out of the home his mother had loved.

CHAPTER 47
VIRGIE

Virgie waited until late afternoon to go talk to Willy. She came to the door in a terry-cloth robe, her hair in big round curlers, her face weirdly featureless under heavy foundation and powder.

"Well, hello, Virgie," she said. "Please forgive my appearance, but you've caught me halfway through my makeup."

"You look fine," Virgie said, trying not to stare. "Is this a good time to talk?"

"Sure," Willy said. "As long as you don't mind me getting ready. I could use the company, actually."

"I don't mind." In truth, Virgie was secretly pleased; this was an opportunity to learn about makeup, a subject on which she was woefully ignorant.

The bathroom was a mess. Pots and jars and lipsticks littered the vanity, and there was a streak of rouge on the sink. As Willy peered at herself in the mirror, Virgie

382

cleaned the streak with a bit of toilet paper.

"Thanks, hon. I wouldn't be so . . . it's just that I don't know exactly when my date plans to pick me up and I need to be ready. He doesn't like to wait."

"Who's your date?" Virgie asked, perching on the side of the tub. "Did you meet him at Gwin's?"

"That's for me to know and you to find out," Willy said with a wink. "You're such a clever little sneak, though, I probably shouldn't say things like that."

Virgie glowed with pride. "Even if I figure it out, I won't tell anyone," she said generously. "Every lady has her secrets."

"You can say that again." Willy picked up a funny little tool and carefully clamped it onto her eyelashes. "Now, what's this big problem you need help with?"

"I didn't say I had a problem," Virgie said. "Just that I need to *talk* about something."

"Forgive me." Willy lowered the tool and gave her a serious look. "You're absolutely right. So, tell me what's going on."

This was why Virgie had decided to talk to Willy — she didn't treat her like a kid. She took her questions seriously and trusted her with adult matters, like going to see Dr. Peabody. Sending the anonymous letter to the police had helped, but it hadn't taken

Virgie's guilt away about what she'd done.

"Did the medicine work, by the way?" she asked politely. "From Dr. Peabody?"

"Sure," Willy said, rolling her eyes. "At least, it will soon enough. A modern miracle, and all that."

Virgie wanted to know more about this miracle, but Willy had that look adults get when they think you're too young to know the truth. Virgie couldn't tell her the entire truth about her situation, either, so they were even.

"Let's say that you found out that someone had done a bad thing," Virgie said carefully, the way she'd practiced. "And the thing they did, it didn't exactly hurt anyone, because the person they did it to — well, they couldn't really be hurt by it."

Willy set the tool down on the sink and folded her arms, giving Virgie a strange look. "Go on."

"Okay, so in a way, the thing they did wasn't even all that bad. But what if, before you knew the whole story, you thought they were a terrible person who probably ought to go to jail. Because you didn't have all the facts. But then you, um . . . maybe you were watching them when they didn't know you were watching them, or even just listening to them when they didn't know — like when you were in the next room — and you heard them talking to someone who was making them cry and you realized that they probably had a good reason to do what they did, like they didn't see any other way out. Not that it makes it right, exactly, but now you wish you wouldn't have thought the bad things about them in the first place."

"Virgie . . ." Willy motioned her to move over, and sat down on the edge of the tub next to her. "It sounds to me like you overheard some things that you weren't meant to hear, things that someone your age couldn't possibly understand. Not because you're stupid — far from it, you're smart as a whip — but because you haven't had the *life experience* to see how it was. Someday, I feel sure you'll look back and it will all make sense to you. The important thing now, though . . . well, there's two things."

"What are they?" Already Virgie was feeling relieved. It felt so good to have an adult take her seriously.

"The first thing is to keep everything you saw or heard to yourself. Like you said, it's a confusing situation, and people could easily draw the wrong conclusion — just like you did."

Virgie considered that. "But what about

the police? I mean, aren't they going to get involved at some point anyway, because of what she — I mean the person — did?"

Willy gave a funny little laugh. "Well. The thing is, it isn't really a *crime,* is it? Because like you said, the person wasn't really hurting anyone. I mean, not to take away from your very good observation, and I agree, in an ideal world things like this wouldn't happen. But — and this is what I meant by things you'll understand more later — life isn't really fair. Some people are born lucky, and some have to fight hard for every bit of luck they can get their hands on. Those people, the fighters, they'd probably love to do everything the nice way — the proper way — but maybe they just never had the chance. And they had to decide, am I just going to accept my fate and be miserable, or am I going to try to make things better for myself? Especially if I have a chance to do it without hurting other people?"

"That's kind of what I thought." Willy was so much smarter than other adults. "So what's the other thing?"

"Well, I think it would be best if you didn't spy on this person anymore. So that you could avoid any further misunderstandings."

"But I did something," Virgie said. "I . . .

took something from her. Something that's worth a lot of money."

"My goodness," Willy said, looking startled. She thought for a moment. "I wonder," she said slowly, "if this thing maybe wasn't worth as much as you thought it was? Like maybe it *seemed* valuable but it was a fake or something. Because I'm thinking that if the person hasn't missed it yet, they've probably either forgotten they even owned it or didn't care much about it in the first place. In which case I'd just keep it and not waste another minute worrying about it."

"You really think it could be fake?" Virgie asked doubtfully.

"Oh, sure. It happens all the time. Even ladies who own expensive jewelry sometimes wear paste copies in public in case they get lost or stolen."

"I didn't say it was jewelry," Virgie said, alarmed.

"No, of course you didn't, that was just an example. What I was trying to say is that you're being pretty hard on yourself, considering that you were trying to do the right thing all along. At this point I think it's best that you forget all about it. And keep whatever it was as a — a souvenir, maybe."

"I guess you might be right," Virgie said, and sighed. "It's just that I don't know if

I'll be *able* to forget. Nothing like this has ever happened to me before."

Willy nodded, and they sat without speaking for a while.

"Do you mind if I smoke?" Willy finally said. "Let's go sit in the other room — it's silly for us to be cooped up in here."

"But don't you have to get ready?"

"Sure — in a minute. But I want to tell you a little story first." They trooped out into her room, where Willy got a coffee cup from the windowsill that she'd been using as an ashtray and lit a cigarette. "Go ahead and sit, honey."

Virgie took the chair, and Willy sat on the bed, tapping her ashes into the cup.

"This is the story of how I ended up here in Reno getting a divorce." She took a puff and let it out slowly, staring at the curling tendrils of smoke. "I grew up in a town so small that all the kids fit in a one-room schoolhouse and our teacher had to teach all of us, from kindergarten through high school. As you might imagine, it made it hard for us to learn much, but we all got to know each other real well. There was a boy in the same grade as me named Peter that I'd been friends with so long I didn't even remember meeting him, because it happened when we were still babies. Anyway,

Peter and I decided to get married when we were only five years old. And when we were seventeen — well, we ran off and did it."

"That's how old my mother was when she met my father!"

"Is that right. For some folks maybe it works out, and God bless them. But for Peter and me . . ." She was quiet for a while. "Everything was harder than we thought it would be. We dropped out of school right at the start of our senior year and moved into this little tiny two-room house on his parents' land. He got a job baling hay and I helped his mother, cleaning and canning and doing the wash and anything else she needed done. We didn't have any money for extras and half the time we didn't even have enough to pay the bills. I worked harder than I ever had before, and my mother-in-law wasn't even nice to me, not unless Peter was around. Anyway, Peter and I started arguing, he came home late from work sometimes, I didn't know where he was going but I knew it wasn't good. I started thinking maybe I made a mistake, wondering if I ought to just move home, maybe finish school. But then I got pregnant.

"That made us both grow up some, I think. Peter stopped staying out late, and he took overtime when he could get it. My mother-in-law helped me sew some maternity clothes and got her daughters to send over things their own kids had outgrown. But when I was about six months along, I went to the doctor for a checkup and my baby had died inside me. No reason they could give me, just that it happens sometimes.

"Now I'm not going to tell you all the details of what happened next, but just trust me on this, Virgie, there's no kind of heartbreak like losing a child, I don't care if you're eighteen or eighty. I'll never forget when the doctor told me it was a little girl — but I never got to see her, never got to give her a name or even bury her. Peter wouldn't talk about it, and I couldn't stand to have my mother-in-law anywhere near me. I went home so my own mother could take care of me while I recovered. It was only supposed to be a few days — but after a week I packed a few things and caught a ride to the train station and bought a ticket to San Francisco with the money I'd saved for the baby, and that was the last time I talked to any of them for almost two years. I sent my mother postcards now and then, so she'd know I was all right, but I didn't want to think about everything I'd left behind. I wasn't even twenty years old and

I figured I'd been sad enough to last me a long while."

"But what did you do for money?" Virgie asked. She'd thought about running away herself, plenty of times — but her imagination took her only as far as Sacramento, where her grandmother lived.

"Worked," Willy said vaguely. "What anyone does for money. Some jobs were worse than others, but I got by. But here's the part of the story I want you to pay attention to. A lot of times since I left home, I've found myself with a few not-very-good choices and no way to choose among them other than to take my best guess. I tried to focus on the next meal or the next rent check or the next job, and I made plenty of mistakes, and there were days I didn't think I'd make it. I was still too sad to fall in love, and I felt guilty about leaving Peter without explaining myself, but men came along anyway, and sometimes I had a little fun with them.

"The thing I came to figure out — and maybe there are girls who figure it out quicker and they're probably better off for it — there's only a few kinds of men. There are the ones to steer clear of — plenty of those, honey. I wish it was different, but you'll learn soon enough. And then there's the ones who want to take care of you, and you learn how to make them believe it was a good idea, to make them feel like their generosity makes a difference, so they keep being generous." Willy stabbed out her cigarette and picked up the pack to shake out another. "And then every once in a while, a man comes along who can't do one blessed thing for you other than make you laugh, help you forget your troubles for a night or two. Now, there are those who'd call me a sinner, but if you ask me you ought to grab hold of that kind of chance whenever you can. Life's short and fun is where you find it — no one hands it to you.

"You're too young to understand how this all connects, but it was a little of all three kinds of men that got me here, to Reno. I'm not asking for anyone's pity, but I'm not going to let anyone shame me either. The bad men taught me to be careful, the generous ones taught me to be grateful, and those good-time fellows . . . well, one of them sent me to Dr. Peabody, truth be told. There's people in this town who think I'm lower than a snake, but your mother treated me well when I needed a little help. I think she and I understand each other. So I'm going to go on this date, and I'm going to act like I haven't got a care in the world, and when

I come home, if my feet hurt from dancing and my face hurts from smiling and my heart hurts from telling lies, well, it still beats standing in my mother-in-law's kitchen with a washboard and sweat pouring off my face and no idea when my husband will come home."

Virgie waited, but that appeared to be all there was to the story. She wasn't sure what she was supposed to have learned from it, but Willy was watching her expectantly, so she said, "I hope your date is nice. Maybe he'll turn out to be nicer than you think he is."

Willy laughed. "Oh, he's plenty nice. Would you like to know a secret?"

"Sure."

Willy got up and went to the closet and removed a large white dress bag, which she hung from a hook on the door. She unzipped the bag and a confection of frothy white lace spilled out.

"That's a wedding dress!" Virgie exclaimed, as Willy took it out of the bag. It had a simple satin bodice with tiny cap sleeves, and layers and layers of tulle skirts. "Are you getting *married*?"

"It certainly looks that way," Willy said with a smile. "He asked, and I said yes, and if all goes well, I'll be married the same week my divorce goes through. I've even picked out the chapel — the Three Bells."

"That's a good one," Virgie said with an air of authority. "They have real flowers there, not plastic."

"I'm glad you like it. There'll be a photographer and a dinner after in a restaurant, maybe even a private room. We'll have a very small wedding party, I expect — I may ask a couple of friends from back home to be witnesses — and then we're going to California to drive along the coast all the way to Mexico for our honeymoon. We're going to swim in the ocean and buy those big straw hats and eat fresh strawberries anytime we feel like it."

"That sounds really nice."

"Maybe . . ." Willy looked at her speculatively. "You're a little old to be a flower girl, but what would you think about being a junior bridesmaid?"

Virgie thought it was a fantastic idea, but she didn't want to seem too excited. "I think that would be lovely."

"Well, then." Willy crushed her second cigarette out and stood. "I think we have a deal. Once we get the date figured out, maybe you and I can go pick out a dress for you, what do you think?"

Virgie got up too. She couldn't wait to

write in her diary about this. She only knew one girl at school who'd been a junior bridesmaid, and it was only for her sister, so that wasn't near as good. She'd have to ask Willy for a photo of the wedding party, so that when school started up in the fall, she'd have it to show the other girls.

"I think that will be fine."

"And about the other thing . . . just remember what we talked about. Mum's the word — keep your souvenir and put the rest of it out of your mind."

Virgie nodded, but her mind was on the wedding. "I should go. But thanks, Willy."

"My pleasure, Virgie. I'm glad we had this little talk."

CHAPTER 48
CHARLIE

Charlie was waiting in the lobby, showered and dressed in a sport coat and one of the two good shirts he'd brought, when Harry and Frank arrived. They took one look at him and burst out laughing.

"What'd you do, try to protect some girl's virtue?" Frank had asked, while his father had clapped him on the back and congratulated him. "Finally decided to stick up for yourself, eh? It's about time!"

A bellboy came toward them, loaded down with their luggage.

"Watch where you're going with that suitcase," Harry scolded. "That's top grain leather. Probably cost more than you make in a month."

"Long drive?" Charlie asked his brother quietly.

"You don't know the half of it. Barely said a word since Tonopah," Frank muttered, rolling his eyes. "I offered to drive, but he wouldn't hear of it. Nearly ran a chicken truck off the road just outside of Hawthorne."

"Been up since goddamn dawn," Harry groused, joining them. His shirt was wrinkled and his tie hung limply around his neck. "I need a nap, but I need a drink worse."

"There's time for both," Charlie said diplomatically. "That is, unless your dinner plans are on the early side . . . ?"

"Nah, they'll hold," Harry said, lurching toward the check-in desk. While his sons trailed behind him, he explained that he was meeting up with a former client who happened to be in town and might have another job for them.

Charlie had his doubts. The frantic days leading up to the grand opening of Atomic Marvel Tours would have left his father no time to court new business.

But Charlie was accustomed to his father's fibs and excuses, and frankly wasn't interested in knowing what Harry was really up to. "You don't have to, Dad. Frank and I would understand if you want to get to your dinner."

"Nonsense. Dinner can wait — I'll just tell Arnie I'm having a drink with my sons first," he said. "He'll understand — he'd better, anyway. Time like this, people need to show some goddamn respect."

"You're absolutely right, Dad," Charlie said — he couldn't help himself. "Respect, decorum, character — now there's the true measure of a man."

Frank snorted, but Harry had already moved on to flirting with the girl at the desk, leaning on his elbow so he had a better view of her bosom while she looked up their reservation.

"There you go, sonny boy," he said, pressing a key into Frank's hand. "Top floor, with the best view in the place. I told that little gal I'd make it worth her while, if you know what I mean."

"I'm just going to assume you mean that you gave her a decent tip," Charlie said. "Now can we —"

"You know what you need?" Harry said, stabbing his finger into Charlie's chest. "You need to relax a little. Go out for a nice steak dinner with your brother, throw a few bucks at the tables, meet some of the locals. Who knows — this might be your lucky night." This suggestion was accompanied by a lascivious wink to indicate that he didn't just mean gambling.

As disgusted as Charlie was by his father's suggestion that he and Frank spend the evening chasing girls the day before their mother's funeral, Frank laughed and slapped their father on the back. Charlie knew that his brother was grieving in his own way, but even as a child, Frank had been loath to show weakness. He used to lie on the floor and challenge his friends to step on him — his arms, legs, even his stomach — with the stipulation that if he could keep a smile on his face the whole time, they had to pay him a nickel. Frank had made a lot of money that way, especially in high school when he graduated to charging a couple bucks to take a punch.

Frank took after their father, who'd been a linebacker at the University of Oregon. Frank might have played for the Cal-Berkeley Bears after the war if he hadn't been injured, but instead he dedicated himself to girls, beer, and skipping classes, and barely managed to graduate, even with an extra semester.

"So listen, son," Harry said, after Frank excused himself to go to the men's room. "You know how Francie gets — has to run the show, no matter what anyone else wants. This whole idea of burying your mother here, well, I'm really sorry it's come to this — it's ridiculous, anyone can see that — but when I tried to talk Francie into doing the right thing, she threw a fit, said she'd already started calling people and making arrangements. I'm afraid it was just too far down the line to change it, especially with people traveling here."

"It's okay, Dad," Charlie had said. He wasn't about to tell his father that he thought it was the right decision.

"That's my boy," Harry said, giving Charlie's shoulder a squeeze. "Your brother was a champ about it too. Showing some real maturity, both of you. Now listen, I need to go upstairs and make a couple calls, and I think your brother wanted to take a shower and change clothes, so let's meet in the bar in, oh, say, an hour. You don't mind, do you?"

"Why would I mind?" Charlie said — but he couldn't help thinking that had he known, he might have spent an extra hour with June.

At a few minutes before four, the first-floor Mapes bar was beginning to fill up with people having a drink before their evening entertainment began. Charlie had staked out a few chairs around a cocktail table and ordered a beer while he waited, gloomily playing the conversation with his father over in his mind. There had been a time when he would have done anything to earn a little praise from his father, but now Harry's words fell on deaf ears. Since going to work for him, Charlie had come to understand that his father used praise as a tool — doling it out when he wanted something, withholding it as a punishment. Frank, who'd received a medical discharge for his battle injuries only a few weeks after shipping out, had been working for their father for two years already when Charlie joined the company, and had been promoted to salesman. Charlie didn't begrudge his brother the position; if Frank was truly happy working at HFC Events Management, Charlie was all for it.

But he wouldn't be sticking around.

He wasn't planning to broach the subject until the desert staging area was fully broken down and all the equipment and staff were back in San Francisco. Originally the Moser brothers had just wanted to run a few print ads and drive people out to the test site in a repurposed school bus to watch the tests, but by the time they signed the contract, Harry had convinced them to expand the idea into a true entertainment venue, so they could charge top dollar, and the scope of the project had tripled.

Charlie figured that after his mother's

service he would return to Vegas and the
early-morning drives into the desert, working extra shifts so they could wrap it up as
quickly as possible.

But then he'd met June — and she'd
thrown his plans, and his heart, into confusion.

At a little after four, Harry and Frank
came walking into the open-plan bar from
opposite directions, dressed in sport coats
and ties nearly identical to his own, and
Charlie groaned inwardly. The sport coats
had been gifts from Harry when each of
them joined the company, the ties and cuff
links doled out for birthdays and Christmas
gifts.

"Hey, sons! Looking sharp!"

"Thanks, Dad!" Frank said.

Harry waved the cocktail waitress over as
he and Frank took their seats. Frank stumbled as he sat; Charlie smelled alcohol and
realized his brother had already started
drinking in his room.

"Boilermakers all around," Harry told the
waitress. "Make 'em doubles. What do you
think of my boys, Miss, couple of handsome
guys, eh?"

"Yes, sir," the girl simpered; she knew a
big tip when she saw one.

"Both single." Harry leered, winking as he

put his hand on Frank's shoulder. "Though I'd put my money on this one — Charlie there's a shy fellow."

"Charlie's not shy," Frank said, shrugging Harry's hand off his shoulder in a rare show of impatience as the waitress walked away. "You shouldn't say stuff like that, Dad."

Charlie looked up, surprised. Now that he took a good look at him, Frank appeared the worse for wear — his face was ruddy, his tie askew.

"Aw, he knows I'm just foolin'," Harry said. "Don't you, Charlie Boy?"

"Mom hated when you called him that."

Now both of them looked at Frank in surprise.

"Did you get into the sauce a little early?" Harry asked. "I mean, don't get me wrong, it's understandable. We're all grieving here. Your mother and I had our troubles, everybody knew that, but I loved her."

"Yeah?" Frank said, leaning across the table and poking his finger in his father's face. "So much that you booked your whore into the same hotel as her? That how you show how much you loved Mom?"

"Hey!" Charlie said, more out of confusion than offense. How did Frank know about Willy? "Frank, you know what, maybe we should let Dad get to his business din-

403

ner, and you and I can go get a steak like he said. What do you say, a nice big rib-eye?"

"Dad isn't going to a business dinner," Frank said, slurring his words and crossing his arms on his chest. "He's going to see his *whore.*"

"Hey, now, listen," Harry said. "I won't have you talking like that."

"Yeah? Well, Mom sure didn't like you *cheating* on her like that, but you never cared."

"What the hell's gotten into you?" Harry said, his face turning red. "For your information, my marriage to your mother was over a long time ago, and she wouldn't say any different if she was here. We stayed together for you kids' sakes, right up until the day she announced she was coming here."

"Okay," Charlie said, standing. He hooked his hand under Frank's armpit and dragged him from his chair. "You know what, Dad, this isn't the time or place. Frank and I are burying our mother tomorrow and we don't need to hear about that right now."

"Or *ever,* you bastard," Frank said, attempting to yank his arm away and stumbling backward into a decorative metal railing. "Ow!"

The waitress had returned with a tray

404

holding their three cocktails. "Is everything all right?"

"No, everything's not all right," Frank bellowed. "Our mother is dead and our father killed her!"

"That's enough," Harry said, pushing back his chair.

Charlie, whose muscles had been hardened by heavy labor, had little trouble dragging his flailing brother away, but he made one miscalculation: he failed to look behind him to see the white-haired dowager passing by, until she fell into a potted palm and screamed. He let go of Frank to help the woman up, but as she got unsteadily to her feet, Charlie heard the sound of a fist connecting with bone.

CHAPTER 49
FRANCIE

"Go away," Francie moaned. She'd made it from the bed to the chair, taking the blanket with her, where she was listlessly reading the same page in an issue of *Vogue* over and over. Earlier in the day, Virgie had brought up a vase of lovely pink and white tulips that Alice had dropped off, which made her feel a little better, only why hadn't Alice brought them upstairs herself? Because her mother was a fool and a disgrace, that's why. Francie wished it was late enough to go to bed.

"It's June," came a muffled voice. "And Patty."

Francie closed her eyes and sighed. Not fair — bringing Patty along was a dirty trick, because who could refuse the little darling? She stuck her feet in her slippers and shuffled across the room.

"Before I open this door," she said, "it's to be understood that there will be no discussion of my appearance."

"Of course not."

Francie opened the door.

June was wearing a dress and a pair of navy peep-toe pumps that had Alice's stamp all over them. She was holding a covered dish, and next to her Patty held a plate with a slice of cake on it.

"We brought your dinner," Patty said, "because you don't feel good."

"Wasn't that thoughtful. Well, you'd best come in, then, hadn't you?"

June looked around the room, taking in the mussed bedcovers, the dishes stacked on the dresser, the dress Francie had worn the night before puddled on the floor. One high-heeled shoe lay upside down next to the bathroom door. The wastepaper basket sat near the head of the bed, close at hand in case Francie had needed to unburden herself of the contents of her stomach again and couldn't make it to the bathroom.

"What happened *here*?"

"I was under the weather. Resting."

"Have you been lying here all day?" June sounded appalled.

"I spoke to Vi's lawyer," Francie said, ignoring the question as she collapsed back into the chair. Frederick Yeske had tracked her down after receiving a letter Vi had posted the morning she left town, letting him know of her death. "It was upsetting. He called to arrange the reading of her will, per her wishes, and wanted to know when to schedule it. I told him I'd talk to Harry and the boys — and Alice too, apparently she was named — but not until after the funeral."

June nodded sympathetically and started tidying. She folded the blanket, picked up the stack of magazines, and made the bed, and only then took a cloth napkin from her purse and draped it over Francie's lap, handed her a fork, and set the plate on her knees.

"Come up here with me," she said to Patty, perching on the edge of the bed. "But no jumping."

"I suppose," Francie said, as she inhaled the aroma of pork chops with creamed onions and found that her appetite was on its way to being restored, "that I owe you an explanation, and an apology."

"I did call three times," June said. "Mrs. Swanson said you hadn't been down for breakfast or lunch."

"I wasn't feeling strong enough to pick up."

June let that pass. "I thought you'd want to hear about our trip to the house — and the mortuary and the florist. Though I had to get Clyde to drive me to the florist, because Charlie had to get back to meet his father and brother."

"Oh dear," Francie said. As delicious as the dinner smelled, she had some amends to make first. She carefully set the plate on the side table. "I've been dreadful to you today, June. I've left you with all the work. And Vi — if she's watching me from heaven she's probably furious with me."

"Are you still sad?" Patty asked, bouncing just a bit, her feet swinging in their little black Mary Janes.

"Yes, darling, Mrs. Meeker is going to be sad for a long time," June said, gathering Patty into her arms. "Remember how sad I was when Mr. Jenkins next door died?"

"He was old," Patty said gravely.

"Yes, but I was sad anyway."

"Do you miss Mrs. Grubbers?"

"*Carothers,* darling."

Francie couldn't help but smile. "Mrs. Grubbers — I think she might have liked that."

"You really should eat," June urged. "You'll need your strength tomorrow."

"But I need to finish my apology. You see, I had dinner with Alice last night, and Arthur, and — and —"

"Mr. Meeker's friend," June said calmly. "Alice told me."

"She *did*?" Francie was shocked that Alice would air the family's dirty laundry to someone she'd met only the day before. Though maybe Alice hadn't explained the exact nature of the men's friendship. "Well . . . did she tell you that I, er, drank more than I should have? And made a fool of myself in front of the entire restaurant? And — and — none of them are speaking to me?"

June shrugged, her expression neutral. "She did say something about a disagreement."

"Well, I behaved abominably. But, June — I had my reasons. Alice has met someone, and she thinks she's in love."

"How *awful,*" June said, with a hint of a smile.

"No, you don't understand. This has happened once before."

"Alice has fallen in love *twice*? Good for her. Maybe there's hope for me."

"You love *me,* Mama," Patty pointed out.

"It's different for Alice," Francie said, her voice beginning to quaver the way it always did when she thought about poor Alice and the hardships she'd been forced to endure, all because of a cruel accident of nature.

410

"No man wants to date a handicapped girl. But certain men . . . unscrupulous men . . . find out about our family's wealth and try to take advantage. Ordinarily circumstances prevent them from getting close to her —"

"What does that mean? What kind of circumstances?"

"Well, obviously, Alice lives at home with us. She can't very well get a job, of course, but she takes classes and volunteers at the hospital and belongs to several clubs. None of which brings her in contact with men, needless to say."

"Hmm."

"Anyway, a number of years ago Alice struck up a conversation with a boy at a lunch counter after one of her classes, and he sensed an opportunity. He flattered her and pretended to be interested in her, and asked her on a date. And I *warned* her, I forbid her to go, but Arthur insisted she be allowed to — we had a terrible fight about it. And I was right, because after two months of courtship, the boy proposed to her.

"June, she was so excited — you should have seen her. He hadn't even bothered to ask Arthur for her hand, but all Arthur could see was that his little girl was happy, talking about dresses and flowers and asking Margie to be her maid of honor. I pointed out that the boy worked as a delivery man and didn't have two nickels to rub together, but Alice didn't care. Not until I had Arthur's lawyer draw up a document to the effect that Alice would receive not one penny from us, ever, if she went through with the wedding — and she *still* didn't care. Can you believe that?"

"She was in love," June said. "So yes, of course I can believe it."

"Well, this is all very rich, because the minute *he* saw the letter, he disappeared, and Alice never heard from him again. Not even to say goodbye. It turns out that the address he'd given her was false, that no one at the delivery company had even heard of him. And yet she cried her eyes out as though she'd lost the love of her life."

"Maybe she was just embarrassed," June said. "And sad. You know, that he'd tricked her like that. I know *I* would be."

Francie sniffed and dabbed at her nose with a hanky and stared at June. There was something different about her.

"Did you do something to your hair?"

June blushed. "Alice insisted. It was terribly expensive, and I told her no, but she wouldn't listen. She said we both should get a trim and a wash and set for tomorrow, and then she and the hairdresser decided that I would look good as a blonde — I mean a real blond, not my old dishwater brown."

"Well, she was *right*." For some reason, this made Francie angry. "You look like a damn beauty queen."

Patty gasped. "She said a bad word, Mama."

"You know what, darling, how would you like to have that lollipop Charlie bought for you?" June took a multicolored confection out of her purse, untied the ribbon holding its cellophane, and handed it to Patty. "Only you must go eat it in the bathroom, so you don't get the carpet sticky. Go on, darling. Close the door behind you."

Patty hopped off the bed and ran to the bathroom.

"I know that trick," Francie grumbled. "But why is Charlie buying candy for Patty?"

"Well, since *someone* couldn't be bothered to help today, it took longer than we expected, and he felt bad for Patty being stuck inside all day."

"What's gotten into you? Why are you taking Alice's side?"

"I'm not taking sides. I just think she's right, Francie. I know it must have been horrible to watch her get hurt the last time she fell in love — I'd just about die if anyone was that cruel to Patty. But you should be proud of her for being brave enough to try again. You know what she told me?"

"I can't imagine." At the moment, Francie felt as if her own daughter was a stranger, and June wasn't helping.

"She says that even if something happens and she and this fellow don't stay together, she still won't regret it, because she's had the best six months of her life."

"Six *months?*"

"She didn't tell you it had been that long because she was afraid you'd be angry."

Francie stewed. "You certainly got her to unburden yourself to you."

"Well, it takes a while for the color, so we had plenty of time to talk. You might want to know that she is in her room back at her hotel afraid to come talk to you because she's worried that you're furious with all of them — her, Mr. Meeker, and Mr. Fitzhugh."

Francie winced; how she wished she would never have to hear that name again. "What on earth does *he* have to do with any of this? Why must you even mention his name?"

"Because," June said, "Alice's beau is his nephew."

CHAPTER 50
WILLY

A man with his forearm wrapped in a bloody towel had been slowly advancing on Willy for the past half hour, sliding from one plastic chair to the next when she wasn't looking, and she had had just about enough.

"I've got a boning knife in my purse," she said, just quietly enough so the nurse at the desk couldn't hear. "You come any closer and you'll be bleeding from *both* arms."

The man quickly retreated and picked up a magazine.

Willy supposed it was partly her fault, for not changing clothes before taking a taxi to the hospital emergency room, but it had taken her the better part of an hour to get ready and she had been hoping that the evening might still be salvaged.

But when she gave her name to the nurse and inquired as to Mr. Harry Carothers's condition, Willy was told that she would need to take her boyfriend straight home to rest if he hoped to make it to his important event tomorrow.

Willy had considered asking the nurse if she was aware that his "important event" was his wife's funeral. Now, almost two hours later, she was running out of patience.

She got up and headed for the nurse's station again, her progress hindered by her red satin stilettos, but before she got there the swinging doors opened and Harry was wheeled out. Bandages crisscrossed his nose, his face was swollen, his eyes were bloodshot, and he was wearing nothing but a hospital gown over his trousers, but he was grinning from ear to ear.

"Hey, gorgeous!" It came out "gor-jush."

"You the girlfriend?" the attendant said, looking her up and down. "Mr. C here told me you were a dish, and he wasn't kidding!"

"How nice," Willy said frostily.

"Be a sweetheart and bring the car around, doll," Harry said, digging in his pocket for his lucky rabbit-foot key chain and tossing it to her. He sounded like a drunk with an adenoid problem. "They won't let me drive."

"Is something wrong with your feet too?"

"Mr. C is feeling no pain, Miss," the attendant said, and chuckled. "He probably shouldn't be doing much walking — wouldn't want him to take a spill and end up right back here. Oh, and he bled all over his shirt so we're sending him home in County General's finest."

"You'll wait with me, Hal, won't you?" Harry said, plucking at the hem of the attendant's scrubs.

"Sure thing, Mr. C."

Willy turned without a word and stalked toward the exit.

Outside, the night sky was obscured by streetlights. Willy fumed as she made for Harry's white Corvette, which was parked in a no-parking area with a ticket stuck under the window wiper. She crumpled the ticket up and tossed it on the ground, wondering how Harry had managed to drive himself to the hospital. She'd seen fellows get their noses broken in bar fights and keep throwing punches like nothing had happened, but Harry wasn't that kind of guy. In fact, he was more likely to run from a fight, which made it all the more infuriating that he'd managed to get himself clocked on the one night they had to be alone together.

Willy was *damn* sure going to get to the bottom of this.

She started the engine and floored the gas

before she put it in gear, just to hear the engine roar. After canceling both of their planned weekend visits since she'd arrived in Reno, Harry had sworn they would make the most of tonight, especially since he would probably not be able to get away again until all of the out-of-town guests were gone — and he'd made an ominous comment about having to get back to Las Vegas as soon as possible.

Willy pulled into the circle drive, where the attendant was helping Harry out of the wheelchair. He looked like an old man with his gown flapping open like that. At least this solved one problem, namely how she was going to get out of having sex with Harry tonight, since there was no way the antibiotic had killed the wretched clap yet.

"You poor darling," she said, feigning concern as the attendant eased Harry into the passenger seat. "Let's get you home."

"Now, Miss, here's his pain pills. He shouldn't have access to them right now — he's likely to forget he already took them and knock himself out. Can I count on you to take good care of him, sweetheart?"

Willy didn't care for the man's suggestive tone. She snatched the bottle and stuffed it in her purse. "I'll take care of him, all right."

"Thanks for everything, Hal!" Harry

called out the window.

"What's that smell?" Willy demanded as she put the car in gear.

"Oh, that — I puked all over myself in the waiting room. Listen, doll, could you stop by a liquor store on the way back to the hotel?"

Willy shot him a look as she rolled her window down to get some air. "You're doped up on painkillers, Harry. I'm pretty sure you shouldn't be drinking right now."

"I'm celebrating," Harry leered, grabbing his crotch. "We can still have a good time tonight, baby — my face got a little beat up, but there's nothing wrong with the rest of me."

"That smell — and your face — aren't doing anything for your sex appeal, Harry. Besides, I don't know what you've got to celebrate. Your wife's funeral is tomorrow. You should probably act like you care, even if it's just for your sons' sake."

Why had she said that? Charlie had treated her like gum stuck to the bottom of his shoe. Frank was probably worse, from what Harry had told her about him.

"My *sons* are the ones who did this to me, for your information," Harry said, sulking.

"What?"

420

"I don't want to talk about it." He turned his face toward the window.

What on *earth* was going on? Harry was thick as thieves with his boys — at least Frank. Chip off the old block, takes after his dad — to Harry, these were the highest compliments he could give his older son. With Charlie he was more critical — the boy was soft, too sensitive, lacked his killer instincts.

Maybe Charlie had gotten tired of playing second fiddle?

Harry's silence didn't last long. "It's not my fault she offed herself," he mumbled.

"Cripes!" Willy exploded. "Could you just show a *little* respect? She's dead!"

"You're the one who called her a she-devil, Willy."

"Only because of all the things you said about her! You know what, Harry? I'm starting to wonder if any of it was even true."

He glanced at her, worry comically rearranging his mangled features. "Of course it was. That woman made my life hell, I can tell you that."

"Well, it's a funny thing, because I spent an evening with her best friend, and she says Vi was an angel. The sweetest woman on earth."

"You did *what*? What did you want to go

421

and do something like that for?"

"I didn't know it was her, obviously! Tell me something, what did you think was going to happen when you put both of us in the same hotel? I mean, how dumb can you get, Harry!"

"I *had* to." Now he was whining, an effect that was heightened by his nasally voice. "I couldn't get my deposit back."

"Are you telling me you put me through hell so you could save a few lousy bucks?"

They were pulling into the drop-off area in front of the hotel, where three or four cars already waited in the valet line. Everyone was returning from their Saturday night out, which made Willy even angrier — she was supposed to have been wined, dined, plied with gifts, and treated like a princess, and instead she was stuck with a foul-smelling old creep who was acting like a spoiled baby.

"What did Francie say about me?" Harry asked.

"What makes you think we talked about *you*?"

"There was always something strange about those two — they spent so much time together I should have dug a tunnel between our two houses. I think Vi loved Francie more than she loved me."

"It would serve you right," Willy said, "considering you probably loved every woman you took to bed more than you loved your wife."

"Don't be that way, baby." It suddenly seemed to have occurred to Harry that he could end up spending the night alone if he didn't patch things up. That, or his medication was wearing off. "Let's not fight anymore. Come up to my room and give me a backrub, and I'll buy you something nice tomor— uh, the day after tomorrow."

Willy eased the car forward. There was only one car ahead of them. "It had better be something *really* nice, given the way you smell."

Harry give her thigh a squeeze. "How about some nice emerald earrings to go with your beautiful eyes?"

Willy turned to glare at him. "The next piece of jewelry you give me had *better* be a diamond ring. You promised!"

Harry cringed. "But that was before all of this. You said it yourself — I need to show some respect. I've been thinking — maybe we should wait. It wouldn't look right, me getting engaged so soon after Vi passed."

"Are you *kidding* me?" Willy shrieked. "Since when do you care what people think of you and me?"

"Since I've got to earn a living, that's since when. My next job is for a goddamn Bible-thumper, for Christ's sake. What's he going to think if you come to dinner in one of your trampy little outfits and —"

"Trampy?" How dare he! She'd spent six dollars on this skirt and another fifty cents to have the hem taken up. And Harry himself had bought her these shoes — and asked her to wear them to bed!

"I didn't mean —"

"Get out."

"Are you nuts? I'm injured! Besides, this is *my* car."

Something in Willy snapped. *His* car, *his* clients, *his* crazy violent sons — and apparently, *his* trashy bit on the side who was good enough to give him head in this very front seat, but not good enough to take to a business dinner. Well, she wasn't having it!

"If you don't get out right now, I'll scream!"

Harry laughed as he reached over and grabbed for the keys, saying, "This is why you broads should never be allowed to drive."

And then, three things happened all at once.

Willy screamed as loud as she could.

Somehow, her foot came down hard on

the gas pedal.

And as the Corvette crashed into the back of the car ahead, she caught a glimpse of Francie's daughter Alice, arm in arm with a tall, skinny red-headed young man, with a shocked expression on her face.

CHAPTER 51
ALICE

"Ow, ow, *ow!*"

"Stop being a baby," Alice scolded, dabbing at Willy's chin with a cotton ball soaked in iodine. "It's just a little sting. You're lucky you don't need stitches."

"It hardly matters if I'm going to be swollen up like a melon," Willy said. "I probably look as bad as Harry!"

"Who cares? It's not like anyone's going to see you. If you come anywhere near the service, my mother's likely to have you arrested."

"For the ten-thousandth time —"

"I know, I know — nothing's your fault, everyone's being horrid to you. Really, Willy, you're going to have to do better than that."

"Are you sure I can't get you anything?" Alice's boyfriend asked. His name was Raymond, or Ronald, or something like that, and now that Willy was past the shock of

426

the crash and had been whisked into the hotel manager's office while the staff dealt with Harry and the police, she had time to look him over more carefully. He was actually rather handsome, in a scrubbed and wholesome kind of way — not her type, but she could definitely see the appeal.

"Thanks, honey, but unless it's forty-proof, I think I'll pass."

"Actually, Reggie, darling, do you think you could see if you could find some coffee?" Alice asked him.

Reggie — that's what it was. He gave Alice an adoring smile before letting himself out the door.

"Well, well," Willy said when he was gone. "You didn't do too badly for yourself, did you? What's he doing here, anyway? I thought this was a family-only sort of thing."

"No one knows he's here," Alice admitted. "I was, um, rather upset when I talked to him last night, and so he took the day off work and drove here to surprise me. He got a room down the street."

"One of the good ones," Willy said — though it came out more sarcastically than she intended.

"Hold still, I'm going to bandage you up now," Alice said. "Though you really should have let the medics do this."

Willy made a face. "There's no way I was going to stay out there with all those cameras!"

"It wasn't 'all those cameras,' " Alice said, rolling her eyes as she carefully applied the bandage. "It was *one* camera, and that was a salesman in town for a convention, not a journalist."

"Oh," Willy said, disappointed. "Then I suppose there's not much chance of me getting a copy of the photo."

"Whatever do you want it for?" Alice had started to repack the manager's first-aid kit. "Forgive me for saying so, but I doubt you're looking your best right now."

Willy laid a hand on her arm. "Listen, Alice. I get that you don't have any reason to think well of me, but Harry and I are finished. I wanted that photo so I can remember what an idiot I was, and not make the same mistake again."

Alice regarded her in surprise before bursting into laughter. "Willy, between the two of us, we're burning every bridge in town! What do you say we get a drink after all when Reggie comes back?"

CHAPTER 52
CHARLIE

Charlie Carothers woke up on the morning of his mother's funeral feeling both better and worse than he had the day before.

Attempting to sit up in bed, the dull ache in his torso became full-on agony. Gingerly, he felt along his rib cage, half expecting to feel ragged shards of bone jutting from his skin. His face was no better: the vision in his left eye was limited to a cloudy band, the eye still swollen nearly shut.

Charlie sighed and tried again, holding on to the bedpost to pull himself up. The marines had taught him a couple things about getting the tar beat out of him: first, it was always worse the second day. And second, the best antidote was to get the blood moving.

He called down to room service and ordered eggs, a rare steak, and two glasses of tomato juice. While he was waiting, he shaved with great care around his scabs and bruises, and then he stared at himself for a long time, wondering when the image in the mirror had started to look so unfamiliar.

He remembered a day years ago, when he was only eleven or twelve, and his mother had marched him to the bathroom and made him look at his reflection. His offense: stealing a slingshot from Montgomery Ward.

"Tell me something, Charlie," his mother had said, her hand on his shoulder. "Do you like what you see in the mirror? Is that someone you could trust? Someone who keeps his promises? Someone who never forgets how fortunate he is?"

That day, Charlie had crumpled, his denial giving way to shame. He'd agonized over the first part of his punishment — a handwritten apology to the store manager promising to pay back every cent — and been grateful for the second, which was to help their elderly neighbor clear out her attic. Physical exertion, even at that young age, helped Charlie make sense of the world; by working himself to exhaustion, he found peace.

But the man who was staring back at him today didn't look as though he could lift a single crate. He looked like hell, and it wasn't just his injuries.

When Charlie had returned from the

Pacific, his mother had encouraged him to take a little time to decide before joining his father's company. "You've earned it," she urged. "Look up your old friends. Take a trip."

Even then, he'd known she wasn't keen on him working for Harry, though she'd never admit it. His mother had been, above all, loyal to her family.

But Charlie hadn't known what else to do with himself. There was a certain kind of restlessness that some of the men came home from war with, a hyperawareness, a vigilance that never seemed to go away. But that wasn't Charlie: his need to keep moving came from elsewhere, from deep inside himself. Even his earliest memories of his father throwing him a football or teaching him a wrestling move or handing him a shotgun were tinged with the knowledge that his path lay elsewhere. There had been no way to escape it, not then and not now — for almost his entire life, Charlie had been on a doomed mission to please a man who could not be pleased.

The food came, and Charlie ate without tasting it. He brushed his teeth and put on his watch. Almost nine o'clock — still two hours before the service was to begin. He'd pick up June and help her get everything

431

ready at the house; anything to keep busy. So far, Charlie had managed to keep his grief mostly at bay, fighting it like a broom whisking floodwater — far from ideal, but effective enough until he found some other outlet.

Another thing: he had no desire to ride in a car with his father. Later, at the cemetery, protocol would need to be observed; a united front would need to be presented. He and Frank would flank their father, and though nearly all the mourners would know that Harry and his wife had planned to divorce — and a few would also know that he had a woman waiting in the wings — they would play the part of a grieving family. But Charlie intended to put that moment off as long as possible.

There was one more thing Charlie needed to do before he drove to the house, however. He put on his suit jacket, grabbed his keys and wallet, took one last look at his neatly made bed, the photograph of him with his mother that Alice had brought him, and let himself out.

Two doors down, he knocked gently. He'd gone to check on Frank last night after Harry drove himself to the hospital, but Frank had refused to open the door.

"Frank?" Charlie called softly. "Hey, let

432

me in, okay?"

There was a long pause, and then the door opened to reveal Frank standing there with his prosthetic hand under his left arm. "Just in time," he said flatly. "The buckles are a bit hard to manage. Besides, I think I bruised my knuckles when I hit Dad."

Charlie tried to mask his astonishment as Frank handed him the rubber prosthetic — this was the first time Frank had ever allowed him to see his stump. Frank had recovered in a field hospital, and by the time he came home, he had been fitted with the hand and even given it a nickname ("Stumpy," which wasn't particularly original but which caught on immediately with his friends in the marines). Their mother, predictably, had kept a stiff upper lip about the whole thing and had a half dozen dress shirts custom-made with a wider cuff on the left sleeve to fit around the brace. After which it was never spoken of within the family — even though Harry always found a way to work Frank's war service into conversations with potential clients.

They sat down on the bed and after a couple of false starts, Charlie got the thing secured in place.

"What's the hardest thing to do with that hand?" he asked impulsively.

Frank got up and went to the mirror and began to tie his tie. "You know, I was going to say something like feel up a girl or flog my log," he said after a moment. "But I guess I'll go with buttons. They have you practice in the hospital — they give you these pieces of old blanket the nurses made up that have big buttons sewn on them and button holes on the other side, and zippers and hooks. I felt like a damn toddler, sitting there in the rec room with that thing — but then you look around and there's guys with no arms or half their face gone or something . . ."

"I'm sorry," Charlie said. "I'm real sorry that happened to you, Frank."

Frank shrugged. "Well, I'm sorry you took all that shrapnel to the chest. Damn Nips, I'd like to carve 'em up and serve 'em to their families for dinner."

Charlie couldn't help being moved — Frank was still looking out for him, after all this time. "Thanks, buddy. But that's all in the past. No point in looking back."

"Listen, is Dad . . ."

"He's fine. I talked to him an hour ago. They patched him up at the hospital — he says he's good as new."

Frank pulled the knot tight — perfect, as always. "I guess I probably shouldn't have hit him. Especially since he didn't see it coming."

"But maybe he *had* it coming."

"Yeah," Frank said thoughtfully. "Yeah, maybe he did."

CHAPTER 53
JUNE

June and Patty were waiting outside the hotel a little before 9:30 for Charlie to take them to the house. There she would meet the florist and the caterer, double-check the arrangements and explain where to prepare the food. Francie had talked to the pianist, but had been vague about when she would be arriving, so June would leave instructions with the caterers to let her in.

After that was done, June would walk over to the cemetery to check on the chairs, the flowers, the tarp the funeral director had promised to lay on the uneven grass to prevent any mishaps with the ladies' high heels. And . . . the casket, of course; she supposed she should be there when it arrived.

Assuming everything went as planned, June would have plenty of time to spare before the service was to start. Everything had gone smoothly so far, and there was only one thing that had her worried: she hadn't heard from Francie since bringing her dinner last night. Maybe it wasn't all that surprising, given that her other children were arriving this morning with their families — but she would have felt better all the same seeing for herself how Francie was doing.

Patty's black velvet hair band kept slipping down. "How about if I just keep that in my purse, sweetheart?" June said, crouching down and sliding it off. She brushed Patty's hair away from her eyes and tucked it behind her ears.

"Can I play the piano when we get there, Mama?"

"No, darling, I already told you, it's just for grown-ups. But maybe after everyone is gone, while I'm cleaning up."

"Is Charlie helping?"

"It's *Mister Carothers*, remember? Listen, I'm just going to run upstairs and get some bobby pins. You can wait on the porch, if you like. Just stay there until I get back, all right? Don't touch *anything* — I don't want a speck of dirt on you."

She checked her watch as Patty climbed obediently into the wicker chair.

Five minutes until Charlie would be there — plenty of time.

Chapter 54
Virgie

Virgie was on her knees with a pailful of coffee grounds and eggshells. Yesterday she'd spread them around the Crimson Glory rosebushes along the side of the house, and today it would be the Peace roses that her mother had the gardener plant in front of the porch after the end of the war. Virgie was hurrying through her chores so she'd have plenty of time to get dressed for the funeral — Willy had given her a lipstick and an eyeliner pencil that she didn't need anymore, and Virgie was hoping that her mother wouldn't notice if she put on a little makeup.

As she worked the grounds and crushed shells into the earth, she heard footsteps on the porch stairs above her, and a man's voice. "Hey, kid, it's me!"

Curious, Virgie crawled out from behind the bushes. A man crouched in front of one of the wicker chairs, then abruptly stood and turned around — with a child in his arms.

Not just any child — *Patty.* She was wearing a little black dress with poufed sleeves and shiny black shoes, and as the man hurried down the stairs, she started to wail.

"Hey!" Virgie shouted. It had to be the man from Mrs. Samples's room, her former accomplice who still thought she had the ring, and now he was kidnapping Patty to force Mrs. Samples to give it to him! "Put her down!"

The man looked over, and then he took off running — just as Mrs. Samples came flying down the front stairs.

"Put her down!" Mrs. Samples screamed, trying to race after them, but she stumbled in her high-heeled black shoes and nearly fell while the man tore down the street toward town.

"Mrs. Samples!" Virgie yelled. She'd never catch up with him, not in those shoes. "Can you drive?"

"What?" she said. "Please, help me! He's got Patty!"

Virgie grabbed her hand and pulled her toward the side of the house. "We'll take Clyde's truck — he always leaves the keys in it!"

Mrs. Samples kicked off one shoe and

then the other, leaving them lying in the dirt, and then she ran so fast toward the truck that Virgie could barely keep up. She was already turning the key when Virgie got in. The engine roared to life, and Mrs. Samples did something that made a horrible sound of metal grinding on metal, and then the truck shot forward and nearly hit the hedges at the edge of the garden before she yanked the wheel and they barreled toward the exit. She barely checked for traffic before she drove into the intersection.

"Which way?" she yelled.

"That way!" Virgie could just make him out, running toward an old black sedan parked on the side of the road. "There he is!"

Mrs. Samples pressed the pedal to the floor.

CHAPTER 55
FRANCIE

Francie stood under the awning at the Mapes Hotel with Jimmy and his wife, Evelyn, who kept repeating that she was perfectly fine, despite her greenish complexion. Francie had seen enough pregnant women in her life to know exactly what the problem was, but she couldn't say anything, of course, until she'd been officially told. Meanwhile, Margie and her husband had checked in early and were up in their room getting the children dressed.

Francie had taken a taxi, planning to tell the driver to wait while she fetched Jimmy and Evelyn and Alice, but Arthur had apparently suggested that he ride with them while Francie rode with Margie and Roy and the kids. He must have called for his car, because it was waiting in the drive, a couple of young valets ogling its sleek styling. She would have been more irritated that Arthur had overridden her plans, but she was worried about Alice, who never kept anyone waiting.

There came Arthur — by himself, thank heavens — dressed in a dark suit she'd never seen before with a yellow silk square in the pocket. Francie wondered if she could go hide in the ladies' room until Arthur and the others had gone so she wouldn't have to face him yet. Eventually, she was going to have to apologize for her behavior at the restaurant, but not today.

But it was too late — he was heading straight for her.

"Francie," he said, his face an inscrutable mask. "Good morning."

She was saved from having to respond when a black sedan went roaring past, honking as pedestrians scrambled out of the way. Seconds later, a familiar old truck whizzed by in hot pursuit — and was that *June* at the wheel?

Francie's confusion instantly turned to horror. For June to look so terrified — for her to take Clyde's truck in the first place —

"Oh *no*, that was Stan! Quick, Arthur, let's go!" Arthur had always been a lead-foot, and if they had any chance of catching up, he'd have to push the Cadillac to its limit. "*Go!*" she said, giving him a shove before sprinting for the passenger side.

442

"Who's Stan?" he demanded as he swung himself into the driver's seat.

"What about us?" Jimmy called.

"Go with Margie! Or call a cab! I'll be there as soon as I can!"

Arthur was already pulling away from the curb. Good old Arthur — he hadn't even hesitated.

Up ahead, both the sedan and the truck had been forced to stop at the Second Street intersection, a tour bus stuck in the middle, unable to make the turn. The driver's door of the sedan opened and a man stumbled out. He lurched around to the other side while cars honked all around him and June jumped out of the truck and started running toward him. Francie was astonished to see that she was in her stockinged feet, but that didn't seem to slow her down — at least not until she collided with a man on a bicycle and fell.

Stan reached into the car and pulled Patty from the passenger seat, slung her over his shoulder and started running down Second Street. Patty was wailing, her face red, struggling to get out of his grasp.

"Stop the car!" Francie hollered as they reached the traffic jam. "He's got Patty! Arthur, call the police! I've got to stop him!"

"Francie, what do you think you're do-

443

ing?" Arthur called, but she was already out the door and running. Thank God she was wearing her sturdy black mid-heels rather than the towering pumps that Alice had wanted her to wear.

"Mrs. Meeker!"

Francie turned her head to see Virgie hopping down from the truck's running board. "Virgie, what are you —"

"I'll get her back!"

"No, it isn't safe! Stay right there!"

Virgie raced past her at an astonishing speed in dungarees and a pair of boys' rubber-soled sneakers, her yellow braids flying, her fists pumping. And sure enough, she started gaining on Stan, whose progress was hindered by the squirming child in his arms.

Stan glanced back over his shoulder and, seeing Virgie gaining on him, made an abrupt turn into an alley between a coffee shop and a hotel. Seconds later Virgie followed him, disappearing from view. Francie's heart sank; here in the heart of downtown, Stan could duck into any of a dozen casinos and disappear in a labyrinth of slot machines and gaming tables. All he'd have to do was exit through another door and he'd escape with Patty.

Francie ran back to June, her heart pounding so hard she could barely breathe. Arthur had made it to her first and was trying to help her up.

"Please, let me go!" June cried. "He's got Patty!"

"Did you call the police?" Francie shouted at Arthur.

"A man in that shop already did," Arthur said. "They'll be here soon, Miss. Stay here with Francie and I'll go!"

"Arthur — your heart!" His doctor had counseled Arthur at his most recent checkup to avoid overexerting himself due to an irregular rhythm. There was only one thing to be done. "*You* stay with June, I'll go!"

Francie turned and started running again. If one of her own children were in danger, nothing would stop her from trying to save them. She reached the alley and ran past garbage cans and produce crates and a man pouring out mop water and emerged onto another busy casino-lined street. A small crowd was forming in front of the Prospector, a dozen people staring up at the enormous sign towering above the building, a figure of a mule loaded up with a pack and pick-ax outlined in colored lightbulbs.

Francie followed their gazes and spotted Stan climbing up the sign, using the bulb casings as footholds, Patty clutched in his free arm. She wasn't fighting him anymore — instead she was looking down at the street in terror, wailing for her mother. The crowd was pleading with Stan to come down, but he paid them no mind as the sound of sirens split the air.

When Stan reached the top of the sign, he set Patty in the crook between the pack and the mule's neck, and rubbed his arm. He had to be extremely strong to have carried her up there, but it had obviously exhausted him. Patty gripped the sign tightly and sobbed.

"Nobody come any closer!" Stan called down, steadying himself with a hand on the mule's pack, his feet resting on the metal that formed the strap.

Stan took off his belt and looped it around the strap to give himself something to hang on to. Never mind that there was nothing to prevent Patty from falling to the pavement below if she got spooked and let go. What was *wrong* with the man?

"Nothing's going to happen if everyone just does what I say," Stan shouted. Four men had moved underneath the sign, joining hands to make a sort of net for Patty to land in if she fell. "I want to talk to my wife."

A buzz went through the crowd, everyone looking around to see who he was talking to, but June was with Arthur, out of sight down the street. Francie pushed through the crowd, breathing hard from all that running.

"Stan!" she shouted, waving her arms above her head. "Stan, over here!"

He scowled as his gaze landed on her. "Who the hell are you?"

Before Francie could respond, a murmur went through the crowd — and then Francie saw why: up on the roof below the sign, inching along the edge, was a small figure with yellow hair. She was moving slowly, only her head visible above the low parapet that ran along the edge, using the sign to block herself from Stan's view. But people in the crowd were beginning to point.

If Stan saw Virgie, there was no telling what he'd do.

"Everyone quiet — please!" Francie yelled, praying they wouldn't give her away. "Stan, I'm a friend of June's."

"You ain't any friend of hers — you're that broad who's been taking her all them fancy places. Filling her head with nonsense!"

"No, you've got it all wrong," Francie said. "I — I needed her help. My best friend died and I didn't know what to do, but June's been — well, she's taken care of everything."

"June don't need people like you taking advantage of her," Stan yelled. "She needs to get home where she belongs. She needs to take care of me and our kid, not some stuck-up rich lady!"

A pair of police cars screamed to a halt behind the crowd, their sirens nearly drowning out his last few words. Two cops got out of the first with their guns drawn. "Drop back!" one of them shouted at the crowd. "Everybody out of the way!"

Francie stayed rooted to the spot, keeping an eye on Virgie, who'd made it almost all the way to the mule's hooves, Patty clinging to the sign a few yards up. Virgie peered over the edge and, seeing Francie, gave her a thumbs-up. When the cops looked up she dropped back down, disappearing from view.

"Bring the little girl down," the other cop boomed into a megaphone. "Nobody wants her to get hurt. If you get her down safely, things won't go as rough for you."

"It ain't my fault any of this happened," Stan hollered, getting worked up again. He leaned closer to Patty, grabbing her arm roughly. "Nothing's gonna happen to her, I got a hold of her. Now get me my wife or I ain't making any promises."

A chill went through Francie — was he

really threatening June with their daughter's safety? What kind of father would do such a thing? For all his many flaws, Francie knew that Arthur would use his dying breath to try to save his children if they were in danger.

"Not like this," Francie yelled. "You think she's going to want to talk to you when she sees what you've done? Putting Patty in danger? Come on, Stan, bring her down and — and I personally guarantee June will talk to you."

"You going to *guarantee* it?" he echoed mockingly. "Where is she, then? Why ain't she with you if you're such good friends?"

"Ma'am, get out of the way!" one of the police officers ordered her.

"I can't," she called apologetically.

"Move, or you'll be arrested!"

Francie had just about had enough. There was a *child* to worry about, and all these men were acting as if they thought they could solve the problem by threatening each other and waving guns around. "Then you'd better come over here and arrest me. I won't even resist. Though I'd appreciate it if you could wait until after you rescue the little girl."

More sirens were approaching. The two cops huddled together, arguing.

"June told me she left because you didn't appreciate her," Francie yelled to Stan, improvising as she went. "She said you never notice when she fixes your favorite supper or dresses nice when you come home. A lady needs those things, Stan."

"Like you'd know!" he said, though there was a note of uncertainty in his voice.

"She's going to be here any minute now. How's she going to feel when she sees Patty in such a dangerous spot?"

"It ain't dangerous," Stan said. "I got a good hold on her — see?"

He shook Patty's arm hard enough that her bottom slipped off the sign and she dangled, screaming, from his hand. Stan jerked her roughly, settling her back onto her perch, and she wrapped her free arm tightly around the sign again.

Underneath her, Virgie had found a foothold and was starting to scale the sign, moving slowly up the front of the mule, clinging to the metal outline like a human spider. In a few moments she would reach the mule's head, and from there she might be able to pull herself up onto the neck next to Patty. But if Stan spotted her, he might cause Patty to fall, either on purpose or by accident — or he could wait until Virgie almost reached him and then push her off and send her plummeting down to the street.

"No — don't do it!" Francie yelled, willing Virgie to understand the danger she was in and turn around.

Instead, Virgie braced herself with an arm around the metal reins dangling from the mule's bit and dug a slingshot out of her back pocket. Working around the reins, she pushed something into the rubber band, then pulled it back and let go. Whatever it was struck Patty's arm and got her attention; she startled and looked down at Virgie, just a few feet out of reach. Virgie put her finger to her lips.

"Stop that, damn it," Stan said, holding Patty's arm all the tighter as she twisted to see Virgie better.

One of the cops was moving slowly toward Francie, nightstick in hand. Fine; let him crack her over the head with it — there was just one thing she needed to do first.

"Stan — June told me to give you this," she called, reaching into her pocketbook and grabbing the first thing she touched, something cold and round and hard — Vi's perfume bottle, which she'd been carrying around with her since that terrible morning. She closed her fist over it before she could change her mind, and then, just like when she was fifteen years old and pitching against the Saint Anne's Panthers, she squinted, took aim, and threw.

Stan saw it coming, the faceted crystal reflecting splinters of light, and he let go of Patty to reach out and grab it, not realizing that Francie had been named MVP two years in a row and pitched a record six shutouts. He wasn't fast enough, and the bottle hit his forehead with a sickening crack that could be heard all the way down below and then, for a slow-motion moment that seemed to go on forever, he teetered on the edge of the sign, arms pinwheeling and mouth contorted in a rictus of terror while Virgie scrambled up the last few feet and, hanging on with one arm, grabbed Patty in the other.

As Stan lost his battle with gravity and sailed forward, falling toward the street with his limbs flailing, Patty wrapped her arms tightly around Virgie's neck and buried her face in her shoulder, so maybe she didn't hear the sickening thud as Stan's body hit the pavement, his weight having been too much for the linked arms of the Good Samaritans below who'd done their best to save him.

Or maybe, as Francie reflected later, at the last minute they'd changed their minds.

CHAPTER 56
FATHER FLETCHER

Father Mortimer Fletcher, who'd been driven to Reno that morning by a pair of spinster sisters who'd attended weekday-morning Mass for many years, remembered Violet Carothers mostly as a silent presence near the back of the church. Recently, the diocese had sent a newly ordained young man from rural Oregon to take on some of Father Fletcher's duties as he approached his eightieth birthday, but when Mrs. Carothers's best friend called to ask if he'd be willing to make the trip, he seized on a chance to escape what felt like the young priest's constant scrutiny, as though he expected Father Fletcher to drop dead at any moment.

He'd been sitting in the chair someone had thoughtfully placed in the shade for quite some time. He wasn't clear on what was causing the delay, but it was a pleasant afternoon and he'd had the foresight to tuck his flask under his vestments before leaving that morning. Also, someone had brought him a plate of little sandwiches and tasty iced cookies, which he was steadily making his way through.

When, finally, the bereaved family members arrived, debarking from a number of shiny, expensive automobiles, they were an astonishingly motley group.

First came a pair of young men, one with a prosthetic hand and the other with a colorful black eye and bruises all over his face, flanking a pretty young woman who carried a sleeping child in her arms and was, inexplicably, wearing torn stockings and a pair of men's brogues. Trailing a few paces behind them was an older man who'd apparently been in the same fight as the younger one, his eyes bloodshot and a large bandage bridging his nose, his sport coat wrinkled and stained.

Next came a distinguished-looking couple and their three adult children — Father Fletcher made that assessment based on strong family resemblance — and their spouses and children: a thin fellow with an unruly thatch of red hair; a petite blonde in a tiny black hat, who looked desperately uncomfortable; and a handsome fellow sweating in his black suit, weighted down with a baby and a toddler, the older child holding her mother's hand.

Father Fletcher studied this group perhaps a bit too long, because when he turned his attention back to the mourners, they were watching him with concern. He wanted to tell them that after nearly sixty years in the priesthood, he was almost never surprised by anything anymore — but unexceptional Violet Carothers had pulled it off.

There were stories here — intrigue and passion, grievances and violence, devotion and betrayal. (It couldn't be proved, of course, but given the thousands of hours he'd spent in the confessional, Father Fletcher knew the signs.) He wanted to tell the mourners that there was more to every one of them than met the eye, that they all carried with them myriad secret desires and craven impulses and burning regrets, and that he had come to believe that *these* were the true substance of the soul. And he wanted to share with them his terror — not just that he would be judged harshly when he faced Saint Peter, but that he wouldn't even be able to explain himself. He wanted, more and more often these days, to ask them all for their mercy.

Instead, he cleared his throat and adjusted his glasses and took the card from his pocket that the parish secretary had prepared for him, with the names of Vi's husband and children and a list of all the duties Violet had performed over the years at Saint Isidore's.

"Dearly Beloved," he began, wondering if there would be liquor at the reception.

CHAPTER 57
JUNE
___

June hadn't even noticed that her feet were bleeding until Arthur had bundled her into the passenger seat of his car.

"Your shoes!" he'd exclaimed, and offered to go back for them, but she'd begged him to just drive as fast as he could. The very next intersection was blocked to traffic, a pair of police officers erecting barriers across the street.

June opened the door before Arthur had even parked and ran to the barrier, where one of the cops stopped her.

"Hold up, ma'am, no one beyond this point."

"But he's got my daughter!"

"Who does?"

"Stan! Oh, please, you've got to let me through!"

"Ma'am! You need to step back *now,* or I'll be forced to move you myself!"

The more she tried to explain, the angrier

the police officers became. Even after Arthur joined her and explained the situation much more calmly, they wouldn't listen, talking into their radios and holding up their hands to stop her every time she tried to come closer. June was certain she was about to be arrested, until one of the cops looked up from his radio and asked her name.

"June. June Samples. I mean Wentlandt! My name is June Wentlandt!"

Only then did the cop grudgingly move the barrier a few inches so she could squeeze by. "Not you," he said, when Arthur tried to follow.

June started running again.

She must have been screaming Patty's name when she reached the crowd behind another set of barriers, because strangers parted to let her through. "Over there," a man told her, pointing to one of the police cars parked askew in front of the Prospector Casino. She climbed over the metal barrier and ran past a bunch of police officers clustered around something lying on the street, sprinting the last few yards to the car. There, sitting in the backseat with the door open, was Virgie Swanson — holding Patty in her lap.

The minute Patty saw June, she started to scream. One of the police officers had broken away from the others and was running toward June, but she dodged around him and ran for the car and grabbed Patty right out of Virgie's arms. People were yelling and flashbulbs were going off, but June ignored them and examined every bit of Patty to make sure she was all right — and then she just held on for dear life.

Much later, when the cops had shooed the reporters away and the crowd had wandered back into the casinos and restaurants and bars, and an ambulance had taken Stan's body to the morgue, and Mrs. Swanson had come for Virgie, and Arthur had taken Francie to the cemetery, and June had answered the detective's questions, and it was agreed that she could return to talk to them after the service was over, Charlie showed up in a truck driven by a man who looked just like him. He jumped out and ran to her and threw his arms around her, then drew back to touch her face, her hands, the hem of Patty's dress, as if to convince himself that they truly were all right. He and his brother had been on their way to the service, he explained, when they overheard the hotel valets talking about the crazy man who'd kidnapped his child and tried to kill them both, and had come straight over.

"They said I could go to the service if I promised to come back to the station after, but the detective hasn't come back yet," June said.

"I'll talk to him."

"I already cleared it with him," a man's voice said.

June looked over Charlie's shoulder to see his brother standing behind him holding a pair of men's shoes.

"Thanks, Frank," Charlie said. "What the hell are those?"

"I, uh, explained the situation," Charlie's brother said sheepishly, a bit of pink creeping up his neck. "The coppers compared shoe sizes and this guy came up short. He says you can bring them back to the station whenever you have a chance. I'm Frank Carothers, by the way. It's a pleasure to meet you."

"Jeez, sorry," Charlie said, smacking his forehead. "Frank, this is June Samples and her daughter, Patty."

"Will you take her for a moment?" June asked, handing Patty to Charlie, who took her as gingerly as if she were made of china. She took the shoes out of Frank's hands and set them on the ground. Then she took both of Frank's hands in hers and looked into his eyes, which were the same shade of

460

gray as Vi's had been.

"Thank you very much, that was so thoughtful. And I'm so very sorry for your loss." She blinked a few times — she hadn't cried yet today, and she wasn't going to start now. "I got to meet your mother, and to know her a little, and she was one of the kindest, nicest, most thoughtful people I've ever met in my whole life."

Frank swallowed hard. He started to say something, then stopped and cleared his throat. "Thank you. And I, uh, hope to see more of you. Charlie says you're a swell girl, and that's good enough for me."

"Okay, okay," Charlie said, jiggling Patty in his arms. She'd snuggled up against him immediately, her eyes sleepy. "Speaking of Mom, how about we get going? I think we've kept her waiting long enough."

CHAPTER 58
OFFICER GREEN

Officer Romeo Green was at the typewriter, finishing up his report at the end of his shift, cursing quietly as he dabbed Eraz-Ex on a mistake, when the receptionist came into the duty room with a girl around his niece's age. Puberty had turned his once-sweet niece moody and unpredictable, and Officer Green looked around hopefully, but the shift change had come and gone, and he was the only one in the room.

"Officer Green, this young lady needs to speak to someone about an urgent matter," Mrs. Wilkins said, winking at him. Mrs. Wilkins had the patience of a saint and a passel of grandchildren; Officer Green resisted rolling his eyes, knowing she could have handled the girl's lost cat or whatever it was by herself.

"My shift actually ended twenty minutes ago," he said. "Maybe you could —"

"I'm sure it won't take long," Mrs. Wilkins

said firmly, already heading back to her post. "And she did say it was urgent."

Officer Green sighed and pulled over a chair.

"How can I help you, Miss —"

"Kitty Warren, sir," the girl said. She had tangled dirty-blond hair and was dressed in a pink blouse and grass-stained shorts that hung low on her skinny hips. "I'm here to retract a complaint on behalf of a friend."

"Excuse me?"

Kitty tugged at her shirttail and blinked. On closer inspection, Officer Green saw that she was trying to cover up the fact that she was nervous — her eyes kept darting to the gun at his belt.

"A person who isn't me thought someone was in danger and made a complaint and, well, they didn't do anything wrong on purpose, but the thing is, if they get investigated, it might make trouble for them. So they just wanted to retract the complaint."

Officer Green raised his eyebrows, trying not to smile. She was a funny kid. "Read a lot of detective stories, do you, Kitty?"

"I — I don't know what you mean," she stammered.

"Okay. Why don't you tell me a little more about this case and how you got wrapped up in it."

"I don't have anything to do with it, sir, other than I happened to overhear the, uh, person talking about it. They — he or she — thought someone was in danger and sent a letter to this police station, but the person is perfectly fine and isn't in danger anymore."

"Ah," Officer Green said, putting two and two together. "As a matter of fact, I think I might know the letter you're talking about. And you're sure you can't tell me anything about your, um, friend?"

"She's not a friend," Kitty said quickly. "Or he. He or she is not a friend, just someone I know. I just don't want them to get in trouble. Their, um, employer wouldn't understand if the cops came around to talk to them."

"If the person was acting out of civic duty, even if he or she was mistaken, there wouldn't be any trouble. We encourage citizens to come to us anytime they fear a crime has been committed. Or is about to be committed."

"Oh." Kitty seemed to relax a bit. "Well, I still can't tell you, though."

"I understand," Officer Green said gravely. "Wait here a moment, please."

He walked out into the hall, two doors down to the little kitchen. Monte Mondini was at the table unwrapping a sandwich, the sports page spread out in front of him.

Officer Green went to the bulletin board and took down a piece of paper that had been tacked next to a pinup calendar from Bob Gamble Chevrolet featuring a busty brunette who was pumping gas wearing nothing but a pair of high-heeled red shoes. Someone had drawn a moustache on the girl.

"What you got there, brisket?"

"Nah, meatloaf," Officer Mondini said gloomily. "Second day in a row. Wife says no more steak until I take the sergeant's exam again."

"You'll do better this time," Officer Green said, clapping him on the shoulder. "I have a feeling."

Back at his desk, the little girl was leaning forward in her chair, trying to read the report he'd been working on. When she heard him coming, she quickly bent over and pretended to tie her shoelaces. Officer Green turned the report facedown and set the sheet from the bulletin board in front of her.

"This the letter in question?" he asked. "I got to tell you, it's had us stumped. Finger-print testing didn't give us anything, and this paper's sold in every stationer in the county. The chief was about to call a press conference for tomorrow morning to ask the public for help."

The girl barely glanced at the paper, on which letters cut from newspaper headlines had been pasted to spell out a message:

WARNING PERSON IN DANGER
GUEST OF HOLIDAY HOTEL.
RECOMMEND 24-HOUR
SURVEILLANCE POSSIBLE KILLER ON
THE LOOSE!

"Is this the complaint in question, Kitty?" Officer Green asked.

"Yes — yes, it is. But the guest is fine. I promise."

"I see," Officer Green said, frowning. "But the thing is, the chief already pulled a third of the department to cover the hotel. All undercover, you understand."

"It was a case of mistaken identity, sir," the girl said earnestly. She was starting to get worked up, twisting her hands in her lap. "The, uh — the guest was not his target. He's left the area. It probably wasn't even him."

Officer Green had only been teasing, not trying to frighten the girl. "Well, that's a relief, I don't have to tell you. A lot of folks around here are going to sleep better to-night."

"Do you need me to sign a statement or something?"

"You know what, I think it's in the best interest of all concerned to protect your identity," Officer Green said. "When I write this up, I'll refer to you as a confidential informant. Does that sound all right?"

Kitty nodded vigorously.

"You'll let me know if your friend learns of any other potential criminal activity, won't you?"

"Oh yes, sir, I definitely will."

Officer Green stood up. "You have the department's gratitude, Miss Warren. It's a shame every citizen isn't as conscientious as yourself. Come on, I'll walk you out."

The girl took a last look around the day room. "You know," she said, "I've thought about becoming a detective myself one day."

Chapter 59
Vi

The night sky was just as she remembered
from all those years ago. The snow on
Mount Rose gleamed in the moonlight, and
there were a hundred times more stars than
she ever saw in the city.

As Vi walked along the river, she remembered Saturdays spent fishing with her
father, drinking cocoa from her small ther-
mos that matched his big green one full of
coffee. There had been lovely afternoons
with her mother picking wild blackberries
along the banks, then going home and making pies and setting them in the kitchen
window to cool, Father teasing that he
might just run off with them so he didn't
have to share.

Very soon, she'd be with her parents again
— and she wouldn't have to go through all
the awful pain and bother that her doctor
had hinted at. She wouldn't have to spend
days lying under a machine, losing her hair

and throwing up, wasting away until she was just a ghost in her own bed, her poor boys having to watch her disappear before their eyes. Sometimes Vi thought that doctors believed they'd failed if they didn't use every new trick and pill they'd discovered just to keep you alive. But staying alive was not the same as living, something that had taken Vi far too long to learn. Now that the moment had arrived, peace had settled around her like a beautiful silk shawl.

Yes, she wished that she could be there on her boys' wedding days. She wished she could hold her grandchildren in her arms. But if heaven truly was awaiting her — and Vi had no reason to believe it wasn't — then she'd be able to watch over them, the failures of her body nothing but a memory. She was looking forward to a deeper knowledge of God, to the answers to some questions that, frankly, the Church had never answered to her satisfaction.

She wouldn't miss having to deal with Harry, either. It was funny — once she'd made up her mind, it was like a switch had been flicked: she felt nothing for Harry, other than mild contempt and embarrassment. And that poor girl! Once Vi reached heaven, she would remember to put in a good word for the girl too — her work was cut out for her if she really intended to marry Harry.

Vi had come to the curve in the river where the water rushed over boulders and then emptied into a deep pool, a place known for good trout fishing. It was as good a place as any. She started to take off her shoes and then stopped, laughing at herself. She looked out over the dark water, the stars reflected like bits of confetti floating on the surface.

Vi had just one regret, one thing she wished she'd been able to fix — and that was Francie. Dear Francie, like the other half of her own heart, who'd been there for every joy and sorrow that mattered, who'd offered every kind of help when she needed it and treated her boys like her own and never stopped making her laugh. Francie, whose own secret sorrow seemed deeper these days, as though it had gotten hold of her legs and was trying to pull her under the surface. As close as they'd been, she and Francie both kept secrets from each other, and now Vi wished they hadn't. Arthur, for instance — Vi had suspected for years, and a nasty rumor among the St. Isidore's women's club had all but confirmed it, but Francie never said a word. And yet, Vi didn't believe that Arthur was the source of Francie's sadness, at least not entirely. Her dear friend was like a beautiful tree that had been cut off from the sun, its branches beginning to grow stunted as they searched for the light they needed to thrive.

Earlier tonight, when Vi had thrown her penny into the river, she hadn't made a wish at all — she wouldn't need wishes where she was going. She'd said a prayer instead, a simple one: *Thank you, dear Lord, for Francie.*

And for June too, she'd added as an afterthought. Meeting her on the train had been a stroke of luck. Vi had immediately seen that she would be good for Francie — giving her a project, something to distract her once Vi was gone. And it was nice to be able to do one last act of kindness for someone in need, especially since Harry would be forced to foot the bill.

But even if Francie had company during her time in Reno, Vi knew that there would be difficult days when her grief and loneliness would be overwhelming. It broke Vi's heart to know that she wouldn't be there to comfort Francie; somehow, that was even worse than knowing that her own life was coming to its end.

"I'll never leave you, Francie," Vi whispered, the very best promise she could make. She would watch over Francie every day of the rest of her life. Francie would be furious that Vi hadn't told her what she planned to do, but in time she'd come to understand it was the only way. And maybe, in time, she'd find something to fill the hole Vi was leaving behind, find happiness and even love again.

All right. It was time. With one last look at the mountains, the moon, the shimmering stars reflected in the water, Vi stepped off the bank and onto her journey home.

EPILOGUE

Three months later

June took a last look around the little attic room that had once housed servants, making sure everything was perfect. The old iron bed was made up with a quilt sewn by Francie's grandmother. A vase filled with asters from the garden sat on the nightstand, along with some books Alice had loved when she was in middle school. The old chevalier mirror had been polished to a shine, and fresh eyelet curtains had been hung in the window, through which she could see all of San Francisco laid out below.

June had already checked the guest rooms on the third floor, which, starting tomorrow, would be filled with relatives and friends in town to celebrate Alice's wedding. But the little attic room was reserved for Virgie, who was taking her first train ride all by herself tomorrow morning. June would meet her at the station, after which they'd go straight to the dress shop to try on her junior bridesmaid dress so it could be altered in time for the wedding in two days, when Virgie would join Margie and Evelyn and June herself in a row of lavender tulle at the altar.

The bridal couple would spend their wedding night at the St. Francis hotel before flying to Paris, and upon their return in three weeks, they would be moving to a slightly larger apartment in Reginald's building. The week following the wedding, movers would come and start boxing up a lifetime of memories, much of it going to auction while only Francie's very favorite things would be delivered to a charming little cottage on Bush Street. Jimmy had made a halfhearted offer for Francie to come live with them once the baby was born, and Margie had made a more enthusiastic offer, with the assumption that Francie would help with her three, but Francie wasn't ready to be a full-time grandmother yet. At least, that's what she'd told June, and judging by the pace she'd kept since returning to the city, she meant it: she'd joined a women's literary club and bought a bicycle, and her friend Helen from Reno was coming for a long visit after the move.

June had stayed on in Vi's suite until the

day Francie stood before the judge to receive her divorce decree, with June and Patty and Mrs. Swanson and some of the ladies they'd befriended in the audience. The most surprising witness, perhaps, was Willy Carroll, who'd stayed in Reno after her divorce was finalized because she'd picked up a regular gig as a Skylette, one of the chorus girls who performed at the Mapes Hotel. She still sang at Gwin's from time to time, and she and Francie and Helen often went out after her performances.

June rarely joined them, because her bookkeeping gigs kept her busy during the day, and she spent her evenings with Patty, who remembered her kidnapping only as a "scary day" and never mentioned her father at all. Stan's body had been shipped back to Bakersfield, where he apparently still had family he'd never told June about, and shortly after that she'd received a letter from one of them threatening to sue her for Stan's pension. Since June hadn't even realized that she was entitled to it, she dug up the business card the old lawyer from the train had given her on the day she ran away, and Mr. Wheeler had made quick work of crushing the distant relative's hopes and getting the pension checks sent to June.

She hadn't told Francie yet, but Mr. Wheeler had offered her a job. He was leaving the bulk of his practice in the hands of his son, but planned to see a few clients from his home office. June would handle his schedule and billing and even, according to Mr. Wheeler, learn to file briefs and research cases. In exchange he would pay her a sum that would cover her expenses twice over and allow her to begin saving for Patty's future.

Francie had promised June that she could live with her as long as she liked — after planning Alice's wedding, there would be Evelyn's baby shower and then the holidays would be upon them, and while the spare bedrooms in the cottage weren't nearly as opulent as those in the big house, there was plenty of room for both her and Patty. But they both knew that June's future lay elsewhere. For one thing, Charlie had been calling on her at the house several nights a week, eventually giving up the pretense that he was checking on Francie or dropping books off for Alice.

June closed the door and made her way carefully down the steep attic stairs. She found Alice and Francie in the library, where they had given up on flashcards and were sitting on the floor with Patty, working on a puzzle.

"Mama, I found a piece!"

"And look, here's another one," Alice said, handing her a puzzle piece and pointing to the hole where it would fit. "You're so clever!"

"Alice, you're due at the caterers' in half an hour!" June scolded. "They really must finalize the menu today. I'll clean this up — you go on ahead."

"I can't bear another boring discussion about hors d'oeuvres," Alice grumbled. "I wish I'd agreed to have the reception at the Little Shamrock the way Reggie wanted."

"With corned beef sandwiches and sawdust on the floor?" Francie teased. "Your father would have a heart attack."

"That reminds me," June said. "Arthur called and wants to discuss the band's set list."

"I wish he'd just decide," Francie said. "I really don't care at this point."

"Silly me, thinking I'd be asked my opinion," Alice said mildly.

"Darling, we just wanted to narrow it down for you. Given your studies and —"

"— and writing thank-you notes for my shower and asking Reggie's mother to tea — yes, Mother, it's all under control."

After Alice left and the library was tidied

and the housekeeper had taken Patty to the park, June asked Francie if she would join her in the office for a moment. They had turned Arthur's former office into a head-quarters for wedding planning, and the credenza was stacked with the gifts that had been delivered and the desk covered with fabric swatches and seating charts and lists, but June had cleared the papers off the two armchairs in the bay window in preparation for this moment.

Once they were seated, she took a deep breath.

"Francie, I hope you'll forgive me, but I didn't really ask you in here to go over the RSVPs."

"You didn't?"

"No . . . there's something I want to give you, before the wedding."

She reached in her pocket and took out the little box. "I had it cleaned, but you'll probably need to get it sized."

Francie took the box and lifted the tiny lid. "Vi's ring!" she exclaimed. "How did you . . . ?"

"It's a long story, actually. I didn't know about the ring until a few days after the funeral. Apparently Vi hid it in my toiletry kit that night before we went to dinner. I think . . . I've thought about it a lot, and what I keep coming back to is I think she wanted me to sell it so I'd have a little money to start over."

"That sounds exactly like something she'd do."

"But then the ring was — well, like I said, it's a long story. It was found by someone who thought it had been stolen, and that person kept it safe, and when they realized they had made a mistake, they asked me to give it back to the rightful owner. Which is you, Francie. You should have it."

"Me? But Vi wanted *you* to have it."

"No, Vi wanted me to have a fresh start — and I've had that, thanks to you. I have everything I need. Besides, the jeweler appraised it and it isn't worth nearly as much as some of Vi's other jewelry, so I'm sure Harry wouldn't mind, and I already asked Charlie and he agrees you should have it."

"It had belonged to her grandmother, and it was the only nice thing her mother owned, and Vi hardly ever took it off."

"Try it on, Francie."

Francie was only able to squeeze it past the first knuckle of the ring finger of her right hand, which made her laugh. "She was so darn skinny. You and her both — appetites like little birds."

"Charlie would disagree. He says he's

never seen a girl eat as much as I do."

"He does, does he?" Francie said shrewdly. "Then moving to Reno is probably a good decision on his part — restaurants are so expensive here."

"He told you?" June said, blushing.

"Of course he did, darling. But not until Harry called first, wanting to know if I'd put Charlie up to it."

"Oh no," June said. "He predicted that Harry wouldn't take it well."

"He didn't," Francie said cheerfully, "but that's his problem. Honestly, he should be grateful that Charlie is setting up in Reno and won't be his competition."

Well, all the cats were out of the bag, it appeared. It was just as well; June wasn't a big fan of secrets.

"Speaking of Charlie," Francie said, "isn't he taking you to dinner tonight?"

"My goodness, you seem to know everything!" June laughed. "Yes, Alice is watching Patty tonight. I'm meeting some of his friends and their wives."

"Then you should knock off a bit early. I'll make myself scarce — I'm going over to Arthur's to figure out these darn RSVPs."

"There's no need," June said, embarrassed. "Please don't leave on our account."

"Oh, sweetheart." Francie tucked the ring

back into the box. "Nights like this are meant to be savored. Hold on to them as best you can — before you know it, you'll look back and wonder where the years went. June, I . . . I can't thank you enough. For the ring, yes, but for everything you've done for me. When I first went to Reno, I felt like I had nothing to look forward to. And then Vi died and I thought I'd never care about anything again. But I do. I *do* care — I almost can't believe it, but I'm looking forward to the future. I worried about all the wrong things, I think. Please don't make the same mistake."

"I'm the one who should be thanking you! I don't even want to think about where I'd be without you. I'll miss you so much."

"I'll be there so often you'll get sick of me," Francie teased. "I need to make sure Patty's keeping up with her studies and that lawyer is treating you well. Now off you go, I need to take over the desk and find all the responses to take to Arthur's."

June left the office, taking one last fond look at Francie, glasses perched on her nose, poring over the papers on the desk, before she closed the door.

A year ago June had been lying in the hospital with a broken pelvis and a fractured eye socket, wondering if she'd survive Stan's

481

next beating. It had taken months to save enough to leave, but she'd done it — and instead of a cramped room she had to share with Patty, she was living in a mansion, wearing clothes from I. Magnin, and Patty played with the children of millionaires. And yet, the biggest change in June was on the inside, where hope had somehow taken root and flourished, and her heart had healed enough to love again.

June headed to her room to start getting dressed. On the way, she paused at the hall table covered in framed photos and picked up her favorite. In it, a younger Francie and Vi were sitting on a sofa in front of a Christmas tree while all five children played on the floor at their feet. The photographer had captured them in a private moment, Vi's head thrown back in laughter while Francie watched her with a look of pure love in her eyes.

Once, long ago, June had thought she knew how life should go: You met a boy, you married, you had a child. You stayed with each other through good times and bad, and someday you grew old together and were buried side by side, together for all eternity.

Her life hadn't gone that way. But somehow, it had turned out better than she'd ever dared hope. Maybe the trick was to stop guessing what would come next and just think about the moment you were in, the only one you could ever really enjoy anyway.

June returned the photo to its place and forgot all about it as she went to her room and started getting ready. She was a bit nervous about meeting Charlie's friends, despite his assurances that they would all adore her. She considered and abandoned half a dozen dresses in her closet, all of them purchased in posh department stores and tailored beautifully and paid for by Francie, before catching sight of jade-green silk in the very back of the closet. She pulled out the dress that Vi had loaned her to wear to dinner the day they met, the only one of Vi's dresses that she'd kept after sending the rest of her things to the Assistance League.

June went to the mirror and held the dress up to her body, remembering how unsure of herself she'd been that night, astonished at the generosity of perfect strangers. She unzipped her day dress and laid it on the bed, and as she pulled on Vi's dress, she caught a faint scent of perfume and powder. She smoothed the full skirt over her hips and slipped on her highest heels, a far cry from the old, scuffed black shoes she'd worn that night, and then she slowly turned in front of the mirror. She knew it was silly, but she couldn't shake the feeling that Vi was with her in that moment.

There were times when June felt as if she were an entirely different person now, one who looked forward without fear, who felt cherished for the first time since her mother had died, who'd discovered talents and skills she never knew she had. And she owed it all to someone she'd known less than a single day. June would never know what Vi had seen in her, why she had placed her faith in her — or if she even knew the magnitude of the gift she'd given her.

The doorbell chimed and June turned away from the mirror. Charlie was never late — he said he couldn't bear to miss a single moment with her. She picked up her evening bag, slipped in her comb and lipstick and a handkerchief, and started downstairs, where she would kiss Patty, say goodbye to Alice, then slip her hand into Charlie's and head out into a night filled with promise.

P.S. INSIGHTS, INTERVIEWS & MORE . . .

ABOUT THE BOOK

AUTHOR'S NOTE

In writing this novel, I took a few liberties with dates, places, and events to fit my imaginary story into a very real chapter in Reno's history. All my characters are fictional, as are the Holiday Ranch, a few street names and other locations, and several of the restaurants, bars, and casinos in the story.

A notable exception is the Mapes Hotel, which was only five years old in 1952, when my story is set. Prior to its closing in 1982 and demolition eighteen years later, the twelve-story art deco hotel and casino was the jewel of downtown Reno. Many Reno residents of a certain age will remember evenings at the swanky Sky Room at the top of the hotel.

I've got no excuse for the inadvertent errors that I'm sure are buried in the novel, but here are several known inaccuracies I included to make my story work:

The Holiday Ranch is not a ranch at all but a repurposed large hotel along the banks of the Truckee River on the west end of Reno. Its fictional location is across the river from some of the grandest homes in town, but the building, riverfront paths, and Gwin's roadhouse are entirely made up. In addition, while there were several hotels catering exclusively to divorcées in downtown Reno, the best known "divorce ranches" were located outside the city in places like Franktown and Washoe Valley.

Those wishing to ride the *City of San Francisco* from San Francisco to Reno in 1952 would have left in the evening, not in the morning as Francie and Vi do.

The medical examiner's building referenced in the story was not actually built until 1959.

Virgie's idols include existing fictional and real-life characters Nancy Drew and Kate Warne, the first known female American sleuth (whose alias Virgie uses when she visits the police), but George Barton, author of the detective manuals Virgie collects, is made up.

For many years, the stories of women throwing their rings into the Truckee River were thought to be apocryphal, and the

Holiday Ranch's ring toss event was my invention. But in the 1970s, divers found nearly five hundred rings at the bottom of the river, proving the stories had been true.

Finally, a quick note about how Reno became the "Divorce Capital of the World," a nickname that stuck for six decades, in the first years of the twentieth century:

In the United States, divorce law varies from state to state. In the 1950s, two factors could make getting a divorce difficult, depending on where you lived: acceptable grounds for divorce and the length of residency required by the state. In 1909, Reno put itself on the map by shortening its residency requirement to six months and offering remarkably generous grounds (many of which required no proof), and during the Great Depression, they lowered the residency requirement even further, with an eye toward filling the city coffers. By the 1950s, only six weeks' residence was required, frequently vouched for in court by the proprietors of the hotels and ranches where women stayed. (Though men also went to Reno to seek divorces, the majority of people who did were women.)

READING GROUP GUIDE

1. At the end of World War II, women who'd worked in America's factories and in the war effort were sent home, whether they liked it or not. Though Vi and Francie were not among those who took on "men's work," how might the war have affected their attitudes about women's roles in both the home and workplace?

2. Virgie is both wise beyond her years and markedly more naïve than modern twelve-year-old girls. How did her unique upbringing shape her views and goals? In what ways did she benefit from her position in the hotel? What lessons and experiences might she have missed out on?

3. Alice shows a great deal of compassion in accepting her father's sexual identity and chosen partner. What makes Alice uniquely able to see past 1950s society's harsh judgment of homosexuality?

4. Vi's death leads Francie to a greater understanding of her complex love for her best friend — platonic, familial, and romantic. In what ways do you think Vi returned that love?

5. As events unfold, it becomes clear that Vi planned her death in advance. How might she have tried to prepare those she was leaving behind, including Francie and her sons? Was her decision an honorable one?

6. Willy accepts her role as villainess with equanimity but privately chafes at others' judgment. What might have contributed to her belief that her choices were defensible? Were you able to forgive her decisions, given their context?

7. In the late 1940s, the widespread use of penicillin provided an effective treatment for gonorrhea, referred to by the slang term "the clap" in the novel. Left untreated, gonorrhea caused ectopic pregnancies and miscarriages, chronic pelvic pain, and infertility in women, not to mention the risk of infecting their partners. Despite penicillin's effectiveness, many physicians refused to treat infected women, citing morality concerns. How might this "wonder drug" have affected women's sexual agency? What might have driven a physician to secretly provide it to women, and what risks would he have been taking?

8. Mary Swanson's role as the manager of the Holiday Ranch is multifaceted: beyond the usual demands of hotel operations, she is responsible for ensuring her guests' safety, witnessing their residence, testifying in court on their behalf, and providing amusement and activities to fill their weeks of waiting — all while keeping the press, the curious, and the unwanted visitors at bay. What prepares Mary for the task, and what qualities ensure her success?

9. The practice of throwing wedding rings into the river was considered apocryphal until divers in the 1970s found decades' worth of rings at the bottom of the Truckee. Would such an act be satisfying? Should the rings be left where they lie, an invisible memorial to those who passed through Reno's hotels and courts?

10. Charlie and Frank are as different as brothers can be, so perhaps it's no wonder that their relationships with their parents were also quite different. How does each react to their father's philandering — and their mother's death? Do you think Charlie makes the right decision to leave his father's company?

11. June's upbringing and life experience are vastly different from Charlie's. What draws the pair to each other, and do you think they might lead a happy life together?

12. Both June and Francie are contemplating major life changes at the end of the book. Are they the right ones? Do you think they will succeed?

ABOUT THE AUTHOR

Sofia Grant has the heart of a homemaker, the curiosity of a cat, and the keen eye of a scout. She works from an urban aerie in Oakland, California.

The employees of Thorndike Press hope you have enjoyed this Large Print book. All our Thorndike, Wheeler, and Kennebec Large Print titles are designed for easy reading, and all our books are made to last. Other Thorndike Press Large Print books are available at your library, through selected bookstores, or directly from us.

For information about titles, please call:
(800) 223-1244

or visit our website at:
gale.com/thorndike

To share your comments, please write:
Publisher
Thorndike Press
10 Water St., Suite 310
Waterville, ME 04901